THE SCRIPTS

WRITTEN BY

NICHOLAS BRIGGS

Published by Big Finish Productions Ltd.
PO Box 1127
Maidenhead SL6 3LW

www.bigfinish.com

Editor: Ian Farrington
Managing Editor: Jason Haigh-Ellery
Consultant for BBC Worldwide: Jacqueline Rayner

Daleks created by Terry Nation

ISBN 1-84435-106-8

Cover art by Clayton Hickman 2004

First published May 2004

With thanks to Gary Finney, Gary Russell and Steve Tribe

The moral rights of the authors have been asserted.

Printed and bound in Great Britain by Biddles Ltd
www.biddles.co.uk

CONTENTS

EDITOR'S NOTE

The scripts reproduced in this book are the versions taken into the studio for the plays' recording sessions.

In the scripts, square brackets are used to denote unsaid dialogue, included in the script for the aid of the actors.

Writer/director Nicholas Briggs explains: 'This is a habit I picked up when I was writing for the Channel 5 soap opera Family Affairs. The script editors told me that if I wrote interrupted lines, the actors wouldn't know what they were going to say before they were interrupted. I thought this was monumentally stupid at the time, but later found that it was quite useful. It enabled me to experiment in the recording sessions, working out just how much of the bracketed words people should say before they were cut off. Sometimes, they ended up saying all of it.'

Each of Dalek Empire's four episodes were written and recorded as seperate productions and therefore each chapter has its own scene numbers. All of Dalek War, however, was written in its entirety and then recorded in one studio block. The scenes are therefore numbered across the series – Chapter One is Scenes 1-36; Chapter Two is 37-72; Chapter Three is 73-104 and Chapter Four is 105-134.

In Project Infinity, there is a character who in the original script is called Dr Johnston. In the credits contained in the CD booklet, however, his name is spelt Johnstone; it is also spelt this way in the script and CD booklet for Dalek War Chapter One. Therefore, Johnstone has been used throughout this book for consistency's sake.

Also, despite the original scripts containing some abbreviations, character names have been spelt out in full throughout the book – 'Dalek Supreme' rather than 'Dal Sup', for example.

Two script abbreviations are used. VO means 'voiceover', whilst FX denotes 'sound effect'.

Each script is followed by a Notes section, which lists annotations that mark where these scripts differ from the released plays. Words or sentences that do not appear in the play are struck through. Words or sentences that were changed or added are emboldened.

Briggs provides a commentary on the scripts in the Q&A sections which appear throughout the book. Original character breakdowns, plot outlines and other features are also included.

For more details on the production of these stories, see Doctor Who: The New Audio Adventures – The Inside Story by Benjamin Cook (ISBN 1-84435-034-7), pp261-267.

SPOLIER! These scripts, and the extra features, will reveal plot points

DALEK EMPIRE

"ATTENTION ALL HUMANS! YOU ARE NOW
SUBJECTS OF THE DALEK EMPIRE!"
THE LARGEST DALEK FLEET EVER ASSEMBLED
BEGINS ITS INVASION OF THE GALAXY!

ON PLANET VEGA VI, SUZ AND ALBY TAKE THEIR FIRST,
DELICATE STEPS TOWARDS ROMANCE. SHE'S A CAREER
GIRL AND HE'S JUST A DRIFTER, BUT THEY'VE KNOWN
EACH OTHER FOR MONTHS NOW, AND THE
ATTRACTION BETWEEN THEM IS UNDENIABLE.

HOWEVER, THE VEGA SYSTEM IS THE DALEKS' FIRST
TARGET! AND THE TOKEN EARTH DEFENCE FORCE
PATROLLING THAT SECTOR IS NO MATCH FOR THE
RUTHLESS DALEK ONSLAUGHT.

WHO IS THE MYSTERIOUS STRANGER SUZ FINDS
AMONGST THE DEVASTATED REMAINS OF VEGA VI?
WHAT IS ALBY'S SECRET? CAN THE DALEKS'
RELENTLESS ADVANCE ACROSS THE GALAXY EVER BE
STOPPED?

DALEK EMPIRE IS A STORY OF HUMAN EMOTION AND
GALACTIC INTRIGUE SET AGAINST THE MOST
DESTRUCTIVE CONFLICT THE GALAXY HAS EVER
KNOWN.

ALBY ALL RIGHT

By Mark McDonnell

'How would you like to fight the Daleks?' enquired Nick Briggs, through the iron grip of an unremorsefully tenacious cold.

Fighting Daleks, eh?

On occasional chilly Sunday mornings in Stockwell?

So that the rest of the nation can enjoy their Sunday papers in bed, without immediate threat of extermination?

Yes... I would do it. 'Dammit, it's my duty! Oh, and here's a box of Kleenex. Bless you.'

The decision must have taken, ooh, 0.5 of a second (and that's only because I didn't want to appear too keen).

'You'll be playing Alby Brook,' said Nick. 'A cynical, out-of-favour Space Security Agent with an authority problem, an eye for a pretty girl and a palate not unaccustomed to a beer'. As I think I've said before, it's me in space!

It's every daft *Doctor Who* lad's dream. (Apart from playing the Doctor of course... hmmm there's a thought...) Travelling round the universe, battling Daleks and having a pint or two along the way. What a joy! And it was. Every minute of it. From the first of Nick's excellent scripts popping with a nice weighty thud onto my doormat, via a fantastic time at the Gallifrey convention in Los Angeles, to Alby's last screamed 'Noooo!'. A joy.

As anyone who's listened to the documentary (on the second CD of *Dalek War* Chapter Four) can attest, there's a lot of laughter in the green room during these recordings. Yes, it's true, and not just in the green room, but in the studio too. That doesn't mean that we didn't take the work seriously. It's a testament to Nick's writing, directing, acting and casting skills that everyone felt relaxed, in safe hands and able to kick back and enjoy. And I think that trust and enthusiasm comes through loud and clear whenever I pop one of these spectacular CDs onto my stereo – as I am wont to do when I need to escape the mundanity of the council tax bill or some other petty trivial matter that can be brought to its knees by the terrifying Dalek Emperor.(That voice chills the blood. Fact.)

And the cast *were* fantastic. Sarah Mowat, or as she should officially be known The Lovely Sarah Mowat, is a superb actress (second fact), a top girl and a privilege to chase around the universe.

Gareth Thomas is a star and an inspiration to work with. On one of those Stockwell Sundays, Kalendorf and I survived a tempestuous journey from Heathrow. We arrived very late and very windswept, and Gareth took it all in his stride while I babbled like an idiot. (I always knew Blake was still a hero!)

But that is naming names. Brilliant cast, all (third fact).

All this reminiscing makes me think we should organise a reunion party. When I've finished this, I'll post a notice on the Dalek Friends Reunited website.

Seriously (for a sec), in *Dalek Empire* Nick was free of the *Doctor Who* format and able to put in some sronger human drama. And this, I feel, is never more evident than the Alby/Suz love story. All of Alby's motivations stem from an overriding love for Suz, but not in a floppy-haired, bumbling Oxbridge fop kind of way. No, this depth of feeling spans galaxies, decades, limb-loss and death.

Now that's love. Actually.

I am genuinely immensely proud to have been involved in these eight fantastic chapters.

Here's to the next part of the *Dalek Empire* journey!

Now. It's time.

'Drudger. Bring me a large pot of strong tea, and get that box of Kleenex back from Briggs – things could get very emotional.

'Right, page one, scene one...

'And, Drudger? No interruptions. This is going to be one hell of an adventure!'

DALEK EMPIRE

NICHOLAS BRIGGS is Dalek Empire's *writer, producer, director, sound designer, composer and chief Dalek voice. Here, he talks about the beginning of the series...*

What are your earliest memories of the Daleks?
Nicholas Briggs: Like many early memories, it's all a bit confused. For many years, I thought I remembered watching [1965/66 Doctor Who serial] *The Daleks' Master Plan*, because I described the bit I remembered, a scene involving a girl being shoved out of an airlock, to an older *Doctor Who* fan friend and he confirmed its authenticity. Then I discovered that this bit had been used as a clip on *Blue Peter*, so I was obviously just remembering that. But then, I do definitely remember seeing Patrick Troughton's first *Doctor Who* story, *The Power of the Daleks* [1966], and I remember already knowing what the Daleks were and being excited about them coming back... I can't work out how, because I would have been round about four-years-old when *Master Plan* was on! I did, however, have *The Dalek Book* – that big, blue-covered bundle of Dalek delights. So maybe I'd only experienced the Daleks through that prior to *The Power of the Daleks*. It's hard to tell what the truth of it is, or, indeed, whether any of this is at all interesting!

Have they always been your favourite *Doctor Who* villains?
Always. In a way, I didn't really relate to them in terms of *Doctor Who* at all. Because of *The Dalek Book*, I saw the Daleks as the stars. I loved seeing them on *Doctor Who*, but as a kid, I always knew that the Daleks should really have their own series. I would spend hours poring over that book; studying every detail of the artwork, always discovering something new each time I read it. It seems odd now, that such an unremarkable book should have had such an influence on me, but it was my most prized possession; a reliable source of entertainment and excitement that I went back to time and time again. And from time to time, I still do go back to it for a comforting fix of nostalgia.

What was the initial impetus for Dalek-only audios? Is it true that the intention was to do Dalek audio stories before Big Finish got the licence to do *Doctor Who*?
I feel as if I've answered this question a million times. It is definitely true that I discussed doing Dalek audios before we had the *Doctor Who* licence, because, back in them there days, strangely, it seemed more likely that we'd get an agreement to do Daleks rather than *Doctor Who* as a whole. I even made some budget calculations and started thinking about adapting the stories from *The Dalek Book*. I soon discovered that, despite my nostalgic admiration for them, I wouldn't be able to bear writing stories about the Daleks invading Saturn! I knew that there had to be a broader scope and that, at the very least, I'd have to write stories that understood the difference between solar systems, galaxies and the universe.

As for the initial impetus... I suppose, at a time when we weren't allowed to do *Doctor Who*, it was an attempt to get as close to *Doctor Who* as possible. My enthusiasm for the series really came through my fascination for the Daleks, so this seemed very much more than an adequate substitute for doing *Doctor Who*. Of course, when we finally did it concurrently with *Doctor Who*, it became, for me, more of a bonus.

Was that original plan the same as what became *Dalek Empire*?
Well, I'd already abandoned the idea of adapting *The Dalek Book*, so in as much as I knew I'd be writing new stories with a kind of flavour of the book, the answer is yes. I'm not sure if I'd actually started writing story ideas at that point. But I know I was thinking about them quite a lot. I always do a lot of thinking – some would call it daydreaming – about stories before I write them.

What would you say are the major influences on *Dalek Empire*?
It's a fusion of all my favourite things. Obviously, I love *Doctor Who*; but I wanted to fuse it with stuff like war films, spy films and, I confess, romantic films. I knew I wanted a love story to underpin it all, as a stark contrast with the ruthlessness and hatred of the Daleks. Much has been said about the Daleks being a kind of Nazi metaphor, and although I don't think one should get carried away with that connection, there's definitely some mileage in that. I remember that, as a teenager, *The Heroes of Telemark* [1965 film starting Kirk Douglas] inspired me to write stories about human resistance groups sabotaging Dalek operations. I even made a frighteningly bad super-8 film about it, using stop-motion animated action men, toy Daleks and my hands for close-ups.

What sort of series did you start out trying to write?
I wanted to write a story that, at its core, would be about the effect a Dalek invasion would have on human beings at a personal level. That was the inspiration for the love story between Alby and Suz. However, in order to create the mechanics of how and why this invasion was taking place, it was necessary to describe the military and more action-packed elements of this. Stylistically, this created a contrast between the more personal, emotional aspects and the action-adventure moments. It meant that, hopefully, balancing the two would make each element seem fresh. After a few scenes with more emotional content, a change of pace to action would re-engage the audience. Likewise, a constant barrage of Daleks exterminating people would become a little tiresome. I feel that the key to keeping an audience engaged is to explore your main theme in different ways. But, essentially, I wanted to make *Dalek Empire* feel like a serious drama. People outside of *Doctor Who* fandom might find that laughable, since it was inevitable that my 'serious drama' would involve scenes of 'robots' barking at each other in funny electronic voices, but it works for me!

How far did you plan ahead?
I wrote the first twenty minutes or so of *Dalek Empire* with a few ideas swimming around in my head. It was just my way of getting going. Then I stopped, thought about the implications of what I was writing, and started to plan out the plot, chapter by chapter.

So, for example, looking back at my scribbled notes, I wrote the following about *Invasion of the Daleks*.

As script... then... Suz's ideas (of making life for slaves bearable) are adopted by the Daleks. Dalek Supreme sends her on her 'good will' mission. After being lost <u>for months</u> (big time lapse), Alby finds the Vega News ship. Meets Pellan there (apparently escaped from Aquitania). Broadcasts from Vega indicate Suz left (with Kalendorf) for the Garazone System – newly conquered by the Daleks. Alby: 'Then that's where I go'. Pellan is going with him.

That was the kind of basic plot I was writing from. It was in no way a scene-by-scene breakdown at this stage. The fleshing out of the story came as I wrote the actual script. Strangely enough, though, some of my storylines contain bits of detail that never made it to the script. For example, there wasn't any 'big time lapse' between Alby escaping from Aquitania and being picked up by the Vega News ship. Also, for *The Human Factor*, my storyline notes that 'Kalendorf [is] doing practical work. Supervising building of shelters'. I also characterised the whole plan for the slave rebellion against the Daleks slightly differently: 'Secret delaying tactics. Kalendorf tells them all a sign will come to turn on the Daleks. Little by little prepared. "Awake!" or "No surrender".'

Of course, the phrase for calling the slaves to action would eventually become the infamous 'Death to the Daleks!'. Not surprisingly, *No Surrender* was the original title of the third episode. As the first series progressed, the planning became more and more detailed, because the story issues became more complicated in the light of developments I'd introduced in the script. So, for example, by the time I got to the planning of "*Death to the Daleks!*", the storylines consist of a more detailed breakdown, including snatches of rough dialogue. This dialogue was never intended to be used. It was more an indication of character motives and the direction in which the scene was going.

For example, the scene in which Suz and Kalendorf discuss who's going to announce 'Death to the Daleks!' to the slaves started out like this:

KALENDORF We have played the long game – but the trick is not to play it too long.
SUZ   When we do call a halt to it... the Daleks will kill us first.
KALENDORF But you want to be with Alby. You have a future. I'll do the dirty work.
SUZ   (*Mysterious*) I have a plan to contact Alby.
DALEK arrives. Direct link-up for SUZ with DALEK SUPREME in one hour.
SUZ   I'll be there.
KALENDORF Where are you going?
SUZ   I need some solitude. One of the privileges of the Angel of Mercy.

As you'll see when reading "*Death to the Daleks!*", the final version bears almost no relation to this at all, but you can see that several of the basic elements are there.

Once I had an idea of where the four parts were going – enough of an idea to put plot teasers on the Big Finish website – I went back to the script writing, stopping to amend the plot as I went along. A lot of this plotting would be done in conjunction with John Ainsworth.

What was John Ainsworth's involvement? Why have a script editor anyway?

John had far more involvement in *Dalek Empire* than he did in *Dalek War*. There's no real reason why it worked out that way, except perhaps there was just more work to be done in order to establish the narrative style of the series. At the scripting level, John's involvement was to read my drafts and suggest changes to lines and story elements. However, before all that, we'd spend time in a Pizza Express discussing the storyline. It was like I was doing a little presentation between courses. With the garlic bread out of the way, I'd shuffle my scribbled notes and tell him the story of *Dalek Empire*, only occasionally changing it on-the-hoof when I saw a disapproving look flicker across his face. I'd also try to enthuse him by showing him the silly little spaceship drawings I'd done in the margins! That never worked. It was at this stage that John and I realised we were really on the same wavelength about the way the story and characters should go. We both wanted a higher level of emotional realism than is generally offered in *Doctor Who*. John really seized on the idea of Suz starting to get a bit carried away by her status with the Daleks. He likened this aspect of her to the Alec Guinness character in *Bridge on the River Kwai*, whose pride in constructing the bridge starts to outweigh his concerns for his men. Unwittingly, he almost begins to side with the enemy. We had fun exploring those possibilities with Suz.

The point of having a script editor is that you need an outside eye on your work. When you're writing something, you're inhabiting the fictional world you're creating. Unless you have lots of time to leave the script alone and come back to it, say, three months later, you can never get an objective perspective on it. A script editor provides that perspective. Luckily, John and I built up a real bond of trust. He trusted my abilities as a writer and never forced a single change on me, and I trusted his abilities enough to do virtually all the changes he suggested, even though I'd always initially moan about them!

DALEK EMPIRE

CAST

SUSAN MENDES	Sarah Mowat
ALBY BROOK	Mark McDonnell
KALENDORF	Gareth Thomas
PELLAN & CAPTAIN MEDEM	John Wadmore
NARRATOR	Joyce Gibbs
ADMIRAL CHEVIAT, ED BYERS, ROBOMAN, WERNEY, DRUDGER, GURIAN, ESPEELIUS, KARIK & ELISONFORD	Ian Brooker
TANLEE & MOREBI	David Sax
DALEK VOICES	Nicholas Briggs Alistair Lock Steven Allen Robert Lock
HIGHNESS	Adrian Lloyd-James
DAUGHTER	Georgina Carter
STRALOS, BARMAN & HERRICK	Jez Fielder
MIRANA & EARTH PRESIDENT	Teresa Gallagher
DR JOHNSTONE	Simon Bridge

PRODUCTION CREDITS

Written by	Nicholas Briggs
Daleks created by	Terry Nation
Story Editor	John Ainsworth
Sound design & music	Nicholas Briggs
Producers	Jason Haigh-Ellery Nicholas Briggs
Executive Producer for BBC Worldwide	Jacqueline Rayner
Directed by	Nicholas Briggs

Invasion of the Daleks
Recorded: 6 May 2001
Released: June 2001

The Human Factor
Recorded: 3 June 2001
Released: August 2001

"Death to the Daleks!"
Recorded: 2 September 2001
Released: October 2001

Project Infinity
Recorded: 11 November 2001
Released: January 2002

INVASION OF THE DALEKS

1. Deep Space.

Rumble of a Star Destroyer's engines. All voices are distorted, as if we're tuning into sub-space radio transmissions.

CAPTAIN MEDEM This is Captain Medem, commander SD *Victorious*, to flagship *Intrepid*. Priority channel message for Admiral Cheviat.[1]

COMMS Acknowledged, *Victorious*. Patching you through. Proceed.

ADMIRAL CHEVIAT I've a feeling you're not the bearer of glad tidings, Julio.

CAPTAIN MEDEM No, Admiral.

ADMIRAL CHEVIAT Let's have it then.

CAPTAIN MEDEM That anomaly we picked up at extreme range on the fringes of the Seriphia Galaxy... Nav-scan now shows it on a steady course for the Vega System. I've had my best people looking over the energy traces... Artificial, almost certainly some kind of drive system.

ADMIRAL CHEVIAT So what do you think it is, a starship?

CAPTAIN MEDEM My people are pretty sure it's a *fleet* of ships, running under cover of an energy-scrambling defence shield.

ADMIRAL CHEVIAT Have you attempted communication?

CAPTAIN MEDEM We've been trying ever since we spotted it, but they either can't or *won't* respond.

ADMIRAL CHEVIAT What's their ETA in the Vega System?

CAPTAIN MEDEM At present, two solar days, but their speed is increasing rapidly.

ADMIRAL CHEVIAT Bring *Victorious* back to the fleet, Captain. I'll deploy our ships in defence formation and appraise Earth Command of the situation before – [2]

A massive, violent crackle of energy.

ADMIRAL CHEVIAT Captain! Captain!

CAPTAIN MEDEM (*Signal breaking up. Urgent*) *Intrepid?! Intrepid?!* Do you read us?

ADMIRAL CHEVIAT Julio, what the hell happened? We lost you for a second there –

CAPTAIN MEDEM Admiral!

Another violent crackle.

CAPTAIN MEDEM We're under fire!

Another crackle.

CAPTAIN MEDEM We have being fired upon. They've dropped their distortion field, increased speed to an incredible rate and – [3]

Another crackle.

CAPTAIN MEDEM Aaargh! (*To other officers*) Damage report, all stations! Bring us about, maximum thrust!

ADMIRAL CHEVIAT Captain! Captain, what do you see? Who's attacking you? Who is it?

Another crackle.

CAPTAIN MEDEM It's a fleet – thousands of ships, *thousands* of them. We don't stand a chance.

ADMIRAL CHEVIAT Get out of there, Julio, get out of there now!
Another crackle.
CAPTAIN MEDEM Heavy damage to all –
A massive, explosive crackle, transforming into a violent sizzle of static. A Dalek voice emerges out of the distortion.
DALEK All humanoid life-forms beware! The invasion of the Daleks has begun!
Crash into theme tune.

2. Vega VI. Marsh Lakes.

The narrator is an older woman with a rich voice. A voice which, in some ways, hints at weariness and dark terrors.

NARRATOR I remember what it was like before the Daleks came to Vega VI.
A soft breeze blows. Water lapping.
NARRATOR In my mind's eye... the air was always fresh, the suns were always high in the sky.[4] The water in the Marsh Lakes... always a sparkling blue. Hmm, that's the way I remember it.
Fade up a high-powered speedboat, ploughing through the waves.

3. Int. Speedboat. Cockpit.

Voices are raised above the engine noise.

SUZ (*Unimpressed*) Do you *have* to drive this thing so fast?
ALBY (*Laughs*) You're scared, Suz, admit it! (*Laughs again and makes 'whooping' noises*)
SUZ Scared I might lose my mineral samples overboard! Scared your male ego's going to get so big it'll explode!
ALBY Very messy!
SUZ Aren't you frightened I'll tell your boss?! I could get you sacked for reckless driving!
ALBY Wouldn't bother me! I can turn my hand to anything!
He revs the engine extra hard.
SUZ Ooh, wait a minute, Alby! Pull in over there! I think I spotted something on the shoreline!
Crossfade to distant acoustic. The speedboat engine drops in tone and motors slowly towards us.
NARRATOR I can still taste that air. Still taste it. Never tasted anything like it since... But the girl, the girl, yes... She was only interested in the rocks (*chuckles*)... her precious rocks.[5]

4. Int. Speedboat.

The boat is moving slowly. Voices are at normal pitch.

ALBY What did you see, Suz?
SUZ Flash of blue, just above the shoreline... caught the sun. Nahh... can't see it now.
ALBY And what does a flash of blue mean?
SUZ Ooh, one of those long, geological words you're too thick to understand.

ALBY   (*Mock annoyance*) Oh, well, don't bore me with it then.
I'm only the taxi driver after all. Where to now, madam?
SUZ   Let's drift around here for a while. Do you mind?
ALBY   *You're* paying, Suz.
SUZ   The Reinsberg Institute's paying. Want some of my packed
lunch?[6]
ALBY   (*Playful*) If Reinsberg doesn't mind.
She opens a plastic container. Rustle of food parcels. She takes a bite.
SUZ   (*Mouth full*) Here. Try a pickled onion...
ALBY   A what?
SUZ   My gran makes them... sends them from Earth.
ALBY bites.
ALBY   Argh! God, they're hot.
SUZ laughs.
SUZ   You've *got* to eat it, or I really *will* complain to your boss.
ALBY   Do it. I don't care. (*Munches*) To tell you the truth, I've
been thinking of moving on anyway.[7]
SUZ   (*Suddenly serious*) Have you?
ALBY   (*Affecting nonchalance*) Yeah.[8]
SUZ   Oh.
ALBY   Nothing personal, Suz. You're my favourite customer...
but the rest of 'em. (*Makes a derogatory noise*)
SUZ   Are they really that bad?
ALBY   (*Eating*) Hmm...
SUZ   Help yourself.
ALBY   Thanks.
SUZ   (*Eating*) Where will you go? What will you do?[9]
ALBY   I used to be a steward on the Star Cruise Line.
SUZ   I know. You told me.
ALBY   Oh, so you *do* listen.
He laughs. Pause.
SUZ   (*Proud to remember*) You got promoted to bar manager
on the *Luciana*.

ALBY BROOK

AN EARTH ALLIANCE security operative who was working undercover on Vega VI when the Dalek invasion began. Alby is an ex-army petty criminal whose two-year hard-labour sentence for racketeering was suspended when Tanlee recruited him for security service duties. If Alby ever steps out of line, there's always the threat that Tanlee will put him straight back in the slammer.

Alby has been playing at being a loveable rogue all his life. Then he meets Suz... and he realises he's fallen in love. But before he can tell her, the Daleks invade and he and Suz are separated. In the chaos of war, Alby ignores mission orders from his boss (Tanlee) and heads off on his quest to find Suz.

His original mission on Vega VI was to make contact with the Velyshaan agent Kalendorf, with regard to the Earth Alliance opening negotiations with the Knights of Velyshaa (a powerful enemy defeated by the Earth Alliance in a terrible war from which the galaxy has only just recovered). The purpose of the negotiations was to form a military pact to defeat the Daleks.

ALBY *Temporary* bar manager. But an old mate of mine has been in touch... reckons he can get me something permanent.[10]

SUZ *Permanent?* On a cruise line?

ALBY I don't think they're going to shut down the Earth run in my lifetime, do you?

SUZ (*Unimpressed*) *Earth?* Oh, you're not going to Earth, are you?

ALBY (*As if quoting from a brochure*) 'Visit the Birth-place of the Species.'

SUZ You ever been there?

ALBY No.

SUZ Don't bother. It's a mess.

ALBY I'd only be there for the end of trip turnaround... I probably wouldn't see much more than the inside of the Southampton Terminus. I'm thinking of the money I can earn.

SUZ Oh... How much?

ALBY Well... Enough for me nest egg.

SUZ Nest egg?! (*Laughs*)

ALBY (*Defensive*) Yeah. What's so funny about that?

SUZ The idea of you settling down with someone.

Pause.

SUZ Are you serious?

An enormous craft starts to fly overhead.

ALBY What the hell – ? Look at that!!!

SUZ Is that a star cruiser?!

ALBY Military! Look, gun ports –

SUZ They don't normally enter the atmosphere, do they?

SUSAN MENDES (SUZ)

A GEOLOGIST WORKING for the Reinsberg Institute on outer planet Vega VI. Suz is single, in her 30s, bright, intelligent, sensitive and, as it turns out, pretty tough. She is not really fulfilled by her job. She needs more of a challenge.

Unexpectedly, she gets that challenge when the Daleks begin their ruthless invasion of the galaxy.

In order to alleviate the suffering of billions of people in the conquered worlds, Suz agrees to work for the Daleks as a kind of liaison officer, promoting better working practices and bringing hope.

She garners a reputation as 'The Angel of Mercy', which puts enormous emotional stress on her. She is constantly wrestling with the dilemma of whether her working for the Daleks is simply alleviating suffering or helping the Daleks to win. Is she only thinking of her own survival, or doing this for the greater good?

The Dalek Supreme seems to regard her as a case for study. Their regular conversations are an unsettling mix of therapy session and Nazi interrogation.

Suz's ultimate goal in all of this is to turn the Daleks' vast slave workforce against the Daleks and completely destroy all networks of suppy and communication, thus bringing the Dalek invasion to a halt.

She and her fellow 'collaborator', Kalendorf, have formulated a plan to telepathically prepare the slave workers for the day when they will hear the unmistakable call to arms. But the struggle towards that day is filled with tragedy and hardship.

ALBY   (*Grave realisation*) She's on fire... Suz, she's on fire and she's going to crash.
Crossfade to the star cruiser, screeching towards the surface. Enormous crash on impact.
NARRATOR   That was the beginning. Everything changed that day. Our lives would never be the same.

5. Int. Speedboat.
The speedboat is travelling at great speed.

SUZ   (*Concerned*) Alby? Alby? Are you all right?
ALBY   (*Preoccupied*) Yeah... Er — yeah... It's just that... I reckon it came down south of the city.
SUZ   Where you live?
ALBY   Yeah. Got a lot of friends there.
SUZ   I can look on one of the news channels. Find out what it's all about.
ALBY   Yeah... yeah...
SUZ   You'd better slow down, then.
ALBY   Er... Yeah.
The speedboat powers down. The engine ticks over. Switches and controls operate. Much interference.
ALBY   What's the matter with it?
SUZ   (*Struggling with controls*) Dunno. (*Tuts*) None of the channels seem to be working.
ALBY   Try the local network.
Interference clears. A news theme tune starts.
ALBY   (*To himself*) Satellites must've been hit.
SUZ   What?
ALBY   Hm?
SUZ   What did you say?
ALBY   (*Preoccupied*) Oh... nothing... nothing.
VO   (*Distort*) Vega VI News, live from Vega City, all day, *every* day.
NEWSCASTER (*Distort*) Only moments ago, a large military space craft crash-landed in the southern sectors of Vega City. Initial reports are unclear, but a picture of carnage is emerging.
SUZ   Oh, God.
The sound of fire blazing and emergency alarms, distorted onscreen.
NEWSCASTER Er... these pictures are coming to you live. Looks... looks very bad. Er... I'm receiving information on the craft which crash-landed, causing this... *this* – An Earth Alliance battle cruiser, name unknown as yet. Planetary traffic control confirm it as a 'repulse' class destroyer; a class of warship employed by Earth's rapid response fleet, currently on patrol in this quadrant. Er... in fact, I'm told we can go live now to Planetary Traffic Control. Er... Ed Byers, officer of the watch, Planetary Traffic Control... can you tell us any more?

6. Int. Planetary Traffic Control.
Much chaotic chatter in background. Alarms going off.

BYERS (*Trying to keep calm*) We've spoken to C-in-C Earth Alliance Rapid Response Fleet, Admiral Cheviat, and she confirms that the fleet have engaged an unknown, hostile alien force at co-ordinates... er, just outside our system, the Vega System. Er – (*lost for words, panicking a little*)[11]

NEWSCASTER (*Distort*) Ed? Are you saying the ship that crashed here was... was a casualty of... of... that, er, engagement?

BYERS Yes. Yes, that's right. We have confirmed ident: Star Destroyer *Victorious*. Er...

The irony sinks in.

NEWSCASTER (*Distort*) Is... is there any news on – ? Er, has the Rapid Response Fleet contained the hostile forces? (*Pause*) Ed?[12]

BYERS (*Grave*) We... we've lost contact with the fleet at this present time. We... we don't know.

Crackle of interference.

NEWSCASTER (*Distort*) Sorry, Ed. We lost you for a moment, there. Could you –

His words are lost in a harsh burst of static.

7. Int. Newsroom.

Burst of static.

NEWSCASTER No... no, I'm afraid we've definitely lost Ed for the moment. Er... What? *What's* interfering with our transmissions?[13]

8. Int. Speedboat.

Crackle of static onscreen.

SUZ What's happening?

ALBY Something's cutting in on the broadcast.

The interference sizzles and crackles loudly.

SUZ Shall I turn it off?

ALBY No. Wait a minute.

The interference resolves into a Dalek voice.

DALEK (*Distort*) Attention! Attention! Citizens of the Vega System! You are now citizens of the Dalek Empire. You will surrender. Resist and you will be exterminated.[14]

The interference fades back in.

SUZ (*The word is unfamiliar to her*) Dalek...? Dalek Empire? What *was* that thing?[15]

ALBY Suz, we've got to get off this planet – *and fast.*

SUZ What? Now, wait a minute, Alby. You're upset... God knows I understand that... because of the crash – so am I! But... I can't take all this in –

The speedboat's engines fire up.

SUZ (*Shouting over the noise*) Alby? Alby!

ALBY It's simple, Suz! The Daleks are going to wipe us out... And if they don't...

Engine revs.

SUZ What? What is it, Alby?

ALBY You'll soon wish they had.

The speedboat zooms off. Fade out. Crossfade with a single, poignant note of music which holds for a while, then begins to fade.

NARRATOR   When the Daleks came, Vega VI put up a fight. They punished us for that. They smashed our cities to pieces, scorched the land for thousands of miles. The clouds of destruction blotted out the suns, filled the air with choking, metallic dust. And then... it was so cold. We thought they were leaving us to starve. But they were waiting. Waiting for our spirit to break. They didn't have to wait for long.

The sound of thousands of Dalek transolar discs hovering fades in. A low, howling wind is blowing.

NARRATOR   It was at daybreak, or what passed for daybreak back then. A dull, cold glow from Vega Prime filtered through the dust clouds. Thousands lay dying and waiting to die on the barren, gnarled, radioactive plains.[16]

People spluttering and coughing violently in the background.

SUZ   (*Weak and totally demoralised*) I... I wonder if we'll ever feel the warmth of the suns again.

The hovering sound comes nearer.

SUZ   Can you hear that? *Can you?*

KALENDORF   (*Wheezing and coughing*) Why don't you just shut your mouth, girl?

SUZ   (*Angry, out of control*) Can you hear it? I'm asking you?! I want to know if I'm imagining things. I want to know what's real and what isn't! Don't you understand!? Answer me!

KALENDORF   Just let us die in peace. (*A coughing fit*)

The buzzing of the transolar discs gets louder and louder. It is a strange, unnerving, threatening sound.

SUZ   (*To herself*) Oh my God... it's them... it's them... thousands of them. Daleks.

KALENDORF   (*Spluttering, through gritted teeth*) As I believe they say on some parts of that old and revered planet Earth... 'The top of the morning to you'.[17]

Screams of panic from the crowd.

NARRATOR   As panic broke out, those who could started to run... run

---

KALENDORF

AN AGENT OF the Knights of Velyshaa. The Knights are an ancient, noble and utterly ruthless race who recently very nearly subjugated the known galaxy. Kalendorf is one of the few agents who has escaped the Earth Alliance blockade around his home planet. Like all the Knights, he has been given one of the best educations in the galaxy and has been trained since birth in telepathic, mind control and combat techniques. He can be a ruthless killing machine, but also has great wisdom and compassion.

He was deeply cynical and suspicious of the Earth Alliance's overtures towards the defeated Velyshaans. This part of his nature is also in evidence when he agrees to go with Suz, the 'Angel of Mercy', to help present the 'human' face of the Dalek invasion. He feels a constant guilt that he accepted this rather than opt for a noble, but ultimately meaningless death. He takes out this frustration on Suz... constantly accusing her of collaboration. Deep down, however, he knows that neither of them really has a choice.

wildly in any direction they thought safe. But there was nowhere safe. The Daleks flew in from all directions. And they soon made their intentions clear.

DALEK   All airborne units, open fire! Exterminate! Exterminate! Fire! Fire! Fire!

Dalek guns rain down death on the crowds. Impact explosions and screaming of the victims. Crossfade to close footsteps. SUZ and KALENDORF are running hard, gasping for breath.

KALENDORF   (*Falling*) Argh! (*Struggles and gasps for a moment*) No, get off me!

SUZ   It's all right, it's all right. Let me help you.

KALENDORF   What's the point? They're going to kill us all.

SUZ   Haven't you got anything to live for?[18]

Crossfade to screams of people being exterminated by Daleks. Transitional music cue.

9. Ext. Space.
The engines of a large space cruiser, Aquitania, *rumbling past. Crossfade to:*

10. Int. *Aquitania*. Lounge Bar.
Muzak plinks away in the background. Burble of sparse conversation. The bar is by no means full. A tannoy pings.

TANNOY   For those of you who've just come aboard at Orion Central, on behalf of the Maximus line, welcome to the Star Cruiser *Aquitania*. We apologise for the delay, which has been caused by essential course alterations due to the current galactic emergency. Thank you for your attention.

Alby gulps a drink down noisily, then slams the glass down. He belches.

ALBY   Hmm... yes, I'm definitely drunk. How unprofessional.

PELLAN   (*The NEWSCASTER*) I wouldn't let it bother you. Huh. I think I'm still too... too scared to *get* drunk. God knows, I seem to have had enough.

ALBY   Whatdya mean...? Scared?

PELLAN   Well, I am.

ALBY   Why?

PELLAN   *Why*? I didn't think I was going to get out alive. That's *why!*

ALBY   Oh, that. Oh... oh, yes. Shocking, isn't it? Yes. Well, my friend... Pellll... Pelululu...

PELLAN   Pellan, Gordon Pellan, Vega VI News. Live from Vega VI, all day, every day... not any more.

ALBY   Yes, er, well... P- (*belch*) -lan, the funny thing is, I'm too drunk to be scared. (*Laughs*)

PELLAN   Lucky you.

ALBY   Yes. (*Laughs*) Er, no, actually. Not luck at all. Time-honoured, tried and trusted planning, old son.

PELLAN   What do you mean?

ALBY   I always do this when things get... (*suddenly drowsy*) When I'm sc... When... (*suddenly alert again*) When I run out on some woman!

PELLAN   Woman? Who?
ALBY   Suzzzz... Suzzz... I... I think I could have... could have loved her.
PELLAN   (*Incredulous. Laughs*) I don't believe you.
ALBY   What?
PELLAN   You escape from a *warzone* by the skin of your teeth... And you're getting drunk because of a woman?
ALBY   I wouldn't waste half a drop of brandy on a Dalek. But a woman... a woman's worth a whole bottle of Southern Comfort... maybe two.
PELLAN   Where is she now?
ALBY   Hm?
PELLAN   This... Suz? Where is she?
ALBY   She... she... wouldn't leave. She didn't understand. I couldn't... couldn't *make* her understand...
Crossfade to:

11. Int. Vega VI. Spaceport.
Crowd panic. Alarms sounding.

ALBY   Come on, Suz! We've got to go! Now!
SUZ   I can't just – I can't *leave now!* Don't you understand?! My mother and father – [19]
ALBY   (*Savagely*) Will be leaving now if they have any sense!
SUZ   No. No, Alby. They'll be waiting for me. I have to go –
ALBY   If you go to them, it'll be too late, Suz. Listen to me, I know the Daleks, they'll –
SUZ   How? How do you know them? I'd never even heard of them until this afternoon. [20]
ALBY   I can't tell you how – you just have to trust me! [21]
SUZ   (*Confused*) I... do... but, I have to find Mum and Dad.
ALBY   They may not be dead yet, but if they're not off this planet already, they might as well be.
SUZ   (*Appalled*) No, *no!* How can you say that? How can you...?
TANNOY   Last boarding call for Star Cruiser *Aquitania*. Last boarding call for Star Cruiser *Aquitania*. [22]
ALBY   Suz, please, I don't mean to be –
SUZ   (*In tears*) Go! Get away from me! Save yourself, if that's all that's important to you! (*Moving off*) But I can't leave the people I love behind!
ALBY   Suz!!! No! Please! (*To himself*) That's why I don't want to leave *you* behind, Suz.

12. Int. *Aquitania*. Lounge Bar.

PELLAN   But you *did*.
ALBY   (*Drowsy*) What?
PELLAN   Leave her behind.
ALBY   Oh yeah... I did my duty.
Bottle and glass smash as he slumps into unconsciousness.
PELLAN   Duty? What do you mean?
Alby snores.

PELLAN   Alby? Alby?
Snoring continues.

13. Int. Dalek Vega VI Command Ship. Control Room.
Dalek Supreme is on radio distort.

DALEK COMMANDER Vega VI Command to Seriphia Galaxy Control.[23]
DALEK SUPREME   (*Distort*) Report!
DALEK COMMANDER Conquest of Vega System achieved. Earth Alliance Rapid Response Fleet destroyed. Dalek Command established on planet Vega VI.
DALEK SUPREME   (*Distort*) Report on enslavement of population!
DALEK COMMANDER As ordered, the weak, wounded and diseased have been exterminated. All surviving humanoids have been incarcerated. Planetary drilling has commenced.
DALEK SUPREME   (*Distort*) Mining of mineral deposits must commence on completion of planetary drilling.
DALEK COMMANDER Understood.
DALEK SUPREME   (*Distort*) Assessment of humanoid efficiency and mental acuity is to be maintained at all times.
DALEK COMMANDER I obey. Robotising plants are now under construction.
DALEK SUPREME   (*Distort*) The Emperor has ordered that those subjects attaining the higher grades of achievement are to be kept under observation.
DALEK COMMANDER I obey.

14. Int. Dalek Vega VI Command Ship. Corridor.
Footsteps along corridor. Coughing, moaning and spluttering of others in background.

DALEK   Move! Move! Those who cannot walk will be exterminated!
Close mic effort of Kalendorf groaning, struggling to walk.
SUZ   (*Quiet, desperate*) Keep hold of me. Keep hold of me.
KALENDORF   (*Through pain*) Just drop me... let them kill me.
SUZ   Shut up.
KALENDORF   Why are you *doing* this?
SUZ   I don't know. I don't know. *Just shut up!*
DALEK   Halt!
Door opens.
DALEK   Prisoners will enter the cell.
Shuffling footsteps of others. KALENDORF stumbles and gasps in pain.
DALEK   Halt! This prisoner cannot walk!
SUZ   Yes, he can!
DALEK   Move away from him!
SUZ   No! He can walk! Are you listening to me? He can walk!
DALEK   Silence!
SUZ   He can walk, don't you understand? He can walk! (*With the effort of dragging KALENDORF to his feet*) You see!
KALENDORF groans.
DALEK   You are supporting him. Release him and move away!
SUZ   Or what? You'll kill me too? Is that what you're saying? Is it?

DALEK   Silence!

SUZ   (*Losing control*) No! No, I won't be silent! Just kill me too! That's what you do, isn't it? Kill! Kill! Kill! That's all I've seen you do since you got here! Alby was right! Alby was right! He said you'd wipe us out. Well, go ahead and do it! What are you waiting for? What are you keeping us alive for? Does it matter whether we can walk or not? Just get on with it, 'exterminate', 'exterminate', 'exterminate', 'ex – ' Go on!!!

15. Int. Dalek Vega VI Command Ship. Control Room.
Communication alarm sounds.

DALEK AIDE   Cell Block 7 patrol leader reports humanoid exhibiting behavioural abnormality within higher-grade response parameters.

DALEK COMMANDER Activate observation screen.

Buzz of activation.[24]

SUZ   (*Distort*) Well go on, then! Do it! What's the matter with you?!

DALEK COMMANDER Advise patrol leader to observe and take no action until ordered.

16. Int. Dalek Vega VI Command Ship. Corridor.

KALENDORF   I think you've confused it.

SUZ   Show it your ankle.

KALENDORF   What?

SUZ   Show it your ankle!

Rustle of material.

SUZ   You see that? His ankle is bruised. Bruised! Do you know what that means? It's not broken. The bruising will go away. It'll get better. He'll be able to walk properly soon. Or is there a time limit? How soon do you need us to be able to walk? How many of us do you need? Can you kill unnecessarily? Have you *got* any plans, or are you making this all up as you go along?[25]

DALEK   You will proceed into the cell! All of you! Move!

SUZ   Why should...?

KALENDORF   (*Harsh whisper*) Don't push your luck! Let's just go!

SUZ   Oh... found the will to live again, have we?

Pause.

DALEK   Move!!!

KALENDORF   Yes... I have.

SUZ   Good. (*Muttering as she moves off*) Good... good... good...

Footsteps. Cell door closes with a hard thud.

17. Int. *Aquitania*. Alby's Cabin.
Alarm buzzing. Alby wakes up, very slowly, with a hangover.

ALBY   Wha...? Shut up... leave me alone...

We hear him thrash around in his bed, then finally flick a switch. The alarm stops buzzing.

COMMS   Good morning, Mr Brook.

ALBY   For God's sake, I didn't ask for a bleedin' alarm call. 'Cancel'!

COMMS Mr Brook. This is not an alarm call. This is the Communications Officer on the bridge. I have a 'Most Urgent' transmission for you on a secure channel. You are required to respond immediately.

During the above, Alby groans, 'Oh, God'.

ALBY (*Groans in defeat*) All right, all right... Patch it through.[26]

A moment of interference. It clears.

TANLEE (*Distort*) Good morning, Mr Brook.

ALBY (*Yawning*) Good morning, Mr Tanlee, sir.

TANLEE Glad to see you got out alive.

ALBY Oh, I'm sure you are, Mr Tanlee, sir. I'm sure you are.

TANLEE A disastrous end to a fairly fruitless mission, by all accounts.

ALBY Well, sir, if I may be so bold –

TANLEE Which you invariably are.

ALBY I don't think so. I had firm information that Kalendorf was on Vega VI.

TANLEE Then why hadn't you found him after six months of looking?

ALBY Because he's a good old pro from the old school, sir. A Knight of Velyshaa. Very good at not being found. Anyway, my contact had got wind of his intention to leave Vega VI on the Star Cruise Line. I was about to go undercover as bar manager on the *Luciana*.[27]

TANLEE Oh, and there was me thinking you were considering throwing it all away for the sake of a pretty face.

ALBY Er... I'm not sure what you mean, sir.

TANLEE (*Reading*) Susan Mendes... known to her friends as Suz... geologist for the Reinsberg Institute, investigating mineral deposits on Vega VI. Never forget, Brook, there's always someone keeping tabs on you.[28]

ALBY Yes, sir. I never forget that, sir.

TANLEE Well you can forget *her*, Brook. She'll be dead by now.

ALBY (*Upset, but trying to hide it*) Yes, sir.

TANLEE *And* Kalendorf.

ALBY Forget Kalendorf, sir?

TANLEE Brook, I know you've probably been drowning your repulsively active libido in alcohol, but do try to engage your brain when called upon to do so by your paymasters... Our intelligence reports all indicate that the Daleks exterminate indigenous populations, occasionally robotising selected subjects or extracting genetic material for their reproductive processes. They tend not to leave people alive just so that B-grade security operatives can save face.

ALBY But, Mr Tanlee –

TANLEE You've missed the boat on Kalendorf, Brook. As we speak, the galaxy is descending into very probably the most catastrophic conflict in its long and turgid history. In short, ex-corporal Alby Brook, two years' penal servitude pending for petty pilfering... you have other fish to fry.[29]

ALBY Other fish, sir?

TANLEE A favourite expression of my ancestors. It means that a scout-ship will rendezvous with the *Aquitania* at 1100 hours your time. You will board it and receive orders for your new mission.

ALBY And what would that be, sir?

TANLEE   Oh, I'm sure the suspense is killing you, Mr Brook.

18. Int. *Aquitania*. Promenade Deck.
Mutter of polite conversation of passengers looking out on the stars. A Tannoy pings.

TANNOY   Welcome to the Promenade Deck. The *Aquitania*'s unique transparent dome, measuring over 5000 metres in diameter, affords passengers a breathtaking, panoramic view of the starscape. We are currently passing the L'Garshoo Nebula, which will be clearly visible for the next three hours.
Alby's determined footsteps.
ALBY   (*To himself, cynical*) How *fascinating*. Time... 1056 hours. Nearly time to leave, Alby.
PELLAN   (*Distant*) Alby! Alby! Over here, old chap!!!
ALBY   (*To himself*) Oh, God... not that bore...
Footsteps as he moves off. Running footsteps after him.
PELLAN   (*Out of breath*) Alby! It's me... Gordon. (*Chuckles*) Don't tell me, you drank so much you don't remember me?
ALBY   (*Faking it*) Oh... oh, yeah. Hi... er, Gordon. Look, I can't stop and talk just now, I'm –
PELLAN   No, listen, old chap. I was thinking about what you were saying about your woman –
ALBY   My... *woman*?
PELLAN   Yes... Oh, don't tell me you've forgotten her already! I went to a lot of trouble for you, old chap. Suz, wasn't it?
ALBY   (*Taken aback at the mention of her name*) Er... yeah... yes.
PELLAN   Yes. I checked in with some of my contacts at the Vega News Agency. They managed to charter a ship. They're still broadcasting... Maybe a job there for me. Could probably do with a decent anchor man... If they don't get themselves shot down, of course! Ha!
ALBY   Yes... yes... Er, what did you mean, exactly? About Suz?
PELLAN   Well, it's just that they've been picking up transmissions from these Dalek creatures on Vega VI. Most of it pretty grim... but one of the things that comes across loud and clear is that they're keeping a lot of the population alive.
ALBY   A – alive? What for?
PELLAN   No idea.
ALBY   (*Lost in thought*) Alive...
Pause.
PELLAN   Well... I just thought... just *thought* that could mean there's a fair chance your lady friend might still be alive. Not much – I mean, I don't want to raise your hopes unnecessarily... but... well... Are you all right, old chap?
ALBY   I... Yes, *yes.* Thanks, Gordon. I... er, I have to go.
PELLAN   Go? Where to?
ALBY   Duty calls.
PELLAN   Duty? You said something about that last –
ALBY's footsteps.[30]
PELLAN   Oh. (*Calling after him*) Well, good luck, Alby! (*To himself*) Extraordinary fellow.

19. Ext. Vega VI.
A harsh wind howls. Establish. Door of Dalek ship opens. A ramp crashes down onto the barren soil.[31]

DALEK TANNOY   Slave workers will disembark from mothership and follow directions! Slave workers will disembark from mothership and follow directions!
The sound of pitiful moans and groans of slaves. Footsteps on rampway.
DALEK   Move! Move!
SUZ   (*Quietly*) Lean on me. Lean on me.
KALENDORF   (*Just about coping*) I wonder what they've got in store for us now? Backbreaking work, no doubt. Maybe you should've let them kill me.
SUZ   You don't mean that.
KALENDORF   No... damn you, I don't. The survival instinct. It's like... an affliction. And I'm so... so hungry. I think I'd do anything just to eat *something*.
SUZ   That's a point. You![32]
KALENDORF   God, no. Don't antagonise them again.
SUZ   You! Listen to me!
DALEK   Slave workers will remain silent!
SUZ   When are you going to feed us? We'll die if you don't feed us! Is that what you want?
DALEK   Food will be distributed while you are working.
SUZ   Working? What are we going to be working on?
DALEK   Move!!!

20. Int. Vega VI. Dalek Control.

DALEK   This humanoid female continues to exhibit behavioural characteristics within high-grade response parameters.
DALEK COMMANDER The Dalek Supreme is monitoring her. Continue transmitting all visual records of her behaviour to Dalek Control in the Seriphia Galaxy.
DALEK   What is the significance of this female?
DALEK COMMANDER It is the order of the Emperor. Obey without question!
DALEK   (*Subdued*) I obey.

21. Int. Vega VI. Mineshaft.
An enormous lift door crashes shut. The lift descends.

DALEK   Slave workers descending to subterranean level 1.
NARRATOR   The Daleks had drilled a series of gigantic shafts deep into the crust of Vega VI. Then they had taken away their sophisticated machinery, preferring to set us to work with little more than our bare hands.[33]

22. Int. Vega VI. Sub-Level 1.
A pickaxe crunches into rock. The groans and coughs of slave workers.

NARRATOR   We laboured at the rockface in an underground chamber...

ceaselessly... thousands of us, breathing in the same stale air. Only a small number of Daleks watched over us, but they had their vicious guard-dogs: human beings whose minds they'd altered somehow.
A whip cracks.
ROBOMAN Get on with your work! Keep working!
NARRATOR (*Contained hatred*) Like a nightmare parody of some paramilitary, fascistic thug from old Earth... They wore blank, dark, ill-fitting uniforms. Their faces were scarred and disfigured with brutally grafted metallic implants... keeping them in constant contact with their alien masters.
Thud of a blow to Suz's body.
SUZ Uugh!
She groans in agony, barely conscious.
ROBOMAN Keep working!
KALENDORF Leave her alone! Can't you see she's tired? We're *all* tired!
ROBOMAN Keep working!
A thud as the Roboman lashes out at Kalendorf.
KALENDORF Argh!
SUZ (*Dragging herself back to life*) It's all right... all right.
Pickaxe hits rock.
SUZ I'm... I'm working. See. I'm working.
Another pickaxe hit.
KALENDORF So am I... so am I.
Pickaxes continue to hit.
ROBOMAN Do not stop!
Footsteps on rock as he walks off.
ROBOMAN (*Distant*) Do not stop! Keep working! All of you!!! Keep working!!!
Suz and Kalendorf continue to work, but they are utterly exhausted. Their efforts are slow and laborious.
SUZ Thanks.
Sounds of effort as they work.
SUZ What *is* your name?
KALENDORF Hm? What?
SUZ Your name... Mine's Suz.
KALENDORF Does it matter? We're just two slaves who died of exhaustion... and for what?
Picks up a rock.
KALENDORF To hack chunks of blue, crystalline rock out of a dead world.[34]
SUZ Veganite.
KALENDORF What?
SUZ That's what we called it... for a joke... at the Reinsberg Institute. Rare deposits of it on the surface... we'd only just located a rich underground strata – [35]
KALENDORF And the Daleks somehow knew it was here. What does it do?
SUZ That's classified.
Kalendorf starts to laugh. In his exhausted state, the laughter becomes uncontrollable. Suz joins in.
ROBOMAN Stop that! You! Stop that!
Their laughter continues.

DALEK   Do not make that noise! Silence! Robomen will restrain them![36]

Footsteps. Much punching and kicking. Suz and Kalendorf groan in pain and agony. Their laughter stops with the first gasps of pain.

DALEK   You will continue with your work!

Sounds of Suz and Kalendorf dragging themselves across the rock. A pickaxe feebly hits rock. Another feeble hit. They gasp and groan in pain and exhaustion.

NARRATOR   What is it that makes a person go on... even when every breath is pain... and all hope is ended? Fear of dying, perhaps, mixed with some involuntary, purely physical desire to live... (*A harsh, empty chuckle*) A lethal cocktail guaranteed to prolong suffering.

A pickaxe hit.

KALENDORF   (*Wearily*) Kalendorf.

SUZ   What?

KALENDORF   My... my name...

SUZ   Your name?

KALENDORF   Kalendorf.

Suz sighs. A pickaxe hit.

SUZ   Suz.

KALENDORF   I know. I remember... It was nice knowing you... Suz.

NARRATOR   But even that desire cannot last forever.

23. Int. Scout-Ship. Flight Deck.

Door slides open. Hovering drudger FX.

DRUDGER   Welcome to Scout-Ship X49, agent Alby Brook. I am your Drudger Pilot. Your flight plan and sealed mission orders are stored in the onboard termin – [37]

ALBY   Any chance of a coffee, pilot?

DRUDGER   I am not programmed to provide –

ALBY   I thought drudgers were programmed for independent thought... flexibility... that sort of thing.

A strangled, confused bleep.

ALBY   Black... two sugars, please.

Another bleep.

ALBY   Well, off you go, then.

DRUDGER   (*Slightly confused*) Coffee... complying.

It hovers off. A door opens and closes.

ALBY   (*To himself*) So, what've we got here?

Sound of information appearing on screen.

COMPUTER   Proceed to Lopra System. Contact Espeelius.

ALBY   (*To himself*) Espeelius? Espeelius... who the hell's that? (*To COMPUTER*) Er... co-ordinates?

COMPUTER   Co-ordinates 0269438089282554 28.

Bleep of controls.

ALBY   Huh, Tanlee's putting me out to grass. That's a long haul... the other side of the galaxy. (*Change of thought*) And a long way from Vega VI... and you, Suz. If you're still alive. (Long sigh) Maybe I should just forget – [38]

Suddenly, a massive explosion.

ALBY   Argh! What the hell was that?[39]

An alarm sounds. Door opens and closes.
DRUDGER   The Maximus Star Cruiser *Aquitania* is under fire from three Dalek assault craft. Intercepting incoming transmission to *Aquitania*.
ALBY   You've spilt my coffee!
DALEK   (*Distort*) Attention Earth passenger cruiser! Prepare to be boarded. All humanoids aboard your vessel are now citizens of the Dalek Empire. Resist and you will be exterminated.[40]
ALBY   Pilot, get us out of here! Now!
DRUDGER   I will set course for the Lopra System.
ALBY   No, I need an evasive course – (*Frustrated*) Oh, God, let me do it.
Controls bleep and squawk. Thrusters firing.
DRUDGER   You are disobeying your orders from Earth Command.
ALBY   To hell with my orders. Disengage scout-ship from *Aquitania* now!
Take-off FX.
ALBY   That's it, we're away.
Impact explosions.
DRUDGER   One Dalek assault craft is pursuing us. The remaining two are docking with the *Aquitania*.
Another impact.
ALBY   Shut up and activate the rear guns. Return fire.
DRUDGER   That course of action is inadvisable.
ALBY   I don't want advice, I need action. Open fire, damn you!
DRUDGER   Complying.
Controls bleep. Guns firing.
DRUDGER   Direct hits. Dalek Assault craft now breaking off pursuit.
ALBY   They gave up pretty easily. (*Laughs*) Seems they've got other fish to fry... (*Chuckles. To himself*) And so have I, Tanlee... so have I. (*Aloud*) Well... No chance of following my mission orders now.
DRUDGER   Explain.
ALBY   The Daleks have obviously made an unexpected advance in this sector. I daren't try to contact Earth Command now. Every Dalek in the area will be listening.
DRUDGER   What course of action do you propose?
ALBY   Ooh... I'm afraid it's on a 'need to know' basis, old son. Sure you understand.

24. Int. Vega VI. Mineshaft.

NARRATOR   The Daleks worked the frightened, exhausted survivors of Vega VI, ceaselessly... for hours... for longer than seemed possible. Hundreds had already collapsed and died at the rock face. But still the Daleks bellowed their commands, still the Robomen brandished their whips and clubs, often lashing and jabbing at corpses... as if they'd forgotten how to recognise the living. Finally, the last few fell to their knees, unable to work a moment longer, their spirits... broken. Even the Robomen were unable to fight off the all-consuming fatigue.[41]
ROBOMAN   (*Exhausted*) Master... they... they will not work. We... we cannot make them work.[42]
DALEK   The work has not been completed. They *must* work. Force them! Force them to work!!!

ROBOMAN   I... I... please, I cannot make them work. Please, master...[43]

DALEK   You will obey your masters! The humanoids must continue with their work!

ROBOMAN   I... I try to obey... I... I... (*Lets out a groan and collapses*) *ROBOMAN collapses onto rubble.*

DALEK   Get up! Get up and obey your orders!!!

ROBOMAN   (*Moaning pitifully*) Please... master... must... must sleep.[44]

DALEK   Exterminate!

Dalek gun fires.

ROBOMAN   Aaaaaargh!

SUZ   (*Very weak*) Are you satisfied now?[45]

DALEK   Silence!

SUZ   Kill me... You might as well... Kill us all. We... we can't work. You've given us no food. No rest.

25. Int. Vega VI. Dalek Control.

Alarm sounds.

DALEK   The humanoids are exhausted and unable to work. The female still defies our orders.

DALEK COMMANDER Establish direct hyper-link to Dalek Supreme in Seriphia Galaxy immediately.

DALEK   I obey.

Hyper-link FX establish. DALEK SUPREME is on 'distort'.

DALEK SUPREME Report.

DALEK COMMANDER The time has come.

DALEK SUPREME Excellent. Show me.

DALEK COMMANDER Activating mineshaft monitor screen.[46]

Monitor screen FX.

SUZ   (*Distort. Exhausted*) Don't you see? You promised us food... but you didn't feed us. You gave us no rest. Don't you understand us...? We can't work forever without rest or food. We'll die. Is that what you want?

DALEK SUPREME Relay my commands to the Dalek in the mineshaft.

DALEK COMMANDER I obey.

Control activates.

DALEK COMMANDER Relay established.

DALEK SUPREME Tell her: 'We will give you food now. Then you will recommence work'.

DALEK   (*Distort*) We will give you food now. Then you will recommence work.

SUZ   (*Distort. Laughs weakly*) You just don't get it, do you? We're not machines... not like you.

DALEK SUPREME If you do not work, we will exterminate you.

DALEK   (*Distort*) If you do not work, we will exterminate you.

SUZ   (*Distort*) Go ahead. You've finally done it, don't you see? You've destroyed our will to live. You've destroyed our hope.

DALEK SUPREME Terminate command relay.

Relay command FX off.

DALEK COMMANDER Terminated. Are they to be exterminated?[47]

DALEK SUPREME No. Everything is going according to plan.
DALEK COMMANDER But the ore quotas have not been achieved.
DALEK SUPREME Correct.
DALEK COMMANDER And veganite is too volatile to be mined by our machinery.
DALEK SUPREME Correct. You will allow the humanoids to rest.[48]
DALEK COMMANDER And the female?
DALEK SUPREME Have her brought to your control centre. I will speak with her.
DALEK COMMANDER To what purpose?
DALEK SUPREME Do not question the Dalek Supreme! Obey!!!
DALEK COMMANDER I obey.

26. Int. Seriphia Galaxy. Dalek Command.

EMPEROR　You have done well.[49]
DALEK SUPREME Yes, Emperor. The fragments of data obtained from the Kar-Charrat Library have yielded invaluable information on the human mind.
EMPEROR　Those fragments have given us access to wisdom on matters previously beyond our understanding. Dangerous wisdom which must not be communicated to the rest of the Dalek race. Is that understood?
DALEK SUPREME Understood, Emperor.
EMPEROR　Only you and I have accessed the Kar-Charrat data. No other must see it.
DALEK SUPREME Understood.
EMPEROR　You will speak to the humanoid female alone. You know what you must do?
DALEK SUPREME Yes, Emperor. I must give her... hope.[50]

27. Int. Vega VI. Dalek Control.
Door opens. Suz's exhausted breathing.

DALEK　　　This is the humanoid female.
SUZ　　　　What are you going to do to me?
DALEK COMMANDER Move to the chair. Move!
We hear Suz's breathing and limping footsteps as she struggles to the chair and sits.
SUZ　　　　What now? Where are you going?
DALEK COMMANDER Look at the screen. The Dalek Supreme wishes to speak to you. (*Moving into distance*) Do not attempt to escape or you will be exterminated.
The door closes.
SUZ　　　　Hello? Hello? Anyone there?
Hyper-link clears.
DALEK SUPREME (*Distort*) I am the Dalek Supreme.
SUZ　　　　Do you expect me to be impressed?
DALEK SUPREME I am speaking to you from the Seriphia Galaxy.
SUZ　　　　Never heard of it.
DALEK SUPREME It is a galaxy we created from a force known as the Apocalypse Element.

SUZ　　　　Why are you telling me this?

DALEK SUPREME For many of your years, we have been creating a powerbase in this galaxy. A force beyond your imaginings in its size and power.

SUZ　　　　I'm not interested in your propaganda. (*Coughing fit*) What do you want with me?

DALEK SUPREME It is important that you understand the futility of resisting the Daleks. We have superior numbers. We have the superior technology. We *will* conquer your galaxy. It is only a matter of time.

SUZ　　　　Oh really... well, it's important *you* understand that you won't get what you want if you work us to death.

Pause.

SUZ　　　　(*Ironic*) Sorry... is this going over your head?

DALEK SUPREME If it is important that I understand... explain it to me.

SUZ　　　　Are you serious?

Pause.

SUZ　　　　All right... It is obviously important to you that we... that we work in your mines.

Pause.

SUZ　　　　Well... is it?

DALEK SUPREME Correct. Continue.

SUZ　　　　The... (*stops herself from saying 'veganite'*) the... blue ore you're making us dig out. It's not exactly friendly to mechanical mining, is it? So you need us to do it. And you obviously haven't got enough of it, have you?[51]

Pause.

SUZ　　　　Have you?

DALEK SUPREME You are correct. Continue.

SUZ　　　　So... Well, if you understood human beings a bit better, you'd let us rest.[52]

DALEK SUPREME But then the work will stop.

SUZ　　　　(*Angry*) It already has stopped, hasn't it?! And if you try to work us any harder, it'll stop permanently, because we'll all be dead.

DALEK SUPREME We can obtain more slaves from other planets we conquer.

SUZ　　　　(*Exhausted*) Yes... yes... of course... you can keep working your slaves to death and keep replacing them until you get what you want. Just do that... I don't care – I don't know why you're even asking me about this anyway.

Pause.

SUZ　　　　Just kill me and get it over with.

Pause.

DALEK SUPREME I have been watching you... Susan.

SUZ　　　　How do you know my name?

DALEK SUPREME I – have – been – watching – you.

SUZ　　　　(*Suspicious*) What do you mean?

DALEK SUPREME You are not afraid.

SUZ　　　　Huh... I am.

DALEK SUPREME But you defy the Daleks. Why?

SUZ　　　　'Why?' I don't know why...

DALEK SUPREME Is it perhaps because you hope to communicate with us?

SUZ   Communicate? What do you mean?

DALEK SUPREME You wanted to show us that your friend would be able to work if we gave his injury time to heal. You wanted us to feed your people so that you would not die of starvation.

SUZ   Well... obviously.

DALEK SUPREME You want us to show... pity.

SUZ   (*Confused*) I... I don't know. (*Defensive*) What are you trying to say? What do you want – ?

DALEK SUPREME You want us to give you hope.

SUZ   Hope? What can creatures like you possibly know of hope?

DALEK SUPREME Susan Mendes... You will sleep now.

SUZ   Sleep? You're going to let me sleep?

DALEK SUPREME The other slaves are sleeping. You can sleep. And when you awaken, we – will – speak – again.[53]

28. Int. Scout-Ship.

DRUDGER   We are now entering the Vega System. This sector is occupied by a high concentration of Dalek forces.

ALBY   You don't say. Funny... I happened to know that already. Plot a course for Vega VI.

DRUDGER   It is inadvisable to proceed any further.

ALBY   Yeah... I knew that too. (*To himself*) Now what... now what? God, what am I doing? Risking extermination just for the sake of a woman? You've got it bad, Alby old son, you've got it bad. And it's only a matter of time before a Dalek ship spots us if I don't think of something soon.[54]

Alarm sounds.

ALBY   Er, why don't I keep my mouth shut?

DRUDGER   Dalek transolar disc patrol approaching.

ALBY   Transolar discs? How many of them?

DRUDGER   I am reading twenty discs with single Dalek occupancy.

ALBY   Oh. And well-appointed bedrooms, I take it?

DRUDGER   Please clarify.

ALBY   Never mind. Any sign of their mothership?

DRUDGER   No other readings at this time.

ALBY   Well, that's something, I suppose.

An impact explosion.

DRUDGER   They are firing at us.

ALBY   I gathered that.

Comms bleeping.

DRUDGER   Incoming communication.

DALEK   (*Distort*) Attention! Attention! You will surrender to the Daleks or be exterminated!

Comms bleep.

ALBY   Hello. Could you say that again, please? I'm a little hard of hearing.

An impact explosion.

ALBY   Obviously not. Open fire forward weapons. Full thrust and 180 turn. Now!

DRUDGER   Complying.

Guns fire. Thrusters fire. Engine power continues to rise.
DRUDGER   Three targets destroyed.
An impact explosion.
DRUDGER   Dalek transolar discs pursuing.
ALBY   Increase speed!
DRUDGER   Increasing speed beyond safety levels will take fuel cells beyond regeneration point.
ALBY   I'm not thinking about what we'll be doing tomorrow! I want to get away *now*! Do it!
DRUDGER   Complying.
Engine whine rises in pitch. Rattling of hull.
ALBY   (*Laughs*) That caught 'em by surprise.
DRUDGER   Dalek transolar discs now increasing speed. They are gaining on us.
ALBY   Fire rear guns.
DRUDGER   Complying.
Guns firing.
DRUDGER   Two additional targets destroyed.
ALBY   Keep firing.
Impact explosion.
DRUDGER   Dalek firepower targeting our engines.
Huge explosion. Whine of engine power falls rapidly.
DRUDGER   Drive units disabled. Engine power nil. Velocity decreasing.
ALBY   You don't say. Damn!
DALEK   (*Distort*) Surrender! Surrender!
Scanner bleeping.
ALBY   What the hell's that?
DRUDGER   Large vessel approaching.
ALBY   Oh great... the Dalek mothership.
Many impact explosions (no more than 15!). The ship rattles and creaks.
ALBY   Oh God. This is it. What the hell was I thinking about, coming back to Vega?
DRUDGER   The Daleks and their transolar discs are being destroyed.
ALBY   What? Let me see.
Controls bleep.
ALBY   That ship... it's... it's an Earth Alliance ship! It's blowing up the Daleks! (*Triumphant laugh*) Yes! Get me a communications link-up.
DRUDGER   Complying. Communications active.
Comms beep.
ALBY   Hello Earth Alliance ship. Come in please, over.
A news theme tune plays on distort.
VO   (*Distort*) This is Vega Free News, live all day, *every* day.
ALBY   (*Laughs*) My God, they did it! Pellan was right! They did it![55]
News theme builds to a crescendo.

29. Int. Vega VI. Mining Area.
Kalendorf stirs and wakes up. Footsteps approach.

KALENDORF   (*Groggy*) Suz? Suz? What happened? Where've you been?
SUZ   They let us sleep. All of us. For hours.
Sounds of people waking up. Spluttering etc.

SUZ   How do you feel?

KALENDORF   Well... better... Still hungry though.

SUZ   Here. They gave me some food.

Sound of plastic container being opened.

KALENDORF   Doesn't look very appetising.

SUZ   Some kind of dried nutrient concentrate... Does the trick though. Makes you feel better. Have you seen the Robomen?

KALENDORF   (*Disbelief*) They're... they're handing out more of that stuff... What's going on? Why the change of heart?

SUZ   You must eat, Kalendorf.

KALENDORF   So I can carry on working?

SUZ   Yes... and living.

Kalendorf sighs. Sound of food being taken. Kalendorf bites and swallows.

SUZ   Not too bad?

KALENDORF   (*Eating*) Hmm... not too bad. So, what happened?

SUZ   After you collapsed... after we'd all collapsed, they dragged me to their control room. I spoke to their leader. The Dalek Supreme.

KALENDORF   (*Surprised*) Dalek Supreme? You spoke to him?

SUZ   What do you know about these creatures? I'd never heard of them before all this.[56]

KALENDORF   (*Secretive*) Never mind how I know. (*Continues eating*) So you spoke to him. What did you say?[57]

SUZ   That we needed food... and sleep.

KALENDORF   And so we got it? That simple?

SUZ   I know. It's like... like he wanted to learn from me... but it was almost as if he knew... knew what I was thinking.

KALENDORF   Suz, listen to me... you mustn't trust the Daleks. It doesn't matter what they say, you mustn't –

SUZ[58]   I don't, I don't... But we're alive, aren't we? We've got... hope.

KALENDORF   Hope? Hope of what? More backbreaking work? Hope of being fried alive if we make a sound or put one foot wrong?

SUZ   But if they feed us... and let us sleep... We'll grow strong. They won't have broken our spirit. We can... we can maybe find a way to fight back.

KALENDORF   With what?

SUZ   I don't know. But at least now we have some time to think about it.

30. Int. Vega News Ship. Airlock Reception.

A huge, echoing, metallic clunk.

TANNOY   Scout-ship now secured in docking bay. Pressurisation commencing.

A massive hissing of air. It reaches a crescendo and tails off. Door opens. Alby's tentative footsteps.

ALBY   Hello? Anyone about?

Another door opens.

ALBY   (*Gobsmacked*) My God, it's... er... it's – [59]

PELLAN   Pellan. Gordon Pellan! Welcome aboard, Alby. The moment the captain spotted a scout-ship, I had a funny feeling it'd be you.

ALBY   What the hell are you doing here? I thought the *Aquitania* was taken by the Daleks.

PELLAN   It was. (*Downbeat*) Not a very pleasant experience.

ALBY   What happened? How did you get away?

PELLAN   Some of the security guards decided to put up a fight.

ALBY   (*Grave, catching on*) Oh, I see.

PELLAN   The Daleks boarded. They went wild, started exterminating indiscriminately. It was chaos... a massacre. Somehow... don't ask me how... I managed to get away in a lifepod.

ALBY   You were lucky.

PELLAN   It doesn't feel that way.

ALBY   What d'you mean?

PELLAN   I just ran. I just... ran. You know? It's like I didn't care a damn about anyone else. Those... voices. And the screaming. I remember... climbing over people... people screaming for help. I didn't care. I just wanted to get out. (*Sighs, reliving it*) Oh, God...[60]

ALBY   (*Awkward*) Yeah... well, steady on, Pellan, old son. All's fair in love and war, and all that. At least you're alive. Don't beat yourself up about it. Tell me, do they have a bar on this ship?

31. Int. Seriphia Galaxy. Dalek Command.

DALEK   Report for the Dalek Supreme.[61]

DALEK SUPREME Speak.

DALEK   Dalek forces continue to advance. Earth Alliance ships are retreating in all sectors.

DALEK SUPREME They will attempt to regroup and counter-attack.

DALEK   Battle computers in all our fleets have anticipated this, but warn of energy and raw material depletion.[62]

DALEK SUPREME All conquered planets will be exploited for their technological and industrial resources. Mineral ores must be mined for the building of Dalek ships and the fuelling of our power units. Slave labour will be used in order to conserve energy.

DALEK   Battle computers warn that slave labour is slow and inefficient.

DALEK SUPREME Not if it is utilised effectively. The Emperor has a plan that will achieve this. Continue with your report.[63]

DALEK   There is an Earth Alliance ship still at liberty in the Vega System. It is transmitting anti-Dalek propaganda. Shall I give the order for it to be destroyed?

DALEK SUPREME No. I will give that order when the Emperor deems it necessary.

DALEK   Understood. Work on Vega VI has fallen behind schedule. Productivity targets have not been achieved. The slave workforce is... resting and eating.

DALEK SUPREME Understood. I will give the order for work to recommence... soon.

32. Int. Vega VI. Mining Area.

General hubbub of contented workers. Some muted laughter.

SUZ   (*Teasing*) You should see your face. Very grim.

KALENDORF (*Grim*) I just don't trust what I'm seeing... It's making me nervous.

SUZ What? People who thought they were going to die regaining some hope?

KALENDORF They're still going to die.

SUZ How do you know? How can any of us know that?

KALENDORF Because it's what the Daleks do. What do you think happens when it's all over? When they've got what they want? Do you think they just say, 'Thanks for the help guys' and then leave?[64]

Pause.

KALENDORF Wake up, Suz. These are the creatures who flattened every city on this planet... blotted out the sun, choked up the atmosphere. They came screaming out of the skies gunning down anyone who wasn't fast enough to get out of the way. These are the creatures who wanted to kill me because I couldn't walk.

SUZ But they didn't kill you, did they? You're alive... We're *all* still alive. Aren't we?

KALENDORF For now. But for how long?

DALEK Susan Mendes. You will come with me.

KALENDORF (*Close*) Time for another cosy chat?

SUZ (*To DALEK*) Very well.

33. Int. Vega News Ship. Canteen.
General canteen hubbub. Clattering of trays. Cutlery etc.

PELLAN (*Approaching*) There's a table here.

Dragging of chairs etc as they sit.

PELLAN No alcohol, I'm afraid... and the food's rationed.

ALBY Oh, no worries... I'm just happy to be alive.

Alby takes a mouthful of food.

ALBY Talking of which, how come you lot are here?

PELLAN Well, I told you Vega News persuaded the Earth Alliance to let them have a ship. When I jettisoned from the *Aquitania*, I set a course for this system.[65]

ALBY Bit of a long shot.

PELLAN You're right there. I'd gone into a coma by the time they picked me up.

ALBY They might never have picked you up.

PELLAN I know. But even that's better than being captured by the Daleks.

ALBY Yeah... yeah. (*Munching food*) But how come this ship hasn't had any trouble with the Daleks? I mean, the Vega System's their bridgehead in our galaxy. It must be swarming with the little bleeders.

PELLAN We've had our fair share of trouble.

ALBY Couldn't see much damage to the hull when I was entering your docking bay. You've been lucky.

PELLAN Maybe the Daleks just think we're small-fry... not worth bothering with.

ALBY Hmm... Maybe. Maybe...

34. Int. Vega VI. Dalek Control.
Door opens.

DALEK   Enter and sit in the chair.

Footsteps. She settles in the chair.

SUZ   Same routine?

DALEK   Face the screen. (*Moving off*) If you attempt to escape, you will be exterminated.

Door closes.

SUZ   Bye-bye.

Hyper-link clears.

SUZ   (*To herself*) Here we go again.

DALEK SUPREME Susan Mendes.

SUZ   Yes.

DALEK SUPREME Do you still wish to die?

SUZ   What?

DALEK SUPREME Do you still wish to die?

Pause.

DALEK SUPREME Answer!

SUZ   I don't understand the question.

DALEK SUPREME When we last spoke, you said, 'Just – kill – me – and – get – it – over – with'.[66]

Pause.

DALEK SUPREME Do you acknowledge that those were your words?

SUZ   (*Reluctant*) Yes... I do.[67]

DALEK SUPREME Do they represent your feelings now?

Pause.

DALEK SUPREME Answer!

SUZ   No... no they don't. But you know that, don't you? Why ask?

DALEK SUPREME Why do you no longer wish for death?

SUZ   What do you want me to say?

DALEK SUPREME I wish you to speak the truth. Answer!

SUZ   (*Sighs*) I was tired... exhausted... *totally* exhausted. Death didn't seem very far away.

DALEK SUPREME And now?

SUZ   All right, you've proved your point.

DALEK SUPREME *And now?! Answer!!!*

SUZ   (*Angry*) And now you've given us hope! Yes, I know! But what's the point? You're only going to work us to death in the end... or kill us when you don't need us any more.

DALEK SUPREME That is what your friend, Kalendorf, believes.

SUZ   You're still watching me?

DALEK SUPREME Every move you make, we can see. Every sound you utter, we can hear.

SUZ   So... is Kalendorf right?

DALEK SUPREME That is up to you.

SUZ   Just say what you mean. Stop playing games.

DALEK SUPREME The Daleks need veganite. It has to be mined in large quantities. We must use slave labour. It is of no concern to us whether you slaves live or die, but if you can devise a system of working which will both satisfy our productivity targets and sustain human life, then we will consider it.

SUZ   Why?

DALEK SUPREME Because we recognise that human beings need hope to survive. If they survive, then they are productive.

34

SUZ   Why not devise such a system yourself? Why are you asking me to do it?

DALEK SUPREME The human factor.

SUZ   What?

DALEK SUPREME That which differentiates human beings from the Daleks.

35. Int. Vega News Ship. Studios.
Door opens. In the background, a news bulletin is burbling away.

BULLETIN   Reports coming in from the remaining comms-beacons in the Vega Prime sector confirm continuous movement of Dalek ships bound for L'Garshoo Nebula. Coded reports from Earth Command confirm that this is the furthermost point of the Dalek advance and that the advance is slowing. Earth forces have already regrouped and retaken a number of key strategic systems. For security reasons, of course, we cannot reveal precise information on this, but sources at Earth Command are optimistic that this may be the turning point.

Jingle plays.

BULLETIN   It's 0450 Vega Time and you're listening to Free Vega News, the voice of liberation in the Vega System. Coming up, Gordon Pellan gives us a rundown of Dalek cruiser movements and discusses anti-Dalek combat measures with Ley Forthal of the Earth Alliance Special Forces.

Music fades in. Over all this...

PELLAN   Hi, come in, Brook.

ALBY   Thanks. Quite an impressive rig you've got here.[68]

PELLAN   Thanks. Oh, by the way, good news about your ship... The engineering guys have managed to fix up your engines.

ALBY   Thanks... (*Melancholy*) Although where I'll be going next, I've no idea.

PELLAN   Well, I did my best for you.

ALBY   Sorry... no, I appreciate it, Pellan. Thanks.[69]

Pause.

ALBY   So... Do you know who exactly is picking up your broadcasts?

PELLAN   There are pockets of survivors all over the Vega System. Our fly-bys have confirmed that. We receive the odd call-sign from them.

ALBY   Risky... for them and you.

PELLAN   We're using low-band audio frequencies only. The Daleks don't seem to pick up on it most of the time... too much hi-definition holographic chatter beaming around their command network.

ALBY   You mean they're too busy to notice? Doesn't sound like the Daleks to me.[70]

PELLAN   How come you're such an expert on the Daleks?[71]

ALBY   Oh... I've done my homework.

PELLAN   Homework?

ALBY   (*Changing subject*) When we spoke on the *Aquitania*, you mentioned something about monitoring Dalek communications on Vega VI.

PELLAN   Oh, I see. You really can't keep your mind off that girl of yours, can you? What was her name... Susan Mendes, wasn't it?[72]

ALBY   Yeah... Suz. Heard anything?

PELLAN   Well, I know she's important to you, Brook... But I honestly don't think we're going to hear her name mentioned in Dalek dispatches, do you? Hardly their number one concern at the moment, is she?

36. Int. Vega VI. Mining Area.
Background burble of slaves relaxing. Footsteps arrive and stop.

KALENDORF   So, what did he have to say for himself this time, your chum the Dalek Supreme?
Pause.
KALENDORF   (*Concerned*) What's the matter, Suz?
SUZ   This whole place is bugged. They know everything we say and do the moment it happens. (*Carefully*) So, if there was something... 'personal' I wanted to share with you... It wouldn't be personal anymore.
KALENDORF   I see. Er... come here.
SUZ   What?
KALENDORF   Closer. (*Quiet and close*) Hold me.
Rustling sound as they hug.
SUZ   (*Close*) What's the matter, you want them to think we're lovers? What are we going to do, whisper in each other's ears? I wouldn't like to bet they couldn't hear that either.[73]
KALENDORF   (*Telepathic echo*) I'd like to see them try to hear this.
SUZ   Oh my God, you're –
KALENDORF   (*Telepathic echo*) Think it, think it, Suz... don't say it.
SUZ   (*Telepathic echo*) Can – you... hear – me?
KALENDORF   (*Telepathic echo*) Good girl. Now listen, we probably don't have long before they split us up. I'm an agent from the Knights of Velyshaa... they train us all in telepathy.
SUZ   (*Telepathic echo*) Knights of...? Didn't we have a war with you once?
KALENDORF   (*Telepathic echo*) Centuries ago, yes. You beat us hollow, you'll be pleased to hear – but never mind that. What has the Dalek Supreme asked you to do?
SUZ   (*Telepathic echo*) He wants me to make a speech... to everyone... Organise work patterns... give us hope.
KALENDORF   (*Telepathic echo*) Do you trust him?
SUZ   (*Telepathic echo*) No. But I don't see what else I can do.
KALENDORF   (*Telepathic echo*) I see your point. You'll just have to –
DALEK   Susan Mendes... It is time.
SUZ   Yes... yes, of course.
DALEK   Move away from that slave! Move!
Footsteps.
SUZ   All right... all right...
DALEK   You will stand here... and speak. Speak to the other slaves.
NARRATOR   The survivors of Vega turned to look at the girl. A dull silence descended in that vast cavern. A simple fear of humiliation welled up inside her... Then she looked at her friend Kalendorf. He nodded the slightest of nods, the corners of his mouth hinting at the most secret of smiles. But his warmth and the sight of a thousand grey faces needing hope made that fear evaporate.[74]

36

Suz's voice echoes around the vast cavern.
SUZ   (*Loudly*) My name is Susan! Can you hear me? There's so many of us... Can those who can hear, pass what I say on to the others? Yes?
Some random shouts of 'yes' etc.
SUZ   (*Amused for a moment*) All right, all right. You'll have to bear with me. (*After a deep breath*) My name is Susan... you can call me Suz. I am like you. A slave of the Daleks. But I stood up to them. And they noticed. I told them we needed food and rest. They gave it.[75]
Some muted cheers.
SUZ   Now they don't care whether or not we live or die. But they do want us to work. That is their only concern. Now... it's as simple as this... If we work in shifts – eight hours on, eight hours off... and work efficiently, we will have rest and food. We will live. If we defy them, they will work us to death – or just kill us – and replace us with other slaves from other planets they've conquered. Now... I believe in hope. I believe that while we're alive, there's hope. Hope for a better future. To the Daleks, hope is irrelevant. They don't care if we have hope or not. But if they see it makes us work harder... then they will *let* us hope.[76]
Begin crossfade to narration...
SUZ   They are sure that they will win... that they will conquer our galaxy...[77]
NARRATOR   And so she spoke to them of hope... that sea of grey faces staring back at her. She told them that it was worth helping the Daleks in order that they, the subjugated human beings, could live to fight another day. She would never know, in her heart, if this was bravery or cowardice. She would think of it often in the years ahead – but she would never be sure. The thought that she was merely clinging to an excuse to justify her instinct to live at any cost... That thought seemed to gnaw at her very soul.[78]

37. Int. Vega News Ship. Corridor.
An enormous impact explosion. An alarm begins to howl. Sounds of panic from the crew and passengers.

TANNOY   Action stations! Action stations! We are under attack! All crew to action stations! Passengers to your emergency disembarkation points immediately!
More explosions. Screams of distress.
ALBY   (*Calling*) Pellan! Pellan!!!
PELLAN   Brook! This way.
They meet, out of breath from pushing through the crowd. (Some vocal improvisation here)
ALBY   Looks like Vega News has finally run out of luck.
PELLAN   (*Distressed*) I've just come from the comms-monitoring centre... It's a full-scale attack, Brook. The Daleks have suddenly swooped on all the known survivor groups in the Vega System – then they headed straight for us.
ALBY   God, I knew it!!! Don't you see? They knew where you were all the time, Pellan.
An explosion. They react.
PELLAN   What do you mean?

ALBY   Come on! We've got to get to my ship! Move it!

38. Ext. Space.
Dalek battle cruiser firing on the Vega ship. Swooping of transolar discs and Dalek gunfire etc.

39. Int. Seriphia Galaxy. Dalek Command.

DALEK   Report for the Dalek Supreme.
DALEK SUPREME Speak!
DALEK   All pockets of human resistance in the Vega System have been destroyed.
DALEK SUPREME Excellent. Continue.
DALEK   Dalek forces in the Vega System have now engaged the Earth Alliance ship responsible for transmitting anti-Dalek propaganda.
DALEK SUPREME Our firepower is superior. It will be destroyed.

40. Int. Alby's Scout-Ship.
Door closes. Footsteps of Alby and Pellan entering. They are out of breath.

ALBY   Right... power up for immediate take-off, please.
DRUDGER   Complying.
PELLAN   Are we just going to leave? What if we manage to – ?
ALBY   Defeat the Daleks? What are you, mad? It's so bleedin' obvious now I think about it... they've known about this ship for as long as it's been here. And all those call-signs you've been valiantly swapping with the survivor groups... I'll lay money that the Daleks have been picking all that up. They've just been using you to get target information.
PELLAN   (*Defeated*) Oh, God.
A huge impact explosion.
ALBY   Right, hang on.
Controls click.
ALBY   Huh, no response on the docking bay door remote activation. I've a funny feeling we're going to have to blast our way out. Strap in, Pellan, old son, strap in.

41. Ext. Space.
Explosion. The whoosh of the scout-ship escaping. Huge explosion of the Vega News ship exploding.

42. Int. Alby's Scout-Ship.
The ship is rocked by the explosion. ALBY and PELLAN cry out.

ALBY   Looks like we got out just in time.
PELLAN   Do you think there'll be any other survivors?
ALBY   Don't ask stupid questions. Now, our only hope is that the Daleks mistake us for a bit of debris. Cut engine power.
DRUDGER   Complying.
Engines shut down.
ALBY   Now... we're adrift.
PELLAN   No sign of any of them following us.

ALBY   No... not yet.
Pause.
ALBY   (*Heavy sigh*) But where to now?
PELLAN   I thought you were on a mission to find that girlfriend of
yours.
ALBY   Don't try to be funny, Pellan.
Pellan starts to chuckle and laugh.
ALBY   Pellan, I'm warning you, I'm not in the mood.
PELLAN   Sorry... I was just thinking about what I said.[79]
ALBY   What? When?
PELLAN   Before... in the studios. That your Susan Mendes was
hardly likely to be the Daleks' number one concern at the moment.
ALBY   What are you getting at?
PELLAN   Just before all hell broke loose... we monitored a Dalek
communication out of Vega VI. A humanoid female, name of Susan
Mendes, top priority transport out of the system.[80]
ALBY   Where to?
PELLAN   Garazone.
ALBY   (*Puzzled*) Garazone? Why...? What are they up to...? (*To
himself*) Suz, what have you done? What do they want with you?
PELLAN   Seems she's somehow pretty important to the Daleks.
ALBY   My little Suz... Well, that's cleared up where we're going,
then, hasn't it? Set course for the Garazone System.[81]
DRUDGER   Complying.
ALBY   (*To himself*) Hang on, Suz. Alby's coming to get you.[82]

CLOSING THEME.

NOTES

1. Line repeated.

2. Line changed to: 'Bring *Victorious* back to the fleet, captain. I'll deploy our ships in defence formation and appraise Earth Command of the situation before **they have a chance** – '

3. Line changed to: 'We are being fired upon. They've dropped their distortion field, increased speed to an incredible rate. **A few seconds ago they were at three sectors, now they're virtually on top of us and** –'

4. Line changed to: '~~In my mind's eye~~... the air was always fresh, the suns were always high in the sky.'

5. Line changed to: 'I can still taste that air. Still taste it. Never tasted anything like it since... But the girl, the girl, yes... She was only interested in the rocks (*chuckles*)... her precious **minerals**.'

6. This line and the following two, changed to:

SUZ	The Reinsberg Institute's paying. **One of the perks of working for a faceless scientific multi-world corporation. Helps to make up for the mind-numbing work.**
ALBY	**Do I sense rebellion in the ranks?**
SUZ	**I don't know. I shouldn't complain really.**
ALBY	**Go on. Enjoy yourself.**
SUZ	**Want some of my packed lunch?**
ALBY	**This another Reinsberg perk?**

She opens a plastic container. Rustle of food parcels. She takes a bite.

SUZ	**No**, **this is a Susan Mendes special**. (*Mouth full*) Here. Try a pickled onion...

7. Line changed to: 'Do it. I don't care. (*Munches*) To tell you the truth, I've been thinking **about** moving on anyway.'

8. Line changed to: '(*Affecting nonchalance*) Yeah. **I mean, it's been six months. Not my style to hang around in one place too long**.'

9. Line changed to: '(*Eating*) Where **would** you go? What **would** you do?'

10. Line changed to: '*Temporary* bar manager. But an old mate of mine has been in touch... reckons he can get ~~me~~ something permanent.'

11. Line changed to: '(*Trying to keep calm*) We've spoken to C-in-C Earth Alliance Rapid Response Fleet, Admiral Cheviat, and ~~she~~ confirms that the fleet have engaged an unknown, hostile alien force at co-ordinates... er, just outside our system, the Vega System. Er – (*lost for words, panicking a little*)'

12. Line changed to: '(*Distort*) Is... is there any news on – ? Er, has the Rapid Response Fleet contained the hostile forces? (*Pause*) Ed?'

13. Line changed to: 'No... no, I'm afraid we've definitely lost Ed for the moment. Er... What? **It seems something is interfering with our signal. We apologise if you are having difficulty** – '

14. Line changed to: '(*Distort*) Attention! Attention! Citizens of the Vega System! You are now **subjects** of the Dalek Empire. You will surrender. Resist and you will be exterminated.'

15. Line changed to: '(*The word is unfamiliar to her*) Dalek...? Dalek Empire? What *was* that thing? **A Dalek**?'

16. Line changed to: 'It was at daybreak, ~~or what passed for daybreak back then~~. A dull, cold glow from Vega Prime filtered through the dust clouds. Thousands lay dying and waiting to die on the barren, gnarled, radioactive plains.'

17. Line changed to: '**Come to finish us off**, **have you**? **Well**, **get on with it**.'

18. Line changed to: '**Come on, we're still alive. Don't give up hope.**'

19. Line changed to: 'I can't just – I can't *leave now*! Don't you understand?! My **father** and **mother** – '

20. Line changed to: 'How? How do you know them? **Until this afternoon, Daleks were just something I vaguely remembered from history lessons as a schoolkid.**'

21. Line changed to: 'I can't tell you how **I know** – you just have to trust me!'

22. TANNOY's line plays throughout the scene.

23. Line changed to: 'Vega VI Command to Seriphia ~~Galaxy~~ Control.'

24. Added dialogue – DALEK AIDE: '**I obey**.'

25. Line changed to: 'You see that? His ankle is bruised. Bruised! Do you know what that means? It's not broken. The bruising will go away. It'll get better. He'll be able to walk properly soon. Or is there a time limit? How soon do you need us to be able to walk? How many of us do you need? **Do you just kill whenever you feel like it for no reason**? Have you *got* any plans, or are you **just** making this all up as you go along?

26. Line changed to: '(*Groans in defeat*) All right, all right... Patch **him** through.'

27. Line changed to:

ALBY   Because he's a good old pro from the old school, sir. A Knight of Velyshaa. **Trained in all the ancient arts of Velyshaa: telepathy, espionage, mortal combat**...

TANLEE   **Yes, all right, Brook.**

ALBY   **In short**, very good at not being found. Anyway, my contact had got wind of his intention to leave Vega VI on **a** Star Cruise Line. I was about to go undercover as bar manager on the *Luciana*.'

28. Line changed to: '(*Reading*) Susan Mendes... known to her friends, **and naturally to you**, as Suz... geologist for the Reinsberg Institute, investigating mineral deposits on Vega VI. Never forget, Brook, there's always someone keeping tabs on you.'

29. Line changed to:

TANLEE   You've missed the boat on Kalendorf, Brook. As we speak, the galaxy is descending into very probably the most catastrophic conflict in its long and turgid history.

ALBY   So, **it's as bad as we thought**? **They're going for the whole galaxy**.

TANLEE   **We've no reason to think not**. In short, ex-corporal Alby Brook, 2 years' penal servitude pending for petty pilfering... you have other fish to fry.

30. Added dialogue – ALBY: '**Bye**!'

31. Added dialogue – DALEK: '**Move**!'

32. Line changed to: 'That's a point. You! **Dalek**!'

33 Line changed to: 'The Daleks had drilled a series of gigantic shafts deep into the crust of Vega VI. Then they had taken away their sophisticated machinery, **apparently** preferring to set us to work with little more than our bare hands.'

34. Line changed to: 'To hack chunks of blue ~~crystalline~~ rock out of a dead world.'

35. Line changed to: 'That's what we called it... ~~for a joke...~~ at the Reinsberg Institute. Rare deposits of it on the surface... we'd only just located a rich underground strata – '

36. Line changed to: '**Silence! Silence**! Do not make that noise! Silence! Robomen will restrain them!'

37. Line changed to: 'Welcome to Scout-Ship X49, agent Alby Brook. I am your Drudger Pilot. Your flight plan and sealed mission orders are stored in the onboard **terminal** – '

38. Line changed to:

ALBY   Huh, Tanlee's putting me out to grass. That's a long haul... the other side of the galaxy. (Change of thought) And a long way from Vega VI... and you Suz. If you're still alive.

DRUDGER   **Coffee**.

ALBY   Maybe I should just forget –

39. Line changed to: '**Woah!** What the hell was that?

40. Line changed to: '(*Distort*) Attention Earth passenger cruiser! Prepare to be boarded. All humanoids aboard your vessel are now **subjects** of the Dalek Empire. Resist and you will be exterminated.'

41. Line changed to: 'The Daleks worked the frightened, exhausted survivors of Vega VI, **without end**... for hours... for longer than seemed possible. Hundreds had already collapsed and died at the rock face. But still the Daleks bellowed their commands, still the Robomen brandished their whips and clubs, often lashing and jabbing at corpses... as if they'd forgotten how to recognise the living. Finally, the last few fell to their knees, unable to work a moment longer, their spirits... broken. Even the Robomen were unable to fight off the all-consuming fatigue.'

42. Line changed to: '(*Exhausted*) Master... they... they will not work. ~~We...~~ we cannot make them work.'

43. Line changed to: 'I... I... ~~please, I~~ cannot... **I cannot** make them work. **I cannot**, master...'

44. Line changed to: '~~Please~~... master... ~~must~~... must sleep... **please**.'

45. Added dialogue – KALENDORF: **'Suz.'**

46. Line changed to: 'Activating mineshaft monitor ~~screen~~.'

47. Line changed to: '~~Terminated~~. Are they to be exterminated.'

48. Line changed to: 'Correct. You will allow the **humans** to rest.'

49. Line changed to:

DALEK   Report for the Emperor.

EMPEROR   Enter.

Door opens.

EMPEROR   You have done well.

50. Line changed to: 'Yes, Emperor. ~~I must give her... hope.~~'

51. Line changed to: '~~The... (stops herself saying 'veganite')~~ the... blue ore, **the veganite**, you're making us dig out. It's not exactly friendly to mechanical mining, is it? So you need us to do it. And you obviously haven't got enough of it, have you?'

52. Line changed to: 'So... Well, if you understood human beings a **little** better, you'd let us rest.'

53. Added dialogue:

SUZ   But...

DALEK EMPEROR Excellent. The human female will now consider what you have said.

DALEK SUPREME Her thought processes may have been impaired by fatigue. When she has recovered, she may not prove susceptible.

DALEK EMPEROR When she has recovered, she will fear death.

54. Line changed to:

ALBY   Yeah... I knew that too.

DRUDGER   **Complying**.

ALBY   (*To himself*) Now what... now what? God, what am I doing? Risking extermination just for the sake of a woman? You've got it bad, Alby old son, you've got it bad. And it's only a matter of time before a Dalek ship spots us if I don't think of something soon.

55.   Line changed to: '(*Laughs*) My God. **My God**, they did it! Pellan was right! They did it!'

56.   Line changed to: 'What do you know about these creatures? I'd **hardly** heard of them before all this.'

57.   Line changed to:

KALENDORF (*Secretive*) Never mind how I know.

SUZ   That's what Alby said.

KALENDORF What?

SUZ   Nothing.

KALENDORF So you spoke to the Dalek Supreme. What did you say **to him**?

58.   Line changed to: '**I know**, I don't, I don't... But we're alive, aren't we? We've got... hope.'

59.   Line changed to: '(Gobsmacked) My God, it's... er... it's... **er**...'

60.   Line changed to: 'I just ran. I̶ ̶j̶u̶s̶t̶.̶.̶.̶ ran. You know? It's like I didn't care a damn about anyone else. Those... voices. And the screaming. I remember... climbing over people... people screaming for help. I didn't care. I just wanted to get out. (*Sighs, reliving it*) Oh, God...'

61.   Line changed to:

DALEK   **Dalek Supreme now entering War Room**.

Door opens.

DALEK 1   **All section commanders will enter the War Room**.

Doors open.

DALEK   Report for the Dalek Supreme **from Logril squadron, leading galactic attack spearhead**.

62.   Line changed to: 'Battle computers in all o̶u̶r̶ fleets have anticipated this, but warn of energy and raw material depletion.'

63.   Line changed to: 'Not if it is utilised effectively. The Emperor has a plan that will achieve this. Continue with y̶o̶u̶r̶ **reports**.' Then, added dialogue – DALEK: '**Vega VI commander reporting via hyperlink**.'

64.   Line changed to: 'Because it's what the Daleks do. What do you think happens when **all this's** over? When they've got what they want? Do you think they just say, 'Thanks for the help guys' and t̶h̶e̶n̶ leave?'

65.   Line changed to:

PELLAN   Well, I told you Vega News persuaded the Earth Alliance to let them have a ship.

ALBY   **Yeah, how did they manage that?**

PELLAN   **Well, High Command knew there were surving pockets of resistance *and* they knew that a single ship operating covertly might just be a life-line and of course we're able to keep High Command up to date and local Dalek troop movements. So**, when I jettisoned from the Aquitania, I set a course for this system. **Wanted to be part of it, to make a difference**.

66.   'Just – kill – me – and – get – it – over – with' is a replay of SUZ saying that line from Scene 27.

67.   Line changed to: '(*Reluctant*) Yes, **of course**... I do.'

68.   Line changed to: '**Hmm**. Quite an impressive rig you've got here.'

69.   Line changed to: '**I'm** sorry... no, I appreciate it, Pellan. Thanks.'

70.   Line changed to: 'You mean they're too busy to notice? **That** doesn't sound like the Daleks to me.'

71.   Line changed to: '**Oh, and you're suddenly** an expert on the Daleks?'

72.   Line changed to: '**O̶h̶**, I see. You really can't keep your mind off that girl of yours, can you? What was her name... Susan Mendes, wasn't it?'

73.   Line changed to: '(*Close*) What's the matter, **do** you want them to think we're lovers? What are we going to do, whisper in each other's ears? I wouldn't like to bet they couldn't hear that either.'

74.   Line changed to: 'The survivors of Vega turned to look at the girl. A dull silence descended in that vast cavern. A simple fear of humiliation welled up inside her... Then she looked at her friend Kalendorf. He nodded the slightest of nods, the corners of his mouth hinting at the most secret of smiles. ~~But~~ his warmth and the sight of a thousand grey faces needing hope made that fear evaporate.'

75. Line changed to: '(*Amused for a moment*) All right, all right. You'll have to bear with me. (*After a deep breath*) My name is Susan... you can call me Suz. I am like you. A slave of the Daleks. But I stood up to them. **I don't know why but I did**. And they noticed. I told them we needed food and rest. They gave it.'

76. This monologue was cut in post-production so that it ran as a montage of different takes, with each clip slightly overlapping the preceeding one. In the following, [/] is used to seperate the clips: 'Now they don't care whether or not we live or die. But they do want us to work. That is their only concern. [/] ~~Now...~~ it's as simple as this... If we work in shifts [/] eight hours on, eight hours off... [/] and work efficiently, we will have rest and food. [/] We will live. [/] If we defy them [/] they will work us to death – or just kill us – and replace us with other slaves from other planets they've conquered. [/] ~~Now...~~ I believe in hope. I believe that while we're alive [/] there's hope. Hope for a better future. To the Daleks [/] hope is irrelevant. They don't care if we have hope or not. But if they see it makes us work harder... then they will *let* us **have** hope.'

77. Line changed to: 'They are sure that they will ~~win... that they will~~ conquer our galaxy...'

78. Line changed to: 'And so **the girl** spoke to them of hope... that sea of grey faces staring back at her. **Their eyes dry and hollow with fear**, **thirsting for hope**. She told them that it was worth helping the Daleks in order that they, the subjugated human beings, could live to fight another day. She would never know, in her heart, if this was bravery or cowardice. She would think of it often in the years ahead – but she would never be sure. The thought that she was merely clinging to an excuse to justify her instinct to live at any cost... That thought seemed to gnaw at her very soul.'

79. Line changed to: '**I'm** sorry... I was just thinking about what I said.'

80. Line changed to: 'Just before all hell broke loose... we monitored a Dalek communication **from** Vega VI. A humanoid female, name of Susan Mendes, top priority transport out of the system.'

81. Line changed to:

ALBY   My little Suz... Well, that's cleared up where we're going, then, hasn't it?

PELLAN   I suppose it has, **since this is your ship and I'm just the hitchhiker**.

ALBY   Set course for the Garazone System.

82. Line changed to: '(*To himself*) Hang on, Suz. **Please. Just hang on**.'

DALEK EMPIRE
ORIGINAL PRESS RELEASE

ON SUNDAY 6 MAY 2001, the first part of *Dalek Empire* was recorded at the Moat Studios in South London.

The cast featured some returning voices from Big Finish's ever-expanding repertory company of actors.

Sarah Mowat stars as planetary geologist Susan Mendes. Sarah played the marathon role of the Sirens of Time in Big Finish's debut *Doctor Who* play, *The Sirens of Time*, appearing as five different incarnations of the same being. Nick Briggs: 'Sarah is a very special actress. I've been trying to find a big role for her ever since *Sirens*. We did at one point consider her to play Paul McGann's new assistant in the *Doctor Who* audios before the character of Charley Pollard was devised.'

Sarah says: 'I've encountered the Daleks before, because my godfather is Roger Hancock, whose company sort of "protects" the Daleks. I know Terry Nation didn't want to have the Mickey taken out of them, and I think that's important because the Daleks can still be terrifying. And they are in *Dalek Empire*.'

Sarah describes the Doctors in *The Sirens of Time*: 'All three of the Doctors were very different. Sylvester McCoy almost ad-libbed around what was written, in a very mad way. He was a sort of mad Doctor, which was fun. Colin Baker was jolly and cuddly. Peter Davison was just gorgeous and really enthusiastic.'

Mark McDonnell plays Alby Brook, a slightly less than dynamic space security agent. Mark featured in *The Fearmonger* and will also be appearing in the next season of Paul McGann plays. He's currently working on the second season of his Radio 4 comedy series, *Velvet Cabaret*, which promises to be the next big comedy cult when it migrates to a BBC TV version entitled *Velvet Soup* this summer. Nick Briggs: 'Mark was one of the "crap commandos", as we called them, in the upcoming *The Time of the Daleks*. The moment I started working with him in that, I knew I'd found my *Dalek Empire* leading man.'

Mark says: 'When Nick first spoke to me about this, he hadn't finished writing it. I said I'd like to do it... So now the character's turned out a bit like me in space... always trying to find out where the nearest bar is!'

Gareth Thomas guest stars as the enigmatic Kalendorf. Gareth is, of course, best known as Blake from *Blake's 7*, but it was his performance in McGann's audio debut *Storm Warning* which led to his casting in *Dalek Empire*. Nick Briggs: 'Aside from being a brilliant actor, he's a thoroughly nice bloke.'

Gareth says: 'It's an interesting character. He has a number of special qualities and is a knight in the old fashioned sense of the word, but in the first part he's acting rather against type... but all will no doubt be revealed as the story moves on.'

Other members of the cast include John Wadmore (another *Sirens* veteran) as newsreader Gordon Pellan, Ian Brooker (regularly heard on *The Archers* and many other Radio 4 productions) and Joyce Gibbs (another *Archers* and Radio 4 regular who will also be familiar to viewers of the BBC1 soap *Doctors* in which she plays Violet Appleby).

Once again, Nick Briggs and Alistair Lock will supply their acclaimed Dalek voices.

Genesis of _Dalek Empire_ Producer Jason Haigh-Ellery explains the genesis of _Dalek Empire_: 'It came about with a conversation between myself and Nick. He was determined to get some Dalek stories done which would stand alone. I wholeheartedly agreed with him. I thought it was a brilliant idea.'

Writer/director Nick Briggs: 'It was before we had the licence to do _Doctor Who_. At that stage, actually doing _Doctor Who_ seemed like a completely unobtainable goal. So my thoughts at that time were that it might be easier just to get the rights to do the Daleks.'

Script editor John Ainsworth explains the premise of the four-part series. '_Dalek Empire_ is about presenting an old _Doctor Who_ situation in a new way. It's a Dalek invasion. And you could say that's all it's about. But it goes further, exploring the real moral issues that people face in terrible situations as well as the relationships they have. And the horrible decisions they have to make for "the greater good", and what that does to you.'

Nick: 'The characters in the series are not in control of the situation. They've been overrun. The Dalek invasion starts and the Daleks are winning! But there's plenty of action in there! Plenty of Daleks! Intrigue, excitement and... transolar discs!'

Part One, _Invasion of the Daleks_, is slated for release at the end of June. Further parts will be released in August, October and December, additional to Big Finish's _Doctor Who_ releases.

Q&A
INVASION OF THE DALEKS

The first episode must have been so important, in terms of helping the audience get into the story. Were there any specific aims you had for the *Invasion of the Daleks*?

Nicholas Briggs: I had three main aims. I wanted to hit the audience with action from the beginning; hence the first scene when the Daleks attack that spaceship. Then I wanted to establish the emotional core of the story, with Suz and Alby having a gentle, romantic frisson. So, in essence, I wanted to tell the audience that this was a war story and a love story. The third aim was to establish the narrative style by having a narrator. So really, it was all a question of creating the flavour of *Dalek Empire*. You know? You open the packet, expecting to taste *Doctor Who*-with-something-missing, and what you get is not *Doctor Who* at all. Something with, hopefully, a slightly spicier, more mature flavour.

How much did you think the Daleks had to be in the story? They're not in it that much.

There wasn't any contractual obligation about how much they had to feature! But it was a difficult balancing act. First off, there's no point playing the 'ooh, who's the monster going to be?' card, since the series is called *Dalek Empire* and there are Daleks all over the CD cover! So I wanted to get them in very early. But the idea was that that should be a sort of tease. Give them the Daleks, then hold them back for a while. It doesn't matter so much if the Daleks don't feature heavily, as long as the drama is shaped by the actions of the Daleks. Everything that happens in that first episode happens because the Daleks have invaded the galaxy. So, even if we're not hearing them, they're always in our thoughts and the thoughts of the characters.

What advantages, storytelling-wise, does a narrator give you?

In this case, the narrator added an extra piece of intrigue. Who is she? Why is this person commenting on events? Of course, most people assumed she was an older version of Suz – which made us secure that Suz would survive. But I deliberately gave her lines which referred to Suz in the third person, which, I hope, added to the intrigue. In general terms, a narrator can really help a story. People expect narrators to give information; so rather than have characters awkwardly relate the plot, you can just leave it to the storyteller herself.

One of the great advantages, not so much used in this part, was that you could advance the story quickly by jumping large chunks of time. I suppose the most effective use of this in *Invasion of the Daleks* is when she talks about the underground mining on Vega. It also allows you to explore emotional issues more bluntly, which I'm rather keen on. I was particularly pleased with the 'What is it that makes a person go on?' speech, which I think is horribly stark.

You must have known who the narrator would turn out to be.
Yes. I always knew that it would be a creature who had all Suz's memories. I always knew that Alby would one day find this woman and ask her what had been going on. So I always knew that the narration we were hearing was this alien woman telling Alby what had happened to Suz. When I started, I'm not sure if I had named her a Seer of Yaldos yet, but the principles were certainly in place.

The character in the opening scene – Admiral Cheviat – was originally a woman.
I've no real recollection of why the sex of Admiral Cheviat was changed. I think I'd forgotten I'd made him a woman until we got into the studio. So we just changed the lines a bit. Massive rewrites, you know. Changing 'she' into 'he'.

***Dalek Empire* is a love story – but the two lovers have only five scenes together at the beginning of *Invasion of the Daleks*. How easily did you think the audience would accept the relationship between these two characters?**
It's a very personal thing. I accepted it. Mark McDonnell and Sarah Mowat accepted it. But it is odd that nothing really happened between them. But, you know, I'm an old romantic at heart. Sometimes there's just a connection between people... or at least, they think there's a connection. The love is very naïve indeed. I think there's a distinct possibility that if the Dalek invasion hadn't happened then Alby and Suz would've had a brief, rather unsatisfactory relationship. But, of course, the Dalek thing is the whole reason it happens the way it does. If it weren't for the threat of the Daleks, Alby wouldn't have been there in the first place. But it's the invasion which gives their brief moment of connection a massive significance. The extreme situation of the war blows their love out of all proportion. It's Alby's flawed character and Suz's need for hope that fuel the love. I also wanted it to be a total contrast to the horrific reality of war. A rather pure, idealised version of love. It also creates anticipation in the audience. Since nothing physical has happened between them, we want to know if it ever will – and how distasteful that'll sound on audio!

Are Alby and Suz based on anyone in particular? Did you know who would play them when you wrote the scripts.
Their names are based on my grandparents, which is why 'Nan and Gramp' appear in the 'thank you's on the sleeve. I didn't know who was going to play them when I started writing. I just tried to make them the best characters I'd ever written. However, at some point during the writing of *Invasion of the Daleks*, I met Mark McDonnell and asked him to do it. Then, I started thinking of the little I knew of him and had fun making Alby a bit like Mark. I didn't know Mark very well at that point; but I was very pleased that when he read it, he said, 'This is just me in space!'. I think he was referring to all the mooning over women and always wondering where the nearest bar was. He's a tremendous actor and a lovely bloke. When I'd finished part one, I had a sneaking suspicion that I should cast Sarah Mowat. She's an absolute delight as a person and as an actress. But I worried that I was making too easy a choice and so we did a lot of auditions. But I kept thinking, 'They're not really as good as Sarah, are they?'. That said, Susan is nothing like Sarah. Susan rocks the boat and stomps about the place making trouble. Sarah is sweetness personified. She's the kind of person who always blushes if you tell her a dirty joke. She isn't disapproving of other people's naughtiness, but she'd never be naughty herself!

'The *Southampton* Terminus'? Of all the places for Earth to have a terminus, why Southampton?
I come from the Southampton area and always used to love seeing the big ships in dock there. I went on board the first *Queen Elizabeth* and I saw the *Queen Mary* set sail for the final time. My Nan actually went aboard the *Titanic* while it was in Southampton. Thankfully, she got off again. My Gramp was a steward on the *Aquitania* – one of the few of those big four-funnelled ships that didn't have a spectacular death. And once, I worked as a book club salesman, for one day only, in the old Ocean Terminus building in Southampton. It was a magnificent building. A real slice of 1920s design. Then, one day, years later, I was driving by and noticed they'd knocked the whole thing down to build a car park. It makes me cry just to think of it. So I thought I'd immortalise it, in a bizarre sci-fi way, by having something of the sort in *Dalek Empire*. I imagine they built it on that bloody car park and squashed all those bloody cars!

One change that occurs a couple of times between script and finished audio is that in Dalek dialogue, the word 'citizens' is replaced by 'subjects'.
I initially toyed with the idea of using 'subjects', but thought that word had too much of a 'royal' association for the Daleks. I substituted 'citizens' because I thought it had a cold, unemotional feel to it. But then I thought, 'Citizens have rights'. And, of course, the Daleks may be cold, but they're not unemotional. They're bursting with emotion. All of it negative! Also, 'subject' had an imperial connotation, and it is called *Dalek Empire* after all. Subjects don't necessarily have rights... and the people conquered by the Daleks would certainly have no rights; so, finally, I thought the word 'subject' was more appropriate.

It's a very evocative, sci-fi-esque title. Other than its literal description of the plot, does it have any meaning?
Invasion of the Daleks is a bit of a 'does what it says on the can' kind of title for the first chapter of *Dalek Empire*; although, I suppose you could think it was about the Daleks being invaded, rather than doing the invading. I used it because it was the opening story of *The Dalek Book*. That lovely piece of artwork of a Dalek blasting away and the words 'Invasion of the Daleks' slicing jaggedly across the page is forever burned into my brain. I just had to use that title. I felt compelled.

The timescale of *Dalek Empire* seems much more fluid than in, say, a *Doctor Who* story. There can be months between scenes, and characters talk of events happening years before.
There's often a tendency for *Doctor Who* stories to seem as if they happen in one day. The action is more often than not continuous and chronological. In my general desire to be more 'realistic' – and I do use the term very loosely – than *Doctor Who*, I wanted to give the impression that, as in life, things take a long time to happen. It gives the whole thing an epic scope and it gives a chance for characters to develop and change. Suz changes quite a lot, for example.

You drew up character biographies for Alby, Suz and Kalendorf. (See pages 11, 12 & 15.) Were they for your benefit or to help the actors?
Both. I definitely wanted to help the actors to get a handle on their characters, especially

since they had only one instalment of the script to go on at first. I was particularly concerned that Gareth could see where Kalendorf was going. Unfortunately, telling him that Kalendorf was strong and warrior-like right from the beginning meant that he kept telling me the character wasn't behaving correctly in the first chapter. It's an odd thing to find an actor telling you that the character isn't right, when you created it in the first place. I suppose he was concerned that there weren't enough seeds planted for his later, heroic behaviour to be credible. Basically, I think he liked the character description very much, but was very disappointed that the character as initially described wasn't immediately on display in the script. His concerns did push me into making Kalendorf stronger. I rewrote sections of *The Human Factor* as a result. I did this partially to keep Gareth happy and partially because I thought he had a very good point. He complained right up until the end that he wasn't giving enough orders and wasn't in command enough. I got quite used to it eventually. I think Gareth was looking for a consistent strength in Kalendorf and felt that the character description was describing a man who'd take the lead more often than was written. I think he thought the story was about him; when, of course, it was, at its core, about Suz and Alby. Interestingly, however, I think it was Gareth's passion for the character that led me to make *Dalek War* more or less all about Kalendorf.

But on the general point about the character biogs, I think it's important to give the actors the initial character flavour you want them to go for. I did the same for my *Doctor Who* audio drama *Creatures of Beauty*, and it worked a treat.

Kalendorf is a Knight of Velyshaa, the race you'd previously used in the *Doctor Who* audio play, *The Sirens of Time*. Why reuse them?
I'm not a fan of continuity and everything tying together. I think it makes the universe too small, and I never set out with that as my aim. However, if you have a need in a story for a particular element which is very similar to one you have created before, then as far as I see it, you have two choices; change the idea altogether and start from scratch, or use the thing you created before. That's what happened here. I wanted this 'agent', Kalendorf, to be a member of an ancient, mysterious race which had had a troubled past with Earth. The Velyshaans fitted the bill... likewise the drudgers. They're handy tools to create a story. It's often easier to use tools you've already got rather than build them all from scratch.

Talking of continuity, there's mention of the Kar-Charrat Library and the Seriphia Galaxy – elements of *Doctor Who* plays you directed. How did they find their way into *Dalek Empire*?
The initial idea was for *Dalek Empire* to be linked quite definitely with the *Doctor Who Dalek Empire* stories. That had been Gary Russell's idea. I didn't like it and forgot all about it. However, when I found I needed the Daleks to have a source of information about the human factor, I suddenly remembered the Kar-Charrat Library in *The Genocide Machine* and all the information that could have been downloaded from the super Dalek that went mad. Once again, it was a ready-made tool that fitted the bill. Likewise, the Seriphia Galaxy... I loved that idea Steve Cole had in *The Apocalypse Element* of the Daleks creating a new galaxy, just to make it a base for operations and a launching pad for invasions. Why create something new when the idea is already in existence? And it ended up giving a partial link with the *Doctor Who* stories, which would make Gary happy. I like it when

Gary's happy! I told him about it and he immediately suggested other links, included one which would have tied in to *Neverland*, involving the Dalek Emperor pleading with Romana for mercy... but I couldn't make that work without slowing the story up.

There's some dialogue that was added about the Knights of Velyshaa. Alby says that Kalendorf is, 'Trained in all the ancient arts of Velyshaa: telepathy, espionage, mortal combat...'
I did a lot of last-minute rewrites on this first part, which I just scribbled on my script. I then read these out to the actors in the studio and they copied them down. This was one of them. It was simply a matter of foreshadowing Kalendorf's telepathy. I'd always intended him to be telepathic, but I didn't mention it in the script until he reveals it to Suz. I thought the audience might feel this was a bit too convenient – so I inserted an earlier mention, which is always the best way of dispelling that sort of criticism. And indeed, no one has ever picked up on that as far as I'm aware.

One of Kalendorf's first lines in the script is, 'As I believe they say on some parts of that old and revered planet Earth... "The top of the morning to you".' This was changed to, 'Come to finish us off, have you? Well, get on with it.' Any reason for the change?
It was one of those lines that, when you're in the studio and an actor is saying it, you think, 'That's a bloody terrible line! Why did I write that?'. So I said as much to Gareth, he seemed to agree, so we just worked out together what might be better and simpler for him to say. That's the beauty of directing your own stuff. You can change it without offending the writer. And sometimes, it only becomes clear that a line is no good when you hear the actor saying out loud. I try to say all my stuff out loud when I'm writing it, but that one slipped through the net!

As you were the producer and director as well as the writer, how did that affect the writing process? Did you know how many actors you'd be able to have, for example?
I established with [co-producer] Jason Haigh-Ellery the number of cast members I could have. Then I worked out a kind of rolling budget which allowed me to spend more on some chapters and save on others. As a result, I came in under budget, then gave Alistair Lock the remainder as a sort of bonus for all the extra work he put in on the Dalek voices. So, yes, knowing the budgetary restrictions as I was writing did make me constantly assess which characters would be doubled-up, *et cetera*. You'll always know when I'm thinking of doubling when I introduce characters with heavy voice effects!

So, who's David Sax then?
David Sax is me when I feel like the credits list is overloaded with my name. I'd use more pseudonyms in the *Doctor Whos* if Gary would let me, but he's dead against them. My theory is that if people know it's you doing a voice, they'll say they could tell anyway. If you don't tell them, a large number of the audience won't be able to tell, no matter how obvious it is, simply and hopefully because they're caught up in the fictional world you're presenting them with. I used to do that when I worked for Visual Imagination. I'd answer the phone to someone who wanted to speak to advertising; I'd tell them I was putting them through, then I'd say, 'Hello, advertising?' in exactly the same voice and, because they were expecting to hear someone different, they'd never be able to tell it was me. The same thing can happen in an audio play. Who's playing this mad Spanish/

Greek/French bloke Morebi? Oh, David Sax – can't be Nick Briggs, then! That's the theory... and I think it's quite funny when people guess it. Dave Owen in **Doctor Who Magazine** [DWM] was quite amusing about being able to see David Sax's huge, false moustache during that Morebi scene. I'm sure he was having a laugh at my acting!

What about the other characters: Tanlee, Pellan, Drudger. Where did they come from?
Since I was going down the Harry Palmer route with Alby Brook, I thought I'd make his boss rather like Harry Palmer's Ross. The name Tanlee is a mish-mash somehow constructed from the names of actors who played Ross and James Bond's 'M'. I wanted him to be initially cold and cynical, so that when things really got bad I could actually show him worrying and being quite genuine. I thought this shift of gear would emphasise just how seriously bad things were going in the war with the Daleks. It was John Ainsworth who suggested that I should play him – we're both big Harry Palmer fans.

My brother is a TV newsreader and journalist, so I suppose that was the initial inspiration for Pellan, but there's no other similarity. I cast John Wadmore, because he's always been a great actor and a close friend. The Drudgers are a blatant plot device. In a movie, Alby would just go off in a spaceship on his own. But on audio, he needs to talk to someone. So the Drudgers are close relatives of every irritating robotic device that has ever featured in sci-fi. I thought Ian Brooker did an excellent job of giving them a kind of chirpy, non-offensive arrogance. It was the strength of his performance that made Gary Russell wonder why I didn't give the Drudger a more touching death scene after the crash-landing on Guria. But I was unaffected. No one cries over a fridge breaking down, do they? The Drudgers were just hovering, talking fridges which I created for the Audio Visuals amateur plays all those years ago.

In the original script, Suz says that she's never heard of the Daleks, but in the play she says, 'Until this afternoon, Daleks were just something I vaguely remembered from history lessons as a schoolkid.' Why the slight change?
I think this was something suggested by John Ainsworth. He felt that, since there had been other Dalek stories before *Dalek Empire*, we should at least acknowledge past battles between Daleks and humans. I thought that was fair enough. I didn't want to make any precise references to the past, so I thought this was enough of a link.

Dalek dialogue is famously difficult. How did you approach writing for them, particularly in scenes with only Daleks in them?
I love writing dialogue for the Daleks. It is difficult in terms of making it interesting, but if you latch on to the idea that they can give out vital plot information, you can have fun giving them revelatory speeches, which makes us think, 'Oh my God, that's what they're up to!'. Also, Dalek scenes where they're planning their tactics give a story a horrible feeling of impending disaster. It doesn't matter what our human friends are up to, the Daleks will always be plotting something dastardly. The challenge is to phrase it all in a Dalek-like way... You must always use 'Dalekese', but the trick is to push the envelope a bit and occasionally include a surprisingly emotional phrase, or have the Daleks discuss something we're not used to them discussing... I think that, in particular, gives a Dalek scene a bit of a dramatic tingle, when they mention 'love' or 'fear'.

Originally, the mineral being mined on the Vega VI is only called veganite 'as a joke', but the reference to veganite only being a nickname was dropped. Also, there was a scripted line of Suz deliberately not using the word veganite in front of the Dalek Supreme; but in the audio, she simply says it – what's all that about?

This was all about simplification. While writing, I thought that 'veganite' sounded a bit cod, and that it might be more believable as just a nickname... but then I thought that nicknames often stick and become the accepted terminology. So rather than get bogged down in that minor detail, I just called the mineral veganite. Likewise, I was toying with Suz being less forthright with information, but this sent the scene up a bit of a blind alley in dramatic terms. The scene is not about Suz being secretive. It's about other, more dramatically interesting stuff, so why distract from the point of it? This often happens to me once I hear the dramatic content of an actor's performance. The piffling little details I've put in sometimes feel too pedantic and less realistic. They can interrupt the emotional flow of a scene and make you ask, 'Would she really have bothered to say that?'.

When Suz gives her speech to the slaves – 'I believe that while we're alive, there's hope,' etc – you scripted it as a monologue, but it was recorded and edited as a montage, with different clauses and sentences being taken from different takes.

The scene was written and recorded as a monologue. I'd always intended to play about with it in post-production, but I wasn't quite sure how. Again, this is the beauty of being involved in all levels of the production in a very hands-on way. You can leave certain issues until later. You can let an idea bubble around in your head and come up with the solution at just the right time. So, when I came to edit and sound-design that scene, I was developing the idea that I wanted to give more of an impression of the impact the speech was having. In a film, you give that by cutting to reaction shots in the crowd. Here, I wanted to give the impression of hearing the speech from different perspectives.

Sarah did it brilliantly, because I wanted her to do it all on that relentless, shouting level – because that's what you'd have to do if you had no microphone and a thousand people to communicate with. I hate it in films and TV when actors address massed armies with only a slightly raised voice. I always wonder why the soldiers don't get bored and start chatting among themselves. To get your words out there, to a vast crowd, you really have to almost exhaust yourself on every sentence. I actually nearly lost my voice demonstrating to Sarah what I wanted her to do.

So, I got this very realistic, shouting delivery from Sarah that had pain and exhaustion in every line. It wasn't pleasant to listen to and it was relentless. That's what I wanted. That was realistic and right. My job in post-production was to enhance that and give us other reasons to want to listen to it. That's why I made it overlap itself and come from different acoustic perspectives. I wanted to make a feature of its length and relentlessness.

Was it always the intention to use cliffhangers? Dalek Empire was praised for its end-of-episode twists, but the end of Invasion of the Daleks is more of a set-up for The Human Factor than a crisis point to be resolved.

I suppose I wanted every episode ending to give a reason for listeners to come back for more. It just felt right for the first part to end on the promise of a change of gear, that things were really getting underway. It was a sort of 'here we go' ending. I think that once the story was more underway, it seemed more logical for there to be more 'gasp, what happens next?' type of endings. Both of those in this series were planned in my initial storylining.

THE HUMAN FACTOR

1. Int. Garazone Bazaar.
The busy atmosphere of the bazaar.

SUZ   (*Upbeat*) Karl! Karl!!!
KALENDORF   Suz! Over here!!!
The sounds of Suz struggling through the crowds.
SUZ   (*Out of breath*) Hi.
KALENDORF   Hi.
SUZ   Fruitful afternoon? Did you...?
KALENDORF   (*Shared secret*) Mmm. Yeah. Yeah.
SUZ   (*Quietly*) Do you think the Daleks can still hear us?
KALENDORF   I wouldn't put it past them. So let's not arouse their suspicions by − [hugging each other/telepathy]
SUZ   (*Cutting in. Artificially bright*) Hard to believe that the Garazone System is under their control, isn't it?
KALENDORF   (*Bitterly*) And has been for the best part of a year.
SUZ   (*Grave*) Yes... yes, but people are still alive, aren't they? Still enjoying some kind of life?
KALENDORF   Well, that's down to you, isn't it? Down to the Angel of Mercy.
SUZ   To *us*.
KALENDORF   They only let me tag along to keep you happy. Which, I might add, is completely out of character for the Daleks.[1]
SUZ   Well, they're happy enough at the moment. The local commander just told me... the Garazone mines and construction bays are running at 110 per cent efficiency.
KALENDORF   You must be pleased. And the war goes on.
SUZ   It would go on without us, Karl.
KALENDORF   (*Irritable*) Don't call me that. It's Kalendorf.
SUZ   (*Playful*) How about Dorf, then? Mr Dorf?
KALENDORF   I'm not in the mood, Suz.
SUZ   Oh, come on, don't be such a misery!
KALENDORF   Or what? You'll report me to your chum, the Dalek Supreme?
Pause.
SUZ   (*Shaken*) Take that back, Karl. Please.
KALENDORF   It's the truth, isn't it? It's no secret... in fact you seem proud to be working for the Daleks.
SUZ   We're *both* working for the Daleks. Everyone here is.
KALENDORF   But only *you* volunteered for the cause.
Music cue as background atmosphere fades.
NARRATOR   Those words hurt the girl. And only the truth hurts. As Kalendorf walked off into the crowded Garazone bazaar, the girl thought back to Vega VI and her speech to the survivors of her home planet. That had been six standard Earth months ago. And it was a speech she had since made on many worlds.[2]
Crossfade into...

2. Int. Vega VI. Mining Area.

Crossfade the speech from Invasion of the Daleks *with later versions of Suz delivering the speech. In these other versions, she speaks into a microphone and is more assured.*

SUZ   (*After a deep breath*) My name is Susan... you can call me Suz. I am like you. A slave of the Daleks. But I stood up to them. I don't know why... but I did. And they noticed. I told them we needed food and rest. They gave it.
Some muted cheers.
SUZ   Now they don't care whether or not we live or die. But they do want us to work. That is their only concern. It's as simple as this... If we work in shifts – eight hours on, eight hours off... and work efficiently, we will have rest and food. We will live. If we defy them, they will work us to death – or just kill us – and replace us with other slaves from other planets they've conquered. Now... I believe in hope. I believe that while we're alive, there's hope. Hope for a better future.
End on the Vega VI version of the speech.
SUZ   To the Daleks, hope is irrelevant. They don't care if we have hope or not. But if they see it makes us work harder... then they will *let* us hope.
Crossfade into narration.
NARRATOR   Six months before... the survivors on Vega VI had agreed and the Daleks had adopted the shift system of work. Everywhere the girl and Kalendorf had travelled since, on planet after planet, the slaves, often on the brink of starvation and exhaustion, had agreed. Well fed and rested, subjugated species became efficient – given just enough strength and hope to want to see the next day... Whether it was a day under Dalek rule or not seemed irrelevant. They were alive, after all. Standing in the Garazone Bazaar, the girl thought back to those early days of the Dalek War on Vega VI. After months of gruelling work under her own shift system, she remembered, she had once again been called to Dalek Control. Once again, she had faced that screen. The image of the Dalek Supreme had formed before her, the cold light of its staring eye burning into her. Each time she faced this creature, she became more and more certain that it had no soul... And yet it somehow knew how to invade the very heart of her.

3. Int. Vega VI. Dalek Control.

DALEK SUPREME (*Distort*) Susan Mendes.
SUZ   (*Weary*) Don't you recognise me?
DALEK SUPREME (*Distort*) Yes. Do you take pride in what you have done? (*Pause*) Answer!
SUZ   I... I don't know.
DALEK SUPREME (*Distort*) You have saved the lives of thousands.
SUZ   So that they can work for you! So that you can win the war... invade our galaxy. Kill more of our soldiers... our people...
DALEK SUPREME (*Distort*) Do you regret what you have done?
SUZ   *I* haven't done anything. Your Daleks implemented the shift system.
DALEK SUPREME (*Distort*) It was your idea.[3]

SUZ   What, and you couldn't have come up with that?
DALEK SUPREME (*Distort*) You gave your idea to the survivors of Vega VI. You gave them hope. They have become efficient.
Pause.
DALEK SUPREME (*Distort*) You – are – troubled?
Pause.
DALEK SUPREME (*Distort*) Answer!
SUZ   I wish you'd killed me.
DALEK SUPREME (*Distort*) You wish to die, Susan Mendes?
SUZ   (*Losing it*) Don't say my name! Don't say it! I hate it when you say it! Don't say it! (*She begins to sob*)
Pause.
DALEK SUPREME (*Distort*) You know you have saved thousands of lives.
SUZ   (*Through tears*) Yes... yes, I know. And I hate myself for it.
DALEK SUPREME (*Distort*) You could save millions... billions of lives.[4]
Suz stops sobbing. Pause.
SUZ   What do you mean?
DALEK SUPREME (*Distort*) You will travel throughout the Dalek Empire in this galaxy. You will speak to the slaves on a thousand conquered worlds. You will save their lives. Give them hope.
SUZ   And make them more efficient? That's what you really mean, isn't it? I won't do it.
DALEK SUPREME (*Distort*) Then – you – will – die.
Suz starts to sob again... almost angrily.
DALEK SUPREME (*Distort*) Susan Mendes?
SUZ   (*Snapping*) I don't want to die! You know that! I know you know that! Let's stop pretending! So, all right, I'll do your dirty work for you! I'll do it! I'll do it, all right!?! Just leave me alone – and stop saying my name![5]
DALEK SUPREME (*Distort*) Transport arrangements will be made immediately. You will leave at first light. This discussion is at an end.
SUZ   Wait – Wait a minute! Wait![6]
DALEK SUPREME (*Distort*) Speak quickly.
SUZ   I'll do this only on one condition.
DALEK SUPREME (*Distort*) No conditions. Obey or die.
SUZ   I want Kalendorf... I want my friend to come with me.
DALEK SUPREME (*Distort*) No.
SUZ   And where do I get *my* hope, then?
DALEK SUPREME (*Distort*) Explain!
SUZ   You want me to give hope to your slaves?
Pause.
SUZ   Well... answer!!!
DALEK SUPREME (*Distort*) Correct.
SUZ   I can't do it if I have no hope to give. Do you understand? Or aren't you as clever as you thought you were? Don't you know as much about the 'human factor' as you thought you did?
Pause.
SUZ   Well?
DALEK SUPREME (*Distort*) Kalendorf gives you hope?
SUZ   (*Exhausted*) Yes. Yes, he does.
Pause.

DALEK SUPREME (*Distort*) Then he will go with you.
Comms-link cuts off.

4. Int. Garazone. Dalek Control.
The sound of the Garazone bazaar distorted on a screen. The Dalek control heartbeat is in evidence. The distorted sound of the bazaar is being filtered by the Daleks, so that they can hear Suz and Kalendorf.

DALEK COMMANDER Increase power to the surveillance systems. It is the order of the Dalek Supreme that all conversations between Susan Mendes and Kalendorf are transmitted from this Garazone Control unit to Dalek Control in the Seriphia Galaxy.[7]
DALEK Adverse signal conditions in the bazaar are inhibiting our scanners.
DALEK COMMANDER Increase the power!!! We must know what they are saying.
Filtering FX.[8]
KALENDORF (*Heavily distorted*) It's the truth, isn't it? It's no secret... in fact you seem proud to be working for the Daleks.
SUZ (*Heavily distorted*) We're *both* working for the Daleks. Everyone here is.
KALENDORF (*Heavily distorted*) But only *you* volunteered for the cause.
DALEK They have parted. There is no more speech.[9]
DALEK COMMANDER The male is unimportant. Hold visual scanners on Susan Mendes. The Dalek Supreme wishes to assess her emotional condition.

5. Int. Seriphia Galaxy. Dalek Emperor's Chamber.

DALEK SUPREME (*Distort*) Dalek Supreme reporting to Emperor.
EMPEROR Enter!
Door opens.
EMPEROR Speak!
DALEK SUPREME Our forces are encountering increased resistance from the Earth Alliance, but the efficiency of our communication and supply network assures that Dalek forces continue to make advances in all sectors.
EMPEROR Excellent. Then the Vegan female is serving her purpose well?
DALEK SUPREME She is. The slaves call her 'The – Angel – of – Mercy'. She brings them hope. It makes them efficient.
EMPEROR Will she continue to help us?
DALEK SUPREME It is uncertain.
EMPEROR Explain!
DALEK SUPREME The emotional complexity of her moral predicament shows the potential to render her inefficient.
EMPEROR That is to be expected. Continue monitoring her for any signs of inefficiency.
DALEK SUPREME I obey.
EMPEROR She may feel compelled to act against us. That is the nature of the Human Factor.

DALEK SUPREME In that event, should we exterminate her?
EMPEROR Only on my command.
DALEK SUPREME Understood.

6. Int. Garazone Bazaar.

Kalendorf is still in a bad mood from his row with Suz.

WERNAY (*Running, out of breath*) Kalendorf! Kalendorf! Quickly!
KALENDORF Wernay? What is it? What's the matter?
WERNAY The Angel of Mercy... where is she?
KALENDORF Er... I don't know... In the bazaar somewhere. Why?
WERNAY There is trouble.
KALENDORF What kind of trouble?
WERNAY I... I...
KALENDORF Well... what?
WERNAY I don't know what to say. You tell us *not* to say. (*With difficulty*) It's... On one of the Garazone moons... A group of slaves... They will not work.[10]
KALENDORF All right, all right. Forget about Suz. I can deal with this. Can you take me there?
WERNAY I landed my skimmer at the docks... I don't know... The Daleks may have impounded it.
KALENDORF How long ago did you land?
WERNAY I came straight here, I don't know –
KALENDORF Not long then. The Daleks are pretty lax here. They think they're sitting pretty. Come on, we should be all right.

7. Int. Wernay's Skimmer.

Establish whoosh of engines taking off and crossfade to interior.

KALENDORF All right. We're clear.
Burble of scanners.
WERNAY No sign of their transolar disc patrols.
KALENDORF No... not yet. Now give me your hand.
WERNAY Here.
KALENDORF (*Telepathic echo*) Now, can you understand me? Answer with your mind. Remember? Don't speak. Use your mind.
WERNAY (*Telepathic echo*) I... understand...[11]
KALENDORF (*Telepathic echo*) Good. The Daleks probably don't have your skimmer bugged, but you can never be too sure, can you?
WERNAY (*Telepathic echo*) No. Never too sure.
KALENDORF (*Telepathic echo*) Now tell me, what the hell's going on? Which moon are we heading for?
WERNAY (*Telepathic echo*) K5000. There's a young hothead there... Morebi... He heard your message... 'death to the Daleks'. He thinks it's time to act now.
KALENDORF (*Telepathic echo*) No!
WERNAY (*Telepathic echo*) I know... I know... But he won't listen. He has got a group of slaves together and they will not start their shift. He says the revolution must start now.
KALENDORF (*Telepathic echo*) It's too soon! It's too soon, don't you people understand?

WERNAY (*Telepathic echo*) We do understand, Kalendorf. But Morebi will not listen.

KALENDORF (*Telepathic echo*) Well, he'd better... or we're all finished. *Fade up engines. Music cue. Time passes.*

WERNAY We're approaching K5000's artificial atmosphere bubble now.

Controls operate. A negative bleeping sound.

WERNAY Something's wrong.

KALENDORF The orbital navigation beacon's not giving off a signal.

WERNAY They must have attacked the communications centre.

KALENDORF Exactly what is this Morebi capable of, Wernay?

WERNAY I don't know... They say that when the Daleks first invaded Garazone, they killed his family... one by one. He surrendered. They say he's never forgiven himself.

KALENDORF Hmm. Then he's got something to prove. (*Sighs*) Anything on the visual scanners?

Buzz of screen clearing.

WERNAY (*Squinting*) I'm getting... That looks like –

KALENDORF Fires. Human bodies burning. (*Grave*) Take us down, Wernay.

8. Ext. Garazone Moon K5000.

Wernay's skimmer touches down. Door opens. Landing ramp folds down. Kalendorf and Wernay walk down the ramp. Fires are burning.

KALENDORF My God, what's happened here?

WERNAY When I left, they were threatening to attack the Robomen.

KALENDORF Well, they did more than threaten. It's a massacre.

Footsteps over gravel.

KALENDORF How many Robomen were there?

WERNAY About fifty, I think.

KALENDORF (*Surveying area*) Yes... Looks like your friend Morebi and his merry band have killed them all. The fools.

WERNAY They've smashed all the security scanners too.

KALENDORF Were there any Daleks stationed here?

WERNAY I think.... just one... in the guard post.

Distant shriek of Dalek creature.

KALENDORF What the hell are they doing?

WERNAY It's... it's coming from that warehouse.

KALENDORF Come on, Wernay! Come on!

Footsteps as they run off.

9. Int. Garazone Moon K5000. Warehouse.

The sound of MOREBI and his cohorts taunting and stabbing at a Dalek creature in its open casing. The Dalek creature squeals in pain. Footsteps of KALENDORF and WERNAY arrive. The sound of their exhausted breathing.

KALENDORF What the hell's going on here?

WERNAY Morebi! Morebi!

MOREBI Ah, Wernay, you brought Kalendorf. Good. My friend, the revolution starts now. Just as you said, death to the Daleks!!!

His cohorts all chant 'Death to the Daleks' and give a few more stabs at the Dalek creature.

KALENDORF   Shut up! Shut up! Stop it!
The chanting tails off.
WERNAY   Oh, Morebi, what have you done?
MOREBI   What's the matter?
KALENDORF   What are you doing to that Dalek?
MOREBI   (*Morbid amusement*) Huh! Don't look so frightening with the top blown off their machines, do they? Eh? Hello in there! Ha![12]
Stabs the Dalek creature. It squeals.
MOREBI   You filthy lump of scum! How long can you survive like that, eh?
DALEK   (*Gurgling*) You... you will be... exterminated.[13]
Morebi leads his men in raucous laughter.
MOREBI   Oh! We will be exterminated, will we? Oh, we're really terrified, aren't we men? Terrified of the little green blob... choking and drowning in its own filth!
He spits at the Dalek.
KALENDORF   It's right, though.
MOREBI   What? What do you mean? How can it hurt us now?
WERNAY   Listen to Kalendorf, Morebi.
KALENDORF   The moment you blew the top off that Dalek, it sent an automatic emergency signal to Dalek Control at Garazone Central.
Pause.
MOREBI   What?
KALENDORF   The Daleks will be right behind us.
MOREBI   (*Defiant*) Then we shall fight them! Death to the Daleks! Death to the Daleks!
His men join in again.
WERNAY   You can't, Morebi! *Morebi!*
The chanting subsides.
KALENDORF   (*Topping them*) And how many of you did it take to defeat this one? Hm? How many of you did it kill first? (*Pause*) This warehouse is full of the burnt bodies of half your friends... Isn't it? So how are you going to stand up to a *hundred* Daleks?
MOREBI   A hundred, a thousand, a million. It does not matter! We will fight.
KALENDORF   And you will die. *Two* Daleks would be enough to deal with all of you. Do you have any ammunition left?
Pause.
KALENDORF   (*Harsh laugh*) No. What's the matter with you people? Why did you do this?
MOREBI   It is as you say, Kalendorf. The secret message you give with your mind. I have heard it. Death to the Daleks... We must rise up and destroy them. Be free.
KALENDORF   Are you just stupid? Is that it? The message... the message the Angel of Mercy and I spread is that you are to listen for those words... One day, you will hear them... when there are enough of us to make a difference. Didn't you understand that?
MOREBI   (*Suddenly exhausted*) Yes... yes... But... how can we wait...? Every day... working till we drop. We sleep, we eat... and then we work again... We are helping the Daleks. That cannot be right. (*Pause*) That is true, isn't it, Kalendorf?
KALENDORF   It isn't a question of right or wrong.

MOREBI   Not a question – ?

KALENDORF   It's about survival! Don't you understand? What you're doing here... it's just a pointless gesture! And you're risking the whole plan. If the Daleks suspect that the Angel and I are doing anything except encouraging slaves to work and be content – then it'll be all over! Over! Do you understand? No more rest, no more food! Just work... until you die.

MOREBI   And you... you and the Angel... They will kill you?

KALENDORF   Of course.

MOREBI   Huh. You are frightened, Kalendorf. Like a cringing little child. You are *frightened.*

KALENDORF   Like you were, when they killed your family?

MOREBI   (*Suddenly caught off guard*) What...?

KALENDORF   Now you listen to me, Morebi... I have spent all of my life training to fight for the glory of my people. Since birth, every fibre of me has been attuned to the needs of combat – and yet in all that time my people have been living under the shame of defeat. So, believe you me, I know what that impulse to strike a blow feels like. It lives in my heart as if the battle has never ceased... as if defeat at the hands of the Earth people had never come about. And yet *I* can still wait, Morebi. So you see, I ask nothing of you... of all of us that I haven't asked of myself for as long as I can remember.

FX: Dalek spaceship landing nearby.

WERNAY   It's a Dalek saucer! Landing right outside!

10. Ext. Garazone Moon K5000.
The saucer completes its landing.

11. Int. Dalek Saucer. Control Room.
DALEK 1 is the taskforce leader.

DALEK 2   Touchdown effected.

DALEK 1   Perceptor readings?

DALEK 2   Perceptors indicate all Robomen destroyed. The Dalek sentry's lifesigns are minimal.

DALEK 1   Prepare assault force for immediate disembarkation.

SUZ   Wait.

Pause. Music cue.

SUZ   The Dalek Supreme has ordered that I should speak to these slaves.

DALEK 1   The slaves have defied the Daleks. They must be punished.

SUZ   Punished, yes, but not killed. If your assault force attacks, the slaves will fight... and your Daleks will kill them.

DALEK 1   It is of no consequence.

SUZ   I have the authority of the Dalek Supreme in this matter! Do you dispute that? (*Pause*) Well?

DALEK 1   No.

SUZ   Then do as you are instructed.

DALEK 1   (*Reluctantly*) I... obey.

DALEK 2   Alert. Alert. Observe visual scanners.

SUZ   (*Taken aback*) Karl... It's Kalendorf... and... who's that? Ah, Wernay... one of the elected Garazone foremen.

DALEK 1   If your associate, Kalendorf, is in league with the rebelling slaves, he will be exterminated.

SUZ   He's not in league with them. Wernay must have contacted him... tried to get Karl to persuade the rebels to surrender.

DALEK 1   You do not know that.

SUZ   I know Kalendorf. And he's under my protection! Now, open the hatch and let me out.

DALEK 1   I will accompany you.

SUZ   No! You will remain in here. Do you understand?

DALEK 1   Very well, but if you fail to convince the slaves to surrender, they will be exterminated.

SUZ   Open the hatch!

12. Ext. Garazone Moon K5000.

Hum of saucer's engines ticking over.

KALENDORF   (*Reflective*) Beautiful simplicity to the design, isn't there?

WERNAY   Mm? The saucer?

KALENDORF   Yes. How can something so smooth and graceful have anything to do with such... hatred?

WERNAY   I... I don't understand, Kalendorf. I can see no beauty in it. To me... it is just... a Dalek ship. Something... evil.

KALENDORF   Yes... yes, you're right, of course. (*To saucer*) Come on, come on, what's keeping you, then?

WERNAY   Do you think they have the Angel of Mercy in there?

KALENDORF   You can count on it, Wernay.

Dalek saucer hatch opens.

KALENDORF   And there she is. Over here!

SUZ   (*Approaching, running*) You're *talking* to me now, then?

KALENDORF   I see you managed to convince them not to come out, guns blazing.

SUZ   Only just. Wernay, how are you?

WERNAY   I... as well as can be expected. Under the circumstances.

KALENDORF   So, what are you going to do, *Angel of Mercy*?

SUZ   You'd better explain the situation for me, Karl.

13. Int. Garazone Moon K5000. Warehouse.

NARRATOR   Have you ever looked into the eyes of someone for whom survival has no meaning? Eyes that betray a fear and desperation which have twisted themselves into an insane, self-destructive anger. It is a pitiful and terrifying sight. Men and women, shaking, sweating... allowing their lives to bleed away into futility. The girl had only just begun to wonder if this would ever happen. If there would be those who could not survive on promises of hope... who could not find it within themselves to have faith that one day the Daleks would be defeated. She could not blame them. She had the same doubts every day.[14]

MOREBI   But you cannot tell us *when*, can you? You cannot tell us if this... this great uprising will even happen in my lifetime – *can you?!*

SUZ   No. But I can tell you that if you don't surrender, you will die.

MOREBI   And if we surrender, what will happen to us? Well?

14. Ext. Garazone Moon K5000

Fade in MOREBI and his men giving their 'Death to the Daleks' chant in the background. SUZ's footsteps approach.

KALENDORF What happened?
SUZ They're brave people.
KALENDORF They're insane.
SUZ Isn't that what bravery is, in the face of the Daleks? I sometimes wish I was mad. That I couldn't think straight. That I didn't care about life anymore.
WERNAY But... Angel of Mercy, it is because you care that so many lives have been saved.
SUZ Oh... Wernay... I...
WERNAY What?
KALENDORF (*Suspicious*) So Morebi decided to sacrifice himself and his people? And he came to that conclusion on his own?
SUZ What are you saying?
Dalek saucer door noise interrupts them.
KALENDORF (*Low and urgent*) And now your Dalek friends are leaving the saucer. Suz, what the hell do you think you're playing at?
DALEK COMMANDER (*Approaching*) The rebels have not surrendered.
SUZ No, they haven't. So you must kill them... Kill them all!
KALENDORF (*Aghast*) Suz?
WERNAY But, you can't just –
SUZ And him! This one! He's one of the ringleaders. You must kill him as well. (*Savagely*) Kill him!!!
DALEK COMMANDER Exterminate.
KALENDORF Noooo!!!
Blast of Dalek gun.
WERNAY (*Screams in agony*) Angel of Mercy!!! (*His words turn into a scream as he dies*)
DALEK COMMANDER Assault force will direct maximum firepower at the warehouse. Fire! Fire! Fire!
Massed Dalek blasts. Massive explosion. Slowly fade mayhem under plaintive music cue. Time passes. Crossfade to:

15. Int. Dalek Saucer.

The Dalek heartbeat. Dalek dialogue dips under SUZ and KALENDORF's exchange.

DALEK 1 Now on course for Garazone Central.
DALEK 2 Rangerscope is tracking replacement slave space transport and security force. Moon K5000 will be fully operational within one Garazone day.
KALENDORF (*Telepathic echo*) So, are you satisfied with your day's work?
SUZ (*Telepathic echo*) There was no other way. If Morebi and his people had been captured, they would have been interrogated. The Daleks would have found out... everything... It would have destroyed everything we've achieved. You know it had to be done.[15]
KALENDORF (*Telepathic echo*) You almost sound like a Dalek.
SUZ (*Telepathic echo*) It – had – to – be – done. Tell me you know that. (*Pause*) Karl, please. Please. (*Pause*) Please.

16. Int. Alby's Scout-Ship. Hypersleep Module.

The gentle, undulating hum of the hypersleep units. A wake-up pinging alarm.

ALBY　　　　　*(Stirring from sleep)* Urrrgh... Ah... that's it, Pellan, m'lad, we're cooked. *(Bad taste in his mouth)* Baargh... Hypersleep. I hate it. Drudger, will you open this damn hyper-pod before I get an attack of claustrophobia.

Pod opens.

DRUDGER　　　Pod open.

ALBY　　　　　Thank God I've got some human company on this trip. If all I had was you hovering about stating the bleedin' obvious, I think the chances are I'd end up chewing the control panels before I ever got near to finding Suz.

DRUDGER　　　Please explain.

ALBY　　　　　And open up Pellan's pod while you're about it, young fella-m'lad.

DRUDGER　　　Pod already deactivated. Pellan is in the control room.[16]

ALBY　　　　　How come? Oh forget it. Pellan![17]

17. Int. Alby's Scout-Ship. Control Room.

Sound of computer chattering. [Plot note: PELLAN has called up the Daleks and told them about ALBY's interest in SUZ.)

ALBY　　　　　*(Distant, approaching)* Pellan! Pellan! What are you up to?

PELLAN　　　　Oh... hi, Alby.

ALBY　　　　　How come you're up already?

PELLAN　　　　Dunno. My pod... well... It just deactivated early, I suppose.

ALBY　　　　　Oh... well... Er, I see. Are we at the Garazone System?

PELLAN　　　　Still some way off. But I don't think you're going to like it.

ALBY　　　　　Full of Daleks, you mean? I was expecting that.

PELLAN　　　　No. I mean... Well, look... I've been intercepting Dalek communications... decoding bits on the computer.

ALBY　　　　　I thought you were a journalist, not a code-cracker.

PELLAN　　　　Huh... No, I learnt a bit from the lads on the Vega News ship. We used to listen in on Dalek stuff... to relay what info we could glean back to Earth Central.

ALBY　　　　　So... What have you got?

PELLAN　　　　It's your friend Suz.

ALBY　　　　　What about her?

PELLAN　　　　They're moving her again. Her and a guy called... er... Kalendorn?

ALBY　　　　　Kalendorf?

PELLAN　　　　Er...

Computer bleeps.

PELLAN　　　　Oh yeah... dorf... you're right, Kalendorf. Do you know him?

ALBY　　　　　*(Covering)* Well, I've heard of him.

PELLAN　　　　Who is he?

ALBY　　　　　Wait a minute, do you know where they're being moved?

PELLAN	Er... The planet Guria.
ALBY	Guria...

Pressing of computer keys.

ALBY	Guria... Guria... Where's that?
PELLAN	Right at the edge of the Dalek advance into the galaxy.
ALBY	Are they still advancing?
PELLAN	Oh yes. (Grave) Yes. Very much so. Things have got far worse while we've been asleep.

Bleep of computer screen readout.

ALBY	Well, will you look at that?
PELLAN	What...? Is that Guria?
ALBY	Yeah. And she's not all that far away. Drudger, set course for Guria.
DRUDGER	Complying.
ALBY	When did they set off?
PELLAN	Who?
ALBY	Suz and... this Kalendorf guy.
PELLAN	Er... Not sure. Pretty recently.
ALBY	Right... well, maybe this time she won't leave before we get there. Drudger, give us all the power you've got.
DRUDGER	Increasing thrust to maximum burn.

Rumble of engines.

PELLAN	Er... Alby. Do you mind if I ask you a question?
ALBY	Depends. Fire away.
PELLAN	What are you going to do when you find her? (*Pause*) Haven't you thought about that?
ALBY	Truth is, Pellan... I've thought about it so much, it doesn't seem real. I'm just hoping that, when I'm confronted with the reality... well...
PELLAN	Well what?
ALBY	Well... that I'll know what to do.

18. Ext. Planet Guria. Oil Rig.

A storm is blowing. Waves crash against the structure of the oil rig. Crossfade to:

19. Int. Main Guria Rig Control.

The sounds of the storm are muted.

DALEK	Gurian planetary weather conditions are worsening. Ocean wave force is increasing to danger levels.
DALEK COMMANDER	Will this drilling platform withstand the force?
DALEK	Structural integrity of all platforms in this oil field is decreasing, but planetary rangerscopes record stress currently within design tolerances.
DALEK COMMANDER	Oil production is 30 per cent below minimum targets. Production must be increased!
DALEK	Drilling cannot proceed under these climatic conditions.
DALEK COMMANDER	And Gurian slave labour is inefficient!!! Where are the slave leaders? I ordered them brought to me!

Door opens.

DALEK 1	Slave leaders will enter.

HIGHNESS (*Chuckling nervously*) Greetings... greetings, Dalek Commander... (*Chuckling becomes a little uncontrollable*) May I say, what an honour it is to be... (*chuckling breaks through*) er... summoned into your noble presence. (*More chuckling*)[18]

DALEK COMMANDER Do not make that disagreeable noise!

HIGHNESS (*Chuckling even more*) I'm sorry, noble commander of the most honourable Dalek race, but I can't help it. You make me nervous.... and when I get nervous. Ha, ha, ha... I just... ha, ha, ha, start to chuckle.[19]

DALEK COMMANDER Silence!!! Silence or you will be exterminated!

Highness stifles his giggles, but they are still somewhat in evidence.

HIGHNESS Perhaps you'd better speak to Daughter. She is next in line to my throne... such that it is these days. (*Tries to disguise a giggle as a cough*)

DAUGHTER (*Mischievous and impish*) Hello.

DALEK COMMANDER Your people are an inefficient slave workforce!

DAUGHTER Sorry.

DALEK COMMANDER You are their leaders! You must instruct them to work harder.

DAUGHTER Yes... we are their leaders. (*Quoting*) I am Daughter of Highness, he who has ruled from birth and he who will rule until that day upon which he hands all High duties to his chosen Daughter. That is me. I am Daughter.

DALEK COMMANDER Your identity is not in doubt. You must instruct your people to work with more efficiency or they will be exterminated and replaced.[20]

DAUGHTER We tell them, noble commander. We tell them, 'Work hard for the noble Daleks. Work hard and all will be well', but it is the bad season. The weather is bad. The great seas of Guria are bad. And when the temper of our biosphere is ill, then its humble inhabitants, the ancient people of Guria, are sick at heart.

DALEK COMMANDER They are infected?

HIGHNESS (*Erupting into more nervous chuckles*) In a way... yes, noble commander.

DALEK COMMANDER Then you must cure their sickness!

HIGHNESS erupts into chuckles.

DALEK COMMANDER Silence!!!

His chuckles stifle into muffled giggles again.

DAUGHTER Our people are without hope, noble commander.

DALEK COMMANDER We allow them food and rest. That is sufficient.

HIGHNESS Well... I'm afraid it isn't, noble commander.

DALEK COMMANDER Do not dispute with the Daleks!

DAUGHTER Noble commander, our people hear rumours... Rumours of... of one who speaks to the peoples of your great empire... There is tell of... of a woman who brings hope and strength wherever she may go.

DALEK COMMANDER You refer to the Angel of Mercy.

HIGHNESS Ah! Ah! We dared not speak that name. I tell my people... we must close our ears to the rumours spread by those who would foolishly oppose you.[21]

DALEK COMMANDER All resistance groups on Guria will soon be exterminated!

DAUGHTER Our humblest apologies for listening to such... such treacherous lies. Please, oh noble commander, we beg you to forgive us.

DALEK COMMANDER Tell your people, the Angel of Mercy is coming to Guria. Tell them they will have hope, that they will no longer suffer from the sickness of emotional despair.

HIGHNESS (*Giggling with delight*) Oh, noble commander, how can we – [thank you?][22]

DALEK COMMANDER Leave! Leave now! Both of you! And cease making that noise!

Highness and Daughter shuffle away giggling and murmuring excitedly. Their footsteps continue until the door closes and the sounds of the control room are shut out.

HIGHNESS (*Confidential. Without a trace of a giggle*) So, the rumours are true. The Angel of Mercy is coming to Guria.

DAUGHTER Yes, father. It will be interesting to meet her.

HIGHNESS Hmm... I do so love irritating them, don't you?

DAUGHTER I could swear that every time you chuckle, those glowing ears of his burn brighter.

They both burst out laughing.

20. Int. Alby's Scout-Ship.

PELLAN We're entering the Gurian System.

ALBY So far so good. Drudger, slow us to half thrust and scan for security detectors.

DRUDGER Complying.

Pitch of engines slowly drops. Scanning FX.

ALBY Maintain full visual sweep... And shut down all non-essential systems... even the coffee machine. The less of an energy signature we're giving off, the better.

DRUDGER Complying.

Whirrs of power shutdown.

PELLAN Doesn't seem to be much Dalek activity out there.

ALBY (*Musing*) No... no... If this really *is* at the tip of their spearhead into our galaxy, you'd expect a bit more fuss and bother going on, wouldn't you? (*Pause*) Hang on a minute, what's that?

PELLAN What?

ALBY There.

PELLAN Oh yeah. It's a long way off... that's what it is. Some sort of navigation buoy... something like that?

ALBY Drudger, can you magnify the image a bit?

DRUDGER Complying.

Magnification FX. Music cue – 'o-oh'.

PELLAN Oh my God...

ALBY A Dalek on a transolar disc. Just *one* Dalek... Sitting out here. Busy doing nothing.

PELLAN (*Nervous*) He's not doing nothing... he's looking straight at us.

Bleeping alarm.

DRUDGER External communication is being received. Patching through.

DALEK (*Distort*) Unidentified craft. Halt and identify.

PELLAN We're dead. That's it. We're dead. Why the hell did I agree to come with you?

ALBY Shut up, Pellan. At least he's not sure we're the good guys yet.

PELLAN I could be happily drifting around the Vega System, not worrying about breathing and frozen to death by now.

ALBY (*Stern*) Which is what you'll be any second now if you don't stop panicking.

PELLAN Sorry... sorry. I'm sorry.[23]

ALBY Drudger, send him back a load of audio distortion. Make him think we're having trouble with our comms system.

DRUDGER Complying.

Distortion FX. In background, Dalek speaks under Alby and Pellan's lines.

DALEK (*Distort*) Unidentified space craft. I am unable to interpret your callsign, you must clarify. I repeat, clarify!

PELLAN Do you think maybe if one of us was to pretend to be a Dalek... Maybe – no that's a stupid idea – He'd expect a special callsign or something.

ALBY Shut up, Pellan – whoa, whoa, wait a minute... You said you worked with the code-cracker boys back on Vega?

PELLAN Well, yeah.

ALBY You monitored Dalek transmissions?

PELLAN Yeah, but –

ALBY Can you remember anything... *anything*...

PELLAN Like what?

ALBY Like a Dalek call sign...? Something to put him off the scent for a moment? Give us time to get away.

Pause.

PELLAN Well... er...

ALBY Come on, think, man.

PELLAN All right... I'll give it a go. Er...[24]

Starts typing on computer. Various bleeps.

DALEK (*Distort*) Identify or I will open fire.

ALBY Come on, Gordon! He's not going to wait forever, mate.

PELLAN Er... I think... I think...

Computer burble.

PELLAN (*Triumphant*) That's it!

21. Int. Main Guria Rig Control.
Establish exterior then crossfade into control room.

DALEK CMDR Report!

DALEK (*Distort*) Unidentified craft has transmitted Vega VI control callsign.

DALEK 1 No arrivals from Vega VI are scheduled.

DALEK CMDR Has the craft's design configuration been matched to existing security data?

Computer bleeps.

DALEK 1 Matching... now.

Alarm sounds.

DALEK 1 (*Excited*) It is an Earth Alliance security scout-ship. Alert! Alert!

DALEK (*Distort*) The ship is moving away at speed.

DALEK CMDR Intercept it immediately! Alert all transolar disc patrols in Gurian orbit. This ship is to be totally destroyed!
DALEK (*Distort*) I obey.

22. Int. Alby's Scout-Ship.
Rise of engine power.

DRUDGER Velocity increasing.
ALBY Steady now. Steady. That's it... I can't believe it, Pellan. You did it.
PELLAN (*Incredulous*) Yeah... yeah... I think I did.
Huge explosion.
ALBY What the hell – ?!
Another explosion. Pellan cries out.
DRUDGER Under fire! Under fire! Squadron of Dalek transolar discs on attack run.
ALBY Pellan, are you okay?
PELLAN (*Recovering*) Yeah... yeah, I think so... argh... my back...
ALBY Drudger, increase speed to emergency thrust. Head for Guria.
DRUDGER Complying.
Power of engines increases again.
PELLAN You must be kidding. We can't land on Guria now. They'll be waiting for us.
ALBY I've not come all this way just to give up now.
Another explosion.
ALBY Drudger, select targets and open fire.
DRUDGER Firing.
Guns firing. More explosions. Alby and Pellan cry out.

23. Int. Main Guria Rig Control.

DALEK Earth Security scout-ship is heading for this planet.
DALEK CMDR Annihilate it!
Door opens.
DALEK 1 Report for Dalek Commander.
DALEK CMDR Speak!
DALEK 1 Hyperlink communication is being received from the Dalek Supreme.
DALEK CMDR Activate hyperlink.
Screen clears.
DALEK SUPREME This is the Dalek Supreme. These are your instructions...

24. Int. Alby's Scout-Ship.
The ship streaks past. Crossfade to interior ship.

ALBY We seem to be outrunning them! I don't believe it!
PELLAN Neither do I.
ALBY How long to planetfall, Drudger?
DRUDGER At current velocity, planetfall –
Bleeping alarm.

PELLAN	It's the comms system. Someone's sending us a signal.
ALBY	Who? What, the Daleks again?
PELLAN	I dunno. It's in code.
ALBY	Well you're the code-cracker now, Pellan. Find out what it says.[25]
PELLAN	Right. Er... here goes...

Typing of computer keys and bleeps etc. A muted explosion.

DRUDGER   Dalek transolar discs still maintaining pursuit. Estimated atmosphere breach in two minutes. Activating heat shield.

Heat shield activation. Crossfade to thrusters firing.

25. Int. Main Guria Rig Control.

DALEK   Rangerscope readings indicate Earth Security scout-ship now entering Gurian atmosphere.

DALEK CMDR Instruct squadron four to continue with pursuit.

DALEK   I obey.

26. Int. Alby's Scout-Ship.

Crack of thunder. Ship swoops through storm. Crossfade to interior.

ALBY	Now that's what I call *really* bad weather.

Explosion.

DRUDGER	Transolar discs closing.
ALBY	How's it going with the code-cracking, Pellan?
PELLAN	I think... Yes, it's co-ordinates. Someone's sent us co-ordinates for a landing site.
ALBY	Eh? Who sent it?

Tapping of computer keys and bleeps.

PELLAN	I don't believe it.
ALBY	What?
PELLAN	It's a resistance group... They're saying we have to change course so that they can give covering fire.
ALBY	Covering fire? Fantastic! Drudger, read co-ordinates from the decoded message and feed them into the nav computer. Now!
DRUDGER	Complying. Course changing.

Explosions.

PELLAN   Will you look at that. They're as good as their word! They're destroying the Daleks.

ALBY and PELLAN cheer triumphantly.

27. Int. Dalek Transport Ship.

Rumble of engines in space as it approaches. Crossfade to interior. Door opens. SUZ's footsteps on metal.

SUZ	Hi. (*Pause*) What are you doing? Counting them?
KALENDORF	I wonder what they're thinking down there. Thousands of Daleks... patiently waiting for the order to disembark. Probably itching to fight the good fight.
SUZ	Do you think that's how they see it?
KALENDORF	Isn't that how every army sees it during a war?
SUZ	Why the sudden interest in Dalek psychology?

KALENDORF   It isn't sudden. I've been thinking about it ever since they let me live... on Vega VI.
Rumble of engines drops in pitch.
KALENDORF   Engines are slowing.
SUZ   We can't have reached Guria yet. Something must be wrong.
KALENDORF   And there she goes again. Thinking like a Dalek.
SUZ   Please, Karl... Can't you just give me a moment's peace? If you feel so morally superior, maybe you should have joined Morebi for a futile gesture.[26]
KALENDORF   I meant... something must be *right*. If Guria's on the front line, and we're slowing down... maybe the Earth Alliance's forces are on the move.
Alarm Sounds.
DALEK   (*Tannoy*)   Emergency!   Emergency!   Battle   alert! (*Continues*)
SUZ   Looks like you're right.
KALENDORF   It'll be ironic, won't it?
SUZ   If the Angel of Mercy is blown to pieces by an Earth battle cruiser? I'd welcome it.
KALENDORF   Oh, you don't get off that easily, Suz. Life's not like that.
SUZ   No. You're probably right.

28. Ext. Guria Coastline.

Waves crash against rocks. The wind howls. Alby's ship streaks down and crashes into the sea with a huge splash. Crossfade to:

29. Int. Scout-Ship.

Alarms sounding. Muted gurgle of water and sounds of sea lapping against the hull. Controls fizzing and fusing.

PELLAN   Alby! Alby! Are you all right?
ALBY   Aaargh! Yeah... no... I dunno. Power cut out on the final descent.
PELLAN   Lucky we crashed in the sea.
ALBY   Yeah... Drudger! Status report! Drudger? Where is it?
PELLAN   Can't see it... any chance you can get the lighting up to full strength?
ALBY   That, among other things, is what I'm trying to find out, dear Gordon. Drudger!
Strangled sounds from Drudger. Its motor whirrs uncertainly.
DRUDGER   Drive systems burnt out. Power minimal.
PELLAN   Yeah, but we're in the sea, aren't we? I mean, are we sinking or what?
DRUDGER   External detectors are offline.
ALBY   We've got to see what kind of mess we're in. Drudger – can you open the main viewport shutters?
DRUDGER   Com... complying
A fizz and a pop as the Drudger shuts down.
ALBY   Drudger?
PELLAN   He's had it.
ALBY   What about the shutters, though?

The shutters open. The sea wash sounds are now louder.

PELLAN   At least we're afloat.

ALBY   Just about. Can you see any land?

PELLAN   Look, we must've come down near enough to those co-ordinates the Resistance gave us.

ALBY   So?

PELLAN   So – they wouldn't have wanted us to come down in the middle of the sea, would they?

ALBY   Why not?

PELLAN   Well... because... Oh, I don't know. Look, just think of something to get us out of this, will you?

ALBY   Why's that just *my* responsibility all of a sudden?

PELLAN   Because you're the reason we're in this mess! Anyone sensible would have headed straight for Earth Alliance territory – but oh no, not you. You wanted to chase around the galaxy after some bint.

ALBY   Gordon... I'm going to ignore that because I know you're frightened and a bit stressed out.

PELLAN   Stressed out? Well funnily enough I am. Because I'm risking life and limb... and for what? Your sex life.

A big metallic crunch.

PELLAN   What was that?

ALBY   I think the ship's bumped into something.

PELLAN   Some – what?

ALBY   We'll have to open the top hatch and have a look. Er... the atmosphere *is* breathable on Guria, isn't it?

PELLAN   What? I dunno – er, yes... yes, I think so.[27]

ALBY   You *think* so? Ah well... (*Vocal noise of effort*)

Hatch opens. Wind whistles in, spray dribbles down.

ALBY   (*Sniffs*) Well, smells breathable to me. Right...

Vocal sounds of effort and FX as he climbs the metal ladder. Crossfade to:

30. Ext. Scoutship. Guria Coastline.

Crashing of waves on rocks. Huge crunch. They shout above the noise.

ALBY   Gordon! Get up here! Now!

PELLAN   (*Approaching up ladder*) What is it?

Another huge crunch as the ship hits the rocks.

ALBY   We're hitting a load of rocks.

PELLAN   What? (*Arriving on deck*) Oh no!

ALBY   That, I believe, is the coastline. And we've got to get ashore or we'll be smashed to pieces with the ship.

PELLAN   Oh come on! What's your ship made of? Glass?

ALBY   Pellan, the power's gone. Remember? So the structural defence barriers are off! Am I getting through to you now?

PELLAN   Well, I'm not climbing up there!

ALBY   Well stay here and sink then. It's your choice, Gordon, old son!

31. Int. Guria Dalek Control.

Bleeping.

DALEK COMMANDER The landing site of the Earth Alliance ship is registering on the rangerscope. Dispatch transolar disc patrol Nine-Zero to capture the intruders.
DALEK I obey.
DALEK COMMANDER They are to be brought here for interrogation.
DALEK Understood.

32. Int. Dalek Transport Ship.
Doors opening and shutting. Dalek chatter in the background: 'Section 493 secured. All damage control units are now in position. Security patrol 79 to forward weaponry launch stations.' etc.

SUZ Getting pretty agitated, aren't they?
KALENDORF Gearing up for a major engagement by the looks of it.
A door opens. The hum of an electric engine approaches.
DALEK Move out of the way! Move!
KALENDORF All right, all right!
The engine gets louder as it approaches.
SUZ (*Over the noise*) What is that thing?
The 'engine' passes by, noisily. A door closes, shutting the noise off.
KALENDORF Some sort of torpedo... I think.
SUZ Then they're preparing for a space battle. Things are hotting up.
KALENDORF And we're right on the front line.
Door opens.
DALEK You two will come with me.
SUZ Why?
DALEK Silence! You will accompany me to the command deck. Now! Move!

33. Ext. Guria Coastline.
Sea crashing against rocks. Vocal and foot sounds of ALBY and PELLAN struggling up the last few feet. PELLAN is really fed up. ALBY is pulling him up. Vocal improvisation here.

ALBY Come on... that's it...[28]
PELLAN (*Exhausted*) Aaargh... (*Getting breath back*) Well... this Susan Mendes better be worth all this.
ALBY Shut up, Pellan or I'll push you back down there.
Distant metallic crunch on rocks.
ALBY That's the end of the ship. Lucky we got out in time.
PELLAN Lucky?! Huh!
ALBY Pellan... I'm warning you.
PELLAN Warning me... what? You mean you're really going to push me down the cliff?
ALBY Look, we're soaked through. We've got to find this Resistance group or some shelter before we catch our deaths out here.
PELLAN Is she rich or something?
ALBY What?
PELLAN This Mendes woman.
ALBY You really don't give up, do you? What is it with you?
PELLAN With me? You're the one who's nearly got us killed for the

74

sake of a woman. Come on, what does she do for a living? Has she got money? Did she steal something from you? What?
Thump.
PELLAN   Aaargh!
ALBY   Now just shut up, Pellan!
PELLAN   She must've really got to you... whatever she did.
ALBY   All right... all right. I'll tell you what she did. It's very simple. She made me happy.
PELLAN gives a dirty laugh.
ALBY   Oh, Pellan... don't make me have to hit you again.
PELLAN   Are you for real?
ALBY   What do you think?
Pause.
PELLAN   I think... There was some pretty high-security stuff going down on Vega VI.
ALBY   (*Puzzled*) What?
PELLAN   Oh... you can learn a lot if you keep your ear to the ground in a news station.
ALBY   And what did you learn?
PELLAN   Ever heard of the Reinsberg Corporation?
Pause.
ALBY   Well... yeah. Suz worked for them.
PELLAN   Uh-huh... Doesn't surprise me.
ALBY   What about Reinsberg?
PELLAN   I heard they had some big, top-secret contract with the Earth Alliance Space Security Service. Something called Project Infinity.
ALBY   Never heard of it. Look, Suz was just a geologist... fairly bored with her job.
PELLAN   And what are you, Alby Brook?
ALBY   What do you mean? What's it to you, anyways?[29]
PELLAN   Well, we're stuck on a Dalek-occupied planet. We're probably going to die here. I'd just like to know who I'm going to die with and what I'm dying for.

34. Int. Dalek Transport Ship. Command Deck.
Busy sounds of activity. Dalek chatter. Door opens.

DALEK   Enter!
Footsteps.
KALENDORF What do you want with us now?
DALEK COMMANDER Silence!
SUZ   We have a right to know!
DALEK COMMANDER You will observe the screen.
KALENDORF That's the planet Guria.
DALEK COMMANDER Correct.
SUZ   Are those your ships moving towards it?
KALENDORF No... it's the Earth Alliance forces, isn't it?
DALEK COMMANDER Correct.
Comms-alarm sounds.
DALEK   Incoming hyperlink communication from the Dalek Supreme.
KALENDORF (*Quietly, to SUZ*) Ah... he must be missing you.

SUZ   Shut up, Karl.

Screen clearing FX.

DALEK SUPREME (*Distort*) This is the Dalek Supreme. Battle computers confirm the unexpected advance of Earth Alliance forces into the Gurian System.

DALEK COMMANDER What are your instructions?

DALEK SUPREME (*Distort*) The Earth force is superior in number and firepower. You will *not* engage them. The life of Susan Mendes is of greater importance to the Daleks. You will protect her.

DALEK COMMANDER I obey.

KALENDORF   Very touching. You really are their star pupil, aren't you?

SUZ   And the reason you're still alive.

DALEK   Rangerscopes now show Earth forces engaging Dalek patrols orbiting Guria.

35. Int. Gurian Slave Quarters.

Chatter of slaves on a rest period. Dripping water. Coughing. Not a pleasant place. HIGHNESS is snoring.

HIGHNESS   (*Waking*) Ah... Daughter... Did you get that food?[30]

DAUGHTER   No...

HIGHNESS   But, you said... (*Sighs*) The Resistance are so ungrateful these days.

DAUGHTER   Never mind that – listen. They've had word from an approaching Earth fleet. The Earth Alliance are going to retake Guria, so the Resistance –

HIGHNESS   But – are you sure?[31]

DAUGHTER   Yes. They've already engaged the Dalek orbital defences. Father, they have the Daleks outnumbered. We could be liberated within hours. So, the Resistance –

Distant explosion. Alarm starts. Distant Dalek Tannoy: 'Emergency'.[32]

HIGHNESS   What's that? The Earth forces attacking already?

DAUGHTER   No – but it won't be long. No, that's what I'm trying to tell you, it's the Resistance. They're sabotaging the Dalek ships – blowing them up.

HIGHNESS   Oh... I don't like it, Daughter. They'll turn this planet into a battleground. And our people will suffer the consequences.[33]

DAUGHTER   They haven't exactly been enjoying the best of times under Dalek rule, have they?

HIGHNESS   No... no... I suppose not. But what do we do now? The Daleks are bound to take reprisals. We're all in danger now.[34]

DAUGHTER   There's a safe place the Resistance have –

HIGHNESS   Look out!

DALEK   Do not move!

HIGHNESS   Oh dear.

36. Ext. Guria Coastline. Cave.

Distant seawash. Footsteps and exhausted breathing of Alby and Pellan. Both shivering with cold as they sit.

ALBY   Still no sign of the Resistance.

PELLAN   No... no...

ALBY   I'm beginning to think that call you deciphered was some kind of hoax... from a Dalek with a bad sense of humour.
PELLAN   Seemed pretty genuine to me.
ALBY   Yeah... well... At least this cave gives us some shelter from that damn wind.
PELLAN   God... I've lost all feeling in my hands.
ALBY   Come here.
Rubs his hands.
ALBY   Any better?
PELLAN   No.
Stops rubbing.
ALBY   Well... tough.
Pause. Pellan starts snivelling.
ALBY   Oh... pull yourself together, Gordon.
PELLAN   (*Blubbing*) Why should I? We're going to die here, aren't we? (*Continues crying*) One way or another. No food... no proper shelter – or the Daleks'll get us first. I don't know how you can be so calm about it.
ALBY   You're wrong about Suz, you know.
PELLAN   What...? You mean she didn't work for Reinsberg?
ALBY   No... I mean yes, she did. But I don't know anything about all that. Huh, ironic really.
PELLAN   Why?
ALBY   Because... well, because I'm... (*Laughs*)
PELLAN   You're what?
ALBY   I'm a spy, Gordon. A security operative for the Earth Alliance. But I just happened to meet her while I was doing my cover job.
PELLAN   What was that?
ALBY   Oh, I'm afraid I'd have to kill you and eat you if I told you that, old son.
PELLAN   You, a spy? I'm not sure I believe you.
ALBY   I'm not sure I ever believed it either, really. It was just the latest chapter in a pretty pathetic little life story. Cue violins.
PELLAN   Eh?
ALBY   Broken home, lived in a slum on Proxima Major, bad education, juvenile criminal – joined the army to escape. Got into trouble in the army – got my sentence suspended for agreeing to work for the security service. A life with no real hope... and certainly... no beauty. Until I met her.
PELLAN   But you never told her how you felt.
ALBY   That's right. So... I have to tell her. I know it sounds... pathetic. But it's like... she woke me up. And then I lost her. It made me realise that, all my life, other people have been making the decisions for me. But now, I know what I have to do. Take control. Find Suz.
PELLAN   You may not ever find her.
ALBY   Then I'll die trying.
Transolar disc descends.
PELLAN   What's that sound? Must be the Resistance... coming to find us. Hey! We're in here! Hey!
ALBY   Oh God, no.
PELLAN   What's the matter?
ALBY   Daleks.

DALEKS Do not move! Do not move! You are our prisoners!
Build transolar disc FX.

37. Int. Guria Dalek Control.

DALEK Patrol Nine-Zero reports capture of intruders.
DALEK COMMANDER Excellent. The Dalek Supreme orders that they must be transported with us when we evacuate this planet.
DALEK Understood.
Distant explosion.
DALEK Gurian rebels are still at liberty. Launch bays on three drilling platforms have been severely damaged.
DALEK COMMANDER Have the Gurian leaders been captured?
DALEK They are being brought here now.
DALEK COMMANDER Dispatch further security units to quell insurrection.
DALEK I obey.

38. Ext. Transolar Disc. In flight.
Distant seas sounds. Disc whooshes towards us... then, we're aboard! Hum of transolar disc motor. Voices raised over the engine sound.

PELLAN Where are they taking us?
ALBY No idea.
PELLAN At least they don't want to kill us.
ALBY Not yet, apparently.
Disc whooshes, descending.
DALEK Transolar disc patrol Nine-Zero. Final descent to control platform.[35]
PELLAN Quite an operation the Daleks've got going here! I've counted fifty drilling platforms so far.
ALBY They were here before the Daleks invaded. Guria used to be one of the Alliance's biggest fossil fuel suppliers.[36]
Distant explosion. Gunfire.
ALBY Whoah! What's going on down there?
DALEK Gurian rebels are attempting sabotage, but they can never defeat the Daleks.
ALBY Right... right... Well, good for you.
DALEK Silence!
Whoosh of disc. Crossfade to:

39. Ext. Guria. Drilling Platform.
Explosion.

DALEK 1 Gurian rebel device has destroyed this launch pad's elevation control units.
DALEK 2 Seek out those responsible and exterminate them!
Gunfire.
DALEK 1 Under attack! Under attack!
DALEK 2 Exterminate Gurian rebels! Exterminate!
Dalek guns fire. Gurian gunfire. Explosion.
DALEKS Vision impaired! Vision impaired. Motive units inoperative. Assist! Assist! Under attack! Under attack! Exterminate!

GURIAN   Attack! Destroy them all! Charge!!!
Much screaming and battle cries etc. Gunfire, explosions and Dalek guns. Huge explosion.

40. Int. Dalek Transport Ship. Command Deck.

SUZ   Why are you holding us here on the command deck?
Pause.
KALENDORF   I think you may have overestimated your authority here. They don't seem to be listening.
SUZ   The Dalek Supreme said we were to be protected! So let us go to our quarters! (*To KARLENDORF*) This is ridiculous. (*Aloud*) I demand that –
DALEK COMMANDER It is the order of the Dalek Supreme that you remain here. Observe the screen.
SUZ   The screen? (*To KARLENDORF*) What's so important about the screen?
KALENDORF   Well... At the moment it's showing the Dalek forces around Guria being well and truly defeated. I'm happy to watch that.
SUZ   But why does the Dalek Supreme want me to watch this?

41. Int. Gurian Drilling Rig.
Door opens. Wind and spray etc.

DALEK 3   Move. Now.
Footsteps on metal. Door closes.
DALEK 3   Forward.[37]
ALBY   Nice to be inside at last, anyway.
PELLAN   I still can't feel my hands.
Distant explosion and gunfire.
ALBY   Sounds like more sabotage from the locals.
DALEK 3   Silence. Keep moving.

42. Int. Guria. Dalek Control .

DALEK   (*Distort – breaking up*) Dalek casualties at 75 per cent. Earth Alliance battle cruisers now breaking through Gurian orbital defences. Battle computer predicts enemy assault craft will breach atmosphere within 500 rels.
DALEK COMMANDER Understood. Planetary evacuation procedures are now underway. But you must fight until your force has been totally exterminated to gain maximum time for our evacuation.
DALEK   (*Distort*) I obey.
Comms bleep off. Distant explosions and gunfire. They continue throughout the scene.
DALEK   Evacuation procedures are being obstructed by Gurian rebel sabotage.
DALEK COMMANDER They must be stopped.
Door opens.
DALEK 2   The Gurian leaders.
HIGHNESS   (*Chuckling*) Noble commander. May I humbly ask the meaning of – [38]

DALEK COMMANDER Silence!

HIGHNESS stifles a giggle.

DALEK COMMANDER Broadcast this message on all frequency wavelengths and on all audio amplification units on this planet.

DALEK I obey.

DALEK COMMANDER Attention! Attention! All Gurian rebels. We have your leader, the one known as Highness. Speak to confirm this. (*Pause*) Speak![39]

HIGHNESS I... I am here... my people.

DALEK COMMANDER Rebels of Guria, if you do not lay down your arms and surrender immediately, your leader will be exterminated.

Distant explosions and gunfire continue.

DALEK Fighting still continues.

DALEK COMMANDER Exterminate him.

DAUGHTER No – father!!!

Dalek gun fires.

HIGHNESS AAAAaaaargh!

His body falls to the floor. Daughter howls in anguish.

DAUGHTER You monsters!!! (*Sobbing*) Father... Father...

DALEK COMMANDER Confirm that he is dead.

DAUGHTER sobs, unable to speak.

DALEK COMMANDER Speak!!!

DAUGHTER He's dead! You've killed my father, Highness of Guria.

Fighting in the background fades.

DALEK COMMANDER Attention! If you do not lay down your weapons and surrender immediately, we will kill the female known as Daughter.

DAUGHTER I am no longer Daughter. By the death of my father, I am now Highness of Guria. And my first command to my people is to avenge my father's death. Fight on!

DALEK Silence!

DALEK COMMANDER Cut broadcast.

DALEK I obey.

DALEK (*Distort*) All Dalek units report Gurian rebels surrendering.

DAUGHTER No!!!

DALEK COMMANDER Isolate next transmission to internal Dalek command network only.

DALEK I obey.

DALEK COMMANDER Attention all Dalek units. When Gurian rebels have been captured, kill them. Kill them all!

DAUGHTER Nooo!!! (*Sobs uncontrollably*) Why do you do such things? Why are you so... so evil? Why? (*Sobs*)

Door opens.

DALEK 3 Enter!

Footsteps.

PELLAN (*To ALBY*) What the hell's been going on here?

ALBY Best not to ask, old son. Best not to ask.

DALEK 3 These are the intruders.

DALEK COMMANDER Activate video link with Dalek transport ship.

DALEK I obey.

43. Int. Dalek Transport Ship. Command Deck.

DALEK   Video link with Dalek Control on Guria now established.[40]
KALENDORF What are they up to now?
SUZ   (*Quietly*) Alby? Is that... Alby?
KALENDORF What...? I don't understand.
SUZ   That man on the screen... I – I know him.[41]
ALBY   (*Distort*) Suz? Suz! Is that you? Oh my God! Suz, it's me...
Alby, I – I –
DALEK COMMANDER Cut transmission.
Transmission cuts off.
SUZ   Alby!!!
DALEK COMMANDER Take her! Take her!
SUZ   Argh – get off me!
KALENDORF Where are you taking her? Whe- ?
DALEK   Silence, or you will be exterminated!

44. Int. Guria. Dalek control.

ALBY   No! Bring her back! Why did you cut the link?! Suz!!!
Suz!!!
A huge explosion. Human and Dalek screams. Slow fade.

45. Int. Dalek Transport Ship. Comms Centre.
Slow fade up on Dalek heartbeat during narration.

NARRATOR   They took the girl... me... They took me to a room. It was
much like that room on Vega VI. A chair. A screen. And the Dalek
Supreme... staring out of it... Watching me. Dissecting my humanity with
mechanical precision.
DALEK SUPREME (*Distort*) You recognised that human. (*Pause*) Answer!
(*Pause*) Answer! Answer!!!
SUZ   (*Subdued*) Yes.
DALEK SUPREME (*Distort*) Who is he? (*Pause*) Who is he? (*Pause*) You
will answer! Who is he? You will answer! Who? Who? Who? Answer!
SUZ   (*Bawling*) Someone I thought was dead! (*Pause. Quietly
realising*) Someone... Someone I'd fallen in love with. But you wouldn't
understand that, would you? (*Venomously*) Just put it down to the
human factor. (*A sudden thought*) Why did you show him to me?

46. Int. Earth Assault Craft. Med-Centre.
Bleep of life support monitors etc. General hospital hubbub.

ALBY   (*Coming round. Much groaning*) Any danger of getting a
drink?
DAUGHTER   What sort of drink would you like?
ALBY   (*Snaps to*) Wh – ? What happened? Who are you? Oh
yeah, I remember. You were there when I saw Suz on that screen and
when... what happened?[42]
DAUGHTER   The Earth Alliance broke through. An assault craft, much
like the one we are in now, scored a direct hit on the rig. You were...
injured. You've been unconscious for days.

ALBY   Days? Oh... Oooooh... well, I feel... er...
DAUGHTER   Sedated. Heavily.
ALBY   Ah... yes. That'd explain the mild euphoria. (*Giggles*) Hey,
where's Pellan?
DAUGHTER   Your friend?
ALBY   Friend? Yeah... yeah, I suppose he is my friend.
DAUGHTER   Helping out with restoring the communications systems
on the drilling platform.
ALBY   Have we taken off and left him behind?
DAUGHTER   No. I would not desert my people. They need me more
than ever now. Now that the Daleks have gone. There's much rebuilding
to do.
ALBY   (*Taking it all in*) I... I see. Can I get up?
DAUGHTER   No... no. Not yet. They've haven't finished... treating your
wounds.
ALBY   (*Suddenly groggy again*) Oh... oh...
DAUGHTER   That woman on the screen. You know her?
ALBY   Suz? Did that really happen? Did I really see Suz?
DAUGHTER   You did.
ALBY   Why was she on that screen?
DAUGHTER   I don't know. She seemed to be important to you.
ALBY   Yes. I... I've been looking for her.
DAUGHTER   Then I will pray that you will find her.
ALBY   That's very nice of you... but why should you do that?
DAUGHTER   Because I know the empty pain of being apart from a
loved one.
ALBY   Loved one?
DAUGHTER   The Daleks killed my father. I feel... dead, inside without
him. There is no... joy any more.
ALBY   I'm sorry.
DAUGHTER   It is clear this Suz is the joy in your life.
ALBY   Is it?
DAUGHTER   It is. And that you love her.
ALBY   I... didn't say that.
DAUGHTER   No. You didn't say that.
Door opens.
PELLAN   Ah! Awake at last. How are the new legs?
DAUGHTER   I thought it best not to –
ALBY   What? New...? Oh my God.
PELLAN   Don't worry. They say you'll be running around in
no time. Apparently they're almost as good as the old ones – maybe
better.
ALBY   (*In shock*) Er... what *happened* to the old ones? I was
rather fond of them.
PELLAN   Blown clean off, old son. You nearly bled to death. Didn't
he, Highness?
ALBY   Highness?
PELLAN   Would have done if she hadn't helped you. I was out for
the count.
ALBY   Oh, God...
PELLAN laughs (annoyingly).

47. Ext. Guria. Drilling Platform.

Brisk wind blows. Approaching, awkward footsteps of Alby. Vocal sounds of him struggling. Sound of Alby grabbing a railing and gasping in relief.

ALBY   Now... let me get this straight –

DAUGHTER   You're improving.

ALBY   What? Oh, it doesn't feel like it. Huh... another month and I'll really get the hang of it... so they tell me.

DAUGHTER   You're lucky to be alive.

ALBY   Thanks to you. Anyway... I want to get this straight... You're telling me that this Angel of Mercy of yours and my Suz are one and the same person?

DAUGHTER   It would seem so. My contacts in the Resistance tell me the Angel's real name is Susan Mendes.[43]

ALBY   (*Almost to himself*) How the hell did she get herself mixed up with the Daleks?

DAUGHTER   Daleks don't tend to give people much of a choice.

ALBY   No... that's true. But... I just don't get it. What's she up to? And why was she on that screen... just there, for me to see? It's like the Daleks did it on purpose.

DAUGHTER   Perhaps they did.

ALBY   What do you mean?

Alarm Klaxon sounds.

ALBY   What's all that about?

Sounds of general panic.

PELLAN   (*Approaching*) Alby! Alby! (*Arrives, out of breath*) Alby! We're screwed![44]

ALBY   What?

DAUGHTER   What do you mean?

PELLAN   The Daleks... They're finally making a counter-attack.

DAUGHTER   When did this happen?

PELLAN   Just now.

ALBY   What about the orbital defence fleet the Alliance left to guard this planet?[45]

PELLAN   Just got knocked out – Alby, the Daleks have been amassing a gigantic attack force ever since they evacuated.

ALBY   How come they weren't detected by the long-range trackers?

PELLAN   Er... I dunno. I heard something about a faulty transmitter interfering with the tracker beams, but look, we – !

ALBY   We've got to get off this planet – fast!

PELLAN   We can't! The last transport just left. They couldn't wait. Earth Alliance haven't got reinforcements within ten light years of this place. The Daleks will be here any minute.

Explosions.

ALBY   Oh no... I don't believe this. Losing my legs I can cope with. But being captured by the Daleks twice in two months – Wait a minute!

PELLAN   What?

ALBY   There's one of those Dalek saucers they left behind still on the launch pad, isn't there?

PELLAN   Well, yes, but we can't. I mean, we don't know how to fly –

ALBY   I can fly anything. That's how I got into trouble in the forces. Come on – you too, Highness.
DAUGHTER   I can't leave my people.
ALBY   But –
DAUGHTER   I think you know it is a waste of your breath and time to argue, Alby.
ALBY   I suppose I do. Yeah.
DAUGHTER   Go!
ALBY   Well... look after yourself. Promise me.
DAUGHTER   You know I cannot.
ALBY   No more than I can, I suppose.
PELLAN   Look – if we're going, we'd better –
DAUGHTER   – Alby, if the Daleks invade again, it is more than likely the Angel of Mercy will come too.
PELLAN   Angel of Mercy?
ALBY   Suz... she means Suz. Look, Highness, if you see her –
Explosion nearby. Vocal reactions.
PELLAN   Come on, Alby!
Explosion.
ALBY   If you see her... tell her... tell her –
A Dalek ship swoops in low, fires its weapons. Another explosion.
PELLAN   Come on, Alby! Move it!!!
ALBY   All right!
DAUGHTER   I'll tell her you love her, Alby.
Explosions.

48. Int. Dalek Saucer.
Door closes.

ALBY   Right... er... This looks like the main drive system... don't you think?
PELLAN   I don't know. You're the expert – apparently. Try it.
Control activates. Engines fire. Rising power hum.
ALBY   (*Jubilant*) That's it! I was right!
PELLAN   Does that thing gauge the altitude?
ALBY   Er... maybe – could do – Yes!
PELLAN   Then it looks like we're going up pretty fast. What's this do?
Control bleep.
ALBY   Don't touch anything... Aha!
Screen activation FX.
ALBY   Main viewer screen. My God, you were right... We're already out of the atmosphere. We must've taken off at a fair lick. Better slow down before we bump into something.
Controls activate. Power hum falls. Buzzing starts.
PELLAN   What does that mean?
ALBY   Er... Er... Dunno. No, wait a minute. None of these controls are responding now. Er... I'd say we were locked onto some kind of homing beam. Oh no... look at the screen. We're heading straight for the Dalek fleet.[46]
Massive jolt.
PELLAN   Was that them?

Alarm sounds.
ALBY   No... we... we're changing course. Something's got hold of us. Probably a retrieval net of some kind.
Dalek ship gunfire.
PELLAN   The Daleks are going to blow us to pieces whatever.
ALBY   No... wait a minute... No, look, they're missing us. They're firing at whoever's got hold of us. Whoever's pulling us in.
PELLAN   But who's pulling us in?
ALBY   Let's hope it's someone friendly.
Crossfade to sound of docking. Massive doors close. Crossfade back to interior of the saucer... Pause.
PELLAN   (*Nervous*) Now what?
TANNOY   Attention! You are inside the Earth Alliance battle cruiser *Horatio*. Your vessel is surrounded by heavily armed personnel. You will open the airlock and surrender.[47]
ALBY   Oh my God – they think we're Daleks.
PELLAN   Well... tell them we're not.
ALBY   I would – but I've no idea where the comm-link controls are... unless you're suddenly an expert on Dalek technology.
FX: burning through bulkhead.
ALBY   Ah... now that's what I call impatient. They're cutting their way through the bulkhead.
FX: burning stops. Metallic clunk as bulkhead section crashes to the floor. Pause.
ALBY   Hello? Hello! No Daleks in here! I'm Alby Brook... Earth Alliance Space Security operative. My friend and I are unarmed.
TANNOY   Move to the opening with your hands up.
ALBY   Come on, Gordon. Do as he says.
PELLAN   (*Nervous*) Right.
Footsteps and stop.
ALBY   This far enough?
TANNOY   Fire![48]
Gunfire. Both cry out. ('Get down!!!' etc. Improvise.)

CLOSING THEME.

NOTES

1. Line changed to: 'They only let me tag along **with you** to keep you happy. Which, I might add, is completely out of character for the Daleks.'

2. This line – and Scene 2 – runs in a differing order, and as a montage of different takes, with each clip slightly overlapping the preceeding one. In the following, [/] is used to seperate the clips:

NARRATOR Those words hurt the girl. And only the truth hurts. As Kalendorf walked off into the crowded Garazone bazaar, the girl thought back to Vega VI and her speech to the survivors of her home planet.

SUZ (*After a deep breath*) My name is Susan... you can call me Suz. I am like you. A slave of the Daleks. But I...

NARRATOR That had been six standard Earth months ago. And it was a speech she had since made on many worlds.

SUZ ~~...stood up to them. I don't know why... but I did. And they noticed.~~ I told them we needed food and rest. They gave it.

Some muted cheers.

SUZ ~~Now they don't care whether or not we live or die.~~ But they do want us to work. That is their only concern. It's as simple as this... [/] If we work in shifts – eight hours on, eight hours off... and work efficiently [/] we will have rest and food. We will live. [/] If we defy them, they will work us to death – or just kill us [/] and replace us with other slaves from other planets they've conquered. [/] ~~Now...~~ I believe in hope. I believe that while we're alive, there's hope. [/] Hope for a better future.

End on the Vega VI version of the speech.

SUZ ~~To the Daleks, hope is irrelevant. They don't care if we have hope or not. But if they see it makes us work harder... then they will~~ *let us hope.*

Crossfade into narration.

NARRATOR ~~Six months before...~~ the survivors on Vega VI had agreed and the Daleks had adopted the shift system of work. Everywhere the girl and Kalendorf had travelled since, on planet after planet, the slaves, often on the brink of starvation and exhaustion, had agreed. Well fed and rested, subjugated species became efficient – given just enough strength and hope to want to see the next day... Whether it was a day under Dalek rule or not seemed irrelevant. They were alive, after all. Standing in the Garazone Bazaar, the girl thought back to those early days of the Dalek War on Vega VI. After months of gruelling work ~~under her own shift system~~, she remembered, she had once again been called to Dalek Control. Once again, she had faced that screen. The image of the Dalek Supreme had formed before her, the cold light of its staring eye burning into her. Each time she faced this creature, she became more and more certain that it had no soul... And yet it somehow knew how to invade the very heart of her.

3. Line changed to: '(*Distort*) **The idea was originated by you**.'

4. Line changed to: '(*Distort*) **It is possible for you** to save millions... billions of lives.'

5. Line changed to: '(Snapping) I don't want to die! You know that! I know you know that! **Look**, let's stop pretending! So, all right, I'll do your dirty work for you! I'll do it! I'll do it, all right?! Just leave me alone – and stop saying my name!'

6. This line and the preceding reordered to:

DALEK SUPREME (*Distort*) Transport arrangements will be made immediately. You will leave at first light.

SUZ   Wait!

DALEK SUPREME This discussion is at an end.

SUZ   Wait a minute! Wait!

7.   Line changed to: '~~Increase power to the surveillance systems~~. It is the order of the Dalek Supreme that all conversations between Susan Mendes and Kalendorf are transmitted from the Garazone Control unit to Dalek Control in the Seriphia Galaxy.'

8.   Added dialogue – DALEK: **'I obey.'**

9.   Deleted dialogue – DALEK: '~~They have parted. There is no more speech~~.'

10.   Line changed to: 'I don't know what to say. You tell us not to say. (With difficulty) It's... ~~On~~ one of the Garazone moons... A group of slaves... They will not work.'

11.   Line changed to: '(Telepathic echo) ~~I...~~ I understand.'

12.   Line changed to: '(*Morbid amusement*) Huh! Don't look so frightening **now** with the top blown off their machines, do they? Eh? Hello in there! Ha!'

13.   Line changed to: '(*Gurgling*) ~~You...~~ you will be... exterminated.'

14.   Line changed to: 'Have you ever looked into the eyes of someone for whom survival has no meaning? ~~Eyes that betray a fear and desperation which have twisted themselves into an insane, self-destructive anger~~. It is a pitiful and terrifying sight. Men and women, ~~shaking, sweating~~... allowing their lives to bleed away into futility. The girl had only just begun to wonder if this would ever happen. If there would be those who **couldn't** survive on promises of hope... who **couldn't** find it within themselves to have faith that one day the Daleks would be defeated. She **couldn't** blame them. She had the same doubts every day.'

15.   This line and the following two were reordered as:

SUZ   (*Telepathic echo*) There was no other way. If Morebi and his people had been captured, they would have been interrogated. The Daleks would have found out... everything... It would have destroyed everything we've achieved. You know it had to be done. It – had – to – be – done.

KALENDORF (*Telepathic echo*) You almost sound like a Dalek.

SUZ   (*Telepathic echo*) Tell me you know that. (*Pause*) Karl, please. Please. (*Pause*) Please.

16.   Line changed to: '~~Pod already deactivated~~. Pellan is in the control room.'

17.   Line changed to: 'How come? Oh forget it. Pellan! **Pellan**!'

18.   Line changed to: '(*Chuckling nervously*) Greetings... greetings, Dalek Commander... (*Chuckling becomes a little uncontrollable*) May I say, what an honour it is to be... (*chuckling breaks through*) er... **to be** summoned into your noble presence. (*More chuckling*)'

19.   Line changed to: '(*Chuckling even more*) I'm sorry, noble commander of the most honourable Dalek race, but I can't help it. **You see**, you make me nervous... and when I get nervous. Ha, ha, ha... I just... ha, ha, ha, **I just** start to chuckle.'

20.   Line changed to: 'Your identity is not in **question**. You must intruct your people to work with more efficiency or they will be exterminated and replaced.'

21.   Line changed to: 'Ah! **Now**! We dared not speak that name. I tell my people that we must close our ears to the rumours spread by those who would foolishly oppose you.'

22.   This line and the next one changed to:

DALEK CMDR Leave!

HIGHNESS (*Giggling with delight*) Oh, noble commander, how can we thank you?

DALEK COMANDER Leave me! Both of you! And cease making that noise!

23.   Line changed to: 'Sorry... sorry, **sorry**. I'm sorry.'

24.   Line changed to: 'All right... **All right**... I'll give it a go. Er...'

25.   Line changed to: 'Well you're the code-cracker now. Pellan. Find out what it says. **Right**?'

26.   Line changed to: '**Oh**, please, Karl... Can't you just give me a moment's peace? If you feel so morally superior, maybe you should have joined Morebi for a futile gesture.'

27.   Line changed to: 'What? I dunno – er, yes... **no**... yes, I think so.'

28.   Line changed to: 'Come on, **come on**... that's it...'

29.   Line changed to: 'What do you mean? What's it too you, **anyway**?'

30.   Line changed to: '(*Waking*) Ah... **Ah**... Daughter... Did you get that food?'

31.   Line changed to: 'But, **but, but** – are you sure?'

32.   Deleted dialogue – DALEK TANNOY: '~~Emergency~~.'

33.   Line changed to: 'Oh... I don't like it, Daughter. They'll turn this planet into a battleground. And **all** our people will suffer the consequences.'

34.   Line changed to: 'No... no... I suppose not. ~~But~~ what do we do now? **I mean**, the Daleks are bound to take reprisals. We'**ll** all **be** in danger now.'

35.   Line changed to:

DALEK   (*Distort*) **Control to** Transolar disc patrol Nine-Zero. **You will now make** final descent to control platform.

DALEK 2   I obey.

36.   Line changed to: 'They were here before the Daleks invaded. I'm sure Guria used to be one of the Alliance's biggest fossil fuel suppliers.'

37.   Line changed to: 'Forward! **Forward**!'

38.   Line changed to: '(Chuckling) Noble commander. May I humbly ask the meaning of **this** – '

39.   Line changed to: 'Attention! Attention! All Gurian rebels. We have your leader, the one known as Highness. **He will** speak to confirm this. (*Pause*) Speak!'

40.   Line changed to: 'Video link with Dalek Control on Guria **is** now established.'

41.   Line changed to: 'That man on ~~the~~ screen... I – I know him.'

42.   Line changed to: '(*Snaps to*) Wh – ? What happened? Who are you? Oh yeah, I remember. You were there when I saw Suz on that screen and... **and** when... what happened?'

43.   Line changed to: 'It would seem so. ~~My contacts in the Resistance tell me the Angel's real name is Susan Mendes.~~'

44.   Line changed to: '(*Approaching*) Alby! Alby! (*Arrives, out of breath*) Alby! **Alby**! We're screwed!'

45.   Line changed to: 'What about the orbital defence fleet the Alliance left to guard **the** planet?'

46.   Line changed to: 'Er... **I**... Dunno. No, no, wait a minute. None of these controls are responding now. Er... I'd say we were locked onto some kind of homing beam. Oh no... look at the screen. We're heading straight for the Dalek fleet.'

47.   Line changed to: 'Attention! **Attention**! You are **now** inside the Earth Alliance battle cruiser *Horatio*. Your vessel is surrounded by heavily armed personnel. You will open the airlock and surrender.'

48.   Line changed to: '**Open** fire!'

Q&A
THE HUMAN FACTOR

Is The Human Factor a reference to the 1967 Doctor Who serial The Evil of the Daleks?
Nicholas Briggs: It's not specifically a reference to *The Evil of the Daleks*, but obviously it's a term that was invented for that story. Like so much other stuff about the Daleks, I was borrowing it. Since these Daleks were being more cunning about their analysis of human behaviour and I was hoping to investigate human behaviour more deeply, I thought it was an apposite title.

You wrote The Human Factor after the recording of Invasion of the Daleks. How do you think that affected the script? Did the actors' performances influence where you went? You could presumably hear their voices as you wrote.
Having worked with the actors on the first episode gave me a great impetus. I now knew for sure that I had cast the right people, thank goodness! I knew I could make the dialogue as truthful as possible within the context of this space opera... I'd discovered that this cast could cope with that as well as I'd hoped they would. In particular, it made me write that big speech that Kalendorf gives to the slaves on the Garazone moon; when he talks about how much he wants to destroy the Daleks and can't stand the humiliation of defeat and servitude. I wrote that while I was waiting for a delayed press screening of some ghastly Japanese film I had to review. Having written that speech was the only thing that made the trip worthwhile!

Early scenes are set in the Garazone Bazaar – again, an element from a previous Doctor Who audio play.
I'm always keen on making alien planets seem sort of grubby and busy and not all about gleaming corridors and sliding doors. I'd already spent a huge amount of time creating that Garazone Bazaar sound effect for *Sword of Orion* [2001 Doctor Who audio play] so, yes, I confess... I took a short cut! I was very proud of that sound effect. It sort of sums up the whole culture in one huge noise. I thought it was also useful in the sense that all that noise very much made Suz and Karl sound as if they were 'in the thick' of something.

Where did the phrase 'Angel of Mercy' come from?
I don't think 'Angel of Mercy' is a particularly original phrase, but it just seemed so right... and so beautifully wrong for the Daleks to say. There were never any alternatives as far as I remember. But I do love phrases that sound wrong when the Daleks say them. You just have to really go for them and make them sound weird, like the Dalek is kind of twitching when it has to say something it would not normally say. 'Angel' and 'Mercy' are words that a Dalek would hardly ever use in any other context. It makes them stand out and gives them greater weight in the story.

The sequence with Morebi and his mob ends with a shock: Suz ordering their deaths.
There was quite a bit of John Ainsworth's very welcome influence here. We talked a lot
about the characters, particularly Suz and Alby. As I've said before, John was very much
thinking of the Alec Guinness character in *Bridge on the River Kwai*. That character became
too good at working with the enemy. He saw it was the only way for his men to survive
and in the process forgot about the greater good.

It's not quite that simple with Suz, but John and I certainly wanted her to waver a bit
and, as a result, make the audience and Kalendorf feel a little uneasy about the direction
in which she was going. I am fascinated by that whole argument about whether or not
you immediately try to smash injustice wherever you see it and risk defeat, or play the
long game and ignore suffering and injustice along the road to a greater and long-lasting
victory. That was the crux of the Suz dilemma.

What made it more interesting was having Kalendorf disapprove of her actions. That
created a real tension between them. There's that point when she begs him to tell her
she's done the right thing, but he simply says nothing. I thought it was appropriate to
push the drama to this level, because it's that kind of thing – when friendships fall
apart – that really hits home emotionally.

**The characters do come across as 'real'. Alby gets drunk and belches, people argue and
have bad moods. It's a leap away from *The Dalek Book*, surely? Are you more interested
in flawed characters than all-shining sci-fi heroes?**
Of course I'm more interested in flawed characters, because that's reality! Even if you're
writing space opera, your characters must be real, not just because that's more honest
and creates more engaging drama, but because real characters with real motivations
push your plot in interesting directions. Alby's flaws get him into all sorts of
dramatically interesting trouble. It's the whole reason he ends up on Guria, for example.
If he was some kind of idealised, heroic character, he'd simply obey orders and you'd
end up with a pretty standard, emotionless and boring plot.

**In the stage directions, it says Pellan 'has called up the Daleks and told them about
Alby's interest in Suz'. How much information did you give to the actors concerning
their character's true motives? Did John Wadmore – and later Teresa Gallagher – know
that their characters were Dalek agents?**
This is an example of something I thought John Wadmore needed to know in order to
play the scene in question. I wrote it into the script to remind myself to tell him this,
because I knew John would never find out from reading his scripts that he was a Dalek
agent, because he dies before that information is revealed. I don't think I told Tree she
was linked to the Dalek Emperor when she was doing "*Death to the Daleks!*". At that stage,
I thought I was going to kill her off anyway (when the link between her and the Emperor
was broken). But, of course, she found out when she read *Project Infinity*. But the point
was that Mirana didn't actually know she was working for the Daleks. The control over
her mind was more subtle than that.

**How important is science fact? How much thought do you put into the practicalities of
space ships and the like?**
In this context, it's almost totally unimportant. The whole problem with travelling over
vast distances of space is the time dilation effect... all that business of the faster you go,

the slower time moves for you. So people who've gone off into space might come back and find everyone they knew had aged 50 years when they'd only aged three years. Now, all that stuff would make a story in itself, but *Dalek Empire* ain't that story. I mean, they try to be relatively scientifically accurate in *Star Trek*, and even *they* ignore that whole time dilation issue. So the 'science' I use is the kind of assumed, bad science that has been accumulating ever since science fiction began. It's the kind of thing that makes scientists grind their teeth in anger. All I do is try to create an internal consistency in the fantasy logic of my science. I go by a gut feeling of what sounds right and what works in terms of what I've already set up. These stories are not about science. They're about characters in a fantasy situation which has some degree of emotional reality. It is not predictive or extrapolating scientific trends.

The two characters introduced in Scene 19 – Highness and Daughter – seem to come in to the story from a different *series*. What's that all about? Comic relief? A change of tone?
They were certainly introduced to create a change of tone after the terrible business of Suz having all those slaves in Garazone executed. But they were new characters, and, in a sense, all new characters arrive from their own fictional reality. I was looking for a race who'd have a reaction to the Daleks which wasn't the norm. I thought of actors who I could cast, and remembered my good friend Adrian Lloyd-James, who's a terrible giggler... suddenly, Highness was born!

The cliffhanger's another corker, and although we don't discover this until "*Death to the Daleks!*", it kills off Pellan. Did you feel liberated, in that you could kill off your characters, unlike, say, in *Doctor Who* where the regulars are pretty much assured of their survival?
It *was* liberating. Jason likes to paint this picture of me being some kind of serial-character-killing writer who he had to restrain in order to prolong the life of the series. I only amended my plans to kill Mirana because Tree turned out to be such a good actress, by the way. But the liberation is more to do with the audience's expectations. They know the series is finite. It is not a continuing format. It doesn't have to end with our heroes moving on to new adventures; but killing Pellan was a useful way of reminding them of that. *Doctor Who* always toys with the idea that the Doctor may die; but we all know that's just a lie, fun though it is. In *Dalek Empire*, I could toy with the audience about whether or not my characters would die, and the audience would genuinely not know what to believe. That's more exciting, isn't it?

DALEK VOICES

Was there ever any doubt that you'd play the Dalek voices? Did you ever give any thought to casting actors who'd played the Daleks on TV?
Nicholas Briggs: No. You must be joking. I love it. Why would I give that job to someone else? Get real.

Tell me about how you recorded the voices in the first series.
As has been said many times before, the 'real' Dalek voices were recorded later. In the main studio session with the 'human' cast, we used 'stunt' Daleks. John Ainsworth would read-in with some rudimentary ring modulation effect on his voice. There were a couple of scenes, especially the Suz and Dalek Supreme scenes in which I actually read the Dalek lines myself, because I wanted to give Sarah something nearer the finished Dalek performance to bounce off. Thinking back to this later is what would convince me that it could work with me actually playing the Daleks in studio with the other actors. However, at this point we recorded them later.

Alistair Lock and I – and later Steven Allen and Robert Lock – would go through the scenes in order, and I'd allocate the lines as we went. I'd worked most of this out in advance, although I was open to a certain amount of 'Oh, can't I do that one too?' from Alistair. Another factor (beyond the financial concerns) which convinced me to do all the Dalek voices myself was that, during some of these sessions, Alistair commented that it was uncanny how I could do the Dalek voices he could do. At one point, he said something like, 'It's like listening to me, but I'm not speaking'.

Strangely, thinking back, no one read in the human lines, we would just read them in our heads and carry on. Another factor that deterred me from using this technique again was my purchasing of my own ring modulator. Unlike Alistair's, mine was an analogue one, far closer to the kind of thing the BBC would have been using all those years ago. Unusually for analogue technology, one of the by-products of this was that I could always set the modulation accurately at the same rate. Alistair's digital set-up would, inexplicably, change every time we did a Dalek session. The result is that the voices are slightly different in each episode of the first series.

Were you impersonating Dalek voices from the TV show? Were you deliberately using a 'Roy Skelton' voice, for example?
Our starting point was always emulating our favourite television Dalek voices. Alistair's forte was doing Roy Skelton and Brian Miller. We called the Brian Miller voice the 'naughty schoolboy' Dalek, because he always sounded pretty pleased with himself in an evil sort of way – like he'd just nicked all the other boys' gobstoppers! Roy Skelton's Dalek is very much like his Zippy voice from *Rainbow*... and both Alistair and I could do that. I learnt the Brian Miller one by listening to Alistair. My mainstay was Peter

Hawkins, which Alistair couldn't do; but he was very good at the Michael Wisher Dalek, which I could do, but I found it hard to sustain – Alistair really had that one nailed... and even created an extension of it when he did an 'Alec Guinness' Dalek. The Dalek Supreme is very much based on the voices Peter Hawkins did from *The Chase* [1965] onwards. The only one I've never really got a handle on is David Graham, although I feel I came pretty close to him in *Dalek War*. But the fact is that, from these starting points, we kind of made the voices our own, because once you get caught up in the manic passion of the Daleks, you start creating your own characters within that rigid, staccato delivery.

Is the voice recorded with the effect on it, or is that done in post-production?
The best way to do a Dalek voice is to hear the modulation while you're doing it. There's something about the way the human voice reacts with the modulation that really informs what you're doing vocally. If you can't hear that interaction between voice and electronic distortion, you can never do a Dalek really effectively.

How much of the voice is the effect, and how much is the performance?
I think it's fifty-fifty. Without the right modulation, a Dalek voice just sounds naff. *Day of the Daleks* [1972] and *Revelation of the Daleks* [1985] are disasters from that point of view. Without any modulation at all, they just sound really, really stupid. But the right modulation with a bad performance just sounds like a bloke with a slightly wobbly voice. All that manic, mechanical delivery has to be done by the actor. It's like playing any part, you kind of have to believe you are a Dalek. I've always found my best, most chilling Dalek voices have come out of those moments when, mentally, I'm totally in the zone... a living, bubbling lump of hate. What I've tried to do over the years – and some listeners have spotted it and liked or loathed it – is push the envelope with the expressive range of the Daleks. By its nature, that range has to be limited, but since this is audio, I feel you just need that extra bit of light and shade to effectively ram home the image of a horrible machine-creature. It also harks back to the Daleks of the mid-Sixties, when Peter Hawkins did a lot of playing around with extending vowel sounds and varying the tempo of his delivery. I think there are a lot of younger fans who are not so familiar with these Daleks, but for my money, these earlier versions are far more interesting and engaging. They actually sound like they're scheming and plotting and thinking of the next nasty thing to do rather than just barking and obeying orders.

Did lots of people want to do the voices?
Lots and lots. Everyone thinks they can be a Dalek. They all want to do it for no money, just so they can say they did one. Rob Shearman just won't shut up about it. I just say yes, then 'forget' to tell him when the studio session is. Maria McErlane was recording [*Doctor Who* audio play] *The Wormery* when I was doing the last session for *Dalek War*. She came bounding in and said, 'Colin Baker tells me you're the man who's doing Dalek voices! Can I have a go?' So we made her day by letting her do a few silly voices... just for fun.

For *Dalek War*, what were your thoughts about the Alliance Dalek voices? They had to be slightly different, didn't they?
The Alliance Dalek voices were worked out at the end of the *Project Infinity* Dalek session.

Alistair, Steve and Robert helped by listening and giving their opinions. It was a sort of Dalek mini-workshop!

What about the Mentor?
I originally described her voice as 'lightly brushed' with a Dalek effect, but I wasn't sure about what I'd do with it in post-production. In studio, I recorded one track with Hannah Smith's voice fully effected with a slightly lower rate of modulation, and one track with no effect at all. I thought that would leave options open to me. The fact that it was effected in studio gave Hannah something interesting to play with as she did the voice. As it turned out, I kept that effected track, but then added a duplicate of that track underneath, pitched down a few semitones, which gave it a more threatening quality.

"DEATH TO THE DALEKS!"

1. Int. Earth Transport Ship. Loading Bay.
Guns firing. Body falls.

TANNOY   *(Distort through mask)* Cease firing!
ALBY's scared breathing. Footsteps approach and stop.
ALBY   Who are you?
TANLEE   *(Through mask)* Sadly, the man who's responsible for looking after annoying little excretions like you.
Servo hiss of helmet being taken off. TANLEE gasps in relief.
ALBY   *(Taken aback)* Tanlee?
TANLEE   *Mr* Tanlee to you, Brook.
ALBY   *(Suppressed anger)* I take it you have an explanation for what you've just done.
TANLEE   Righteous indignation from you? Congratulations. I never thought I'd see the day.
ALBY   *(Angry) Why* did – ?
TANLEE   Why did we shoot your friend Pellan? *(Pause)* He's got a small metal disc somewhere in his brain.
ALBY   A...? What are you saying?
TANLEE   *(Impatient)* The Daleks put it there.
ALBY   *(Penny drops)* You mean he was working for them?
TANLEE   Controlled by them. A slightly more sophisticated version of a Roboman, if you like.
ALBY   *(Incredulous)* Roboman...
TANLEE   If you'd paid any attention to your pocket computer download on Dalek methodology – [1]
ALBY   *(Snapping back)* It got left behind on Vega VI – but I *did* read it and I *do* know what a Roboman is, thank you. I'm just trying to get used to the idea that I've spent the best part of a year getting to know a Roboman.
TANLEE   *(Ignoring him)* Sergeant, search the craft for Dalek bugging devices.
SERGEANT   *(Distorted through mask)* Sir. *(Moving off)* Right, you three, with me!
Heavy footsteps as soldiers depart.
ALBY   Did you have to shoot him? Couldn't you have – ?[2]
TANLEE   The process is irreversible, I'm afraid. The Daleks have seen to that.
ALBY   I see... It's just that... I'd just got round to liking him.
TANLEE   Don't punish yourself unnecessarily. The Daleks are good at what they do. And your friend Pellan here was a key element of the Dalek counter-attack upon Guria.
ALBY   What?
TANLEE   Didn't you wonder how the Dalek fleet got so close without setting off the planetary alarms?
ALBY   He said something about a faulty transmitter interfering with the tracker beams, but I – My God.

TANLEE   Yes. We believe it was Pellan who disabled the systems.
ALBY   (*To himself*) Pellan... Huh, and you seemed like such a harmless prat.
TANLEE   (*Ignoring him*) This way...
ALBY   Oh... right...
Sound of ALBY's efforts to walk with his new false legs.
TANLEE   If you can manage to walk with those wretched new legs of yours.
ALBY   (*In some discomfort*) I'm trying, sir... I'm trying...

2. Dalek Transport Ship. Control Room.

DALEK COMMANDER Signals from the agent Pellan have now ceased.
DALEK SUPREME (*Distort*) It is of no consequence. Proceed with recapture of the planet Guria.
DALEK COMMANDER I obey.
DALEK SUPREME (*Distort*) The Angel of Mercy...

3. Int. Seriphia Galaxy. Emperor's Chamber.

DALEK SUPREME ...must speak to the inhabitants of Guria. Efficiency of the slave workforce must be increased.
DALEK COMMANDER (*Distort*) I obey.
DALEK SUPREME Hyperlink terminating.
Hyperlink termination FX.
DALEK SUPREME Our agent was unable to determine the significance of the relationship between Alby Brook and Susan Mendes.
EMPEROR   The emotional connection between them is enough.
DALEK SUPREME It is a weakness we can exploit.
EMPEROR   It will play its part in our plan. Report on veganite status.
DALEK SUPREME All veganite deposits from Vega VI have been refined and secured in Imperial Command Ship storage bays.
EMPEROR   Then we must depart for the Lopra System immediately. Transfer this chamber to Imperial Command Ship.
DALEK SUPREME I obey.
Comms bleep.
DALEK SUPREME Dalek Supreme to Command Ship.
DALEK   (*Distort*) Command Ship receiving.
DALEK SUPREME Open docking bay doors. Imperial Chamber Module will now enter Command Ship.
DALEK   (*Distort*) I obey.
DALEK SUPREME Activating Imperial Module motive power.
A huge clunk and rumbling.
DALEK SUPREME Emperor, we are now proceeding towards Command Ship. Docking will be completed in 30 rels. Blast-off will take place in 50 rels.
EMPEROR   Set galactic circumnavigation course co-ordinates.
FX of co-ordinates being set.
DALEK SUPREME Co-ordinates are now set.
EMPEROR   Excellent. It is time for us to fulfil the true destiny of the Daleks!

4. Int. Tanlee's Cabin.
Door opens, footsteps. ALBY is struggling with his legs.

TANLEE	Do sit down, for God's sake. And try not to look quite so

sour in the presence of your commanding officer.

ALBY   (*Sullen*) Any chance of a drink?
TANLEE   Brook, this isn't one of your sordid rendezvous in a seedy
nightclub.
ALBY   (*Sullen*) Pity.
Pause.
TANLEE   Dear me... Feeling a little love-sick, no doubt.
ALBY   (*Aggressive*) What do you mean?
TANLEE   Tell me, was she worth the risk of being shot for desertion
of duty?
ALBY   Who?
TANLEE   Don't be tiresome.
ALBY   You mean Suz. (*Pause*) So are you going to have me shot?
TANLEE   Regrettably, no.
ALBY   How did you know about Gordon?
TANLEE   Pellan? Oh... We picked up his transmissions to the Daleks
when he arrived on the Vega Free News ship. We were about to have him
killed by our agents on board when you dropped in. He seemed to show
some interest in you; we wanted to know why. After the Vega ship was
destroyed, we finally traced his signals here.
ALBY   Why would the Daleks be interested in me?
TANLEE   Because, it seems, they are very much interested in your
precious Susan Mendes. That's something you have in common with
them. Isn't that cosy?
ALBY   Is it... to do with... (*Remembering*) Project Infinity?
TANLEE   (*Sharp*) And what would you know about Project Infinity?
(*Pause*) Come on, speak up.
Pause.
ALBY   (*Thinking hard*) Er... Well, the mission you sent me on
after Vega VI. I was about to set off for the... er... the Lopra System, wasn't
it? But the *Aquitania* was attacked by the Daleks and... and... well...
TANLEE   And who was to be your contact in the Lopra System?
ALBY   Er... contact... contact... (*Remembers*) 'Contact Espeelius',
that's what the computer said, anyway. But that's all I know.[3]
TANLEE   Hmm... Let's keep it that way, shall we?
ALBY   (*Taken aback*) What?
Rumble of impact on ship.
TANLEE   Ah... the battle doesn't seem to be going well. Do excuse
me.
Comms bleep.
TANLEE   Patch me through to Admiral Elisonford, please.
Burst of static.
ELISONFORD (*Distort*) Tanlee?
TANLEE   Admiral... How are things looking?
ELISONFORD (*Distort*) We're outnumbered and outflanked. The Daleks
have retaken Guria.
TANLEE   Pretty much as predicted then. I take it you intend to
retreat.

ELISONFORD (*Distort*) If your... er, business here is concluded.
Rumble of another impact.
TANLEE   Oh... please, let's not stay here on my account. The ride's getting far too bumpy for my liking.
ELISONFORD (*Distort*) I'll give the order for the fleet to withdraw. Out.
Comms bleep. Another rumble of impact.
ALBY   So that's it... you just leave the people of Guria to the Daleks.
TANLEE   Well, we could all stay here and get killed, if you'd prefer.
Comms bleep.
TANLEE   Excuse me. Tanlee.
TECHNICIAN (*Distort*) It's ready, sir.
TANLEE   So soon? I am impressed. Very well.
Bleep.
TANLEE   Now then... Time is short. It seems we've established what you *don't* know. Let's find out what you *do* know. This way.
Door opens. TANLEE's footsteps move off. ALBY struggles with his new legs.
TANLEE   (*Distant*) Oh do come along, Brook!

5. Int. Earth Transport Ship. Lift.
Door closes. Lift starts.

ALBY   (*Leg discomfort*) Where are we going?
TANLEE   You'll find out.
ALBY makes a grunt of discomfort.
TANLEE   If we had time, I'd suggest having those legs of yours replaced. Obviously the field surgeon was playing some sort of practical joke on you.
ALBY   (*Dubious*) Er, thank you for the thought, sir.
TANLEE   Now then... Susan Mendes. What can you tell me about her?
ALBY   Well...
TANLEE   And spare me any romantic glorification.
ALBY   They call her the Angel of Mercy, apparently. As far as I can gather, she and Kalendorf are being taken on some kind of... well, *tour* of Dalek occupied planets.
TANLEE   Why?
ALBY   To improve the morale of the slaves...
Crossfade to:

6. Ext. Guria.
Dalek transport ship landing. Crossfade to:

7. Int. Dalek Transport Ship. Suz's Quarters.
Door opens.

KALENDORF Suz? Suz, are you in here?
SUZ   (*Morose*) What do you want?
KALENDORF We've landed on Guria. The Daleks want their Angel of Mercy outside. There are slaves to cheer up. (*Pause*) Suz? (*Sighs. Gentle*) Are you going to tell me about him?
SUZ   Who?

KALENDORF Alby? The man you saw on the screen.

SUZ *(Almost as if she's talking to ALBY)* Alby? *(Drifting back to reality)* Alby... *(Pause)* No.

Crossfade to:

8. Int. Earth Transport Ship. Lift.

TANLEE So she's a traitor?

ALBY Not necessarily.

TANLEE *(Pointedly)* And what makes you say that?

ALBY I was told by the ruler of Guria that, apparently, Suz has been saving lives. That she's getting better working conditions, proper food and healthcare for people who would otherwise die.

TANLEE And why would the Daleks be interested in that?

ALBY I... I don't know.

TANLEE And why is Kalendorf involved? What's in this for the Knights of Velyshaa?

ALBY I don't know.

TANLEE He was due to begin unofficial negotiations with us to form an anti-Dalek pact with the Velyshaans. We were going to allow the Knights of Velyshaa to re-arm. They would have been formidable allies... like Earth, Velyshaa is an ancient enemy of Dalek power. And now, the chief Velyshaan emissary, Kalendorf, is apparently working *with* the Daleks. It doesn't make sense.

ALBY No, sir.

TANLEE None of this damn business does.

ALBY No...

Lift door opens.

9. Int. Earth Transport Ship. Launch Bay.
Footsteps.

TANLEE This is your new ship.

ALBY *(Impressed)* What... this one?

TANLEE Yes, I agree... far too impressive for the likes of you. It's the latest thing, an experimental prototype... packed full of everything the top-flight Special Space Security agent should need.

ALBY So why are you giving it to me?

TANLEE Because I want you to find Susan Mendes.

ALBY Find her? She'll be on Guria by now.

TANLEE Yes. And going there now would be a suicide mission. You'll have to wait until she leaves, then track her down. Find some way of... at least speaking to her. We intercepted the video link from Guria to the Dalek transport ship... She saw you, Brook. She knows you're still alive. Maybe she'll try to contact you.

ALBY She may not be able to.

TANLEE Look, you're the security operative who, according to your file, works best under conditions of extreme pressure. So live up to your reputation.[4]

ALBY What do you want me to do?

TANLEE I want you to find out what *she* knows about Project Infinity.

ALBY	How am I going to do that, if I don't know anything about

ALBY How am I going to do that, if I don't know anything about it myself?

TANLEE She trusts you. She'll tell you the truth.

ALBY Maybe.

TANLEE If she knows anything about it... kill her.

ALBY But... (*Pause*) You've got to be kidding.

TANLEE I feel I need hardly ask you if I *look* like I'm 'kidding'.

ALBY I won't do it!

TANLEE (*Sighs*) Brook, I'm not entirely without feelings.

ALBY You could have fooled me.

TANLEE I know you have an affection for this woman... And... And I don't ask you to do this lightly.

ALBY Then tell me what Project Infinity is.

TANLEE It's better you don't know.

ALBY Why?

TANLEE It's too dangerous.

ALBY What? The project, or me knowing about it?

TANLEE Both. (*Pause*) Project Infinity may be our only hope of defeating the Daleks. If they were to find out about it... find a way of destroying it... then... Well, I'm afraid it leaves very little hope for the freedom of the galaxy.

ALBY But Suz was just a geologist. (*Remembering*) I mean, when Pellan said that the Reinsberg Corporation were involved in Project –

TANLEE (*Urgent*) Pellan? Pellan knew about the Reinsberg Corporation?

ALBY Oh my God... That means the Daleks –

TANLEE – it really depends on how *much* they know. And if your friend Mendes is working for them, with whatever good intentions, she may – even inadvertently – give them the vital piece of information they need.

ALBY But she may not know anything about it.

TANLEE Then why are the Daleks so interested in her?

ALBY I... I don't know.

TANLEE Then find out.

ALBY And kill her if she does know?

TANLEE If she's betrayed the secrets of Project Infinity to the Daleks, you might as well kill *yourself* as well.

ALBY It's really that important?

TANLEE Yes... yes it is...

ALBY (*Grave*) I see.

Pause.

TANLEE So what's it to be... Alby Brook?

10. Narration.

NARRATOR The years passed... The Angel of Mercy did her job well. The Dalek war machine had never been so efficient. Slavery was its lifeblood, the force which created its power, leaving every particle of technological might free for the purposes of destruction. The scale of the war increased. Nobody ever knew how many billions died. There wasn't the time to stop and count. For every Dalek defeat, the Earth Alliance suffered ten. No matter how ingenious, inventive and determined the humans were, it seemed they couldn't stand against the endless metallic onslaught. While Earth's commanders begged and scavenged for reinforcements... there were always more Dalek ships... Always more Daleks... Always... And for the Angel of Mercy... the work was becoming her life... my life. Worlds without end... hard to remember their names. All of them, planets conquered by the Daleks... populations enslaved.

11. Int. Celatron. Suz's Office.
Fade in on...

DALEK ...and production quotas have exceeded productivity targets by 27 per cent.[5]
SUZ Good. Has the Dalek Supreme been informed?
DALEK The Dalek Supreme is informed of all developments.
SUZ Where is he? I haven't spoken to him for some time.
DALEK I have no information.
SUZ Well... find out.
DALEK I... obey.
SUZ That's all. You can go.
DALEK The Supreme Controller of this sector is arriving on this planet at zero-four-five-zero hours.
SUZ Supreme Controller? Who's that?
DALEK The Supreme Controller commands all Dalek forces in this sector of the empire.
SUZ *(Unimpressed)* How fascinating.
DALEK You will report to the Supreme Controller.
SUZ I don't deal with underlings. I was sent on this mission by the Dalek Supreme, under direct orders from your Emperor. If your 'Supreme Controller' wishes to see me, *it* will have to report to *me*.
DALEK That is not acceptable.
SUZ Well, it'll have to be. Now get out!
DALEK You must obey –
SUZ – 'obey the Daleks'? Is that what you were going to say? Well, I do obey the Daleks... I obey the Emperor and no one else. So, what are you going to do now? Kill me? *(Pause)* I thought not. Now, get out of my sight.
DALEK I... obey.
Door opens and closes. SUZ takes a deep breath. Comms bleep.
SUZ *(Startled, then recovers)* Yes?
KALENDORF *(Distort)* It's Kalendorf.
SUZ Oh... come in.
Door opens. KALENDORF's footsteps.
KALENDORF The local commander was looking a little twitchy as he left your office, just then. Did you say something to agitate him?[6]
SUZ *(Superior)* Er... I might have done.
KALENDORF Don't push them too far, Suz.
SUZ Don't patronise me, Karl. Did you speak to the mine-workers in the outer provinces?
KALENDORF *(Cautious)* Suz, I don't think –
SUZ It's all right, we can talk freely. I had a slave maintenance detail check this office from top to bottom and remove all the surveillance devices.

KALENDORF That may be, but you can't be sure that –

SUZ Oh, the Celatrons are brilliant technicians. They used to have a reputation as the galaxy's technocrats.

KALENDORF Before the Daleks invaded.

SUZ Yes, before the Daleks invaded. So, you see, we are free to –

KALENDORF Free to what? Take stupid risks? Suz, please, take my hand. (*Pause*) What's the matter?'

SUZ I would've thought you'd be relieved not to have to make telepathic contact with me –

KALENDORF (*Reacting to mention of 'telepathic'*) Suz!

SUZ (*Continuing*) not to have to *touch* me.

KALENDORF Suz, please, you must –

SUZ Don't deny it. Remember, I've been inside your mind, Kalendorf. I can sense... the resentment you feel towards me. (*Pause*) No... you *don't* deny it. (*Pause*) Why are you looking at me like that?

KALENDORF Suz, *please* –

SUZ (*Snapping*) Keep away from me! I've told you. We can speak aloud here. There's no need for us to project clandestine thoughts into each other's minds. We don't need your... your special powers!

KALENDORF And I'm telling you... that if we're not careful... if the Daleks –

SUZ – were to find out that as well as making their slave empire run efficiently we were planting the seeds of its downfall ...? (*Pause*) There. I've said it. Have the alarms gone off? Have the walls come tumbling down? Have a thousand Daleks descended on us, screaming for our blood? *Well?!*

KALENDORF Obviously not.

SUZ No. Because no matter how careful we've been over all these years, there've been countless opportunities for the Daleks to find us out. But they haven't. And do you know why?

KALENDORF (*Sighs*) Why?

SUZ Because they trust me.

KALENDORF starts to laugh. His laugh gets bigger and more derisive.

SUZ (*Over him*) *They trust me!!!*

KALENDORF If you could just hear yourself! The Daleks don't trust. They're *using* us, Suz.[8]

SUZ And we're using them.

KALENDORF Are you? (*Pause*) Doesn't it ever occur to you that you're being rather too efficient on the Daleks' behalf?

SUZ If I held back, they might suspect –

KALENDORF I'm not saying you should hold back. But you've been doing... you *are* doing *more* than your best, Suz. Whole sectors of the galaxy have been lost to the Daleks because of your zealous devotion to duty. I sometimes think there are more Dalek communication relays drifting in space than there are stars in the sky. And they seem to have very nearly as many ships at their disposal. And who is it who's responsible for the high morale of the slaves – the efficiency of their factories? You.

SUZ We agreed we had to convince the Daleks we were working for them –

KALENDORF Yes, but not –

SUZ   (*Continuing*) – *wholeheartedly*. No small, subtle acts of sabotage, nothing that could be interpreted as even the slightest undermining of their operations. No holding back. Total obedience.
KALENDORF   (*Bitter*) Total obedience to the Daleks.
SUZ   Until we can be sure that we have enough support to make a difference – to throw their empire into chaos.
KALENDORF   And when is that going to be, Suz? In your judgement... as the legendary Angel of Mercy?
Pause.
SUZ   Not yet.
KALENDORF   Not yet. And what happens in the meantime?
Door bleep. Intercom click.
SUZ   Yes? What is it?
DALEK   (*Distort*) You must open the door and come with us.
SUZ   Why?
DALEK   (*Distort*) You must report to the Supreme Controller.
SUZ   I've already told you, I won't –
DALEK   (*Distort*) You will obey. You will –
Bleep as SUZ cuts the comms-link.
SUZ   (*To herself*) Who do they think they are?
KALENDORF   Your masters. Let them in. What was it you were saying? No holding back? Total obedience?
SUZ   This is different.
KALENDORF   How?
SUZ   This is a question of... of...
KALENDORF   Of authority? Power?
SUZ   Yes, power!!! I have power over the Daleks. I've made their empire a success, you're right! They couldn't have done it without me!
KALENDORF   They could. It would have just taken them a lot longer.[9]
SUZ   They need me!!!
Muffled Dalek blasts.
SUZ   What the hell are they – ?
Door explodes. Dust settles.
SUZ   How dare you – ?!
DALEK   Silence!
DALEK 1   You will come with us! Now!
SUZ   And if I refuse?
DALEK   We will kill Kalendorf.
Pause.
KALENDORF   You see? You don't have power over the Daleks. You just have power over the rest of us. Every slave in their empire. The Daleks may never kill you... they don't have to.

12. Int. Orearlis Comms Relay. Control Control.
The Orearlisians are an insectoid life-form. They make various chirruping and screeching sounds during their speech. I mention this here, as the fact that they are insects is not mentioned for some some time in the dialogue. Bleeping of tracking system.

KARIK   This is the signal I reported, Hive Leader Stralos.
Bleeping frequency increases.

STRALOS	You acted correctly, Karik.
KARIK	The space vessel is now changing course, heading towards us.

Bleeping.

KARIK	It seems to be in something of a hurry.
STRALOS	Quite so. Quite so. We must warn it. Activate a signal beam.

Beam FX. Sustain.

KARIK	It is done.
STRALOS	This is Hive Leader Stralos of the Orearlis Communications Relay Platform, calling approaching vessel. This space platform is protected by high-intensity molecular disrupter fields. Please do not encroach further into our territory, or your ship will sustain damage.
MIRANA	(*Distort*) This is Officer 274 Mirana of Earth's Interplanetary Police. Sorry to disturb you, Hive Leader, but I've reason to believe you've an intruder onboard.
STRALOS	Intruder? That is not possible. Nothing can enter through the disrupter fields... and I can assure you that they are intact.

Bleep.

STRALOS	(*Urgent*) Karik – check that the fields are intact!
KARIK	Right away, Hive Leader.

Bleeps.

STRALOS	Well?
KARIK	All defence fields unbroken.

Bleep.

STRALOS	Officer Mirana, there is no sign of incursion.
MIRANA	(*Distort*) I don't doubt it, Hive Leader. But I've been tracking this suspect for some time. I believe he has the means to overcome such defence systems and remain undetected.
STRALOS	I presume your objective is to arrest your suspect?
MIRANA	(*Distort*) Er... yes, it is... Hive Leader.

STRALOS makes some agitated insectoid noises.

STRALOS	It is forbidden to allow civilians on board this platform without prior authorisation from the Space Security Service.
MIRANA	(*Distort*) I'm sure I need hardly remind you that your government and mine have a well-established extradition treaty relating to the arrest of known and suspected criminals.
STRALOS	And I need hardly remind you, Officer, that this is a time of war. This platform is a vital communications relay for transmissions containing classified material.
MIRANA	(*Distort*) Which is why this matter is so urgent, Hive Leader. I have firm evidence that my suspect is in possession of a stolen hyperlink beam decoder. If he is on board your platform, he may be gaining access to classified transmissions as we speak.
STRALOS	What course of action do you propose?
MIRANA	(*Distort*) In light of the security issues involved, I would not suggest that you should lower your defence field to allow my ship to dock, but... perhaps you might consider transmatting me over to your space platform so we can investigate the issue further?
STRALOS	What is the exact purpose of this supposed intruder's incursion?

MIRANA (*Distort*) Well... I'm not sure. But if his intentions are lawful, wouldn't he have contacted you openly?
STRALOS clicks and tuts as he considers the matter.
STRALOS Your point is well taken, Officer Mirana.
MIRANA (*Distort*) I'm obliged to you, Hive Leader.
STRALOS Very well. We will transmat you through our defence shield. But be warned, if this is a deception on your part, Orearlisian justice is swift and ruthless.
MIRANA (*Distort*) Er... *your* point is well taken, also, Hive Leader Stralos. I'm ready to transmat at your earliest convenience.
STRALOS Karik.
KARIK Activating transmat beam... now.
Transmat FX.
MIRANA (*Recovering*) Ah... thank you, Hive Leader.
STRALOS Welcome aboard, Officer 274 Mirana. And now perhaps you would care to explain how we track down this intruder of yours if his methods are sophisticated enough to overcome our defences?
Click of a device. Some beeps.
MIRANA I have a stored record of a DNA sample I was able to take from him some time ago. Perhaps if we were to enter this into your security systems, we might be able to find him.
STRALOS Very wise.
FX: whirr of computer.
STRALOS Please inject your sample into this data tray.
KARIK (*Jittery*) Security tracer now activating.
MIRANA (*To herself*) Now, let's see precisely what you're up to, Alby Brook.

13. Int. Celatron. Dalek Control.
Door opens.

DALEK Enter.
Footsteps.
KALENDORF (*Quietly to SUZ*) What's the set-up here? Is this shiny red chap more or less important than your chum the Dalek Supreme?
SUZ Less.
KALENDORF You hope.
DALEK Silence!
DALEK 1 Supreme Controller, this is the Mendes woman and her associate, Kalendorf.
DALEK SUPREME CONTROLLER Report!
SUZ (*Sullen*) What is it you want to know?
DALEK SUPREME CONTROLLER Do not question the Daleks. Make your report.
SUZ All your productivity targets have been exceeded. If you want any more detail than that, I suggest you download the full report from your command net. I'm not a walking computer and I don't see why I should report to you –
DALEK SUPREME CONTROLLER Silence!
SUZ I want to speak to the Dalek Supreme!
DALEK SUPREME CONTROLLER Silence! What is the purpose of this humanoid, Kalendorf?

SUZ He is under my protection.

DALEK SUPREME CONTROLLER That does not answer the question.

SUZ If you want to know more, talk to the Dalek Supreme.

DALEK SUPREME CONTROLLER Silence!

KALENDORF I can speak for myself!

DALEK SUPREME CONTROLLER Silence! Explain your purpose!

KALENDORF Well make your mind up. What do you want? Silence or an explanation?

DALEK SUPREME CONTROLLER You have been observed with slaves on many of our conquered planets. Often there is no audible conversation between you. What is the meaning of this? (*Pause*) Answer!

KALENDORF We're praying.

DALEK SUPREME CONTROLLER A meaningless religious ritual?

KALENDORF That's your opinion.

DALEK SUPREME CONTROLLER Why do you pray?

KALENDORF Why? Why does anyone pray?

DALEK SUPREME CONTROLLER Answer!

KALENDORF I don't know... We pray for the day when every last Dalek has been smashed into the ground. Is that what you want to hear? We pray... we *hope* that one day... we shall be rid of you.

DALEK SUPREME CONTROLLER And you believe that this will happen? (*Pause*) Answer!

KALENDORF (*Pointedly to SUZ*) What do you think, Angel of Mercy?

SUZ It's asking *you* the question.

DALEK SUPREME CONTROLLER Do not communicate with each other! Answer the question!

SUZ Well?

KALENDORF Yes. We... I believe that one day we shall be rid of you.

DALEK SUPREME CONTROLLER Your belief is mistaken.

KALENDORF We shall see.

14. Int. Orearlis Platform.

Breathing and footsteps of Mirana in spacesuit.

MIRANA Which way now, Stralos?

STRALOS (*Distort*) Take care, Officer Mirana. You are now traversing this platform's central power grid. If you were to fracture any part of the superstructure, the release of energy would destroy you.

MIRANA Er... right. I'll... er... I'll be careful then.

STRALOS (*Distort*) Proceed to the third conduit on your left.

MIRANA What's the security tracer showing now?

STRALOS (*Distort*) The intruder Alby Brook has moved further out into the deep-space transceiver array. It may be that he is aware of your approach, and is attempting to evade you.

MIRANA Or he may just be up to more mischief. Right... here we go.

Footsteps and breathing.

STRALOS (*Distort. Alarmed*) Officer Mirana!!!

MIRANA What is it? What's the matter?

STRALOS (*Distort*) Alby Brook's signal has vanished from the tracer.

MIRANA (*To herself*) What the hell's going on now? (*Aloud*) Brook!

Do you hear me? If you don't give yourself up now, you won't get off this platform alive! Brook? (*Pause*) Any sign of him, Stralos? (*Pause*) Stralos?

ALBY   Stralos can't hear you, Mirana. I'm jamming your suit comm – don't turn round! I've got a gun –

MIRANA   – at the back of my head?

ALBY   You guessed it.

MIRANA   Brook, you're just making it worse for yourself.[10]

ALBY   Oh, shut up and get moving. I haven't got time for this. Go on, move.

MIRANA   Why are you in such a hurry?

ALBY   I'm expecting a call. And when you hear it, I'm hoping you'll realise that it's best not to poke your snooty little nose into my business. Now, move.

15. Int. Celatron. Dalek Control.

KALENDORF (*Impatient*) This is ridiculous. What's it doing? Contemplating its metallic navel? How long are we supposed to wait here?

SUZ   It must be accessing the command net, checking up on me. (*Aloud to DALEK*) Er... if you've finished with us, 'Supreme Controller', I have duties to perform.

DALEK SUPREME CONTROLLER Stay where you are! Both of you!

KALENDORF What do you want with us? We've answered your 'fascinating' questions. Just let us get on with our work.

DALEK SUPREME CONTROLLER Mendes! We know you had the surveillance devices removed from your office. A security squad of Daleks is currently installing further surveillance devices. Any Celatron slave ordered by you to remove *these* new devices will be exterminated.

SUZ   (*Defiant*) I don't know what you're talking about.

DALEK SUPREME CONTROLLER Observe the screen.

Screen activates.

DALEK SUPREME CONTROLLER Are those the slaves you ordered to remove the first surveillance devices? (*Pause*) Exterminate them!

SUZ   Noooo!!!

Onscreen distort FX of Dalek guns and screaming of Celatrons dying. Pause.

DALEK SUPREME CONTROLLER Do you wish to cause more deaths? (*Pause*) Answer!

SUZ   (*Subdued*) No. I don't. (*Pause*) Can we go now?

DALEK SUPREME CONTROLLER No. A hyperlink communication beam is being established. You will await commands from the Dalek Supreme.

16. Int. Orearlis Platform. Deep-Space Array.

Burbles of comms-net in background. Hovering motor of drudger robot. Footsteps and breathing of MIRANA.

ALBY   Right. Stop there.

MIRANA   Is this *your* drudger connected to the deep-space array, or does it belong to the Orearlisians?

ALBY   It's mine.

MIRANA   Can I ask what it's doing?

ALBY   How's it going, Drudger?

DRUDGER   Hyperlink beam still scanning for control call sign. Dalek interference is considerable in this sector.

ALBY   Keep at it.

DRUDGER   Complying, Alby Brook.

MIRANA   Who are you trying to call up? And why did you have to come here to do it?

ALBY   I've got the gun, so I think I'll be asking the questions, Mirana.

MIRANA   What could *you* possibly want to ask *me*?

ALBY   Well, for starters... Hasn't an interplanetary police officer anything better to do than follow me through four star systems?

MIRANA   Not when my informant on Orearlis III told me you were prepared to pay any amount for a hyperlink decoder... no questions asked.[11]

ALBY   (*Chuckle*) God. I knew you were trouble when you tried to arrest me in that bar on Quelador.

Crossfade to flashback. Busy bar.

ALBY   Sorry. Someone's already sitting there.[12]

MIRANA   Doesn't look like it to me.

Sounds of her sitting.

ALBY   Look. I'm expecting someone... and gorgeous and irresistable though you are, darling, he's not going to be very pleased to find you in his chair.

MIRANA   Ah... you mean Mr Auderlon.

Pause.

ALBY   Wha...? Who are you? Did he send you?

MIRANA   I've come straight from him.

ALBY   So... What's the deal?

MIRANA   The deal is, you come with me; I show you the merchandise, then you pay me.

ALBY   When?

MIRANA   Now.

Crossfade to exterior bar. Footsteps.

ALBY   So where exactly are you taking – ?

Footsteps stop.

ALBY   You – [13]

MIRANA   – ve got a gun pointing at the back of your head, yes. Alby Brook, off-world immigrant of no fixed abode, you are under arrest.

ALBY   What for?

MIRANA   You don't have to say anything, but I am now recording all your responses for the purposes of evidence. What for? Illegal trade in Earth Alliance government property, namely a stolen hyperlink decoder. And I've a funny feeling that's just for starters. (*Pause*) Nothing to say? Have it your own way.[14]

Crossfade to INT. INTERROGATION CELL. Cell door opens and closes. Footsteps to table. Chair drag. Sit down.

MIRANA   It's been 36 hours. Thought of anything to say yet?

ALBY   No. But you'd be saying something a bit more substantial if you actually had any evidence you could back up. (*Pause*) Let me guess... Having trouble finding Mr Auderlon? (*Pause*) Thought so.

MIRANA   All right. You can go.

ALBY   Thanks.

Drag of chair as he gets up. Hiss and click of DNA sampler activated.
ALBY   Argh! Ow, that hurt! What the hell was that?
MIRANA   (*Defiant*) What was *what*?
Crossfade back to Orearlis platform.
ALBY   You took a DNA sample that night, didn't you? Isn't that illegal?
MIRANA   These are unconventional times – and I had a bad feeling about you.[15]
ALBY   Well, I can't fault your instincts. I got my hyperlink decoder and you followed my trail.
MIRANA   And what did happen to your Mr Auderlon?
ALBY   Oh... people like him are very good at disappearing when they need to.
MIRANA   So what *are* you up to?
ALBY   Trying to beat Dalek jamming signals.
MIRANA   Why?
ALBY   There's a war on, or haven't you heard?
MIRANA   And what's that got to do with you?
ALBY   Something well beyond your jurisdiction, darling. And if I was any good at my job, I'd have already blown a hole in your head.
DRUDGER bleeps.
DRUDGER   Attention, Alby Brook. Message decoding.
ALBY   Is it Tanlee?
Bleeps.
DRUDGER   Negative correlation. Message is of Dalek origin.
MIRANA   Why would the Daleks be sending us a message?
ALBY   This is a relay station, right? The cheeky beggars are using an Earth Alliance relay station to boost their signal. Drudger, where's the message being beamed from?
DRUDGER   Co-ordinates 847348493 –
ALBY   – No! *Where?!* I was never good with numbers.
Bleeps and buzzes of an electronic diagram appearing on a screen.
DRUDGER   Please observe star map.
ALBY   Wait a minute... the source is showing up somewhere outside the galaxy.
DRUDGER   Correct.
ALBY   Where's it being transmitted to?
DRUDGER   The Planet Celatron.
ALBY   Let's see what they've got to say for themselves.
Minor alarms start up.
DRUDGER   Call sign decoded. Transmission commencing.
DALEK SUPREME (*Distort*) This is the Dalek Supreme.
ALBY   Bingo. Big time.
DALEK SUPREME (*Distort*) Susan Mendes.
ALBY   What?
MIRANA   Who?
ALBY   Shut up!
DALEK SUPREME (*Distort*) You wished to speak to me?

17. Int. Celatron. Dalek Control.

DALEK SUPREME (*Distort*) Answer!

SUZ   (*Taken aback*) Er... er, yes. Yes, I did.
DALEK SUPREME Then speak!
KALENDORF (*To SUZ*) Well, say *something*. Perhaps you should do your little speech about how the Daleks trust you. He'll love that.
DALEK SUPREME Speak!
SUZ   *You* sent me on this mission. I... I... was merely... concerned that – I thought that I should report directly to you.[16]
DALEK SUPREME All Daleks are responsible to the Dalek Supreme. The Dalek Supreme obeys the Emperor.
SUZ   (*Feeling stupid*) Yes... yes... I understand. I... I'm sorry.
KALENDORF (*Concerned*) Suz... are you all right?
SUZ   (*To KALENDORF*) Shut up.
DALEK SUPREME You wish for... emotional support?
KALENDORF (*To himself*) What? Well... I never thought I'd see the day –
SUZ   (*To KALENDORF*) What do you mean?
DALEK SUPREME Answer!
KALENDORF (*To SUZ*) Daleks don't discuss emotions.
SUZ   (*To KALENDORF*) Well, he does. He always has done.
DALEK SUPREME Answer!!!
SUZ   Yes... yes, I suppose I do. But you can't help with that, can you?
DALEK SUPREME Reports of surveillance data indicate there is animosity between you and Kalendorf. Is that correct?
SUZ   Well... Yes. There is... animosity.
DALEK SUPREME Then he will be exterminated.
SUZ   No!
DALEK SUPREME If he is not giving you hope, he is not fulfilling his purpose. He is useless.
SUZ   He isn't useless!
KALENDORF Oh, thanks.
SUZ   He... We just... (*Runs out of words*)
DALEK SUPREME Explain! (*Pause*) Explain!!!
SUZ   Relationships between human beings –
KALENDORF I'm not human.
SUZ   All right – relationships between *people*! Friendships don't always... well, they don't always run smoothly.
DALEK SUPREME Your relationship is not efficient.
KALENDORF I really can't believe we're having this discussion.
DALEK SUPREME Silence! If we could replace Kalendorf with the human being called Alby Brook –
SUZ   What?
KALENDORF Alby Brook... the man you saw on the screen back in the Guria System? The man you won't talk about?
SUZ   Yes.
DALEK SUPREME The man you love.
Pause.
SUZ   (*Aloud*) Why do you mention him?
DALEK SUPREME Susan Mendes, intelligence reports indicate he is attempting to locate you.
SUZ   You know where he is?
DALEK SUPREME Yes.

During above section, crossfade to...

18. Int. Orearlis Platform. Deep-Space Array.

ALBY   You lying piece of scum!
MIRANA   What the hell is all this about?
ALBY   Just shut it!
Gradually crossfade back to...

19. Int. Celatron. Dalek Control.

DALEK SUPREME We could have him brought to you. He is of the same race. You love him. He will give you hope. He would then replace Kalendorf.
KALENDORF Ah, so you're still threatening to kill me. At least we're back on familiar Dalek territory.
DALEK SUPREME Silence!
SUZ   You're asking me to choose?
DALEK SUPREME We only wish you to be efficient.
SUZ   I don't believe you know where Alby is. You're trying to trick me. Why are you doing this?
DALEK SUPREME Alby Brook is an Earth Security agent. He is intercepting this conversation.
SUZ   What?
Crossfade to...

20. Int. Orearlis Platform. Deep-Space Array.

ALBY   How the hell did he know that? Drudger! Disconnect! They must have a trace on us!
DRUDGER   Disconnecting.
Buzz FX.
MIRANA   So, you're a security agent. Is that true?
ALBY   Do you always believe what Daleks say? They *are* the enemy, you know. Anyway, it's none of your business, darling. And you've seen and heard too much already.
MIRANA   (*Panicked*) What are...? No – wait a minute. Can't we talk this over – er...[17]
ALBY   No! Drudger, get to the ship – fire her up for launch! Go!
DRUDGER   Complying.
FX: DRUDGER hovers off.
ALBY   All right, Officer. I think I've amply demonstrated how crap I am at my job by leaving you alive. So, let me compound that admission. Come on, I need one good reason why I shouldn't kill you. Come on.
MIRANA   Er... you like women in uniform?
ALBY   Ah... clever move. Using humour to deflate my murderous intent. But not good enough. Try again.
MIRANA   Er...
STRALOS   (*With a screech*) Drop the weapon, Earth creature.[18]
ALBY   Wha – Aaargh!
Gun fires. Screech from STRALOS.

21. Int. Celatron. Dalek Control.

DALEK SUPREME Then you wish Kalendorf to live?
SUZ   I do.
DALEK SUPREME You do not wish him to be replaced by the man you love.
SUZ   No.
DALEK SUPREME There is no discernible reason to your emotional responses.
SUZ   I... I know.
DALEK SUPREME You and Kalendorf will continue with your work. But your relationship must be efficient. The Dalek Empire needs your total obedience. Is that understood? (*Pause*) Answer!
SUZ   (*Bitter*) Yes... It is... understood.

22. Int. Dalek Imperial Command Ship.

EMPEROR   This confirms my theory of Kalendorf's significance. He is a Knight of Velyshaa. He has telepathic capabilities. The Mendes woman needs him for her plan.
DALEK SUPREME Susan Mendes and Kalendorf are plotting against the Daleks?
EMPEROR   Correct.
DALEK SUPREME Shall I order their extermination?
EMPEROR   It is not necessary. Now that they know we have suspicions, they will redouble their efforts to convince us of their loyalty to the Dalek cause. It will make them more efficient.
DALEK SUPREME But in time, they will betray the Daleks – attempt to overthrow our empire.
EMPEROR   And that attempt will serve its purpose in our plans. Time to arrival in the Lopra System?
DALEK SUPREME On this course, at current velocity, planetfall will be achieved in one solar year.
EMPEROR   Excellent. Nothing Susan Mendes and Kalendorf can do will harm us now. Victory for the Daleks is assured.

23. Int. Alby's Ship.
ALBY's ship shoots past. Crossfade to interior. Buzzes and fizzes of DRUDGER performing 'surgery' on ALBY's artificial legs.

ALBY   How are the repairs to my legs going, Drudger?
DRUDGER   Almost complete.
ALBY   Lucky that damn insect went for my legs, eh? I don't think my head would be *quite* so easy to fix.
DRUDGER   Please elaborate.
ALBY   Any sign of that Mirana woman pursuing?
DRUDGER   No vessels pursuing.
ALBY   Good. I've never been a fan of the police... and that woman is beginning to irritate me. I shall be very happy if I never see her again.[19]
DRUDGER   Security shield is functioning. This vessel cannot be detected by any known scanning system.
ALBY   Thank God for top-of-the-range gadgets. Ow!

DRUDGER Apologies.
ALBY Just be careful with that laser thing, will you?
DRUDGER Please keep still.
Fizz of laser.
ALBY Drudger, do you think it's possible the Dalek Supreme really could have known we were listening in?
DRUDGER It is possible, if the Daleks were aware that they were using the Orearlis Platform to relay their hyperlink signal.[20]
ALBY Hmmm. (*Reflective*) It was... weird, hearing her voice. Suz. After all these years. She sounded... I don't know... different. Harder. Suppose it's nice to know she hasn't forgotten me...
DRUDGER Do you require a response?
ALBY No. (*Back to reflecting*) No, no easy answers... And no way of getting to the planet Celatron. That's *deep* in Dalek waters.
DRUDGER Repairs to your leg are now complete.
ALBY Thanks.
DRUDGER Do you require coffee, Alby Brook?
ALBY I require... something stronger. Set course for Carson's Planet. I know a good bar there.
DRUDGER Complying. Course set.
ALBY One thing's for sure. Without that hyperlink decoder, and a transmitter as powerful as that Orearlis array, I'm never going to be able to report back to control. Sorry, Mr Tanlee... but I tried my best... and failed.

24. Int. Earth Transport Ship. Tanlee's Cabin.

EARTH PRESIDENT (*Distort. Signal breaking up*) Tanlee! Tanlee! Are you reading me? Are you reading me?
TANLEE Just about, your presidency. But the signal carrier is getting weaker by the moment.[21]
EARTH PRESIDENT (*Distort*) The Daleks are jamming us. We're using all available power to send this last message. Now listen to me, Tanlee. I've ordered the home fleet to evacuate the solar system. Do you hear me?
TANLEE Yes, but – ?
EARTH PRESIDENT (*Distort*) The fight is lost here, Tanlee. Our bases in Jupiter and Saturn orbit have been destroyed. The Mars colony is fighting a Dalek invasion force that outnumbers them 100 to 1. The fight is lost. Our only option is surrender. Do you understand?
TANLEE I... Surrender the Earth?
EARTH PRESIDENT (*Distort*) Tanlee? Tanlee? Are you reading me?
TANLEE Er... Yes, your presidency. Yes. Proceed.[22]
EARTH PRESIDENT (*Distort*) I'm transferring operational command of all Earth forces to you. Do you know what that means?
TANLEE Understood, your presidency. I understand. Good luck.[23]
EARTH PRESIDENT (*Distort*) If the home fleet gets through, I suggest you add them to the outer planet flotillas... but the decisions are yours now, Tanlee. Do your best. You must go to final phase at all costs. The future of the –
Transmission cuts out in a cacophony of static. A deep sigh from TANLEE.
TANLEE My God...

Comms bleep.
TANLEE   Comms centre. Do you have that link-up with the Lopra System yet?
Comms bleep.
TANLEE   Comms centre! Comms!
COMMS   *(Distort)* We're just pinpointing now, sir, but –
TANLEE   Earth is surrendering to the Daleks... Get me that link-up at all costs. Comms.
COMMS   *(Distort)* Er... yes, sir. *(Pause)* Link-up has just been established, Mr Tanlee. But we're not certain how long we can hold off Dalek jamming signals.
TANLEE   I want this beam encrypted with our best codes. Do you understand?
COMMS   *(Distort)* Sir. Signal incoming.
Much crackling and cutting-in and out of signal etc during ESPEELIUS's speech.
ESPEELIUS   *(Distort)* This is Project Director Espeelius.
TANLEE   Espeelius. We must keep information to a minimum. This message is encrypted, but no hyperlink beams can be considered secure now. The Daleks comms-network is... well, they've pretty much got the galaxy sewn up.[24]
ESPEELIUS   *(Distort)* Understood. Proceed.
TANLEE   The President of Earth has transferred all operational authority to me. You must go to final phase as soon as possible. Do you understand?
ESPEELIUS   *(Distort)* Understood... but power supplies are low.
TANLEE   You must conserve as best you can.
Violent interference and crackles fade in.
TANLEE   *(Over the crackling)* Espeelius? Espeelius, do you hear me? Conserve power and go to final phase immediately.
Crackles crescendo.

25. Int. Planet Lopra Minor. Project Infinity Operations Room.
Equipment ticking over. Chatter of scientists etc. Static of message cuts out.

ASSISTANT   We've lost the signal, Director.
ESPEELIUS   You heard what Tanlee said?
ASSISTANT   Yes, Director. Then the Earth is lost.
ESPEELIUS   But not the galaxy. Not yet.
ASSISTANT   No, but –
ESPEELIUS   Now... Our supply of veganite is too low for the full testing schedule. We can proceed with only one run-up to full power before final phase. *(Sighs)* All personnel to their stations. Prepare Infinity Scan. Activate central power.
ASSISTANT   But, Director – !
ESPEELIUS   I know! It is madness. But the only alternative... is destruction.

26. Int. Carson's Planet. Bar.
Sleazy music playing in background. Clinking of drinks etc. (BARMAN is alien.)

BARMAN	So you know this Angel of Mercy dolly, then?
ALBY	(*Drunk*) Hmm.
BARMAN	How come? I mean... she's been with the Daleks for years.
ALBY	Before all that.
BARMAN	Before? You wanna move on, mate. Get yourself a life.

Stop chasing around after some dolly who's probably forgotten all about you.

ALBY Stop chasing? Huh... I haven't got within a planetary system of her for three years. She's probably so deep in Dalek territory now, I wouldn't be able to get near her even if I painted meself silver and started (*Dalek impression*) 'talking like this'.

BARMAN And if I were you, I wouldn't go shootin' me mouth off about her here on Carson's Planet either.

ALBY Why not?

BARMAN We're right on the frontier. We had the Daleks running this planet a couple of years ago, you know.

ALBY You did?

BARMAN Oh yeah. Then the Earth bods retook us. Terrible fighting, there was. Terrible. Left me half blind and homeless. I thought I was a goner, you know? Then I got this job here. Up until then, all I could do was beg on the streets.

ALBY Oh...

BARMAN Oh yeah. But the point is, this place is a kind of halfway house now. Meant to be neutral. But it's not only full of thieves and murderers now... there are spies from... well (*whispers*) spies from both sides. I swear half me customers are Dalek replicants.[25]

ALBY Really?

BARMAN For sure. I mean, *you* might be one for all I know. Oh. (*Pause*) Er... and, er, well, no offence if you are. (*Suddenly nervous*) I mean, takes all sorts to make a galaxy. Ha, ha. Drink on the house?

ALBY I'm not a Dalek replicant.

BARMAN Ah, but you see... now I'm confused, aren't I? I mean, you *could* be, but you're just not saying. Get my drift?[26]

ALBY I think I'm drifting *off*.

BARMAN No... no... Don't take offence. Go on, have another drink anyway. You can pay for it if you like. I... I don't mind either way.

Bar stool screeches and ALBY's footsteps.

ALBY No thanks. I'm away back to my ship. Reality seems to be getting more confusing than drunkenness. Night!

27. Ext. Carson's Planet. Backstreet.

Dog barks in distance etc. ALBY hums drunkenly as he walks. He trips over something.

ALBY Argh! Who put that there?

He struggles noisily to his feet.

ALBY (*Seeing someone*) Oh. Who are you two? Ah... wait a minute guys – no need for the hardware. Look, what d'you want? Money?

TANLEE's footsteps.

TANLEE (*Approaching*) And before you try to shoot them while pretending to find your wallet, please bear in mind we're all on the same side.[27]

ALBY (*Aghast*) Mr Tanlee? What the hell are you doing on Carson's Planet?

TANLEE Looking for you.

ALBY I tried to call you, you know?

TANLEE No. But it doesn't surprise me. Presumably you were unable to cut through all the Dalek jamming signals.

ALBY (*Hiccoughs*) Er... yeah. Something like that. Seemed like the Daleks were on to me. Anyway, why are you looking for me?[28]

TANLEE God help us... I know it's been a long time Brook, and you're evidently ridiculously drunk, but I'm your commanding officer.

ALBY Yeah – I mean, obviously I know that. Obviously.

TANLEE (*Sighs*) Give me strength. Now listen to me carefully, Brook. And if *this* doesn't sober you up, nothing ever will...

28. Ext. Yaldos. The Lakes.

Gentle lapping of water. Footsteps on shoreline approach and stop.

KALENDORF I've been sent to get you. They're expecting a hyperlink from the Dalek Supreme in five hours. Apparently he wants to talk to you.

SUZ If I close my eyes and just dip my hand in the water... wash it around gently...

Washing of water FX.

SUZ I can believe I'm back on Vega VI.

KALENDORF I'm surprised they let you come out here on your own in the first place.

SUZ Well, the Daleks are full of surprises, aren't they? Have they set the time for the broadcast yet?

KALENDORF No. But it must be any day now.

SUZ sighs, relaxing.

KALENDORF You know, after what happened on Celatron, I thought they'd never let us out of their sight again.

SUZ Hmm. (*Pause*) Have you ever considered...? (*She stops*)

KALENDORF Considered what?

SUZ That they might know what we're up to?

KALENDORF That wouldn't make sense.

SUZ Perhaps not.

KALENDORF If they had even the slightest suspicion, why would they give you the chance to make a live broadcast to every planet in the Dalek Empire? To let you do that... they must be absolutely sure that you'll do nothing but toe the party line. Praise the slaves for all they've achieved. Tell them how many lives they've saved.[29]

SUZ And I shall say all that... to begin with.

KALENDORF So... You think it's time?[30]

SUZ You know it is.

KALENDORF I *had* come to that conclusion. (*Warm*) But, as I've been told on many occasions, the final decision is yours.

SUZ Hmm.

KALENDORF Suz, I know it must have been difficult for you, back on Celatron... When the Dalek Supreme – [31]

SUZ – offered to kill you and replace you with Alby Brook? (*Pause*) Karl... listen... I know we haven't always... (*Sighs*) There've been bad times.[32]

116

KALENDORF Suz, you don't have to say –

SUZ I don't have to, but I want to. (*Pause*) What you've done... over all these years... What *you* have done is what may save... all of us. You are the important one. I've just been... the window dressing. The public face of our... deception... of our betrayal of the Daleks.

KALENDORF No. You can't dismiss it that easily –

SUZ And anyway, even if the Dalek Supreme hadn't been bluffing, even if he really had known where Alby was, even if I had been prepared to see you die... what would've been the point of that?

KALENDORF Being with someone you love? You tell me.

SUZ And how would Alby and I have ever been happy... as slaves of the Daleks? With probably the whole galaxy enslaved?

KALENDORF But you love him.

SUZ Alby Brook. My feelings for him are like... a very old fantasy – replayed so many times. And yet... in reality... it never really started. And if it had, it would probably have been over long ago.

KALENDORF You don't know that.

SUZ No. But that's what I feel.

KALENDORF No, that's what you want to feel – because it makes what you've got to do easier.

SUZ I don't think this is helping me, Karl.

KALENDORF Suz, listen. We both know that when you stand up in front of all those billions of slaves and say those words –

SUZ 'Death to the Daleks'.

KALENDORF You'll be killed – immediately. The Daleks will turn on you without a thought.[33]

SUZ But it will have begun. As soon as they hear those words, 'Death to the Daleks', billions of slaves will know that I'm asking them to sacrifice themselves. Lay down their lives in a struggle where their only chance of winning is based on sheer numbers... They can only win, or at least make a difference if the Daleks are overwhelmed. And to achieve that, they must just keep on fighting... without fear of death. (*Pause*) Karl... It's my job to inspire them to do that.

KALENDORF But you love Alby. I know that. I know what's in your heart and mind. You can't hide it from me.

SUZ All right. So?

KALENDORF You have a reason to live.

SUZ I can't think about that now –

KALENDORF You must, Suz. You must have hope. You must be there to lead everyone, when it's all over. When we've won.

SUZ What are you saying?

KALENDORF Tell the Daleks you want me to oversee security in the transmission centre. From there, I can interrupt the broadcast.

SUZ *You* want to deliver the message? But then the Daleks will kill *you*.

KALENDORF There can be no greater glory for a Knight of Velyshaa. For all of my people. (*Pause*) Well? Suz... I'm begging you. What we've been doing has been a living hell for me. Hating the Daleks. Standing by and... just watching atrocity after atrocity being committed. Hating myself. Hating you. Hating life itself. Wishing for it all to go wrong, for us to be found out and killed... just so all of this would come to an end.

SUZ Karl...

KALENDORF   Give me the chance to make sense of all these years of betrayal... of working for the enemies of civilisation.
Pause.
SUZ   Give me two hours. I'll meet you back here.
KALENDORF   Where are you going?
SUZ   (*Mysteriously*) I need solitude. One of the privileges of the Angel of Mercy. And this is just the right place to give me real peace of mind.

29. Ext. Carson's Planet. Backstreet.

ALBY   So when is this broadcast likely to happen? And what's she going to say?
TANLEE   Soon. And we're not sure. Sober now?
ALBY   Getting there.
TANLEE   Good – now, listen to me. All we know is that something big is about to happen.
ALBY   About Project Infinity?
TANLEE   We don't know. But you have to get to her first and find out. If you leave now, at maximum speed, you should make the planet Yaldos in two days.
ALBY   Yaldos?
TANLEE   That's where she is. And, Alby, you'd better pray that's quick enough.
ALBY   You still want me to kill her?
TANLEE   If necessary. I'd order an attack on Yaldos if I had a big enough force within striking distance.
ALBY   But you haven't?
TANLEE   There's virtually nothing left of our forces. But there's just a chance you may get through.
ALBY   Huh, 'a chance'... Well, why not...
TANLEE   (*Confidentially*) The fact is... we are losing the war with the Daleks. Our fleets have been decimated... and the Daleks command all the major space lanes and have accessed every communications network in the galaxy. Last month... Earth surrendered after being besieged for years.
ALBY   (*Shocked*) What?
TANLEE   So, Alby... it's up to you. Get straight to your ship. There's not a moment to lose. And be careful, for God's sake. As we landed here, we picked up Dalek readings.
ALBY   Daleks? Here on Carson's Planet?
TANLEE   They're either after you or me... or both... or just up to no good. So, please, just get the hell out of here. Go!
ALBY   Yes, sir.
TANLEE   Good luck, Alby. You are our last hope.
ALBY   Oh... great.
Footsteps as ALBY walks off.
TANLEE   Right, you two, let's get back to the ship.
A Dalek gun blast.
TANLEE   Get down!!!
Two more blasts and the men are killed.
DALEK   Do not move.[34]

TANLEE I'm not moving.
DALEK Proceed to space dock. Capture the one known as Alby Brook.
DALEK 1 I obey.

30. Int. Alby's Ship.
Door opens and shuts. Fast footsteps of ALBY running in. ALBY is out of breath.

ALBY Drudger! Immediate take-off – and don't wait for clearance from traffic control.
DRUDGER Complying.
MIRANA You're not going anywhere.
ALBY Oh, God, not you again.
MIRANA More criminal activity? I already have you booked on seven counts of traffic and excise violations.
ALBY You just can't leave me alone, can you?
MIRANA And this time, I have the gun. It occurred to me that you didn't offer a shred of proof for your –
ALBY Drudger – Protocol 5!!!
Drudger gun fires. Gun clangs to floor, fizzing.
MIRANA Argh!!!
DRUDGER Protocol 5 carried out. Intruder's weapon destroyed.
ALBY What were you saying about a gun?
MIRANA Are you going to kill me?
ALBY Ah, that old chestnut again.
Alarms sound.
DRUDGER External detectors indicate Daleks approaching.
ALBY Let's go! Move it!

31. Ext. Carson's Planet. Spaceport.

DALEK Open fire on that ship, immediately! Fire! Fire! Fire!
Dalek blasts. ALBY's ship takes off.
DALEK 1 Squad 4 to transolar disc patrol in planetary orbit. Intercept escaping vessel.

32. Int. Alby's Ship.
Engines rising in pitch. Various alarms.

DRUDGER Dalek transolar disc patrols closing.
MIRANA What the hell's happening?
ALBY You're witnessing some proof of what I told you last time we met.
Impact explosion. Vocal reaction from both.
MIRANA I thought Carson's Planet was neutral.
ALBY Perhaps someone forgot to tell the Daleks that! You'd better hold onto something, my lovely.[35]
Impact explosion. Vocal reaction.
DRUDGER Transolar discs attacking – port and starboard.
ALBY Switch on security shield.
Buzz of activation.

DRUDGER   Shield activated.

33. Ext. Space. Carson's Planet Orbit.

DALEK   Escaping ship no longer detectable. Lay down wide-angle blast pattern. Maximum power. Fire! Fire! Fire!!!
Dalek guns fire.

34. Int. Alby's Ship.
Buffeted by impacts.

DRUDGER   Daleks firing blind. Attempting to hit us.
ALBY   Steer us away. Set course for Yaldos.
Bleeps.
DRUDGER   Complying.
MIRANA   Yaldos?
DRUDGER   Dalek fire successfully evaded.
MIRANA   I suppose you realise that kidnapping an interplanetary police officer is a crime, punishable by –
ALBY   And I suppose it hasn't escaped your attention that there *is* a war going on? I mean, you are aware of that fact, are you? Considering we've just been shot at by a squadron of Daleks on transolar discs. That fact did penetrate your shiny red police helmet, did it? (*Pause*) Nothing to say? No citations to issue?
DRUDGER   Maximum velocity achieved.
MIRANA   (*Subdued*) Why are we going to Yaldos? Are you into ancient cultures or something?
ALBY   What?
MIRANA   You've heard of the Seers of Yaldos...?
ALBY   No. Who the hell are they?
MIRANA   Nobody really knows. Legend has it they're... well, sorcerers... that they bring the dead back to life.
ALBY   (*Dismissible chuckle*) Yeah... right. Then we might be needing them soon.
MIRANA   What do you mean? What are you going to do on Yaldos?
ALBY   Er... I don't actually know. Funny that. But... very probably... I shall have to kill the woman I love.
MIRANA   Why?
ALBY   Oh, to save the galaxy from the Daleks. How's that for you?
MIRANA   How's that for *you*?
ALBY   It stinks.

35. Narration.

NARRATOR   The Seers of Yaldos... I had heard of them a long time ago. And then, one day, the Daleks had told me that our next planetfall would be on Yaldos. This was my chance. Chance. My only chance... to speak to Alby... to speak... to history. That sounds rather grand, doesn't it? (*A little chuckle*) Perhaps I have been a little grand. Some may say this whole terrible business has filled a vacuum in what I had begun to feel was a rather empty life. They may say I seized upon my role as the Angel of Mercy with a little more vigour than was perhaps necessary. They may be right. But, Alby, I did love you. Do love you. No matter how much I've tried to deny it, to be tough... ruthless. Underneath it all, I've always felt that you were... with me somehow. That girl on Guria told me about you, that you'd said you loved me and were prepared to die finding me. She said I would find a way to be with you forever. And I have found that way, my love. Here I am.

36. Int. Yaldos. Dalek Control.

DALEK   Hyperlink beam from Imperial Command Ship to Yaldos Dalek Control now established.
Door opens.
DALEK 2   Enter.
Footsteps.
DALEK   The Dalek Supreme wishes to speak to you.
SUZ   I know. Leave us.
DALEKS   We obey.
Door closes. Hyperlink activates.
DALEK SUPREME (*Distort*) Susan Mendes.
SUZ   So... Why do you want me to make this broadcast?
DALEK SUPREME (*Distort*) Earth has fallen.
SUZ   Earth...?
DALEK SUPREME (*Distort*) The Daleks are victorious. This galaxy is now under our control. It is the new Dalek Empire.
SUZ   You... you've conquered every planet in the galaxy?
DALEK SUPREME (*Distort*) All planets not yet occupied by the Daleks pose no military threat. They will be unable to defend themselves.
SUZ   So it's over, then. How does that make you feel?
DALEK SUPREME (*Distort*) You will tell the citizens of the new Dalek Empire that the war is ended. You will tell them that their work has hastened our victory. That they will obey the Daleks forever.
SUZ   And that's it? That's what it's all been about? Why didn't you answer my question? How does it make you feel?
DALEK SUPREME (*Distort*) The Emperor of the Daleks will now speak to you.
SUZ   The Emperor...? Why?
Hyperlink signal readjusts.
EMPEROR   (*Distort*) Susan Mendes.
SUZ   (*Afraid*) You... you are the Emperor?
EMPEROR   (*Distort*) I am.
SUZ   You've never spoken to me before. Why are you speaking to me now?
EMPEROR   (*Distort*) Because you have reached the end of your long journey.

37. Int. Lopra Minor. Project Infinity Operations Room.

ESPEELIUS   (*Over speakers*) May I have your attention, please?
Bustle in the room settles.
ESPEELIUS   (*Over speakers*) This is Project Director Espeelius. The Infinity Scan is prepared for its first and only test run. We had hoped for more supplies of veganite to give us power for more tests... but the Dalek

conquest of the Vega System has prevented this... and now the galactic situation is critical. If this test run is successful, we will have justified centuries of painstaking research and work. We will, God willing, have begun the last journey towards saving the galaxy. I know you will all do your best. Good luck to us all.
Clicks off.
ASSISTANT   Director. The Scan Probe is now targeted on the dimensional fissure's weakest point.
ESPEELIUS   Hmm. Good. Begin!
Scan Probe activates. A high-power, piercing sound.
ESPEELIUS   Increase energy levels. Set cut-off at 120 units.
Rise of power hum. Electronic tinkle of data.
ASSISTANT   (*Gobsmacked*) D... Director... It's incredible... The data banks – They're... they're *uploading*. They're... Oh my God. It's working... The sheer volume of data is... incredible.
ESPEELIUS   Well, we are dealing with infinity, are we not?
Comms bleep.
COMMS   (*Distort*) Director! Director! We've picked up transmissions coming from the Yaldos System.
ESPEELIUS   What? That's of no concern to me. Don't bother me now.
COMMS   But, Director... there's been a rebellion.
ASSISTANT   A rebellion? What are the transmissions saying?
COMMS   'Death to the Daleks'... we're hearing those words, transmitted over and over again. It's like it's some prearranged call to arms. All over the Dalek Empire, slaves are turning on the Daleks, taking control of communications and supply networks. It's ... it's just... chaos.
ASSISTANT   Do you think the tide is turning against the Daleks?
ESPEELIUS   I doubt it. Hm. Perhaps in the short term, yes... But whatever has happened in the Yaldos System... it's just a sideshow. Project Infinity is the main event.[36]

38. Ext. Yaldos.
Millions cheering. Firing of guns. Sporadic chants of 'Death to the Daleks'. ALBY's ship comes in to land.

39. Int. Yaldos. Comms Centre.
Cheering is muted in the background. Door opens. Cheering volume up slightly.

SLAVE   (*Out of breath*) Kalendorf! Kalendorf?
KALENDORF   (*Brooding*) What is it?
SLAVE   There is a ship... an Earth Alliance ship.
KALENDORF   So?
SLAVE   An agent... His name is Alby Brook. He's asking for you... and... and (*tails off*)
KALENDORF   The Angel of Mercy?
SLAVE   (*Subdued*) Yes... yes, I'm sorry.
KALENDORF   (*To himself*) The Angel of Mercy.
ALBY and MIRANA's lines in the distance, coming closer.
ALBY   Look, just let me through.
MIRANA   I'm an interplanetary police officer... Do you know the penalty for...?

ALBY	Are they in here... Ah.
MIRANA	Is that him?
ALBY	Kalendorf? Are you Kalendorf?
KALENDORF	Yes. And you are the 'legendary' Alby Brook. I remember

your face.

ALBY	You look very different from the pictures I saw of you.
KALENDORF	Huh. We were supposed to meet on Vega VI, weren't we?
ALBY	You were very good at avoiding me, I seem to remember.
KALENDORF	I was... biding my time.
ALBY	Are you and Suz responsible for this... revolution that's

taking place?

KALENDORF	It's something we'd planned and worked at for a long

time.

MIRANA Well... you've caused quite a stir. On the way in, we were picking up nothing but 'Death to the Daleks' on all frequencies. It's like the galaxy's gone mad.

KALENDORF We've certainly given the Daleks something to think about.

ALBY	They'll counter-attack, that's for sure.
KALENDORF	Yes. Yes. That's for sure. (*Pause*) Alby Brook. You don't

ask. I know you want to. Are you afraid to ask?

Pause.

ALBY	(*Quietly*) Yes. I am afraid.
KALENDORF	Do you want me to tell you?
ALBY	(*Breaking down*) Oh, God, no...
KALENDORF	They killed her, Alby. The Angel of Mercy is dead.

CLOSING THEME.

NOTES

1. Line changed to: 'If you'd paid any attention to your pocket computer download on Dalek methodology, **you'd know** – '

2. Line changed to: 'Did you have to shoot him? Couldn't you **just** – ?'

3. Line changed to: 'Er... contact... ~~contact~~... (*Remembers*) 'Contact Espeelius', that's what the computer said, anyway. But that's all I know.'

4. Line changed to: 'Look, you're the security operative who, according to your file, **which I wrote**, works best under conditions of extreme pressure. So live up to your reputation.'

5. Line changed to: '...~~and production~~ quotas have exceeded productivity targets by 27 per cent.'

6. Line changed to: 'The local commander was looking a little twitchy as he left your office, just **now**. Did you say something to agitate him?'

7. Line changed to: 'Free to what? Take stupid risks? Suz, please, take my hand. (*Pause*) **Why won't you take it**?'

8. Line changed to: 'If you could just hear yourself! The Daleks **can't** trust. They're *using* us, Suz.'

9. Line changed to: 'They could. It would have just taken them a **little** longer.'

10. '**Oh**,' added at the beginning of the line.

11. Line changed to: 'Not when my informant on Orearlis III told me you **would pay anything** for a hyperlink decoder.'

12. Line changed to: 'Sorry, **love**. Someone's already sitting there.'

13. The switch between this line and the following line was actually:

ALBY You**'ve got** –

MIRANA – ~~ve got~~ a gun pointing at the back of your head, yes. Alby Brook, off-world immigrant of no fixed abode, you are under arrest.

14. Line changed to: 'You don't have to say anything, but I am now recording all your responses for the purposes of evidence. What for? Illegal trade in Earth Alliance government property, namely a stolen hyperlink decoder. And I've a funny feeling **that** that's just for starters. (*Pause*) Nothing to say? Have it your own way.'

15. Line changed to: 'These are unconventially times – ~~and~~ I had a bad feeling about you.'

16. Line changed to: '*You* sent me on this mission. I... I... was merely... concerned that – **well**, I thought that I should report directly to you.'

17. Line changed to: '(*Panicked*) What are...? No – wait a minute. Can't we talk this over – ~~er~~...'

18. This line was moved to after the following line.

19. Line changed to: 'Good. ~~I've~~ never been a fan of the police... and that woman is beginning to irritate me. I shall be very happy if I never see her again.'

20. Line changed to: 'It is possible, ~~if the Daleks were aware that they were using the Orearlis Platform to relay their hyperlink signal~~.'

21. Line changed to: 'Just about, **Madam President**. But the signal carrier is getting weaker by the moment.'

22. Line changed to: 'Er... Yes, **Madam President**. Yes. Proceed.'

23. Line changed to: 'Understood, **Madam President**. I understand. Good luck.'

24. Line changed to: 'Espeelius. We must keep information to a minimum. This message is encrypted, but no hyperlink beams can be considered secure now. The Daleks comms-network is... well, they've pretty much got the **whole** galaxy sewn up.'

25. Line changed to: 'Oh yeah. But the point is, this place is a kind of halfway house now. Meant to be neutral. **That actually means the place is such a mess, no one bothers with it.** ~~But~~ it's ~~not only~~ full of thieves and murderers ~~now~~... **and of course**, there are spies from... well (*whispers*) spies from both sides. I swear half me customers are Dalek replicants.'

26. Line changed to: 'Ah, but you see... ~~now~~ I'm confused, aren't I? I mean, you *could* be, but you're just not saying. Get my drift?'

27. Line changed to: '(*Approaching*) And before you try to shoot them while **you're** pretending to find your wallet, please bear in mind we're all on the same side.'

28. Line changed to: '(*Hiccoughs*) **Yeah**... yeah. Something like that. Seemed like the Daleks were on to me. Anyway, why are you looking for me?'

29. Line changed to: 'If they **even had** the slightest suspicion, why would they give you the chance to make a live broadcast to every planet in the Dalek Empire? To let you do that... they must be absolutely sure that you'll do nothing but toe the party line. Praise the slaves for all they've achieved. Tell them how many lives they've saved.'

30. Line changed to: '**Ah**... So... You think it's time.'

31. Line changed to: 'Suz, I know it must have been difficult for you, back on Celatron... **I mean**, when the Dalek Supreme – '

32. Line changed to: ' – offered to kill you and replace you with Alby Brook? (*Pause*) Karl... listen... I know we haven't always... (*Sighs*) **Well**, there've been bad times.'

33. Line changed to: '**Yes**. You'll be killed – immediately. The Daleks will turn on you without a thought.'

34. Line changed to: 'Do not move. **Do not move.**'

35. Line changed to: '**Well**, perhaps someone forgot to tell the Daleks that! You'd better hold on to something, my **love**.'

36. Line changed to: 'I doubt it, Hm. Perhaps in the short term, yes... But whatever has happened in the Yaldos System... ~~it's just a side show~~. Project Infiinity is the main event.'

Q&A
"DEATH TO THE DALEKS!"

By the time you came to record "*Death to the Daleks!*", the first two CDs had been released. How did the reaction to those plays affect your writing, recording or post-production?

Nicholas Briggs: Well, the initial review-reaction to the series was quite bad. *Dreamwatch* and *SFX* just didn't get it and simply moaned that Daleks were boring and where was *Doctor Who* anyway? The positive reaction started to filter through to me from people who read the reviews on the internet and through personal contact with other fans. But I'm not sure when that kicked in. The review in **Doctor Who Magazine** seemed to take ages to come out, because they'd just adopted their policy of not reviewing things in advance... That was very lovely when it came, but I can't exactly remember when that was. I think, at this stage, I was still just beavering away, trying to get everything done on time. I had a theatre job in the summer and another one in the autumn, so it all got a bit tight time-wise. Also, when I'm away doing theatre, I tend to become very disconnected from the *Doctor Who* world; so I don't think the reaction was affecting the way I worked at all, at this stage.

What were your writing habits like for *Dalek Empire*?

I wrote *Dalek Empire* at my home in South-East London and at my parents' place down in the New Forest. When I was writing at home, I think I was using my Mac G4 and when I was at my parents', I used pen and paper. I also did a lot of strolling in the park near where I live, writing in exercise books. I used to do this a lot back in the Audio Visuals days, and it's a method of writing that I've re-adopted more and more ever since I discovered that Rob Shearman writes like this! Just trying to emulate his genius, of course. But writing out in the open air can free your imagination quite a bit. I tend to feel stifled if I stay indoors all the time – which I do a lot! It's the reason I couldn't just be a writer. I have to go out and work with other people, for the sake of my sanity. Oh, and by the way, I wrote it in Microsoft Word. I love my hanging indents.

How long did it take?

It took most of 2001. I always take lots of breaks, because people generally are more productive just before and just after a break. Between these times, productivity sags somewhat. So I do a little and very often, which seems to work well. I do my longest periods of concentrated work very late at night – or in the early hours of the morning, I should say – because there's a great stillness round about that time. You know no one is going to ring you and there are only bad, late-night movies to distract you.

I do loads of rewriting, because I constantly re-read my work. And every time I re-read, I rewrite something. When I'd finished a first draft of a chapter, I'd send it to John Ainsworth. He'd make notes and then we'd meet up to discuss them. As a result of that,

I'd do anther draft. I think, on average, each chapter went up to about four drafts. When both John and I were happy with the script, I'd send it to Terry Nation's Estate and to Jacqueline Rayner [Executive Producer for BBC Worldwide]. The Nation Estate never asked for any changes, which was nice, and neither did Jac. In fact, Jac was kind enough to say things like, 'Very exciting! Can't wait to find out what happens next!' in her official approval emails. I did send the first couple of chapters to Jason, but I visited his house a month or so later and found them discarded, unread somewhere and so didn't bother sending him any more.

"Death to the Daleks!" has very few changes between script and finished audio – were you particularly happy with it?
Well, just because there weren't many changes doesn't necessarily mean I was more happy with it than I was with the other chapters. It just means I thought I got it more right the first time. I'm not sure why. It is a very character and dialogue-based episode with very little action. That stuff on Celatron, in particular, did dig to the root of Suz's growing psychological problems. And in many ways, this chapter was the pay-off to a lot of set-up. Since that was all planned out in advance, maybe it just came together quicker.

The title's an unusual one – not only does it have speech marks and a exclamation point, but it's also noticeably similar to a certain 1974 *Doctor Who* serial.
I knew that chapter three's title should be whatever I decided was going to be the 'call to arms' phrase Kalendorf and Suz were spreading amongst the slaves. Once I'd decided that 'Death to the Daleks!' would be that phrase, I had to go with it as a title. Gary Russell, in particular, thought I was bonkers and said that the Nation Estate would object. Jac also voiced some worries about it, so I asked her, 'Are you telling me on behalf of the BBC that I can't do it?' or something like that. She said she wasn't officially objecting at all. The Nation Estate made no comment about it at all.

I really did think it was a good title for this chapter. I also stand virtually alone in liking the original *Death to the Daleks*, which is a bit of a running joke with some friends of mine, so I also wanted to pay tribute to that original story in this way. It's also a bit of a talking point, and that's never a bad thing in terms of drawing audience attention.

One final point, I said there was the precedent of the *Star Trek* movie *First Contact*. As all *Next Generation* fans know, there was also an episode of that series called *First Contact*. I rest my battered case.

One of the few notable changes you made was that Tanlee calls the Earth President 'Madam President' rather than 'your presidency'. Any reason for the change?
I thought 'your presidency' just sounded a bit stupid. It sounded as if he was referring to her period in office rather than addressing her office by name.

"Death to the Daleks!" introduces a new regular, Mirana. In what kind of detail had you mapped out her story? Was it a deliberate ploy to make people accept her as a regular so you could then kill her off?
Her story had been mapped out in the plot-line, but I didn't prepare a character biog for her, which, in retrospect, perhaps I should have done. But you're absolutely right, I did want to give the impression that she was a new regular and at that stage I did think I was going to kill her off. It was a bit of audience expectation management going on! I wanted

the audience to accept her as a new regular, and to that end I gave her that whole introductory scene with the strange insect aliens and the hilarious Jez Fielder doing the most outrrrrrag-g-g-geous voice I've ever heard. I was on the floor laughing in the control room. I got everyone else in to have a listen. They thought he was mad. They were right.

When you're writing a series in which the episodes are released two months apart, how much thought do you give to recapping events? How much can you assume that the listeners will have remembered from the earlier instalments?
I only recapped events when I thought the characters, rather than the audience, would actually need to remember. Otherwise, I wanted the audience to rely on having heard the previous CD or having read the 'story so far' section. That's why I included that as part of the packaging. I was a bit worried that someone might buy *"Death to the Daleks!"* first and not know what was going on. I thought the info in the CD booklet might help. In reality, though, I think it's unlikely that people bought a later chapter and listened to it without having heard the previous CDs. But I have no firm research to back that up.

Giving Alby false legs was a bit harsh, wasn't it? Were you just being sadistic or something?
I was just being as realistic as possible. I wanted him to be caught up in a major planetary assault, so I thought, 'What are the chances of everyone getting out of that alive?' Quite slim. I didn't want to kill a main character off at that point, so I just thought I'd give him a nasty injury. It also made a good transition point in the plot. Waking up in a hospital is always good for that, I find. Where am I? What happened? It's a good excuse for people to ask the bleedin' obvious, which is always helpful on audio.

Tanlee turns up in *"Death to the Daleks!"* – what made you decide that he would be your character?
At some very early point, I was considering asking Mark Gatiss to be Tanlee; but he was terribly, terribly busy and I didn't want to have to worry about finding recording dates that would fit in with his busy schedule. I never actually asked him to play the part, but I did chat to him about *Dalek Empire* generally and I kind of scoped out his availability, which wasn't good. It was John Ainsworth who suggested that I should play the part, since in discussions about the character he thought I was very definite about how I wanted to play it. It was fun to do, because he does change somewhat as the story progresses. It's an indication of how serious the situation is getting towards the end of the story that he becomes quite emotional when he realises that Earth is going to be invaded. I'm thinking of that bit when the comms cut off and he's left on his own saying, 'My God'. I enjoyed giving that a bit of emotional weight.

When Alby and Mirana meet up, we get a flashback to their first meeting. You'd also done something similar in *Invasion of the Daleks*, with Alby and Suz's last scene together being dramatised as a flashback. Does non-linear storytelling interest you? Of course, you use it a lot more in *Dalek War*.
The more I write, the more I realise just how absolutely vital it is that you tell your story in the right order. I know... that sounds blindingly obvious. But the fact is that it's not always obvious for me to figure out what the most effective order is. If you think of the

way you tell people stuff in real life, you quite often don't tell them things in strict chronological order. Sometimes it's more effective to tell people up-front what happened at the end, which gives the process of the unfolding of your story more significance; or sometimes it works to suddenly go back and let people know what happened earlier, which gives you a kind of retrospective shock. Leaping forward to finding Alby on the *Aquitania* is a slightly disorientating thing to do. For a moment or two, we flounder a bit, wondering what is going on. Then, when I let you know how he got there, the idea was to give you the emotional blow of his last scene with Suz at the same time – so you get vital information and, hopefully, emotional impact at the same time, which I think is more powerful and engaging for an audience. That's the theory, anyway.

The *Dalek Empire* CD booklets contain comic strips depicting scenes from the episodes. The inspiration for the comic strips was, of course, *The Dalek Book* and the TV21 comic strips. I asked Tim Keable to do them, because he's just as in love with those things as I am. He loves drawing Daleks and I've known him for many years. How could I not ask him? I selected bits of the script for him to do, I think, although he sometimes suggested bits. I seem to remember he particularly suggested the bits for "*Death to the Daleks!*" and *Project Infinity*, which I agreed with. I would always send the scripts to Tim as soon as they were finished, so he could get an idea of what was coming up. I also thought it was important for him to have a broader story context for his illustrations, so he wasn't just creating scenes in isolation. I wanted him to have a general feel for the overall story.

The cliffhanger is a right humdinger – Kalendorf telling Alby that Suz is dead. You were being very cagey here, weren't you? You must have known that people would say, 'Well, how can Suz be dead if she's been narrating the events?'
Yes, I was playing around with audience expectations. I knew that everyone would assume it was Suz narrating. And in case anyone was still doubting it, I had the Seer suddenly start referring to Suz in the first person. This, of course, was the Seer's personality becoming more enmeshed with Suz's – but in the absence of other evidence at the time, it sounds like a confirmation that it is indeed Suz who is narrating. So, in a way, it's a cliffhanger that leaves the audience wondering about two things: is Suz really dead? Is it really Suz narrating? Well, with those sorts of questions hanging in the air, I hoped no one could resist getting the next instalment.

Q&A
SCRIPT EDITING

When Nicholas Briggs finished the first draft of each chapter of Dalek Empire, he would send it to script editor John Ainsworth. Ainsworth would read the script and make notes, then the two of them would arrange to meet somewhere to run through the script. In the lead-up to the recording of the fourth Dalek Empire play, Project Infinity, Briggs was heavily involved in theatre productions of A Midsummer Night's Dream and Closer in Chesterfield, whilst Ainsworth was based in London. Therefore, Briggs drove south on Sunday 14 October 2001 – his only day off from a busy rehearsal schedule – and met up with Ainsworth just off Caledonian Road in North London at 10.30am. Dismayed that none of the local cafes were open, they sat in Briggs's old Vauxhall Astra and had their meeting. They recorded their discussion, initially intending extracts of it to be used on one of Big Finish's behind-the-scenes CDs. However, the recording was then mislaid until recently...

This is a transcript of director and script editor discussing the early scenes of Project Infinity. It shows how John was keen to introduce a new element of mystery and how Nick was keen to emphasise the developing character traits of Alby Brook.

John Ainsworth   There are two particular things which are possible criticisms, but I have a way in mind that will improve them. Though you may disagree and throw it all away, and that's fine. Firstly... more an observation, in that I think compared to the other three episodes, this one goes much more into action and there's much less plot. I mean, in the sense that there's the revelation of what Project Infinity is, and that really is your only plot. We've just got to get there and stop them, or try to. That's it, really. I know that's a horrific simplification. You know what I'm saying?

Nicholas Briggs   More or less. There is the revelation of Mirana being under the Emperor's control, but that's the impetus for them to go to Project Infinity in a way. OK, yeah.

Ainsworth   The other point is one that we've talked about, but I'm still having difficulty... about the whole thing of having Alby sort of running away up the mountain and refusing to give this information to Kalendorf and Mirana. And then it turns out not to be a huge amount of information anyway. I know we talked about this before, but just reading through again, it still feels a little bit... I can't really grasp why he's doing that.

Briggs   Well, I think that it's less that he's running away and refusing to give them information, it's more that he's just running away and not even thinking about the information he's got. And Kalendorf thinks Alby has information. That's what it's to do with. It's Kalendorf who's saying, 'You know something' and Alby's saying, 'I don't know anything'. He's not lying. As far as he's concerned, he believes he doesn't know anything. So he finally says, 'OK, you wanna know what I know? I know this and that... and that's all there is to it! And that fact means there's no point in knowing it anyway, because we're all going to be dead in five minutes' time' or whatever.

Ainsworth   I think what tips the balance towards making the audience think Alby knows more is the fact that Kalendorf keeps saying, 'There's that look in his eye'. It's almost like, when Alby heard the mention of the Lopra System, he flinched.

Briggs   Oh... right.

Ainsworth   Perhaps Kalendorf is planting too big a seed of an idea here.

Briggs   Yeah...

Ainsworth   What you're saying is that Kalendorf imagined this 'look' in Alby's eye.

Briggs   No, Alby definitely has a reaction when he hears about the Lopra System.

Ainsworth   He clocks it. But it's not quite as significant as Kalendorf – and therefore the audience – will think it is.

Briggs   For Alby, it has this whole resonance of him being sent on a mission to kill Suz if she knew about Project Infinity. And Tanlee said to him that if the Daleks do know about Project Infinity, then we're finished. So when he hears that a Dalek ship has been spotted in the Lopra System – and he knows Project Infinity is in the Lopra System – Alby just thinks, 'We're screwed'.

Ainsworth   Yeah.

Briggs   Which is why he focuses on Suz more. Now that's all well and good, isn't it? But I haven't actually said any of that in the script. [*Laughs*]

Ainsworth   Well, you have. All those explanations are there, but I think the trouble is that there's a false build-up because of what Kalendorf seems to believe. We're expecting Alby to give more of a revelation than he does. So when he doesn't –

Briggs   But that's what the revelation is... that there isn't one! They chase after him, all the way to the top of this mountain, thinking 'What's he doing? Where's he gone?'... and when they find him, he just says, 'I'm looking for pickled onions'. It's the art of bathos... anti-climax. But it does trouble me that it creates a sense of disappointment in you.

Ainsworth   Right. Well, have a think about that.

Briggs   On the general point, I did want to make it more action-packed.

Ainsworth   Right.

Briggs   Because episode three has virtually no actual 'kerpow!' action at all. Which really came home to me when I'd finished editing it. I thought, 'My God, this is a really talkie episode'.

Ainsworth   Episode threes always are, aren't they?

Briggs   And I thought that we really need to go off with a bang, which is why I put the whole battle scene thing in.

Ainsworth   Oh, I think you're absolutely right. I think not having that would be a let down, dramatically speaking. But the thing that I was going to suggest about both the points I've brought up, is... I wondered if it might be interesting – and this is an extra bit of plot which won't change anything structurally – if Alby was slightly suspicious or fearful that Kalendorf could be a Dalek duplicate, because, of course, the Daleks have had every opportunity to make a duplicate of him.

Briggs   Oh, my God.

Ainsworth   So therefore Alby would be a little bit reluctant to discuss the Lopra System and Project Infinity with someone he suspects of being a duplicate. And, of course, Kalendorf will be unwittingly reinforcing Alby's suspicion by pursuing him on all these points. So Alby's thinking, 'Oh my God, the Daleks want to know what I know'... which, of course, is true, but then it turns out to be Mirana who wants to know, because *she's* the Dalek agent. I just think that plays around with the surprise element. It will redirect people's suspicions, perhaps.

Briggs   [*Liking the idea*] Yeah...

Ainsworth   And Kalendorf could, quite conceivably be a duplicate.

Briggs   No, I follow that. It's just that –

Ainsworth   You think it's muddying it all a bit.

Briggs   No. You're absolutely right. Alby would think that. My first thought is that it will just make all those scenes longer. I think that what's there already is more or less necessary – although I know that introducing this idea would largely just change stuff rather than add to it – but it would make it *longer*. And it's already very long indeed. My gut feeling – and you know me, I'll have to think about this –

Ainsworth   I'm saying it more for you to think about it rather than make a decision now.

Briggs   My gut feeling is that I quite like the way it happens now, because it's all just about Alby being depressed and feeling that everything he's done has been wasted – and he doesn't want to fight any more. It's all about stuff which is more realistic human emotion, rather than thriller stuff like, 'You may be a spy!' and all that. But maybe I'm not satisfying the needs of the genre.

Ainsworth   I think it would be a great shame to get rid of the human emotion stuff. But, there's no reason why there can't be a combination of the two. If you said that Alby did really think Kalendorf is a replica, you might wonder why he isn't doing anything about it, reporting his suspicions to the authorities or something. And the reason why he's not is because he just doesn't care about anything anymore.

Briggs   This is it... If someone burst into Alby's room and said, 'Did you know that Kalendorf's a Dalek replicant?' he'd just say, 'Oh, piss off!'. I don't think he gives a damn about it.

Ainsworth   But, at the same time, he wouldn't want to start spilling vital information to Kalendorf.

Briggs   But I think Alby thinks it's all too late anyway. Which is why I put in the scene at the beginning. I want Mark to do that as if the poor guy is really in a mess... You know? Alby's disengaged from the thriller plot completely now. But... Hmmm

Ainsworth   I think, go home and think about it. I'm not saying the story is completely missing this element. I'm just saying it's something that might work and that it might give an extra twist to the duplicate thing. It might give another little strand of plot.

Briggs   I'm more inclined to have Alby throw this element in when he's being angry. For him to throw it in and say, 'For all I know...'. You know? 'This whole situation is bad and, for all I know, it could be even worse. I don't actually care, but as far as I'm concerned you're talking out of your arse for two reasons. One, because I'm not interested in what you're saying. Two, because you could actually be working for the Daleks anyway. And it's all too difficult for me to think about', you know, that sort of attitude.

Ainsworth   I don't think it does need much more than that.

Briggs   OK... Hmmm. Thank you.

Ainsworth   Well, anyway! Think about that.

Briggs   It's interesting you say that there's not much plot and it's all action, because I kept thinking, 'Oh, there's so much plot to get across!'

Ainsworth   I suppose I meant that there's not enough mystery. The rest of it is what I'd call the mechanics of it.

Briggs   By the way, did you want a pen?

Ainsworth   I've done all my pen work.

Briggs   Well, there's one here if you want one.

And then began the line-by-line analysis of the script. As is evident from the scripts reproduced in this book, Briggs did indeed take Ainsworth's advice by throwing in a reference to Alby suspecting Kalendorf of being a duplicate.

PROJECT INFINITY

1. News Broadcast.[1]
News theme tune begins. Dip volume for...

NEWSREADER This is Galactic Free News, broadcasting on all wavelengths and hyperbeams. The galaxy-wide revolution against the Daleks continues, but its leaders warn against complacency.
Music fades.
NEWSREADER Seven standard months have passed since the death of Angel of Mercy Susan Mendes triggered the rebellion on almost every planet enslaved by the Daleks. And although in the initial fighting the Daleks lost control of a number of key planetary systems and communications networks, it is claimed that the rebellion is in danger of losing momentum. And with the mysterious disappearance of Space Security Chief Ernst Tanlee, the Operational Commander of Earth's Forces, more worrying developments are signalled. Rebellion leader Kalendorf, one of the fabled Knights of Velyshaa, had this to say when we spoke to him via direct hyperlink to the planet Yaldos.
KALENDORF (*Distort*) The Daleks have not been beaten. We must be clear about that. The fight *has* to go on.

Crash in Dalek Empire *theme tune.*

2. Int. Yaldos. Alby's Room.
Bleep of comms alarm. Liquid being poured from bottle into glass, messily. ALBY takes a big gulp. Bleep of comms alarm again. ALBY burps. Click of button.

ALBY (*Drunk and morose*) I told you. No calls! I don't want to talk to anyone!
COMPUTER Priority message.
ALBY I said, I don't want to talk to *anyone!* That means anyone... at all... in the whole bleedin' universe! Including you! So get lost.
COMPUTER Priority message reads... 'Try a pickled onion... My gran makes them...sends them from Earth. Grid reference 059249786.
ALBY (*Over computer voice*) Look, stop it! I'm just not interested in any messages from any – (*stunned*) What?[2]
COMPUTER Priority message reads... 'Try a pickled onion... My gran makes them...sends them from Earth. Grid reference 059249786.
Glass drops and smashes. Crash as ALBY falls to the ground. Groans in pain.
ALBY (*Gasping*) Suz? Suz... is that you?

3. Int. Dalek Imperial Command Ship.

DALEK SUPREME (*Distort*) Dalek Supreme reporting to Emperor.
Door opens.
EMPEROR Speak!

DALEK SUPREME Course alteration to this vessel's trajectory has been effected. At this range, Earth Alliance deep-space scanning beams will no longer be able to detect us –

EMPEROR Until our final approach to the Lopra System. Is it certain that we were detected?

DALEK SUPREME Readings indicate momentary contact only.

EMPEROR We underestimated the tenacity of the humans and their allies. That must not happen again.[3]

DALEK SUPREME Understood, Emperor. Our new course will delay planetfall on Lopra Minor by five solar months.

EMPEROR A high-speed advance attack force with augmented delta-ray shielding must be dispatched to Lopra Minor as soon as possible. They will be undetectable.

DALEK SUPREME Preparations will be instigated immediately.

EMPEROR They will secure Project Infinity and begin conversion of the systems in preparation for my arrival.

DALEK SUPREME Understood.

EMPEROR Our human agents report that no reinforcements have been allocated to defend the Lopra System. Our attack force will encounter no significant resistance. Victory is assured!

4. Int. Yaldos. Comms Centre.[4]

Knock on door.

KALENDORF (*Sighs*) Come in.
Door opens. Footsteps.
KALENDORF Ah, Officer Mirana.
MIRANA Hi... Are... are you okay?
KALENDORF 'Okay'? Do I look okay?
MIRANA Not really.
Pause.
MIRANA I've got the latest hyperbeam reports. Do you want me to go through them with you now?
KALENDORF Is there any point?
MIRANA Well... Not really. But I guess that's for you to decide. You're in charge after all.
KALENDORF Apparently. I didn't ask for the job. Nobody voted for me.
MIRANA Nobody else *wanted* the job. I mean, I'm *apparently* head of communications. How did *that* happen?
KALENDORF (*Chuckles*) Nobody else –
MIRANA – wanted the job... that's right. (*Shares the chuckle*) Anyway, the reports are here if you want to take a look.
KALENDORF Talk me through them.
MIRANA Okay, but there's nothing new.
KALENDORF There's always something new.
MIRANA If you say so...
Computer activated. Electronic sound of graphics.
MIRANA (*Routine*) This is the picture we'd built up with the first round of reports. Which you've seen. And... here's that pattern of successful rebellion we know so well. A kind of split, right from the Vega System, through Garazone, Guria... the Celatron worlds here... like an arc across the galaxy, more or less ending here on Yaldos.

KALENDORF That's no surprise... an arc of rebellion travelling through almost every planet Suz and I were taken to by the Daleks.
MIRANA Just a month after the rebellion started...
More graphic sounds.
MIRANA And our influence has spread quickly. Dalek forces are scattering, retreating... mainly in the direction of the Seriphia Galaxy.
KALENDORF Where they came from in the first place.
MIRANA And you can see that arc of rebellion is getting thicker.
More graphic sounds.
MIRANA *Three* months in, and the Dalek forces look pretty patchy. They're just concentrating in ten or more strong-points... most significantly in Earth's solar system.
KALENDORF And then the slow-down of activity. Maybe you were right... there *is* nothing new. Is that the latest picture?
MIRANA More or less.
KALENDORF (*Suddenly curious*) Open *that* file.
MIRANA Sure. But it just confirms the way things are going.
More graphics noises.
KALENDORF (*Worried*) What...? What are they playing at?
MIRANA Running scared.
KALENDORF (*Studying the graphics*) Hmm... Is that what you think?
MIRANA Despite everything you've said in the media, there's still a lot of gung-ho attitude from our people
KALENDORF An army's state of mind is important, but you need more than just attitude to win a battle. A lot of our fleets are badly equipped and poorly organised. But look... these attacks here... The Daleks shouldn't have been defeated; but they're simply retreating at the first sign of trouble.
MIRANA Maybe. Maybe they just know it's all over for them.
KALENDORF No.
MIRANA Kalendorf, what's the matter?
KALENDORF I don't know. Hmmm...
MIRANA What are you thinking?
KALENDORF I'm thinking... They're trying to make us lazy.
MIRANA (*Unconvinced*) By losing the war?
KALENDORF By treating us like over-excitable children. Letting us win, over and over again when we've no right to.
MIRANA That doesn't sound like Dalek thinking to me.
KALENDORF A few years ago I would have agreed with you... But not now. You'd be surprised what constitutes Dalek thinking these days.
Taps a few keys. Graphics bleep.
MIRANA What are you doing? (*Dismissive*) Oh, the Lopra System.
KALENDORF (*Deep in thought*) Why do I keep coming back to that?
MIRANA I've no idea. It's in the middle of nowhere.
KALENDORF On the opposite side of the galaxy to Seriphia.
MIRANA We haven't had any more sightings of that Dalek trace – and anyway, it was some way out from Lopra.
KALENDORF But it was heading in that direction.
MIRANA We can't be sure of that. My money's on it being just another scanner shadow. We get them all the time... A lot of the equipment we're working with is... well, pretty beat up.
KALENDORF Hmmm. I've never believed in shadows, Mirana.

MIRANA   I think you should get some rest.
KALENDORF   (*Ignoring her*) You know... Suz once said to me that she thought the Daleks knew what we were planning all along.
MIRANA   That doesn't make sense.
KALENDORF   That's what I said. (*Sighs. Change of thought*) Do you think Alby knows more than he's telling us?
MIRANA   Alby? Why do you say that?
KALENDORF   I noticed him get a bit tight-lipped when the first report of that Dalek sighting came in.
MIRANA   Did you? Oh.
KALENDORF   Yes. Where is he?
MIRANA   Er... I don't know. I haven't seen him in quite a while. He's been rather... distant, lately.
KALENDORF   Drunk, you mean. He hasn't said much to anyone ever since he found out Suz was dead.
MIRANA   He'd been looking for her a long time.
KALENDORF   (*Pensive*) Yes...
Comms bleep.
KALENDORF   Kalendorf to Alby Brook. Respond please.
Negative bleep.
KALENDORF   Alby, this is Kalendorf. Where are you?
Negative bleep.
KALENDORF   Comms centre, can you locate Alby Brook for me, please?
COMMS   (*Distort*) Traffic control reports he left the city about an hour ago, sir.
KALENDORF   Not drunk, then. (*Urgent*) Where was he heading?
COMMS   (*Distort*) Er... Oh. It seems he didn't log a flight plan, sir.
Door opens.
MIRANA   Where are you going?
KALENDORF   To find Alby... and ask him what he really knows about the Lopra System.

5. Ext. Lopra Minor. Jungle.
A spaceship lands. Establish jungle atmosphere. Crossfade to:

6. Int. Lopra Minor. Project Infinity. Director's Study.
An old-fashioned clock ticks sedately. ESPEELIUS's distinctive, staccato breathing. A sharp buzzer sounds.

ASSISTANT   (*Distort*) Director! Director!
Pause. The buzzer again.
ESPEELIUS   I gave orders that I was not to be disturbed.
ASSISTANT   (*Distort*) But, Director –
ESPEELIUS   The calculations for full activation of the Infinity Scan must be precise. Any inaccuracies could result in –
ASSISTANT   (*Distort*) A spacecraft has just landed on the jungle perimeter!
ESPEELIUS   What? Are we under attack?
ASSISTANT   (*Distort*) No... no, the call sign identifies the ship as the personal transport of the Operational Commander of Earth's Forces.
ESPEELIUS   Tanlee? Tanlee has come here?
ASSISTANT   (*Distort. Distracted*) Er... yes, sir. That's confirmed. We've

just received another signal. Commander Tanlee wishes to oversee the final activation in person. He's... he's on his way to your study now!

ESPEELIUS   Tell him I'm not to be disturbed –

Door opens.

TANLEE   (*All smiles*) Director Espeelius!

ESPEELIUS   Tanlee?!

TANLEE   Good to see you. I'm glad to hear I haven't missed the main event.

7. Int. Alby's Skimmer.

Howling of mountain wind. A skimmer streaks by. Crossfade to interior.

ALBY   (*To himself*) Come on, come on... must be around here somewhere. Nav computer, hurry up with triangulation.

Bleep of nav computer.

NAV COMPUTER Co-ordinates shifting randomly.[5]

ALBY   What? But... I thought we were just about there.

NAV COMPUTER Unidentified energy barrier emanating from Yaldos mountains is preventing precise co-ordinate reading.

ALBY   Barrier? What kind of energy barrier?

NAV COMPUTER Unidentified.

ALBY   Oh, very clever.

Comms bleep.

NAV COMPUTER Incoming transmission.

ALBY   Hello? Who is it?

SUZ   (*Distort*) Alby... Is that you?

ALBY   Suz? Suz! Er... yes, yes it's me – but –

Comms bleep.

NAV COMPUTER Co-ordinates triangulating now.

ALBY   What? Oh good. Look, never mind that. Suz! Suz? Do you read me, over?

Hiss of static.

ALBY   Computer, play back that last message.

NAV COMPUTER What message?

ALBY   What'd'ya mean, 'What message'?

NAV COMPUTER Nav computer received co-ordinate triangulation signal. No other message received.

ALBY   (*To himself, confused*) No other...? But I heard... Suz.

Comms bleep.

ALBY   (*Urgent*) She's calling again. Put her through!

NAV COMPUTER Incoming transmission.

ALBY   Suz?

KALENDORF   (*Distort. Confused*) Suz? It's Kalendorf!

ALBY   Kalendorf? What... but...?

KALENDORF   (*Distort*) Alby, are you all right? What the hell are you doing out here flying around a mountain range?

ALBY   What are *you* doing out here?[6]

MIRANA   (*Distort*) Following you.

ALBY   Mirana? God, can't I get *any* peace?

KALENDORF   (*Distort*) It's time you and I had a conversation.

ALBY   About what?

KALENDORF   (*Distort*) The Lopra System.

ALBY   (*Dismissive*) I don't know what you're talking about.

8. Ext. Yaldos Mountains.
Skimmer lands on rock. Crunch of touchdown. Crossfade to:

9. Int. Alby's Skimmer.

KALENDORF   (*Distort*) Come in. Alby. Where are you?
ALBY   (*Sighs*) Go away!
MIRANA   (*Distort*) Got him pinpointed. He's landed.
KALENDORF   (*Distort*) We're right behind you.
ALBY   (*Unimpressed*) Oh... great.[7]
MIRANA   (*Distort*) We're coming in to land.
ALBY   No!

10. Ext. Yaldos Mountains.
Howl of distant wind. Crunch of ALBY's approaching footsteps. Bleep of a tracker.

NAV COMPUTER Now approaching final co-ordinates.
ALBY   (*To himself*) Must be that cave.
Clicks tracker off.
KALENDORF   (*Distant, echoing*) Alby! Alby!
MIRANA   (*Distant, echoing*) There he is!!!
Their distant footsteps fade in and approach.
ALBY   I thought I told you this was personal!!!
As their footsteps get closer, we hear them breathing with effort.
KALENDORF   Air's pretty thin up here. We should've brought some respirators.
ALBY   Why don't you go back and get some?
MIRANA   We'll be all right. Won't we, Kalendorf?
KALENDORF   Hm. Well, we're here now. You might as well tell us what you're up to. (*Pause*) Come on, Alby.
ALBY   If you must know...
Pause.
MIRANA   Yes?
ALBY   I'm looking for some pickled onions.
KALENDORF   Some what?
Footsteps as ALBY moves away.
ALBY   (*Moving off*) You heard.
KALENDORF   (*To MIRANA*) What's he talking about?
MIRANA   (*Faintly amused*) Onions. A terran vegetable, I seem to recall.
KALENDORF   This isn't making any sense. Alby! Come back here!
We change perspective. ALBY's footsteps approach. He's a little out of breath.
ALBY   (*Taken aback*) My God. I... (*Starts to laugh*) Pickled onions.
The sound of a jar being picked up. The lid is unscrewed. Crunch of ALBY biting into an onion.
ALBY   Argh! (*Laughs*) Just as hot as they were on Vega VI.
Footsteps approach. Some breath from KALENDORF as he approaches.
KALENDORF   Don't tell me... Those are pickled onions?

ALBY	Yeah.
MIRANA	What are 'pickled onions' doing halfway up a mountain?

Takes another bite.

ALBY	Mmmm.
KALENDORF	Are you sure they're safe to eat?
ALBY	No.
KALENDORF	(*Insistent*) Alby?
ALBY	(*Sighs*) I got a message.
KALENDORF	A message?
MIRANA	About pickled onions?
ALBY	It said, 'Try a pickled onion... My gran makes them...

sends them from Earth'. Then it gave this grid reference.[8]

MIRANA	I don't understand. Do you?
KALENDORF	No.
ALBY	It's something Suz said to me... on Vega VI. The last time...

the last time we were... well, happy.

KALENDORF	What do you think it means?
ALBY	She's here.
KALENDORF	Alby...
ALBY	She must be.
KALENDORF	Suz is dead. You know that.
ALBY	Do I? These are *her* pickled onions. I know they are.
MIRANA	(*Laughs, then stops herself*) Sorry... Sorry...
KALENDORF	Are you still drunk?
ALBY	No!

Pause.

ALBY	Oh look, I know this all sounds stupid, but, I heard her –

Distant crunch of gravel, echoing from a cave.

ALBY	Wha – ?
MIRANA	(*Quietly*) What was that?
KALENDORF	(*Quietly*) It came from the cave.[9]

Footsteps approach out of the cave. Mysterious music cue. (The SEER is the NARRATOR. To begin with, her voice is mingled with SUZ's. This is indicated by SEER/SUZ.)

SEER/SUZ	Hello, Alby. I've been waiting for you.
ALBY	Who are you?
SEER/SUZ	Don't you recognise me?
ALBY	S... Suz?
MIRANA	She's one of the Seers... Aren't you? One of the –
KALENDORF	– Seers of Yaldos?
SEER	Come with me, Alby. Please. Your friends are welcome too.

11. Int. Seers' Cavern.

Muted howl of mountain wind. The tinkle of alien wind-chimes. Their footsteps enter cave.

KALENDORF	(*Hushed*) So... who exactly are these Seers of Yaldos?
ALBY	Mirana said they were sorcerers... didn't you?
MIRANA	That's what I'd heard.
KALENDORF	And where are the others?
SEER	Alby Brook. You must listen to me.
ALBY	Where did you get those pickled onions?

SEER	Ssssh. Listen, and all will become clear.
ALBY	Okay... okay, I'll listen.
SEER	You wish your friends to hear also?
KALENDORF	He does.

Pause.

ALBY	Yeah. Why not...
SEER	Then sit. All of you.

Shuffles and scuffs as they all sit on rock.

SEER	I remember what it was like before the Daleks came to Vega VI.
ALBY	You do?
SEER	In my mind's eye... the air was always fresh, the suns were always high in the sky. The water in the Marsh Lakes... always a sparkling blue. Hmm, that's the way I remember it.[10]
ALBY	*You* remember?
SEER	I can still taste that air. Still taste it. Never tasted anything like it since... But the girl, the girl, yes... She was only interested in the rocks (*chuckles*)... her precious minerals.

Crossfade into audio montage of narration from the first three episodes.
Crossfade to:

SEER/SUZ	But, Alby, I did love you. Do love you. No matter how much I've tried to deny it, to be tough... ruthless. Underneath it all, I've always felt that you were... with me somehow. That girl on Guria told me about you, that you'd said you loved me and were prepared to die finding me. She said I would find a way to be with you forever. And I have found that way, my love. Here I am.
ALBY	Suz...? I don't understand.
SEER	I came to see the Seers. (*Chuckles*)
KALENDORF	(*Remembering, to himself*) When she left me at the lakes.
SEER	That's right, Karl.
KALENDORF	Only Suz ever called me that. I used to tell her not to.
SEER	I know. I remember.
ALBY	*I* still don't understand.
MIRANA	Sorcerers... Are you sorcerers?

SEER chuckles.

MIRANA	Did you know they say you can bring the dead back to life?
SEER	Is that what they're saying about us now? Hmm... Flattering, in a nice sort of way.[11]
ALBY	(*A little impatient*) Please, will you just *explain*? Please?
SEER	A permanent link was formed between Susan Mendes and me.
KALENDORF	Permanent?
SEER	When Suz came here, she was anxious that those she cared for should one day know of what was about to happen to her.

Crossfade to:

12. Int. Yaldos. Seers' Cavern. (The Past)

SUZ   You see... (*Sighs*) It's difficult to explain – I've come to believe that these Dalek creatures I told you about are... Well, I don't think they've been telling me the whole truth. And I'm worried that if I

find out what they're really up to *after* I leave you... then my friends will never find out – and... and it's vital that they do. Do you understand?
SEER   Susan... I have no understanding or wish to know of affairs beyond these mountains. Our people learnt long, long ago that the universe is a chaotic place, where one life, one race, one planet means nothing. Where attempts to control the flow of history always ultimately fail.
SUZ   Well... Following that line of thinking, that means the *Daleks* will ultimately fail. But I rather want that to happen sooner and not... well, *ultimately*.
SEER   I understand your concern. But you needn't worry. When you link with a Seer of Yaldos –
SUZ   'Link'?
SEER   Yes. Part of my mind will not only *become* your past and present... The connection between us will last as long as you remain on Yaldos.
SUZ   I see.
SEER   Will that suffice?
SUZ   (*Warmly*) Yes. Yes, it will. Thank you.
FX: the sound of a jar being placed on stone.
SUZ   And will you take these.
SEER   What are they?
SUZ   They're for Alby. If he ever finds you.
Music cue. Crossfade to:

13. Int. Yaldos. Dalek Control.
Recap from previous episode...

DALEK SUPREME (*Distort*) The Emperor of the Daleks will now speak to you.
SUZ   The Emperor...? Why?
Hyperlink signal readjusts.
EMPEROR   (*Distort*) Susan Mendes.
SUZ   (*Afraid*) You... you are the Emperor?
EMPEROR   (*Distort*) I am.
SUZ   You've never spoken to me before. Why are you speaking to me now?
EMPEROR   (*Distort*) Because you have reached the end of your long journey.
(*New section...*)
SUZ   Journey? You mean you're not going to send me to any other planets? You've finished with me now?
EMPEROR   (*Distort*) That decision is yours. But your journey has been inside your own mind... inside your conscience.
SUZ   I don't know what you're talking about.
EMPEROR   (*Distort*) Do not resist! Why have you helped the Daleks?
SUZ   You know why. Because you threatened to kill me if I didn't.
EMPEROR   (*Distort*) The survival instinct?
SUZ   Yes.
EMPEROR   (*Distort*) But we have learnt that the Human Factor is infinitely more sophisticated than the survival instinct. Our history tells

143

us that despite our superior might, the complexity of human thought and emotional instincts is able to defeat us.

SUZ   That's very big of you to say so.

EMPEROR   (*Distort*) Susan Mendes... Are you the one who will defeat us?

SUZ   Why would I risk you killing me?

EMPEROR   (*Distort*) Because you have betrayed Humanity.

Pause.

SUZ   Well... It's too late to do anything about that now, isn't it?

EMPEROR   (*Distort*) To achieve greatness, human beings often feel it is necessary to make sacrifices. Will you make the ultimate sacrifice, Susan Mendes?

Pause. Music cue.

EMPEROR   (*Distort*) I will not force you to answer. But know this, any treachery you plan against us is insignificant in the face of the infinite possibilities the Daleks will soon have at their disposal.

SUZ   Infinite?

EMPEROR   (*Distort*) Do you know of Project Infinity?

SUZ   No. I've never heard of it. What is it?

EMPEROR   (*Distort*) That is of no importance to you now. But the Earth Alliance fear that you know of Project Infinity, and that you would betray its secrets to us.

SUZ   So it's something to do with the Earth Alliance? What? (*Pause*) Why don't you answer?

EMPEROR   (*Distort*) We have known of Project Infinity for centuries.[12]

SUZ   For centuries? How?

EMPEROR   (*Distort*) Do you know of the Kar-Charrat Library?

SUZ   Er... no.

EMPEROR   (*Distort*) It is of no consequence. The time draws near for your broadcast.

SUZ   So you still trust me?

EMPEROR   (*Distort*) You must do what you must do. Empires will rise and fall. It is the nature of history. Go, do as you will. But before you strike at us, the Daleks will have already defeated you.

14. Int. Yaldos. Dalek Control. Corridor.

NARRATOR   I didn't know what the Emperor meant. I didn't care. I just knew what I had to do. They were taking me to Central Square in Yaldos City. I would make my speech in front of an audience of thousands... and that speech would be simultaneously broadcast to billions of others across the galaxy.

Door opens. Footsteps of SUZ.

DALEK   Move! The time grows near.

SUZ   All right! Stop pushing.

Door opens.

KALENDORF   (*Approaching*) Suz! Suz, what's going on?

DALEK 1   Silence!

KALENDORF   I was in the transmission centre when a Dalek patrol arrived. They're taking me to the outer zone production plants. They said you'd ordered it.

SUZ	That's right, Karl.
KALENDORF	But –
SUZ	(*Firm*) But *what*, Karl?
KALENDORF	I thought we'd agreed –
SUZ	Take him to the outer zone. Obey my orders.
DALEKS	We obey the Angel of Mercy.
KALENDORF	Suz, don't do this. I'm begging you, don't – !

SUZ cries out as KALENDORF grabs her.

DALEK	Release her!

Crossfade to telepathic background.

KALENDORF	(*Telepathy*) Suz! Please, you must let me deliver the message. You'll be killed if you don't let –
SUZ	(*Telepathy*) I know, Karl. Don't forget me.
KALENDORF	(*Telepathy*) Suz...
SUZ	(*Telepathy*) Goodbye, Karl.

Crossfade back to reality.

SUZ	(*Shaking him off*) Get off me!!! Take him away! If he disobeys, kill him. Do you understand?
DALEK 1	Understood.
KALENDORF	Suz? You – [13]
DALEK	Silence or you will be exterminated.

Door opens.

15. Ext. Yaldos. Central Square.

NARRATOR	Did you understand, Karl? I hope you do.

The rumble of a crowd full of anticipation.

NARRATOR	I wondered what all those people expected from me. I had always given them hope. And now... I was about to ask many of them to die. I had to set an example.
SUZ	Peoples of the galaxy. We all knew this day would come. Perhaps some of you doubted it. I never did. (*Pause*) I have just spoken with the Dalek leaders. They tell me, Earth has been conquered. That the Daleks have won. That the war is over. (*Pause*) We will all live as citizens of the Dalek Empire... forever! That is what they tell me. They want me to say that we slaves should be commended for hastening the Dalek victory. But I only have one thing to say to that. DEATH – TO – THE – DALEKS!!!*[14]*

A great roar from the crowd. Music cue. A sustained note.

DALEKS	Silence! Silence! Exterminate! Exterminate![15]
NARRATOR	The thousands immediately surged towards me. Barriers crashed to the ground. Dalek guards were overpowered, submerged beneath a sea of screaming slaves.

Alarmed squeals of Daleks. Explosions. Crashing of barriers etc.[16]

NARRATOR	It had begun. And I hoped... I *knew* that on a thousand other worlds, the same was happening. Dalek armouries raided, ships captured, secret plans put into immediate operation... a rebellion on the move... years in the making. My two Dalek guards turned to me. One was suddenly overpowered as the front row of the crowd crashed into it.

Cry of Dalek and slaves crying out in triumph.

NARRATOR	But they could not reach the other Dalek in time. I turned to face it. Cold light from its eye. Point blank. Burning bright.

DALEK   *Exterminate!!!*

Dalek gun fires. SUZ screams. Scream echoes through sustained note of music. Music fades. The scream's echo slowly fades. Crossfade to:

16. Int. Yaldos. Seers' Cavern.

ALBY   *(Contained)* Thank you. I... I... appreciate you... Er...?
SEER   What is it, Alby?
ALBY   They... Well, Kalendorf tells me, they never found her body.
SEER   I see.
KALENDORF   *(To the SEER)* There was a lot of fighting... A lot of... Much of the city square was flattened when we destroyed Dalek control there.
ALBY   But there were no... [remains]. There was nothing. When they went through the wreckage, they found nothing. *(Pause)* Nothing left of her.
KALENDORF   Alby... I don't understand. Are you really saying that you don't accept that she's dead?
ALBY   Did you *see* her die?
KALENDORF   No... but I can point you in the direction of several hundred people who did.
ALBY   And why the hell should I believe you? You worked with the Daleks for years! For all I know, you could *still* be working for them! *(To the SEER)* Is she dead? Can *you* tell if she's dead?
SEER   I feel... There is nothing new from her in my mind.
MIRANA   And does that mean she's dead? Didn't you say that you'd stay linked to her only as long as she was on this planet?
KALENDORF   Mirana! There's no point –
ALBY   Well, is that true?
SEER   Yes. There are many possible reasons why I'm not linked to Suz anymore. She may have left the planet. She may be in a deep coma. She could have – [17]
KALENDORF   But it's an irrefutable fact that she was blasted at point-blank range by a Dalek! She's dead, Alby! She's dead! Do you think I like that? Do you think that's what I wanted? What I *want*?
Pause.
ALBY   *(Quietly)* No.
KALENDORF   She died for all of us! She did it because she felt overwhelming guilt – but, by God, the reason why we're all still alive is because she was prepared to give her life!
ALBY   I know.
KALENDORF   I wanted it to be me! I wanted her to live. *I* wanted to be the one who was remembered as the dead hero. And you know why? Because *I* couldn't bear the guilt either. I still can't. But I know for sure that she's dead, Alby. And we now know the lengths she went to – to ensure that we found out what the Daleks are *really* up to. *That's* what we should be thinking about now. This... Project Infinity. And there's that look on your face again. [18]
ALBY   What?
KALENDORF   The same look I saw when we first heard news about that Dalek trace heading for the Lopra System. Come on, Alby. Tell us what you know.
MIRANA   Alby? *(With compassion)* It's all right.

ALBY   (*Morose*) I don't know anything. Do you hear me? I don't know a damned thing. Nobody tells me *anything*. So don't expect me to play the hero. All right? Is that what you were expecting? Eh? You want me to pick up my trusty sword and ride off, side-by-side with my comrade-in-arms, the mighty Kalendorf, Knight of Velyshaa? Eh? Ride off to the Lopra System to find out just why the hell Project Infinity is so damned important for us and for the Daleks? Eh? Well, forget it! Do you think I've waded through this whole *bloody* war just to pick another fight with the Daleks? To start it all off, all over again? Well, forget it! *Forget it!* I did everything I did for one reason. And that reason is dead. (*Starts to sob uncontrollably*) She's dead... Oh God, she's dead.
ALBY's sobs continue and then subside.
KALENDORF   (*Quietly*) Alby... The war isn't over.
ALBY   (*Through tears*) Just shut up.
KALENDORF   The Daleks are tricking us – I know it! Don't you see? The Emperor knew what Suz was going to do. But he didn't seem to care. He let her set his shiny, new Dalek Empire ablaze. He just *let* her do it. *Why?*
ALBY   I don't care.
KALENDORF   All right, you don't care. She left this message, this legacy for you. But *you* don't care. You don't want it.
ALBY   Don't try to be clever.
KALENDORF   (*Quietly*) But it *is* the point, isn't it? She wanted you to know everything she'd been through, so that it would count for something. Isn't that true?
SEER   It is. And, Alby, you were very... strong in her mind. She wouldn't have wanted you simply to give up.
MIRANA   But what Suz did *has* counted for something. The Daleks have been defeated.
KALENDORF   Have they? Alby?
ALBY   What are you asking me for? How should I know?
KALENDORF   The Daleks are being defeated because they're not interested in fighting us any more. Why is that? Is it because that one little Dalek ship, or whatever it is, heading for the Lopra System is more important than anything that's happened throughout the entire galaxy?[19]
ALBY   Oh, God, you don't give up, do you?
KALENDORF   So just tell me what you know about this Project Infinity!
ALBY   Nothing!
KALENDORF   You've just told me it's in the Lopra System. That's not nothing.
ALBY   All right, it's in the Lopra System – so what?
KALENDORF   Come on! I don't believe that's all you know! Come on!
MIRANA   Kalendorf... I don't think he does – [20]
KALENDORF   Oh wallow in self-pity if you like! If you think it makes you a better person just to waste the rest of your life because the woman you loved is dead, then *you do that*. If that makes you feel noble and guiltless, go right ahead. But at least give the rest of the galaxy a chance. Will you? Will you just do us all that one favour before you slouch off back to a bottle to ferment in self-indulgence?
SEER/SUZ   Alby? *Alby...?*
ALBY   (*A long intake of breath*) All right, I'll tell you what I know.
KALENDORF   Good.

ALBY　　　　But there's not much to tell. And if the Daleks *are* heading for Lopra, it's too late anyway.

KALENDORF　　That's for me to judge.

MIRANA　　　What do you know, Alby?

ALBY　　　　My boss, Tanlee... that's the mysteriously missing Ernst Tanlee, Operational Commander of Earth Alliance Forces, by the way... He sent me on a mission to find out if Suz knew anything about Project Infinity. He said, if she knew anything about it, I was to kill her rather than risk the Daleks finding out.

KALENDORF　　I see. I see...

ALBY　　　　Oh, wait a minute. You haven't had your money's worth yet, old son. Tanlee said that if Suz had already told the Daleks about Project Infinity, then I might as well kill myself... because that meant it was all over for us.

MIRANA　　　For you and Suz?

ALBY　　　　No... for everyone! For everyone except the Daleks, I suppose. Well, don't you see? Suz didn't tell the Daleks about Project Infinity, but they *already* knew. They're already on their way there... probably there already – So it's all over! Do you see, now? *It's – all – over.* There's no point doing anything any more.

KALENDORF's footsteps.

KALENDORF　　*(Starts to move off)* Well, that may be your point of view, but it isn't mine.

MIRANA　　　Kalendorf, where are you going?

KALENDORF　　To find Project Infinity. In the Lopra System.

MIRANA　　　Why? If what Alby says is true, then –

KALENDORF　　Then what? What would you have me do? Organise another galaxy-wide broadcast? 'Hello everyone, it's all over, time to follow Alby Brook's noble example and get drunk'? Don't you see? This whole invasion of the galaxy has been a massive distraction. Something to divert us from what the Daleks are really doing. And the rebellion? That was something else to keep us all occupied, just in case we noticed a tiny flicker on a space scope screen. The flicker of one Dalek ship up to no good... heading for Project Infinity in the Lopra System.

MIRANA　　　You don't know that for sure. There could be hundreds of possible –

KALENDORF　　– possible explanations? Yes, let's just sit around and discuss those. That'd be another distraction the Dalek Emperor would be only too pleased about.

ALBY　　　　She's right, Kalendorf. You can't be sure –

KALENDORF　　You play the Emperor's game if you like. I'm going to the Lopra System.

MIRANA　　　I'm afraid I can't let you do that.

Gun clicks.

ALBY　　　　Mirana, what are you doing?

KALENDORF　　If you want to stop me, you'll have to use that gun.

MIRANA　　　That's precisely what I intend to do.

Gun fires. KALENDORF cries out and falls to the ground. His groans of discomfort and pain continue.

ALBY　　　　Mirana, what the hell – ? Oh no.

MIRANA　　　There must be no interference in our plan.

ALBY　　　　Whose plan?

148

MIRANA   And now you mu — aaargh! (*Various groans of pain*)
A high-pitched psychic effect.
ALBY   What's the matter with you? What's the matter with her?
MIRANA screams in pain.

17. Int. Dalek Imperial Command Ship.
Alarms sound.

EMPEROR   Aaaargh!
DALEK SUPREME Emergency! Emergency! Psychotropic link with Emperor's cerebral functions is under attack!
EMPEROR   (*Confused*) What is happening? Assist me! Assist me![21]
Crossfade to:

18. Int. Yaldos. Seers' Cavern.

MIRANA   Assist me! Assist me! (*Her cries of confusion and pain continue throughout the scene*)
SEER   (*In pain*) Alby! Alby, quickly... Disarm her!
ALBY   Wh – what's going on?
Gun fires.
MIRANA   Stay back! Do... do not... Do not approach me!!!
Gun fires again.
SEER   I am holding her mind in mine. I don't know how long I can... quickly, take her gun!
Another shot.
ALBY   Argh! You must be joking... I can't get near her.
MIRANA   Stay back!!!
Crossfade to:

19. Int. Dalek Imperial Command Ship.

EMPEROR   Stay back!!!
DALEK   Source of psychotropic interference detected.
DALEK SUPREME Identify!
DALEK   Readings indicate the presence of a highly concentrated psychic energy beam.
EMPEROR   Aaargh!
Crossfade to:

20. Int. Yaldos. Seers' Cavern.

MIRANA   Aaaargh!
ALBY   Kalendorf! Kalendorf!
KALENDORF   (*Badly injured, in pain*) Alby... argh! What's happened to Mirana?
ALBY   I don't know. She seems to be having some sort of fit.
SEER   Her mind is linked to the mind of another.
ALBY   What?!
SEER   Her mind is... is...
MIRANA   (*Struggling*) Psychic energy beam emanating from...
Crossfade to:

21. Int. Dalek Imperial Command Ship.

EMPEROR   ...Seer of Yaldos.
DALEK   Seers of Yaldos. Ancient inhabitants of planet Yaldos. Possessing highly developed psychic abilities.
EMPEROR   Increase energy supply to my cerebral functions. The Seer must...
Crossfade to:

22. Int. Yaldos. Seers' Cavern.

MIRANA   ...be exterminated!
ALBY   Exterminated?
KALENDORF   (*Struggling*) It's... the Daleks.[22]
ALBY   The Daleks?
KALENDORF   She's working for the Daleks, she must be.
SEER   (*In pain*) Yes! Daleks... she's linked to... a Dalek mind. Something implanted in her brain.
ALBY   How the hell did they manage that?
KALENDORF   (*Bitter*) The same way they manage everything – by outwitting us.
MIRANA   (*Stronger*) I am the Emperor of the Daleks. You will all be exterminated.
ALBY   The Emperor? Oh, God![23]
SEER   I can't... can't maintain... Argh. She's becoming too powerful for me. My mind is weakening.[24]
KALENDORF   Alby, quickly – move me closer to the Seer. I must help her.
ALBY   Kalendorf, you're bleeding to death! For God's sake just –
KALENDORF   Alby! Just apply pressure to my wound and – and help me! Argh!
Crossfade to:

23. Int. Dalek Imperial Command Ship.
Energy hum rising.

DALEK   Energy supply to Emperor's cerebral functions now increasing.
DALEK 1   Data indicates Emperor will regain full control over agent Mirana's mind in 10 rels.
DALEK SUPREME Excellent! Increase energy flow! Increase!!!
DALEK 1   I obey.
Energy hum rises faster. Crossfade to:

24. Int. Yaldos. Seers' Cavern.

KALENDORF   Seer! Give me your hand!
Slap of hands meeting.
SEER   (*Weakening*) Help... help me...
MIRANA   You cannot resist my power. Your minds will be destroyed.
KALENDORF   (*Vicious*) We'll see about... *that!!!*
Psychic blast.

25. Int. Dalek Imperial Command Ship.
Explosion.

EMPEROR   AAAaaargh!!!
DALEK   Alert! Alert! Psionic energy burst has damaged cerebral receptors! Psychotropic link overload imminent!
DALEK SUPREME The overload must be contained immediately.
DALEK   I obey.
Controls operate. Negative bleeps.
DALEK 1   The Emperor's cerebral receptor controls are non-operational. The overload cannot be contained.
EMPEROR   Aaaaargh!!!
Crossfade to:

26. Int. Yaldos. Seers' Cavern.

MIRANA   Aaargh!
KALENDORF and SEER gasp in relief.
ALBY   Kalendorf! Kalendorf, I think you've done it.
SEER   (*Gasps. Very weak now*) My... mind is free.
KALENDORF   (*Recovering*) That gave it something to think about.
MIRANA   No! No! Assist me! *Assist me!!! (Screams continue)*
KALENDORF   If the Emperor doesn't disconnect from her mind now... he'll be destroyed.
ALBY   What about her? What about Mirana?
MIRANA   Aaaaargh!!!

27. Int. Dalek Imperial Command Ship.

EMPEROR   Aaaargh!
DALEK SUPREME Disconnect link! Disconnect immediately or the Emperor's mind will be destroyed!!!
Explosion. Energy hum drops immediately.
EMPEROR   (*A final gasp*)
DALEK   Psychotropic link with agent Mirana has been disconnected.
DALEK 1   Emperor's cerebral functions returning to normal levels.
EMPEROR   We have lost her!!!

28. Int. Yaldos. Seers' Cavern.
KALENDORF's exhausted breathing.

ALBY   I'm going to get back to my skimmer. You need an emergency medical team up here, fast.
KALENDORF   (*In extreme pain*) No, wait...
ALBY   What?
KALENDORF   Just... argh... Check on Mirana first.
ALBY   Are you sure it's safe to touch – ?
KALENDORF   Do it!
ALBY   (*Moving off*) Okay, okay... I'm doing it.
SEER   (*Exhausted*) Kalendorf... thank you for saving me.
KALENDORF   (*Through pain*) It's lucky I did, isn't it? Since you're the last of your people.

SEER   You saw that in my mind?

KALENDORF   Yes, I did. But that's not all I saw. (*Aloud*) How is she, Alby?

ALBY   (*Distant*) Still alive... but out cold. (*He approaches*) Don't know why you're so concerned about a Roboman anyway... the process isn't reversible, you know. Huh, I should've trusted my instincts about her. I've never been a big fan of the police –

KALENDORF   She isn't a Roboman.

ALBY   What do you mean? She's controlled by the Daleks. She has an implant in her head. What else *could* she be?

KALENDORF   Something very different.

SEER   She was linked directly to the Emperor.

ALBY   The...? So?

KALENDORF   Ever wondered what it might be to look into the mind of your enemy?

ALBY   But – What? Do you mean that's what you just did? You two?

SEER   For a moment, yes.

KALENDORF   Just a glimpse. But what a glimpse it was. There was a clear link from the Emperor's mind to a Dalek command network. And there was something else... (*with difficulty*) I can't... can't quite...[25]

SEER   Infinity.

KALENDORF   Infinity, yes.

ALBY   (*Realising*) Project Infinity. That's why you wanted to know if Mirana was still alive. You think you can find out about Project Infinity through her mind... through her contact with the Dalek Emperor's mind. Don't you?

KALENDORF   (*To SEER*) Is it possible?

SEER   Mirana's mind was not merely controlled by the Emperor. It had been... interacting, sharing its alien thoughts for many years. The device in her brain is likely to have retained that information.

KALENDORF   Don't you think it sounds like a little piece of hope, Alby? Almost as if it might not be 'all over' for us? Hm?

ALBY   I'm going to call for that medical team.

KALENDORF   Argh... I'd tell them to hurry if I were you. Argh.

ALBY   (*Moving off*) Right. I will.

KALENDORF   Oh, and Alby!

ALBY   (*Distant*) What?

KALENDORF   Is a little piece of hope grounds enough for you to pick up your trusty sword and ride off, side-by-side with your comrade-in-arms, the mighty Kalendorf, Knight of Velyshaa – ?

ALBY   – to the Lopra System?

KALENDORF   – to find out just why the hell Project Infinity is so damned important for us and for the Daleks?

ALBY   Do you ever give up?

KALENDORF   Never.

29. Dalek Imperial Command Ship.[26]
Sharp negative bleeps from mind-link controls.

DALEK SUPREME Psychotropic link with humanoid agent cannot be re-established. No response to destruct signals.

EMPEROR   Has the humanoid female survived?

DALEK SUPREME Readings indicate her mind was conscious when the psychotropic link was severed.

EMPEROR   She was linked to my mental processes and through me to the Dalek Command net. The humans may now gain knowledge of our plan if they are able to access the implant in her brain. We must set a direct course for Lopra Minor.

DALEK SUPREME If we deviate from current trajectory, this vessel will be in range of Earth Alliance deep-space scanners for a sustained period. We will be detected.

EMPEROR   That is of no consequence now. Speed is of the essence.

Comms bleep.

EMPEROR   Report on advance attack force status.

DALEK 1   (*Distort*) Advance attack force coded signals indicate they are on final approach to planet Lopra Minor.

EMPEROR   Excellent!!!

30. Int. Lopra Minor. Project Infinity. Operations Centre.[27]

ESPEELIUS   My calculations are complete. The Infinity Scan is set to automatic activation the moment alignment occurs.

TANLEE   So when *will* this spacio-temporal anomaly next be in the correct alignment, Espeelius?

ESPEELIUS   We call it a dimensional fissure... Not for three point five eight solar days.

TANLEE   And exactly how long is a solar day in the Lopra System? It doesn't matter. I'll take your word for it.

ESPEELIUS   Now... if you'll forgive me, I must rest.

TANLEE   Well, under normal circumstances I –

Comms bleep.

TANLEE   Er, excuse me for a moment. Tanlee? (*Pause*) I understand.

ESPEELIUS   What is it? Who was that?

TANLEE   One of my men. As I was saying, under normal circumstances, I would allow you to rest.

ESPEELIUS   *'Allow'?*

TANLEE   But unfortunately for you, these are far from normal circumstances.

ESPEELIUS   I don't understand.

TANLEE   Well, under normal circumstances, if, say, a Dalek attack force were to land on this planet... even a modest Dalek attack force, your security alarms would make enough noise to wake the dead, wouldn't they?

ESPEELIUS   What are you saying?

TANLEE   I had my men deactivate your security systems.

ESPEELIUS   Wh – Why did you do that?

TANLEE   You're about to find out, my dear old friend.

ESPEELIUS   Tanlee, what are you talking about? This is no time for childish games. The events that are about to unfold here –

TANLEE   Are not quite the events you expected, I'm afraid.

Door opens.

ESPEELIUS   My God... Tanlee... What have you...? You've betrayed –

DALEK   Do not move! This facility is now under Dalek control. Resist and you will be exterminated.

31. Int. Battle Cruiser *Courageous*. Sickbay.

MIRANA awakens with a start.

JOHNSTONE   How are you feeling?
MIRANA   Er... confused. Disoriented.
JOHNSTONE   Anything else?
MIRANA   Anything... anything *else*? I don't know how I got here. Where is here, by the way? (*Pause*) You don't wanna tell me?
JOHNSTONE   I'm Dr Johnstone. I'm a life sciences specialist from Earth.
MIRANA   Earth?
JOHNSTONE   Where are *you* from?
MIRANA   Oh... er... I was born on a freighter passing through Orion's belt. So... I never really know how to answer that question.[28]
JOHNSTONE   I see.
MIRANA   My parents were from the Gal-sec colony.
JOHNSTONE   Hmm.
MIRANA   Is that the answer you wanted?
JOHNSTONE   Well, at least you didn't say you were from Skaro.
MIRANA   Skaro?
JOHNSTONE   It's the home planet of the Daleks.
MIRANA   Is *that* why there are armed guards at the door... You think I'm working for the Daleks?
JOHNSTONE   You have been... for several years now. Through no fault of your own, admittedly – but we're not quite sure how free your mind is yet.
MIRANA   How free my mind...? What are you – ?
JOHNSTONE   You don't remember? You don't remember any of it?
MIRANA   (*With difficulty*) Well... er...
JOHNSTONE   Fascinating.
MIRANA   (*Suddenly*) Oh my God.
JOHNSTONE   Ah, you do, then?
MIRANA   Only... only... pieces. I can't quite... can't quite...[29]
JOHNSTONE   You're lucky you can think at all after what you've been through. You've been in a coma for nearly five months. Just relax.
MIRANA   Relax?! Ow, my head hurts. Argh! Bandages? Why have you – ? Oh my God. You've been rooting around in my head, haven't you?
JOHNSTONE   I'm afraid so.
Door opens.
KALENDORF   Well, what have you discovered?
MIRANA   Kalendorf?
JOHNSTONE   So you remember *him*?
MIRANA   Yes, but... (*A noise of frustration*) I can't think straight.
JOHNSTONE   She's confused.
KALENDORF   And that's all you've found out? I could have guessed that, doctor. I was hoping for something a little more inspiring; especially since we're just about to enter the Lopra System and badly need to know exactly what we're letting ourselves in for.
MIRANA   About to enter...? We're on a ship?

KALENDORF (*To JOHNSTONE*) You're sure there's no longer any link between her and the Dalek Emperor?

JOHNSTONE Oh, positive. Virtually.

KALENDORF Virtually? You did extract the device from her brain, I take it?

JOHNSTONE Er, no... We couldn't. Not without killing her.

MIRANA Er... excuse me?

KALENDORF So there *is* still a risk?

JOHNSTONE No, we burnt out all the transceivers.

KALENDORF Are you certain?

JOHNSTONE Well... pretty certain. It *is* alien technology, you know.

KALENDORF So how are we going to access any useful data if you've left the device in her brain?

JOHNSTONE We identified the memory circuits and cracked their entry codes... more or less. With the right electronic stimulus, she'll tell us all she knows.

MIRANA She? You mean me?

KALENDORF Yes. And in answer to your question, you are onboard the Battle Cruiser *Courageous* – and we're about to enter the Lopra System –

MIRANA I heard that part –

KALENDORF – so there's no time for niceties. Shall we begin, Dr Johnstone?

JOHNSTONE Be my guest.

KALENDORF How do we go about this?

MIRANA Go about what?

JOHNSTONE Ask her the questions and I'll activate the memory circuits of the Dalek device in her brain from this panel. Theoretically, she should just tell us the answers.

KALENDORF Theoretically?

MIRANA I'll try not to disappoint you.

KALENDORF All right... What is Project Infinity?

Bleeps of Johnstone's equipment. Pause.

KALENDORF Well? Doctor, is that thing working?

JOHNSTONE It should be. Mirana, will you answer the question, please?

MIRANA I... can't...

KALENDORF Can't or won't?

MIRANA I... I just don't know the answer.

An alarm sounds.

KALENDORF Ah...

Comms bleep.

KALENDORF Kalendorf to bridge, what's happening, Alby?

32. Int. Battle Cruiser *Courageous*. Bridge.

Alarm still sounding. Chatter of activity in the background.

ALBY Kalendorf, we've just entered the Lopra System and the space scope has detected Dalek readings on the third planet... er... Lopra Minor.

KALENDORF (*Distort*) What sort of readings?

ALBY Heavily shielded by delta rays, but at this close range, our scanners are picking up chatter on a localised command net.

KALENDORF	(*Distort*) What are they saying?
ALBY	It's coded, and we can't crack it. Not yet, anyway.
KALENDORF	(*Distort*) Right, this is it. All weapons to full power.
ALBY	Already done. And I've ordered our assault units to board

their landing craft. Should be ready for launch in a couple of minutes. Do
we go straight in?

KALENDORF	(*Distort*) We do.

33. Int. Battle Cruiser *Courageous*. Sickbay.

MIRANA	Lopra Minor.
KALENDORF	What?
JOHNSTONE	You recognise that?
MIRANA	Yes.
KALENDORF	What about it?
MIRANA	The Daleks are there.
KALENDORF	(*Irritated*) I know that. You just *heard* that.
MIRANA	Project Infinity is there.
KALENDORF	That's hardly an inspired conclusion to reach – [30]
MIRANA	Project Infinity is there. 'It must be protected at all costs

until the Imperial Command Ship arrives. Attack units to be deployed on
jungle perimeter. Do not open fire until the Earth Alliance troops have
landed.'

KALENDORF	What's she talking about? What's happening?
JOHNSTONE	I... I don't... I think she's picking up Dalek transmissions.
KALENDORF	I thought you deactivated the transceivers in her implant.
JOHNSTONE	I thought I had –
MIRANA	'Secure all exits. Continue augmentation of the systems.'
KALENDORF	Do they know you're listening to them?
MIRANA	'Firepower to maximum. Special Weapons units will move

in on attack grid pattern logril nine zero four – '

KALENDORF	Mirana, listen to me!!!
MIRANA	What?
KALENDORF	Do they know – ?
MIRANA	No. They don't know I can hear them. Why can I hear

them? Oh yes, the implant. But they know you're here.

JOHNSTONE	We gathered that.
KALENDORF	What about Project Infinity?
MIRANA	'Installation of Dalek augmentation devices continues.

Augmentation must be complete for arrival of Imperial Command Ship.'

KALENDORF	(*Thinking*) Imperial Command... that sounds bad... Er...

What is Project Infinity?

MIRANA	What is...?

Pause.

KALENDORF	(*Close*) What is it?
MIRANA	It... It is...

Bleeping.

JOHNSTONE	That's it!
KALENDORF	What's it?
JOHNSTONE	The memory cells of the implant have activated. I sent a

stimulus signal again. I'm getting a response.
Another bleep.

KALENDORF Mirana?
Pause.
MIRANA Project Infinity... 'We will use it to gain total control of...' Of the entire universe.
KALENDORF The universe? And we thought they just wanted our galaxy.[31]

34. Int. Lopra Minor. Project Infinity. Operations Centre.

DALEK 1 Infinity Scan augmentation procedure now at 35 percent.
DALEK COMMANDER Increase augmentation rate immediately!
DALEK 1 All processes are running at maximum efficiency.
DALEK COMMANDER Understood. The augmentation is vital to our plan. These systems must be defended at all costs.
DALEK 2 Rangerscopes confirm that the approaching Earth Alliance craft is carrying an assault force superior in number and firepower to the Dalek force here on Lopra Minor.
DALEK COMMANDER But we possess the element of surprise.
Door opens.
DALEK COMMANDER Report![32]
TANLEE All facility personnel have been secured in the lower storage areas.
DALEK COMMANDER Understood. You will proceed as ordered.
TANLEE I obey.
Alert signal.
DALEK 2 Rangerscope readings indicate the Earth Alliance craft is now entering planetary orbit. Its landing craft are now penetrating Lopra Minor atmosphere.
DALEK COMMANDER Battle alert! Battle alert! All units to defence positions immediately!

35. Int. Battle Cruiser *Courageous*. Sickbay.[33]

MIRANA ...'All units to defence positions immediately!'
ALBY (*Distort*) Our landing craft are entering Lopra Minor atmosphere now.
KALENDORF We know, Alby. The Daleks have just told us.
ALBY (*Distort*) Are we sure we can trust her?
JOHNSTONE The information is only travelling one way, I'm sure of it.
KALENDORF I think we have to, Alby. She's the only advantage we've got.
ALBY (*Distort. Laughs*) I don't suppose she can give us precise co-ordinates for every Dalek position! That'd be nice!
MIRANA (*Realising*) Yes... Yes, I can!
ALBY (*Distort*) What?
KALENDORF She says 'yes she can'.
ALBY (*Distort*) I heard.
KALENDORF (*Surprised*) How can you *do* that?
MIRANA The Daleks are constantly transmitting their co-ordinates through their command net, so that the squad commander can keep updating its orders. It's kind of like a very fast game of chess.
KALENDORF Between the Dalek commander and us.

MIRANA   Yes.

KALENDORF   Doctor, can you link Mirana up to our tactical computer and beam her information direct to our assault force?

JOHNSTONE   I can try.

ALBY   (*Distort*) All the assault force guys are patched in to the tactical computers on board each of the landing craft. They've all got heads-up displays on their visors.

KALENDORF   And we can supply data direct to each tactical computer.

MIRANA   And if you create a direct tap from my implant to our tactical computer... It should work.

JOHNSTONE   It should... It should. Right... er...

Various bleeps and electronic buzzes as JOHNSTONE starts work.

KALENDORF   Alby, tell the assault force to sit tight at ten thousand metres altitude and wait for further orders. I'm on my way to the bridge. Johnstone, keep me informed. And Mirana...

MIRANA   Thank you?

KALENDORF   Yes.

MIRANA   It's the least I can do...

36. Int. Battle Cruiser *Courageous*. Bridge.

ZERO 2   (*Distort*) Landing craft Zero 2 reporting steady at ten thousand metres. Do you want us to circle?[34]

ALBY   Confirmed, Zero 2. We have you at 15 degrees NorWest of Project Infinity base, at a distance of... (*reading it off*) 5 point 6 kilometres.[35]

ZERO 2   (*Distort*) Acknowledged.

ZERO 1   (*Distort*) This is Zero 1. We have visual contact with Zero 2. We are now circling.

ALBY   Steady as you go.

ZERO 1   (*Distort*) Weather conditions are good. No problems with visibility.

ALBY   Acknowledged, Zero 1. Zeros 3 and 4, continue to hold your positions 15 degrees NorEast of the base.

ZERO 3   (*Distort*) Zero 3 acknowledging.

ZERO 4   (*Distort*) Zero 4 acknowledging.

ALBY   Mr Herrick, let's have an aerial scan of the area on the main screen, please.

Screen FX.

HERRICK   Onscreen, now, sir.

ALBY   Sir? This is reminding me of my days in the forces... (*To himself*) Except nobody ever called me sir, then.

Door opens.

KALENDORF   (*Approaching*) Are they all in position, Alby?

ALBY   They're ready and waiting.

HERRICK   Sir, we're picking up Dalek activity in and around the base, but delta-ray interference is distorting the signals. We can't get any precise fixes on Dalek positions.

KALENDORF   Hopefully, that's not going to matter. Kalendorf to sickbay.

JOHNSTONE   (*Distort*) Sickbay responding.

KALENDORF   How's it going, Dr Johnstone?

JOHNSTONE   (*Distort*) Bear with me, I'm working as fast as I can.[36]

KALENDORF   Let us know when you make any progress with the link-up, please.

JOHNSTONE   (*Distort*) I will. Out.

Radio chatter of Zeros continues in background.

ALBY   (*Confidentially*) Have we found out anything about Project Infinity?

KALENDORF   Only that the Daleks intend to use it to conquer the entire universe.

ALBY   I wonder what *the Earth Alliance* were going to use it for... So, what do we do if and when we get to it?[37]

KALENDORF   I don't know. Destroy it?

ALBY   Tanlee said it was our last hope of defeating the Daleks. Might be a bit silly to blow it up.

KALENDORF   It might be a good deal more than silly to leave it hanging around for the Daleks to use. But let's deal with one problem at a time, shall we?

A buzzing alarm.

KALENDORF   What's that?

ALBY   Another problem... I think. Mr Herrick?[38]

HERRICK   We've picked up a large ship on the outer galactic edge of the Lopra System. Drive systems suggest –

KALENDORF   – a Dalek ship?

HERRICK   Yes, sir.

KALENDORF   The Imperial Command Ship.

ALBY   The Emperor?

KALENDORF   Who else?

ALBY   (*Whistles*) They really mean business.

KALENDORF   What's its course and speed?

HERRICK   On current course and speed, it'll be with us in a couple of hours, sir.

Comms bleep.

KALENDORF   Johnstone, hurry up with that computer link. We have important company.

MIRANA   (*Distort*) I know. It *is* the Emperor. Send your landing craft in. I'm ready.

HERRICK   (*Distort*) Link-up to tactical computer... complete.

Activation signal.

ALBY   Oh, that is beautiful. Look at the screen. All the Dalek positions around the base are showing up.[39]

Comms bleep.

KALENDORF   *Courageous* to landing craft, confirm Dalek positions on your tactical displays.

ZERO 1   (*Distort*) Zero 1 confirming.

ZERO 3   (*Distort*) Zero 3 confirming.

ZERO 2   (*Distort*) Zero 2... we've got them.

ZERO 4   (*Distort*) This is Zero 4... we can see them.

KALENDORF   Commence attack run. See how many Daleks you can hit from the air before making planetfall.

ZERO 1   (*Distort*) Zero 1 acknowledged. All landing craft arm DX missiles.

ZERO 3   (*Distort*) Zero 3 acknowledged.

ZERO 4   (*Distort*) Zero 4... arming missiles.

ZERO 2   (*Distort*) Zero 2 confirmed. All missiles armed.
ALBY   The Dalek position markers are moving.
KALENDORF Mirana, what are they doing?
MIRANA   (*Distort*) They've spotted the landing craft. 'Special Weapons Daleks to aerial defence mode.'

37. Ext. Lopra Minor. Jungle.
Dalek hover engines rising in pitch.

SPECIAL WEAPONS DALEK Special Weapons Daleks obey! Climbing to attack altitude. Firing now.[40]
Several Special Weapons Dalek blasts. A whoosh of a landing craft shooting past and an explosion.

38. Int. Battle Cruiser *Courageous*. Bridge.
A distorted explosion.

ZERO 2   (*Distort*) This is Zero 2, we are hit. Request covering fire. Making emergency landing.
ZERO 3   (*Distort*) Covering fire! Now firing.
Distorted sound of missles. Explosions.
ALBY   (*Tense*) Looks like a hit.[41]
MIRANA   (*Distort*) Three Special Weapons Daleks destroyed by missiles. 'Rangerscopes now tracking landing trajectory of human craft.'
KALENDORF Zero 2! Dalek ground units are moving to intercept you on landing. Zero 2! Respond!!!
ZERO 2   (*Distort*) Acknowledged.
ZERO 1   (*Distort*) Zeros 3 and 4, continue with attack on airborne Special Weapons Daleks, then make your designated landings. I am moving to support Zero 2. Firing DX missiles at surface targets.
Distorted FX of missiles firing. Explosions.[42]
ALBY   So far... not so bad.[42]

39. Int. Project Infinity. Operations Centre.

DALEK 1   Four Dalek attack units destroyed by airborne fire. Special Weapons Daleks under attack.
DALEK CMDR The humans have unexpectedly penetrated our delta-ray shielding. They are able to track our movements. All Daleks, break cover and attack immediately!

40. Int. Battle Cruiser *Courageous*. Bridge.

ALBY   That's it! We've really upset the hornets' nest now!
KALENDORF Zero 1!
ZERO 1   (*Distort*) We see them! We see them! Firing now!

41. Ext. Lopra Minor. Jungle.
Jungle atmosphere. Landing craft swoops. Missile fire. Explosions. Daleks cry out.[43]

DALEK   Regroup and exterminate! Exterminate!

42. Int. Battle Cruiser *Courageous*. Bridge.

ZERO 2   (*Distort. Running*) This is Zero 2, we are on foot and moving towards the base! Fanning out to intercept Dalek forces advancing towards us.

MIRANA   (*Distort*) Zero 2, watch your left flank, an order has just been given to encircle you. The last surviving Special Weapons Dalek is now ordered to make an air attack on you.[44]

ALBY   There they go! We see them, Mirana!

ZERO 2   (*Distort*) Open fire!!!

43. Ext. Lopra Minor. Jungle.[45]
Jungle atmosphere. Handgun fire.

DALEK   Under attack! Under attack!
Daleks cry out and explode.

DALEK 2   Exterminate! Exterminate!
Dalek gunfire. Soldiers cry out.

44. Int. Battle Cruiser *Courageous*. Bridge.
Muted gunfire etc on distort.

ALBY   Come on! Get out of there!

KALENDORF   It's too late. They're caught in a trap.[46]

ALBY   Zero 1, take out that Special Weapons Dalek, it's going to finish them off!

ZERO 1   (*Distort*) Targeting now. Firing!
Distort missile blast and explosion.

ALBY   Got him!!! (*Laughs triumphantly*)

KALENDORF   (*Grim*) They still don't stand a chance.

ZERO 2   (*Distort. Screaming*) This is Zero 2! We are surrounded and outnumbered. We're digging in, but –
Comms cuts off with a burst of static.

HERRICK   We've lost them.

ZERO 4   (*Distort. Running*) This is Zero 4 with Zero 3, we are on foot and have the base perimeter in sight. Have destroyed four or five sentry Daleks. No casualties. Do they have any big surprises for us?

MIRANA   (*Distort*) You are clear, Zero 4. Repeat, you are clear. They made a big mistake moving their main force to hit Zero 2.[47]

KALENDORF   Mirana, the display shows that main Dalek force retreating to the base. Are there new orders?
Distorted sound of missiles firing and exploding.

ZERO 1   (*Distort*) This is Zero 1. We are hitting them hard on the retreat!

KALENDORF   Mirana! What's happening?

ZERO 3   (*Distort*) This is Zero 3. We are forcing entry to the base. Should be through in 3 minutes.

KALENDORF   Mirana? Are you getting anything?

MIRANA   (*Distort*) Oh my God.

ALBY   What is it?

MIRANA   (*Distort*) Hostages... They have the base personnel in the lower storage area!

HERRICK   We're receiving a transmission from the Dalek commander.
ALBY   If they've got hostages, you know what's coming, don't you?
KALENDORF   (*Grim resignation*) Patch it through.
Comms bleep.
DALEK COMMANDER (*Distort*) This is the Dalek Commander. If you do not cease your attack, we will begin extermination of Project Infinity personnel.
ALBY   (*Close*) What do we do?
Pause. Tense music cue builds.
ZERO 1   (*Distort. Running*) This is Zero 1, we have disembarked and eliminated all Dalek defences and have sustained minimal casualties. Now approaching main entrance to the base on foot.
DALEK COMMANDER (*Distort*) We detect that your forces are still advancing. The first hostage will now be exterminated. Observe.
Distorted sound of Dalek blast and hostage screaming in agony as he dies. Comms bleep.
KALENDORF   All units... halt your advance.
ALBY   Zero 3, stop cutting through that door now!
ZERO 3   (*Distort*) What the hell's going on?
ALBY   The Daleks have got hostages. If you enter the base, they'll kill them all.
ZERO 1   (*Distort*) All units, shut down cutting equipment and stay where you are.
ZERO 3   (*Distort*) Acknowledged.
ZERO 4   (*Distort*) Acknowledged.
Pause.
ALBY   Now what?
Another distorted Dalek blast and scream. Comms bleep.
KALENDORF   (*Angry*) We've done what you asked! Stop the killing![48]
DALEK COMMANDER (*Distort*) Your forces must now return to your ship, or the exterminations will continue.
Another distorted Dalek blast and scream.
MIRANA   (*Distort*) Kalendorf, they mean what they say.
KALENDORF   I know.
Another distorted Dalek blast and scream.
KALENDORF   How much death can you witness before it becomes meaningless?
ESPEELIUS   (*Distort*) Listen to me!
ALBY   Who *is* that?
ESPEELIUS   (*Distort*) I am Project Director Espeelius.
DALEK   (*Distort*) Silence!
ESPEELIUS   (*Distort*) Our lives don't matter. Whoever you are! Listen to me! You must press home your attack! If the Daleks gain control of Project Infinity it will be the end of everything – [49]
DALEK   (*Distort*) Exterminate!!!
ESPEELIUS   (*Distort*) Aaaargh!
DALEK COMMANDER (*Distort*) Withdraw, or exterminations will continue! Withdraw!
KALENDORF   All units! Continue the attack!
ZERO 1   (*Distort*) Acknowledged. All units, continue attack!
MIRANA   (*Distort*) No! Kalendorf, you can't – !

KALENDORF   Mr Herrick, steer a course to land the *Courageous* at a safe distance from the base. Take us down. Do it!
HERRICK   Aye, sir!
Controls operate. Rumble of engines. Distorted exterminations and repeated chants of 'Exterminate' on the screen.[50]
KALENDORF   *Shut that off!!!*
Bleep and the sound of gun blasts and screams shuts off. Rumble of engines increases.
MIRANA   (*Distort*) Just because you're not looking at it, doesn't mean it isn't still happening. I don't know how you –
Bleep as MIRANA is cut off.
ALBY   Kalendorf, I –
KALENDORF   (*Quiet, determined*) I can't... hear... *anything.* I can't hear anything.
The engine rumble crescendos with big music cue. Hold silence for a moment.

45. Int. Lopra Minor. Project Infinity. Operations Centre.
Slow fade up. Footsteps of KALENDORF and ALBY.

ALBY   They really did fight to the last... Dalek, didn't they?
Sound of Dalek metal casing smashing to the ground.
ALBY   That's what I call devotion to duty.
KALENDORF   Blind obedience.
ALBY   So... Project Infinity! Well... it looks impressive. Maybe a touch damaged during the battle. But what is it supposed to do?
KALENDORF   (*Subdued*) Let's hope Johnstone can jog Mirana's Dalek implant memory.
ALBY   Then what?
KALENDORF   If we can find out how to operate it... and if it's not too damaged, we use Project Infinity against the Daleks.
ALBY   And if we can't, we destroy it?
KALENDORF   Yes. Before the Emperor gets here.
ALBY   Which is in about... 45 minutes' time. Fair enough.
Door opens. Footsteps enter.
KALENDORF   Well, Mr Herrick?
HERRICK   The base is secured, sir. All Daleks were destroyed in the attack.
KALENDORF   And the hostages? (*Pause*) I see.
HERRICK   But we did find *someone* alive, sir. Just now.
ALBY   Who?
HERRICK   We're not sure. He was out in the jungle. Apparently seems a bit shaken up. There were some others with him, all killed by Dalek fire.
ALBY   Where is he?
HERRICK   He's being brought here now, sir.
Footsteps approach.
TANLEE   (*Groggy*) It's all right... it's all right... I can walk. You don't need to – My God.
ALBY   (*Gobsmacked*) Tanlee?
TANLEE   Alby Brook.
ALBY   What the hell are you doing here?

TANLEE   I *was* doing my job. Who's this?

46. Int. Dalek Imperial Command Ship. Emperor's Chamber.

EMPEROR   We are now approaching extreme transmaterialisation range. You must distract the humans. They must not suspect.

47. Int. Lopra Minor. Project Infinity. Operations Centre.

TANLEE   Well, well, well... the great and noble Kalendorf.
KALENDORF   You haven't answered Alby's question.
TANLEE   I was here to oversee the final phase of Project Infinity. When the Daleks attacked, my men and I went into the jungle to put up a fight. But... well, there were too many of them. We got caught in a pretty fierce fire-fight and... To tell you the truth, I'm rather surprised to find myself alive.
ALBY   You were lucky.
TANLEE   Is that what they call it. Anyway, where's Espeelius? Has he started yet? Is the dimensional fissure aligned? (*Pause*) Why do I get the feeling you don't know what I'm talking about?
ALBY   Espeelius is dead. The Daleks killed everyone before we could get here.
TANLEE   God... It sometimes feels like all this killing is never going to end.
KALENDORF   Oh, it's far from over yet, by my reckoning, Tanlee. Unless you can activate this thing and destroy the Daleks.
TANLEE   Destroy... What do you mean?
KALENDORF   The Dalek Imperial Command ship will arrive here in less than an hour. And we have no meaningful way of stopping them unless *someone* can make Project Infinity work.
TANLEE   (*Laughs*) How extraordinary.
ALBY   What's so bleedin' funny, Tanlee?
TANLEE   You think it's a weapon, don't you? You don't know what Project Infinity is, do you? You came all this way to stop the Daleks getting it – and yet you don't know what it does. What a remarkable devotion to duty. I take it this wasn't your idea, Brook.
KALENDORF   (*Losing patience*) It was my idea.
TANLEE   I thought as much –
KALENDORF   So tell us what Project Infinity is.
TANLEE   It's no good at stopping Imperial Command Ships, I'm afraid.
KALENDORF   (*Roar*) *Tell us!!!*
TANLEE   Quantum realities. Have you heard about that? An infinite number of possible universes, based on an infinite number of possibilities.[51]
KALENDORF   I've heard of it.[52]
ALBY   So have I, actually.
TANLEE   (*Sarcastic*) Oh, well, that's a relief.
KALENDORF   (*Warning growl*) Time is running out, Tanlee.
TANLEE   Well, this was set up after the last Dalek war... centuries ago. They knew the Daleks would try again. And they knew there was a good chance that the Daleks would learn from their mistakes and very

probably succeed this time. So, some of our cleverest people hypothesised... What if there was a parallel, quantum reality, an alternative universe in which we defeated the Daleks for all time? If we could just see into that universe and see how the humans there did it, then we'd know what to do in this universe. We'd have *their* answer for defeating the Daleks.

ALBY   Sounds a bit like... well, a bit like cheating to me.

TANLEE   I would've thought that might appeal to you, Brook.

KALENDORF   How does it work?

TANLEE   Well, they scoured all of the known galaxy for a weakness in the fabric of space and time. They found it out here. Then they bombarded it for a few centuries... and eventually came up with... this. Do you mind if I activate the main viewer?

Control bleep. Screen activates.

ALBY   Wow.

KALENDORF   What is it?

TANLEE   They call it a dimensional fissure. And the theory is that they punch a beam through it, which they call the Infinity Scan.

ALBY   And with that, they find this alternative universe where the Daleks were totally defeated?

TANLEE   Well, eventually. But of course, they pick up a lot of useless data on the way. It was going to take them a while to sift through it all. Several years, I expect. And they've already done a preliminary scan. So the hypothesis was sound. Which is a relief.

ALBY   None of which helps us now. Even if we could get it to work.

TANLEE   Oh, it'll work all right. As soon as that fissure is aligned, the Infinity Scan is set to fire off automatically. It's powered by veganite, you know.[53]

ALBY   (*Realising*) Which is why the Daleks attacked the Vega System first. *They* want to use Project Infinity to find out how to defeat *us* for all time.

TANLEE   Perhaps.

Comms bleep.

KALENDORF   Kalendorf. Who is it?

JOHNSTONE   (*Distort*) Kalendorf, we've just detected some kind of spatial anomaly just outside the Lopra –

KALENDORF   I know. We're looking at it. It's a called a 'dimensional fissure' and it's a vital part of Project Infinity.

JOHNSTONE   (*Distort*) You mean you've found out what it does?

KALENDORF   Yes. And it's no help to us at the moment.

JOHNSTONE   (*Distort*) Oh... well, er... seems it jogged Mirana's implant memory. She's on her way to you – pretty fired up. She says she knows what the Daleks wanted it for.

KALENDORF   We know that as well.

JOHNSTONE   (*Distort*) Oh... I... er... I see. So what are we going to do?

KALENDORF   (*Deciding*) Well... We're going to take off and blow this base to pieces from orbit. That's about all we *can* do.

TANLEE   I wouldn't advise it.

ALBY   Oh yeah? Why's that?

MIRANA   (*Distant, approaching*) Kalendorf! Kalendorf!

Footsteps as she arrives, out of breath.

MIRANA	I know what the Daleks –
ALBY	So do we. Tanlee's just told us.
TANLEE	Have I?
MIRANA	(*Terrified*) Who are you?
KALENDORF	What's the matter, Mirana?
TANLEE	My name is Ernst Tanlee, I'm –
MIRANA	No!!!
ALBY	What is it, Mirana?
TANLEE	My dear young lady? I'm sorry if I –
MIRANA	Daleks! Daleks! I can hear... *see* Daleks!
ALBY	What?!

MIRANA In his mind! He's working for them. They're communicating with him. The Emperor! It's just as it was with me!

ALBY But – Tanlee?

Gun click.

TANLEE Nobody move! (*Pause*) That's better. And I assure you. I will kill you if you do move.

MIRANA He's told you what the Daleks are going to do?

ALBY Yeah. They were going to find out how to defeat us for all time by tapping into information from another universe.

TANLEE starts to laugh.

ALBY Yeah, you *would* find it funny, wouldn't you?

MIRANA But that's not what they're going to do.

TANLEE Quite right, my dear. You tell them. Why not?

KALENDORF Well, Mirana?

MIRANA The veganite. You must know about the veganite. The Emperor is bringing a massive amount of veganite in its ship. They're going to increase the power of the Infinity Scan to an incredible level.

Pause.

ALBY So?

MIRANA Don't you understand? They're not just going to *scan* other realities. They're going to find the one they want, then create a *gateway* between the two realities. They're going to bring the Daleks from that reality into this one. Daleks from a universe where they have found the perfect way to become... to become –

TANLEE Totally invincible, yes. Thank you, my dear.

KALENDORF You can't kill all of us at once with that gun. Not if we rush you.

TANLEE Perhaps. But which of you will make the sacrifice first? I expect it will be you, Kalendorf... since you missed your opportunity last time. *But before you do...*

KALENDORF What?

Pause.

ALBY You know, I never liked you, Tanlee. Even when you weren't working for the Daleks. (*Pause*) What are you waiting for?

TANLEE Hm? What makes you think I'm waiting.

MIRANA Oh no... Oh no...

KALENDORF What is it, Mirana?

MIRANA It's too late.

TANLEE Yes. I'm afraid it is.

Several transmat FX as Daleks materialise.

KALENDORF Daleks!

MIRANA	The Emperor's ship... It's just entered transmat range.
DALEK	You are our prisoners. If you attempt to escape, you will be exterminated.
KALENDORF	Why don't you just exterminate us now?
ALBY	Hey, speak for yourself.
DALEK	You are of superior intellect. You will be robotised.
TANLEE	Yes. Even you, Brook. Hard to believe, I know.
DALEK	You will go with them.
TANLEE	I obey.
DALEK	Assault party to Imperial Command. Kalendorf, Brook and agent Mirana are being transmaterialised for robotisation as ordered.

48. Int. Dalek Imperial Command Ship. Emperor's Chamber.

DALEK (*Distort, continued form previous scene*) Requesting transmat of full attack force to exterminate Earth Alliance troops on Lopra Minor.

DALEK SUPREME They will be dispatched immediately. Veganite energy will be beamed directly from this ship to the Infinity Scan at the moment of alignment with the dimensional fissure. Proceed with final preparations.

DALEK (*Distort*) The Infinity Scan controlling interfaces sustained damage during the Earth Forces' attack.[54]

DALEK SUPREME Make repairs to the systems.

DALEK (*Distort*) I obey.

DALEK SUPREME Imperial Command Ship will enter Lopra Minor orbit in 70 rels.

DALEK (*Distort*) Understood.

Comms bleep.

DALEK SUPREME Emperor! All is prepared!

EMPEROR Prepare me for transmaterialisation to Lopra Minor.

DALEK SUPREME I obey.

EMPEROR Nothing can defeat the Daleks now! We will be invincible!

DALEK SUPREME Invincible! Invincible![55]

EMPEROR *Invincible!!!*[56]

A nightmarish crescendo of chanting.

49. Int. Dalek Imperial Command Ship. Robotisation Bay.
Door opens. Vast reverb.

DALEK	Enter!
TANLEE	Beautiful, isn't it?
MIRANA	Oh my God, no.
ALBY	There's millions of them.
TANLEE	Oh yes. Millions of human beings... and their close cousins, Kalendorf. Millions. Sleeping. All the best specimens. Waiting for rebirth.
KALENDORF	Why? You're going to put us to sleep... cryogenic sleep?
TANLEE	Something of the kind.
MIRANA	(*With dread*) I remember now. I saw this in the Emperor's mind.
ALBY	I thought you were going to robotise us.

TANLEE   That's the initial phase, yes. But then... you sleep... and the processes begin.

KALENDORF   What processes?

MIRANA   To become a Dalek. They're going to turn us into Dalek creatures.

TANLEE   Accelerated mutation. And with the help we will get from our brothers who cross from that other reality... You will become the ultimate beings of the universe. We all will.

KALENDORF   I'd rather die –

TANLEE   Die fighting? Making a break for it? Smashing a few harmless dents into a Dalek casing or two as you go? Be our guest. But Dalek guns don't always kill. Our guards have orders to paralyse any who cause trouble. So you see, there's no escape. That's something even Susan Mendes discovered.

ALBY   What? Suz?

DALEK   Move! Move now!

TANLEE   This way, please.

ALBY   Suz is here? Tell me!

DALEK   Move!

ALBY   You've got to tell me! Is Suz here?

TANLEE   Why shouldn't she be?

ALBY   Suz? Suz! *Suzzzz!!!*

His cry echoes.

50. Int. Project Infinity. Operations Centre.
Massive energy of Infinity Scan winds down.

DALEK   Infinity Scan has terminated. Processing of data from alternate universes now underway.

DALEK SUPREME Continue!

Faint electronic chatter of data processing. Transmat beam begins.

DALEK   Emperor materialising.

Transmat beam completes.

EMPEROR   Report!

DALEK SUPREME Initial readings indicate scan data volume is smaller than predicted.

DALEK   Damage sustained by the systems has inhibited scanning effectiveness. But data volume remains within optimum parameters.

EMPEROR   That is acceptable for our purposes.

DALEK   Processing of data continues.

EMPEROR   Data is to be fed directly to my cerebral processors.

DALEK SUPREME The Emperor possesses the greatest mind in the universe!!!

Electronic chatter of processing reaches a crescendo. Time passes. Alarm sounds.

DALEK   Parallel universe located where readings indicate *total* Dalek control.

EMPEROR   Activate the dimensional gateway![57]

Gateway activation effect.

EMPEROR   Launch command beacon through gateway.

DALEK   I obey.

Command beacon is launched.

DALEK SUPREME Command beacon launched.

EMPEROR   Monitor for response signal.

DALEK   I obey.

Bleep of monitor. Response signal.

DALEK   Response signal received. Readings indicate dimensional gateway has been breached.

EMPEROR   A Dalek army is entering the dimensional gateway in the parallel universe.

Gateway rumbles ominously.

Bleep of readouts.

DALEK SUPREME Daleks now entering our universe.

Gateway rumble subsides.

EMPEROR   Greetings! I am the Emperor of the Daleks in this universe. You have become the invincible rulers of your universe.

ALTERNATE DALEK Correct. The Daleks have absolute power.

EMPEROR   We seek your absolute power for our universe.

ALTERNATE DALEK We are accessing your command network.

EMPEROR   Our achievements are humble. We seek your absolute power.

ALTERNATE DALEK You Daleks have conquered this galaxy.

EMPEROR   Correct.

ALTERNATE DALEK You have waged war against its peoples. You have destroyed. You have subjugated.

EMPEROR   Correct!

Pause.

ALTERNATE DALEK You have committed the greatest crimes our universe has ever known! Neutralize them! Neutralise![58]

Strange Dalek neutraliser guns firing. Crash into

CLOSING THEME.

NOTES

1.   Scene deleted.
2.   Line changed to: '(*Over computer voice*) Look, stop it! I'm just not interested in any message ~~from any~~ (*Stunned*) What?'
3.   The last six lines of Scene 3 were deleted.
4.   Scene 4 was substantially changed:

KALENDORF   ~~(*Sighs*) Come in~~.
Door opens. Footsteps.
KALENDORF   ~~Ah, Officer Mirana~~.
MIRANA   ~~Hi... Are... are you okay?~~
KALENDORF   ~~'Okay'? Do I look okay?~~
MIRANA   ~~Not really.~~
The next 11 lines are then as scripted.
MIRANA   (*Routine*) This is the picture we'd built up with the first round of reports. Which you've seen. And... here's that pattern of successful rebellion we know so well. ~~A kind of split, right from the Vega System, through Garazone, Guria... the Colatron worlds here~~... like an arc across the galaxy, more or less ending here on Yaldos.
KALENDORF   That's no surprise... an arc of rebellion travelling through almost every planet Suz and I were taken to by the Daleks.
MIRANA   Just a month after the rebellion started...
More graphic sounds.
MIRANA   And our influence has spread quickly. Dalek forces are scattering, retreating... mainly in the direction of the Seriphia Galaxy.
KALENDORF   Where they **come** from in the first place.
MIRANA   ~~And you can see that arc of rebellion is getting thicker.~~
More graphic sounds.
MIRANA   *Three* months in, and the Dalek forces look pretty patchy. They're just concentrating in ten or more strong-points... most significantly in Earth's solar system.
KALENDORF   ~~And then the slow down of activity. Maybe you were right... there is nothing now. Is that the latest picture?~~
MIRANA   ~~More or less.~~
KALENDORF   (*Suddenly curious*) Open *that* file.
MIRANA   Sure. ~~But it just confirms the way things are going~~.
More graphics noises.
KALENDORF   (*Worried*) ~~What...?~~ What are they playing at?
MIRANA   Running scared.
KALENDORF   (*Studying the graphics*) Hmm... Is that what you think?
MIRANA   Despite everything you've said in the media, there's still a lot of gung-ho attitude from our people
KALENDORF   An army's state of mind is important, but you need more than just attitude to win a battle. A lot of our fleets are badly equipped and poorly organised. ~~But look~~... these attacks here... The Daleks shouldn't have been defeated; but... **but**... they're simply retreating at the first sign of trouble.
MIRANA   Maybe. Maybe they just know it's all over for them.
KALENDORF   No.
MIRANA   ~~Kalendorf, what's the matter?~~
KALENDORF   ~~I don't know. Hmmm...~~
MIRANA   ~~What are you thinking?~~
KALENDORF   ~~I'm thinking~~... They're trying to make us lazy.
MIRANA   (*Unconvinced*) By losing the war?

KALENDORF By treating us **as** over-excitable children. Letting us win, over and over again when we've no right to.

MIRANA **Well**, that doesn't sound like Dalek thinking to me.

The next 11 lines are then as scripted.

MIRANA **Well**, that doesn't make sense.

KALENDORF That's what I said. (*Sighs. Change of thought*) Do you think Alby knows more than he's telling us?

MIRANA Alby? Why do you say that?

KALENDORF I noticed him getting a bit tight-lipped when the first report of that Dalek sighting came in.

MIRANA **You did**? Oh.

KALENDORF Yes. Where is he?

MIRANA Er... I don't know. I haven't seen him in quite a while. He's been **kind of**... distant, lately.

KALENDORF Drunk, you mean. He hasn't said much to anyone ever since he found out Suz was dead.

MIRANA He'd been looking for her a long time.

KALENDORF (*Pensive*) Yes...

Comms bleep.

KALENDORF ~~Kalendorf to Alby Brook. Respond please.~~

Negative bleep.

KALENDORF ~~Alby, this is Kalendorf. Where are you?~~

Negative bleep.

KALENDORF Comms centre, can you locate Alby Brook for me, please?

COMMS ~~(*Distort*) Traffic control reports he left the city about an hour ago, sir.~~

KALENDORF ~~Not drunk, then. (*Urgent*) Where was he heading?~~

COMMS ~~(*Distort*) Er... Oh. It seems he didn't log a flight plan, sir.~~

Door opens.

MIRANA ~~Where are you going?~~

KALENDORF ~~To find Alby... and ask him what he really knows about the Lopra System.~~

5. This line and the following five were deleted.

6. Line changed to: 'What are *you* doing ~~out~~ here?'

7. The final three lines of Scene 9 were deleted.

8. We also hear Suz's reading of 'Try a pickled onion... My gran makes them... sends them from Earth.'

9. Line changed to: '(Quietly) It came from **that** cave.'

10. Line changed to: '~~In my mind's eye~~... the air was always fresh, the suns were always high in the sky. The water in the Marsh Lakes... always a sparkling blue. Hmm, that's the way I remember it.'

11. 'Oh,' added at the beginning of the line.

12. Line changed to: '(*Distort*) **That is of no importance to you now.** We have known of Project Infinity for centuries.'

13. Line changed to: 'Suz? You **know what will** – '

14. Line changed to: 'Peoples of the galaxy. We all knew this day would come. Perhaps some of you doubted it. I never did. (*Pause*) I have just spoken with the Dalek leaders. They tell me, Earth has been conquered. That the Daleks have won. That the war is over. (*Pause*) We will all live as citizens of the Dalek Empire... forever! That is what they tell me. They want me to say that we slaves should be commended for hastening the Dalek victory. But I ~~only~~ have one thing to say to that. DEATH – TO – THE – *DALEKS!!!*'

15. Line changed to: 'Silence! Silence! **Silence**! ~~Exterminate!~~'

16. Added dialogue – DALEK: '**Exterminate! Exterminate! Exterminate**!'

17. Line changed to: 'Yes. There are many possible reasons why I'm not linked to Suz anymore. She may have left the planet. She may be in a deep coma. She ~~could have~~ – '

18. Line changed to: 'I wanted it to be me! I wanted her to live. *I* wanted to be the one who was remembered as the dead hero. And you know why? Because *I* couldn't bear the guilt either. I still can't. But I know for sure that she's dead, Alby. And we now know the lengths **that** she went to – to ensure that we found out what the Daleks are *really* up to. *That's* what we should be thinking about now. This... Project Infinity. And there's that look on your face again.'

19. Line changed to: 'The Daleks are being defeated because they're not interested in fighting us any more. Why is that? **It's** because **the** one little Dalek ship, or whatever it is, heading for the Lopra system is more important than anything that's happened throughout the entire galaxy?'

20. Line changed to: 'Kalendorf... I don't think he does **know** – '

21. Added dialogue – DALEK: **'All tactician Daleks report to Emperor's chamber immediately.'**

22. Line changed to: '(*Struggling*) ~~It's~~... the Daleks.'

23. Line changed to: '~~The~~ Emperor? Oh, God!'

24. Line changed to: 'I can't... **I** can't maintain... ~~Argh~~. She's becoming too powerful for me. My mind is weakening.'

25. Line changed to: 'Just a glimpse. But what a glimpse it was. There was a clear link from the Emperor's mind to a Dalek command network. And there was something else... (*with difficulty*) I ~~can't~~... **I**... I can't quite...'

26. Scene 29 was substantially changed to:
Sharp negative bleeps from mind-link controls.
DALEK SUPREME Psychotropic link with humanoid agent cannot be re-established. No response to destruct signals.
EMPEROR ~~Has the humanoid female survived?~~
DALEK SUPREME ~~Readings indicate her mind was conscious when the psychotropic link was severed.~~
EMPEROR ~~She was linked to my mental processes and through me to the Dalek Command net. The humans may now gain knowledge of our plan if they are able to access the implant in her brain.~~ We must set a direct course for Lopra Minor.
DALEK SUPREME If we deviate from current trajectory, this vessel will be in range of Earth Alliance deep-space scanners for a sustained period. We will be detected.
EMPEROR That is of no consequence now. Speed is of the essence.
~~Comms bleep.~~
EMPEROR ~~Report on advance attack force status.~~
DALEK 1 ~~(Distort) Advance attack force coded signals indicate they are on final approach to planet Lopra Minor.~~
EMPEROR ~~Excellent!!!~~

27. Scene 30 was substantially changed. The first eight lines are as scripted, then:
TANLEE ~~One of my men. As I was saying, under normal circumstances, I would allow you to rest.~~
ESPEELIUS ~~'Allow'?~~
TANLEE ~~But unfortunately for you, these are far from normal circumstances.~~
ESPEELIUS ~~I don't understand.~~
TANLEE ~~Well, under normal circumstances, if, say, a Dalek attack force were to land on this planet... even a modest Dalek attack force,~~

172

ESPEELIUS ~~What are you saying?~~

TANLEE ~~I had my men deactivate your security systems.~~

ESPEELIUS ~~Wh~~ Why did you do that?

TANLEE ~~You're about to find out, my dear old friend.~~

ESPEELIUS Tanlee, ~~what are you talking about?~~ This is no time for childish games. The events that are about to unfold here –

TANLEE Are not quite the events you expected, I'm afraid.

Door opens.

ESPEELIUS ~~My God~~... Tanlee... What have you **done**...? You've betrayed –

DALEK Do not move! This facility is now under Dalek control. Resist and you will be exterminated.

28. Line changed to: 'Oh... er... I was born on a freighter passing through Orion's belt. So... I never really **knew** how to answer that question.'

29. Line changed to: 'Only... only... pieces. I can't quite... I can't ~~quite~~...'

30. Line changed to: '**Well**, that's hardly an inspired conclusion to reach – '

31. Line changed to: 'Project Infinity... "We will use it to gain ~~total~~ control of..." Of the entire universe.' The next line, the last of the scene, is then deleted.

32. This line, and the following three, are all deleted.

33. Scene 35 was substantially changed. The first 12 lines are as scripted, then:

MIRANA The Daleks are constantly transmitting their co-ordinates through their command net, so that the squad commander can keep updating its orders. ~~It's kind of like a very fast game of chess.~~

KALENDORF ~~Between the Dalek commander and us.~~

MIRANA ~~Yes.~~

KALENDORF Doctor, can you link Mirana up to our tactical computer and beam her information direct to our assault force?

JOHNSTONE I can try.

ALBY ~~(Distort) All the assault force guys are patched in to the tactical computers on board each of the landing craft. They've all got heads up displays on their visors.~~

KALENDORF ~~And we can supply data direct to each tactical computer.~~

MIRANA ~~And if you create a direct tap from my implant to our tactical computer...~~ It should work.

The scene then continues as scripted.

34. Deleted dialogue – ZERO 2: '~~(Distort) Landing craft Zero 2 reporting steady at ten thousand meters. Do you want us to circle?~~'

35. Line changed to: '~~Confirmed, Zero 2. We have you at~~ 15 degrees NorWest of Project Infinity base, at a distance of... (reading it off) 5 point 6 kilometers.'

36. Line changed to: '(*Distort*) ~~Bear with me~~, I'm working as fast as I can.'

37. This line and the following three were deleted.

38. Line changed to: '~~Another problem... I think~~. Mr Herrick?'

39. Line changed to: 'Oh, that is beautiful. Look at **that** screen. All the Dalek positions around the base are showing up.'

40. Line changed to:

SPECIAL WEAPONS DALEK Special Weapons Daleks obey! Climbing to attack altitude.

DALEK   **Tracking enemy craft approaching**.

SPECIAL WEAPONS DALEK Firing now.

41.   Line changed to: '(*Tense*) **Yes**. Looks like a hit.'

42.   Deleted dialogue – ALBY: '~~So far... not so bad.~~'

43.   Added dialogue – DALEK 1: '**Have sustained damage. Have sustained damage.**'

44.   Line changed to: '(*Distort*) Zero 2, watch your left flank, an order has just been given to encircle you. ~~The last surviving Special Weapons Dalek is now ordered to make an air attack on you.~~'

45.   Scene 43 was changed to:

Jungle atmosphere. Handgun fire.

DALEK   Under attack! Under attack! **Vision impaired! Vision impaired!**

Daleks cry out and explode.

DALEK 2   Exterminate! Exterminate! **Fire! Fire!**

DALEK 1   **Crush all resistance**.

DALEK 3   **Exterminate**

Dalek gunfire. Soldiers cry out.

DALEK 3   **They are surrounded. There is no escape. Destroy. Destroy.**

46.   The first two lines of Scene 44 were deleted.

47.   Line changed to: '(*Distort*) You are clear, Zero 4. ~~Repeat, you are clear.~~ They made a big mistake moving their main force to hit Zero 2.'

48.   Line changed to: '(*Angry*) We've done what you asked! **Now**, stop the killing!'

49.   Line changed to:

ESPEELIUS (*Distort*) Our lives don't matter.

DALEK   (*Distort*) **Silence!**

ESPEELIUS (*Distort*) Whoever you are! Listen to me! You must press home your attack!

DALEK   (*Distort*) **Silence!**

ESPEELIUS (*Distort*) If the Daleks gain control of Project Infinity it will be the end of everything –

50.   Added dialogue – DALEK CMDR: '**Withdraw!**'

51.   Line changed to: 'Quantum realities. Have you heard **of them**? An infinite number of possible universes, based on an infinite number of possibilities.'

52.   Line changed to: '**Yes**, I've heard of it.'

53.   Line changed to: 'Oh, it'll work all right. As soon as that fissure is aligned, the Infinity Scan is set to fire off automatically. It's powered by veganite, **by the way**.'

54.   Line changed to: '(*Distort*) The **controlling interfaces of the Infinity Scan** sustained damage during the Earth Forces' attack.'

55.   Line changed to: 'Invincible! Invincible! **Invincible!**'

56.   Line changed to: '*Invincible!!! **Invincible!!!***'

57.   Line changed to: 'Activate ~~the~~ dimensional gateway!'

58.   Line changed to:

ALTERNATE DALEK You have committed the greatest crimes our universe has ever known! Neutralise them! ~~Neutralise!~~

DALEK   **Exterminate!**

ALTERNATE DALEK Neutralise them!

Q&A
PROJECT INFINITY

It's noticeable that the first scene of *Project Infinity* – the scene of Kalendorf being interviewed on a news programme – is missing from the finished audio. Did you record it? Why was it cut?

Nicholas Briggs: The scene was recorded and later cut. Alistair Lock played the newsreader. It was cut because the play was overrunning; but also because it just wasn't necessary. One of the few good things I learnt when I worked in publishing was that you can often easily cut the first paragraph from an article. The reason is that the first paragraph is just the writer kind of getting himself into gear, settling his bum into the seat as it were. He usually goes on to repeat, in more detail, what he says in the first paragraph. This was exactly the case in this first scene. I was recapping for my own sake. This often happens in first drafts. Writers work through ideas to solidify them in their own minds, but in the final analysis this 'working through' is often not necessary for the audience to hear. Everything that's mentioned in this scene is referred to and explained later.

On the same topic, the scene is longer in the first draft. In your first version of the script, the scene continues as:

NEWSREADER And with the mysterious disappearance of Tanlee, the Operational Commander of Earth's Forces, more worrying developments are signalled.
KALENDORF (*Distort*) Our tactical assessment is that the Daleks are playing a waiting game. They are regrouping. And now our long-range scanners are picking up traces of Dalek activity beyond the boundaries of our galaxy.
INTERVIEWER (*Distort*) You mean in the Seriphia Galaxy, where they made their attack from?
KALENDORF (*Distort*) No... I mean on the opposite side of the galaxy. It seems that while we were busy trying to fight their main invasion force – and failing – a small group of Daleks was circumnavigating our galaxy.
INTERVIEWER (*Distort. Taken aback*) Well... do – do we know why?
KALENDORF (*Distort. Sighs*) No. No we don't. All we can be sure of is... they're up to something.

It's telling that I decided to cut it down before recording it. I clearly already had the instinct that it wasn't really necessary. The version that was recorded was the slightly cut version. The material that was cut after the first draft is even more plot-heavy and over-explanatory. Yuk.

Was the play overrunning because there was a lot of plot to fit in?
It wasn't so much that there was a lot of plot, but that it was all a bit overstated. The only bit of plot that was actually cut concerned the Dalek Supreme sending an advance squad to attack Lopra Minor before the Emperor's ship arrived. That meant that every scene with the Emperor and the Supreme ended with an exchange on this subject. In post-production, I found that by cutting these final exchanges in each of these scenes, I saved a hell of a lot of time, made the story flow more easily and – what's best of all – you don't even miss those bits! Nobody has ever questioned why or how those extra Daleks turn up to help Tanlee. It was an interesting lesson in what audiences do and don't need to know. The moment I cut those bits, it's almost as if I forgot they ever existed.

Were there any other deleted scenes?
I toyed with the idea of having a Yaldos council chamber scene. In this unfinished fragment, it is clear that Alby and Kalendorf are arguing that resources must be diverted to pursuing the Dalek ship which was detected on the fringes of the galaxy...

Int. Yaldos. Council Chamber.
A crowd of delegates arguing. Proceedings are out of control.

MIRANA   Members of the council! Are we to believe that Kalendorf and Brook are seriously suggesting that we weaken our forces here in the inner sectors of the galaxy to... what? Send them on some wild chase to find an insignificant group of Daleks who may or may not be approaching the Lopra System for some unknown purpose?
Noises of agreement from crowd.
KALENDORF   *(Close)* Well... Alby?
ALBY   What can I tell them? I don't really know anything. And it may be too dangerous to tell them the little I do know.

Who sends the message to Alby, telling him to try a pickled onion?
It's a psychic message from the Seer. The same as the message that Alby receives on the radio as he approaches the mountain in the skimmer.

Is there any significance to 'pickled onions'? Are you a fan?
I'm a great fan of pickled onions! I have all their albums! They are my favourite food, which is socially embarrassing for at least two reasons; but I'll leave you to guess those.

In the first draft, Kalendorf says he saw Suz die, which contradicts what we later find out.
That's probably why I cut it. I did, however, want to get across Kalendorf's certainty that Suz was dead. I always knew that she wasn't going to be, but I was keen for Kalendorf to be so grief-stricken that he could not even dare to entertain the possibility of hope. His saying that he actually saw her die could have been viewed as this; but its factual inaccuracy would have just been confusing.

The first draft is quite different to the finished play. Mirana was originally killed off...

12. Int. Yaldos. Seers' Cavern.

[...]

MIRANA   Kalendorf, where are you going?

KALENDORF   To find Project Infinity.

MIRANA   Why? If what Alby says is true, then –

KALENDORF   Then what? What would you have me do? Organise another galaxy-wide broadcast? 'Hello everyone, it's all over, time to follow Alby Brook's noble example and get drunk'? This whole invasion of the galaxy has been a massive distraction. Something to divert us from what the Daleks are really doing. And the rebellion? That was just something else to keep us all occupied, just in case we noticed a tiny flicker on a space scope screen. The flicker of one tiny Dalek ship up to no good...

MIRANA   You don't know that for sure. There could be hundreds of possible –

KALENDORF   – possible explanations? Yes, let's just sit around and discuss those. That'd be another distraction the Dalek Emperor would be only too pleased about.

ALBY   She's right, Kalendorf. You can't be sure –

KALENDORF   You play the Emperor's game if you like. I'm going to the Lopra System.

MIRANA   I'm afraid I can't let you do that.

Gun clicks.

ALBY   Mirana, what are you doing?

KALENDORF   If you want to stop me, you'll have to shoot me.

MIRANA   That's precisely what I intend to do.

Gun fires. KALENDORF cries out and falls to the ground.

ALBY   Mirana, what the hell–? Oh no.

MIRANA   It is a pity you did not manage to convince Kalendorf of the futility of resistance. And now you mu- aaargh! (*Various groans of pain*)

ALBY   What's the matter with you? What's the matter with her?

SEER   Quickly... I am holding her mind in mine. Disarm her.

ALBY   Right. (*Sound of effort*) Got it...

Scuffing of feet.

ALBY   Kalendorf! Kalendorf!

KALENDORF   (*Severely injured*) Alby... aaargh. Damn, she's a Dalek spy... aargh... damn!

SEER   No... not just spy... Her mind... Her mind... (*Gasps in pain*)

MIRANA   (*Fighting against SEER's mental powers*) The Seer's mental powers will soon be overcome.

ALBY   Who are you?

MIRANA   You are addressing... the Emperor of the Daleks.

SEER   (*Gasps in pain*) Their minds are linked! There is... a device... implanted in her brain. I can... I can see... See into the mind of the Emperor. No! Noooo!

MIRANA   You will all be exterminated!

KALENDORF   Alby, shoot Mirana... kill her!

Gun fires several times.

MIRANA   You cannot kill me. I have the Emperor's strength of purpose.

A punch. ALBY gasps, falls. Gun clatters. Footsteps, gun is picked up.
SEER　　　　It's... infinity... I can see what you seek... Infinite possibilities... infinite power...
MIRANA　　　Power that your puny mind cannot comprehend. The very thought will destroy you.
SEER　　　　Aaargh! Kalendorf, Alby! This Emperor seeks infinity.
KALENDORF　What?
ALBY　　　　Infinity? Project Infinity?
MIRANA　　　And now, old woman, you will die.
Gunshot. SEER cries out. MIRANA cries out.
MIRANA　　　(*In pain, confused*) What? What is happening?
SEER　　　　Our minds are linked. I die... you die (*A final gasp*)
MIRANA cries out and dies.

13. Dalek Imperial Command Ship.
EMPEROR cries out.

DALEK SUPREME Psychotropic link with humanoid agent relinquished.
EMPEROR　　(*Recovering*) The... the humans now know something of our plan. They will try to stop us. Set direct course for the Lopra System.
DALEK SUPREME A direct course will be detected by the human beings' scanning devices.
EMPEROR　　It does not matter now. Speed is of the essence.

I came to a bit of a halt with it. It's true that one of the reasons why I decided to keep Mirana was because of Teresa's strong performance, but I also realised that she would be a good focus of the story. I could use her to take us on six months and move things on to the final approach to Lopra Minor. So we wake up with Mirana, as confused as she is, so we can learn as she learns. I seem to remember it took me quite a while to work this out.

How would the rest of the story have gone?
Here are extracts from the original plot of *Project Infinity*, which show what might have been if I'd followed my initial plans to kill Mirana. We pick up the story in the Seer's Cave, immediately following the flashbacks to Suz being exterminated on Yaldos...

- Alby upset (devastated)
- Project Infinity discussion with Kalendorf. What did Suz know?
- Seer: 'Veganite fuels it. Top Secret. Lopra System, Lopra Minor.'
- Alby & Karlendorf: 'Earth Alliance seeking alliance with Knights of Velyshaa – against big threat, probably the Daleks.'

- Kalendorf had heard of Project Infinity.
- Alby: Big – if Suz was right and Dalek Supreme seemed to know about revolution, Project Infinity must really hold the key.
- Mirana: 'It does.' (She's a Dalek replicant. She will now destroy them.)
- Seer links with her mind and distracts Mirana.

- Kalendorf kills Mirana.
- Seer was linked, for a moment, to Dalek neural net.
- She has seen Project Infinity.
- Alby & Kalendorf: 'What is it?'
- The thought kills the Seer.
- Alby & Kalendorf must go to Lopra.

- The Dalek Supreme and Emperor are circling the Milky Way from Vega IV to reach Lopra. Dalek duplicate with Alby and Kalendorf killed. Info on Project Infinity. They'll be heading for it. Their goal – Project Infinity.
- Alby and Kalendorf arrive on Lopra Minor. Split up. Alby arrested. Questioned by Espeelius. Alby mentions mission ordered by Tanlee. Tanlee enters.
- Alby: 'Daleks on Carson's Planet?'
- Tanlee: 'I escaped. Were you able to report in on what Suz told you about Project Infinity?'
- Alby suspicious – how would Tanlee know etc?
- Disguised, Kalendorf breaks in and discovers what Project Infinity is. 'Oh, God etc.' (But we don't know at this point)

- Tanlee apparently satisfied.
- Espeelius enters. 2nd activation is about to commence.
- Tanlee says Alby might as well see what all the fuss is about.
- Espeelius is not happy.
- Kalendorf is caught.
- Dalek Sup and Emp arriving in Lopra System. 'Our agent reports all is going according to plan. Extra supplies of Veganite we carry will boost the process/ augment Project Infinity.'
- Main chamber.
- Tanlee, Espeelius & Alby enter.
- Impressive etc.
- Kalendorf brought in.
- Starts to explain Project Infinity from what he's seen.
- Espeelius continues, 'All dimensions, all possibilities – ideas for defeating Daleks'

- Alarms sounds.
- Daleks landed. Attack.
- Kalendorf & Alby help with defence.
- Daleks relentless.
- Kalendorf: 'Must destroy project. If Daleks get it... It could do same for them.'
- Tanlee – gun. 'That's right. Nobody move.' (duplicate)
- Alby and Kalendorf are restrained.
- Daleks enter. Install extra veganite. Espeelius impressed that this will not just take dimensional readings, but will open gateway.
- Dalek scientist plugs in & selects correct dimension. One where Daleks rule.
- Gateway opens.
- Civil war ending.
- Alby and Kalendorf observe it.

As you can see, this original storyline, written long before any idea of a second series was suggested, did envisage a chaotic, inconclusive ending. The main difference would have been that Alby and Kalendorf were left watching the galaxy burn in the fires of the civil war between the two Dalek factions. However, it's clear that I hadn't actually worked out how Alby and Karl would survive long enough to witness this. Also, it isn't clear whether or not Tanlee or Espeelius would survive.

It's interesting that I tried several times to plant the information about Kalendorf's original mission. I never really found an appropriate place for it – it certainly doesn't fit very well here.

The planet that the story begins on is still being referred to as 'Vega IV', not 'VI'. Obviously Clayton Hickman's comment about 'Vega IV' sounding like 'vague guffaw' hadn't yet been made!

In The Human Factor, Daughter tells Alby that if she sees Suz she will tell her that he loves her. In Project Infinity, Suz (the Seer) says, 'That girl on Guria told me about you, that you'd said you loved me and were prepared to die finding me. She said I would find a way to be with you forever. And I have found that way, my love. Here I am.' The meeting must have happened 'off-stage'.

That's precisely what happens. It happens 'off-stage'. That's why the Seer reports it. This is the primary source of information for us on the subject, not the reiterating of information from another scene. That scene doesn't exist. There's plenty of talk about the Daleks coming to Guria. I don't think it's too much of a leap to assume that Suz did go there. And if she went there, Daughter would certainly have kept her word. She was a nice kind of girl, you know. Georgina Carter, who played Daughter, is always ribbing me that 'the Princess is coming back in the next one, I think'. Actors are always doing that, postulating that you're actually going to create a whole series based on their character!

Again, you were playing around with narrative – a large part of *Project Infinity* is taken up with explaning events that, chronologically speaking, happened in "*Death to the Daleks!*"
And earlier! That's the whole point of meeting the Seer. She will fill us – and the characters – in on the stuff we hadn't already found out.

It's a bit of a cheat, isn't it, having the Seer able to narrate events that occured to Suz after they'd met?
Well, it's a bit of cheat having people dash around the galaxy with no time dilation effect. It's a bit of a cheat that there are matter transmitters and ray guns. It's only a cheat in that way. It's explained perfectly clearly that the Seer maintains a mental link with Suz as long as she remains on Yaldu. Suz is most concerned that those left behind find out what happens to her. The fact that it is possible is part of the science fiction or fantasy. If you don't like science fiction or fantasy, then go and watch *EastEnders* and stop moaning to me about things being a cheat!

When you were writing *Project Infinity*, was it your intention that Suz had been killed, or were you being deliberately vague about it? You play it as if she's dead right until the last scene and then we get the hint that she was simply paralysed and put into cryogenic sleep.
In all honesty, I think I was playing a game with myself. Daring to entertain the idea that she was dead. But I think I always knew that she couldn't be. It's difficult to remember exactly what I was thinking. I certainly wanted the audience to believe she was dead; so I didn't want to give any little clues. There was one, however. The Seer says that the break in the link between her and Suz could have been caused simply by Suz leaving Yaldos.

Even though Mirana wasn't killed off, it's still revealed that she was unwittingly working for the Daleks, as was Pellan earlier in the series. And later in the episode, Tanlee is uncovered as a Dalek agent. Double-crossing characters seem quite abundant.
Dave Owen picked up on this in his **DWM** review. He wrote a very funny thing about Alby going home to see his parents, only to find that they were Robomen. I laughed a lot. I think the whole theme of betrayal and double-crossing is a vital element of any war story and, for that matter, any Dalek story. It's the idea that in extreme situations, the enemy resorts to any trick to outwit the good guys. It also adds to that unnerving feeling that you can't trust anyone.

Though they met in "*Death to the Daleks!*", *Project Infinity* sees Alby and Kalendorf get a lot of time together. Was it fun writing for new combinations of characters?

I particularly enjoyed writing their first meeting. It's always interesting when two people only know each other by reputation. I thought Mark and Gareth did a particularly good job on that. There was also, of course, the whole feeling of dread in Alby when he meets Kalendorf. He knows that something awful has happened. I was particularly proud of having him start to cry before Karl gives him the bad news. Later, their interaction was interesting because it wasn't that clear who was in charge. Kalendorf was supposed to be, but Alby is very self-reliant. Gareth actually queried why Alby was giving some of the orders. Bless him, Gareth just wanted Kalendorf to be the biggest, toughest guy in the story!

When the characters arrive at Lopra Minor, there is the attack on the Infinity installation. How difficult is it to realise large-scale action on audio?
It's a great challenge. I took as my template the rebel attack on the Death Star as presented in the LP version of *Star Wars*. I was impressed at how they were able to convey the detail and drama of the attack without any narration. Having people talking to each other over communicators is always a good way of doing that. People keep asking what's going on, and the other people have to report. I loved that sequence.

Who played all the 'Zero' characters?
Ian Brooker, Jeremy James, Simon Bridge and Sarah Mowat. Interestingly, Jez developed a voice which he later adapted, with an American accent, for Control in the *Judge Dredd* series.

The ending is a double whammy of cliffhangers: first off, it appears that Alby and co have lost and are going to be turned into Daleks; then, the Alternate Daleks turn up and aren't what we expect. Was it intended to be a cliffhanger? Did you know what would happen next?
It was intended to be an ending that wasn't a definite resolution. Initially, I wanted Alby and Kalendorf to be observing the chaos into which the galaxy was descending, but the whole cryochamber thing changed that. But I didn't know what would happen next, because I'd planned it as the end of a stand-alone four-part series.

Q&A
DALEK WAR

Okay – so, seriously now: when did you first start to think about doing a second series?
Nicholas Briggs: I'd always approached *Dalek Empire* as a one-off four-part series. That's how I planned the plot. And after *Invasion of the Daleks* was released to quite poor reviews – from *Dreamwatch* and *SFX*... I think I'll keep mentioning that! – I thought, 'Oh well, it was worth a try and at least I'm having fun.' But, little by little, good vibes started to filter back to me. Jason picked up on these vibes, and, more importantly for him, the respectable sales figures. So it was round about the time of "*Death to the Daleks!*" that he started talking to me about the possibility of doing another series. But, you know, everything in Big Finish is done in a very vague sort of way. Nobody really ever communicates clearly, and Jason does a lot of mumbling and talking around the subject. He's usually knackered (he's always massively busy with his 'day job') and can't remember what he said to you half an hour ago; so there was no real, official commissioning. He just sort of mumbled about how it might be a good idea. So, I suppose I was bearing that in mind when I wrote "*Death to the Daleks!*" and *Project Infinity*. Somehow, by the time I'd finished writing *Project Infinity*, I still wasn't absolutely certain about doing a second series; but I discovered that Jason was. So, in that meandering, Big Finish sort of way, I very gratefully accepted the challenge. But I can't remember any dates of when I actually started writing the second series. There were a few false starts – one of them reprinted later in this section.

There's one version of the beginning of *Dalek War* I'd started scribbling down in an exercise book, which actually got left on a train. I'd written quite a lot of it and had taken it with me to a *Doctor Who* convention in Newcastle-upon-Tyne. I got a bit stir-crazy during the train journey home and was so pleased to get off that wretched train that I left the exercise book in that little magazine thingy on the back of the seat in front of me. I wonder if anyone ever picked it up? I suppose it ended up in a Virgin Trains bin somewhere.

Tell me about the evolution of the story – how much was stuff you'd thought of during the writing of Dalek Empire? How much of it was extrapolated from the events of Dalek Empire? Did you want to introduce new characters?
I hadn't thought of any of the plot elements of *Dalek War* when I was doing *Dalek Empire*. There was one sequence I started writing for the end of *Dalek Empire*, in which Mirana in a semi-frozen state witnessed, through her link with the Dalek neural net, what happened when the Alternate Daleks arrived. When I cut that from *Project Infinity*, I toyed with the idea of using it in *Dalek War*. But when I actually started to write *Dalek War*, I discarded that idea almost immediately as, frankly, too boring.

The plot of *Dalek War* was only extrapolated from *Dalek Empire* in that it was a continuation of the story. But I wanted to create something entirely new, and not rely on too much knowledge of the first series. I doubt if many people who bought *Dalek War* hadn't heard *Dalek Empire*, but I was still keen that no previous purchase was necessary, folks.

So, the Saloran and Tarkov scenes fulfilled the needs of plot reiteration, but with the added twist that they were getting some of the facts wrong, or looking at them from a slightly different point of view. You see, I'd had this mad idea, when I was working up to writing *Dalek War*, that I should do the whole thing as a documentary. I was watching this BBC2 documentary about some lost civilisation or other, and – I must have been in a really strange frame of mind – I started to feel that the documentary format was more intriguing than drama. Well, I soon got over that nonsense; but I did keep that feeling in mind. I started to treat the plot of *Dalek War* like it was a series of historical fragments. Ironically, that allows you to say stuff like 'we just don't know what happened' and 'somehow, things changed, but no one knows why'. Depending on how you handle this, it can lend a story a kind of epic quality or just be a terrible cop-out. But I'm a great believer in drama feeling as real as possible, and the fact is that one of the most dominant feelings many of us have about our lives is that things don't quite make sense or tally up properly... or turn out the right way. It's certainly a dominant feeling in my life, so it usually finds its way into my scripts. And it's that feeling of events moving on beyond the control of individuals that I tried to have sneaking around in the background of *Dalek War*. Just as the Seer narration in *Dalek Empire* had been effective in moving the story along, the Saloran and Tarkov scenes in *Dalek War* also allowed me not only to move the plot along but, additionally, it allowed me to ask questions that the audience might be asking (like, why did Kalendorf never tell anyone about his plan?) – but instead of giving answers, I usually just asked more questions.

As for new characters... I didn't have a specific goal to introduce new ones; in fact, I was very keen to stick with and develop the strong characters that'd emerged in *Dalek Empire*. However, because of what I wanted to do with the story – have the future perspective and split the characters up – I had, by necessity, to create new characters for my regulars to speak to. So Mirana got Marber, Alby got Morli and Kalendorf got the Mentor.

How much of a problem was that fact that you'd 'killed off' Suz?
It wasn't really a problem because, by the time I'd written the cryo-chamber scene in *Project Infinity*, I was entertaining the idea that she had been frozen by the Daleks. It also gave me the opportunity to make the overriding thrust of *Dalek War* Chapter One the recovery of Suz. Everyone, including me, wanted Suz back. I'd already given myself a way of bringing her back, so why resist?

You again used a narrative framing device – Saloran and Tarkov.
Aside from the reasons of moving the plot along more quickly and having my narrators articulating and asking questions from a 'sort of' audience perspective, there are two other, less noble reasons for using a narrative framing device. Firstly, it just seemed part of the style of *Dalek Empire* and made it very different from our *Doctor Who* releases. Secondly, narration gives a story an epic quality. It's that sense that, if somebody is bothering to talk about the story from a distant perspective, then it takes on a higher level of significance. You know, if you start a drama with someone walking down the

road and going into a shop, it all seems a bit mundane and unimportant. However, if you do exactly the same scene and put in a narrator saying, 'It all started that day I walked down the road and went into the shop... and after that, things would never be the same' you suddenly invest it with all sorts of potential significance. It means you have to deliver more later and could easily screw it up; but it does get you off to a rollicking good start!

As for 'non-linear storytelling', which sounds very grand and complex, I'm keen on it to the extent that I actually think it's part of the natural way we all tell stories. We like to think that we tell people stuff from the beginning to the end, but if you actually analyse the way most people impart information, they do it largely in a sort of thematic order. You find that people who tell the most entertaining stories often suddenly wind back in their storytelling and use phrases like 'Of course, what we didn't know was that...' and 'In the end we...' and 'But before all that...'. So it's something that we're all quite used to in real life. People often do it deliberately to heighten the impact of what they're telling you. So, sometimes, to write your script in strict, chronological order – with the beginning, the middle and the end adhering strictly to what happened first, what happened second and what happened last – is not the most effective and engaging way of telling your story. For example, to start *Dalek War* with the scene of Kalendorf, Alby and Mirana waking up in the cryo-chamber is just very dull. It's much more interesting to catch up with the characters at a later point in their timeline. Then, by the time you actually do the scene in which we discover exactly what happened when they woke up, the audience is chomping at the bit for this information. It gives the scene far more impact, but you've done that thing of delayed gratification. I feel very strongly that the most important thing to work out about storytelling is not just what to tell the audience, but when to tell it to them.

I think I first really thought about this when I saw a fantastic Canadian film called *The Sweet Hereafter*, about a school bus crashing and the consequences of this for a village community. It was told in a completely non-chronological order, but made perfect sense and was one of the most moving, powerful films I've ever seen.

Unlike *Dalek Empire*, all four *Dalek War* scripts were written in one go. Tell us about how you went about writing them. Did you write them in episode order?
The first thing I wrote for *Dalek War* was the background to the future world of Saloran and Tarkov. This led me to writing the 'beginning' of the story as the whole sequence with them. So I certainly intended to write the thing in order, but after I'd finished the Velyshaa sequence, I realised that most of it should actually be at the end of the story. So I cut it up and made a mental note to distribute it throughout the story. I then started off with the 'Kalendorf at war' sequence. But, as you know, that changed a couple of times before it was finalised. But once I'd done that, I wrote the script in order. I stopped to write a more detailed plot synopsis (with drawings, of course!), but, interestingly, this finishes at the point of the Vaarga men entering Kalendorf's ship. I can't find any plot documents after that. I do remember writing the last segment really quite quickly, so I just think I kind of flew from that last bit of plot synopsis until I reached the end. I remember John Ainsworth being quite shocked that I'd suddenly finished. There were rewrites, of course, but it largely stayed the same.

Did the fact that you wrote them all at once change the emphasis, do you think? In your eyes, is *Dalek War* more of a serial – less episodic – than *Dalek Empire*?

I hadn't really thought about it like that. But yes, I suppose that's true. The thing about *Dalek Empire* is that, largely speaking, it never goes backwards. It's a bit like a James Bond film in that it always moves on to the next location and very rarely goes back to it. Our characters are always moving forward, physically. *Dalek War* doesn't do that so much. It takes a long time for Alby and Suz to move off that scout-ship... Alby by dying and Suz by being captured. So, yes, I suppose *Dalek War* does fold back on itself more than *Dalek Empire*. There's more of a sense of one story unfolding rather than different adventures that form a story.

DALEK WAR

KALENDORF	Gareth Thomas
SIY TARKOV	Steven Elder
SALORAN HARDEW	Karen Henson
MARBER, DRUDGER & SPARKS	Ian Brooker
MIRANA	Teresa Gallagher
ALBY BROOK	Mark McDonnell
THE MENTOR	Hannah Smith
Dr JOHNSTONE & SCIENTIST	Simon Bridge
HERRICK, TROOPER & VAARGA MAN	Jeremy James
SUSAN MENDES	Sarah Mowat
MORLI	Dannie Carr
THE DALEKS	Nicholas Briggs
TROOPER	David Sax
ALLENBY	Mark Donovan
GODWIN	Helen Goldwyn
COMMAND, COMPUTER & TECHNICIAN	Jack Galagher

PRODUCTION CREDITS

Written by	Nicholas Briggs
Daleks created by	Terry Nation
Story Editor	John Ainsworth
Sound design & music	Nicholas Briggs
Producers	Jason Haigh-Ellery Nicholas Briggs
Executive Producer for BBC Worldwide	Jacqueline Rayner
Directed by	Nicholas Briggs

Dalek War
Recorded: 27 October and
3, 4, 6 and 10 November 2002

Chapter One
Released : January 2003

Chapter Two
Released : February 2003

Chapter Three
Released : March 2003

Chapter Four
Released : April 2003

DALEK WAR

Basic Plot

Nicholas Briggs: I really am quite surprised at how similar my original ideas for the plot of Dalek War are to the finished production. I expected to look back and find that it had changed beyond all recognition. There are even lines of dialogue in my original notes which stayed more or less the same.

I'm a great believer in letting a story and its characters take on a life of their own when I'm writing a script. So, because I tend to let my writing go wherever the fancy takes me, I always make sure I have the whole thing mapped out in as much detail as I can muster beforehand. As you will see from the document below, that doesn't amount to that much detail at all, but it does give me something I can keep referring back to... just to make sure I'm on the right track.

There are two things that make me laugh about this document. Firstly, that Saloran Hardew was originally a man, so I referred to him as 'Hardew'. When he became a woman, I referred to her as 'Saloran'. Is that sexist? Secondly, I hadn't formulated a way of Kalendorf implanting a destructive impulse in Suz's mind. Considering this was a pretty pivotal plot element, the phrase 'in a clever way yet to be decided' hardly seems adequate forward planning!

Two thousand five hundred years after the final events of *Dalek War*, the galaxy is sparsely populated and undeveloped. It was devastated 2,500 years ago by a terrible war that nobody really remembers. Populations were fragmented, technologies lost. There is no social/political cohesion in the galaxy. Many believe that galactic civilisation is on the brink of extinction.

A small alliance of races is attempting to co-ordinate efforts to re-establish order and prosperity in a largely lawless, poverty-stricken galaxy, but their resources are pitifully inadequate. They are known as the Galactic Union.

One man, Saloran Hardew, has made it his mission to discover what happened to the galaxy all those years ago. He is a learned and determined man. He has dedicated his whole life to his quest. Nothing else matters to him. In his heart, he knows that if the peoples of the galaxy do not discover the nature of the terrible fate which once befell their ancestors, then there is every chance the same thing may happen again. He believes that all attempts to re-establish galactic order and progress are short-sighted and foolish if lessons from the past are not learnt. His views are not widely shared. He is thought to be an eccentric and an obsessive. He is essentially an outcast from mainstream thinking and society (what little there is of either).

Saloran's quest has taken him to the planet Velyshaa. All his research has shown that the events which led to the 2,500-year-old catastrophe are connected with a being who originated on this planet. This being is known by many names – all of them variations of 'Dark One', 'Bringer of Death/Darkness' and the like. Saloran's controversial theory is that the historical figure upon whom this mythical fiend is based was a Knight of Velyshaa known as Kalendorf.

For some years now, Saloran has been in isolation, working amongst the ruins of the ancient Velyshaan civilisation. He is intent on discovering the truth about Kalendorf. He believes that this will unlock the secrets of the galaxy's terrible past.

One day, the tracking stations of the Galactic Union pick up a transmission fragment conveyed to them through a freak wormhole. The wormhole has caused the message to travel an incredible distance in a short amount of time. The Galactic Union's tracking stations would otherwise not have been able to pick up the message for centuries.

The transmission fragment is a distorted image. But analysis of the image reveals it to be an unidentified portion of a metallic object with a molecular structure similar to 2,500-year-old relics catalogued by Saloran Hardew, before he set off for Velyshaa. A junior member of the Union's ruling council, Siy Tarkov, brings the correllation to the attention of the council, insisting that Hardew should be contacted. The council are unimpressed, but agree to let Tarkov take the image to Hardew.

Tarkov makes the long journey to Velyshaa. He finds an embittered Hardew, but shows him the image. Hardew immediately spots the correllation, but cannot throw any further light on the origin or nature of the object. He says that maybe his latest findings will help. Tarkov begs him to tell him what he has discovered so far.

Hardew subjects the image to analysis by his computers... eventually, they will come up with a full image.

Hardew gives a potted and somewhat inaccurate history of what happened in *Dalek Empire*. He identifies the key players. Then the story moves forward a little.

We begin the *Dalek War* story...

We return to Hardew's 'narration' throughout, occassionally with conversations between him and Tarkov. Hardew uncovers more and more of what happened as he accesses the 'thought history' left behind by Kalendorf.

As the story unfolds (already plotted), we learn that Kalendorf and Mirana's plan was to give the Enemy Daleks Suz in order that they could have their Emperor back. (Suz contains the Emperor's celebral matrix in condensed form.) In return, the Enemy Daleks will rid the galaxy of the Alternate Daleks.

Kalendorf explains that Suz has to do this. Alby is furious. His involvement in the plan was motivated purely by his desire to be with Suz again. Kalendorf joins psychically with Suz as he used to. They share something. She then understands and tells Alby she has to do this. Alby is convinced Kalendorf has 'brainwashed' Suz. But Suz leaves with the Daleks.

Alby tries to kill Kalendorf, but is killed in the fight/struggle.

The terrible war between the Daleks begins, with the old alliance forces now on the side of the Enemy Daleks. The war lasts for many years. There is terrible destruction.

The Mentor has one last conversation with Kalendorf. He is captured. The Mentor wants to know why he betrayed the Alternate Daleks, when all they wanted to do was make their universe a peaceful place. Kalendorf lists all the bad things the Alternate Daleks did in the name of 'peace' and 'order'. The Mentor says that the ends justify the means. Kalendorf disagrees. The Mentor says that their battle computers predict this war will never end and that it will eventually lead to the destruction of all living matter. Is Kalendorf prepared to let that happen rather than live under the protection of the Mentor and his Daleks?

Kalendorf says yes.

MENTOR   I believe you. Then we will leave. Of course, you realise that the Enemy Daleks will betray you once we have gone. They will attempt to conquer your galaxy again.

KALENDORF	I know.
MENTOR	And still you would prefer that?
KALENDORF	Perhaps we shall defeat them.
MENTOR	You could not defeat them before.
KALENDORF	Perhaps things are different now.

The Mentor and his Daleks leave through the gateway. The Enemy Daleks destroy the gateway, sealing it forever.

Kalendorf is brought before the old Dalek Emperor... Except that it is now in the form of Suz. The Daleks plan to use her 'Angel of Mercy' image as a way of tricking the Earth Alliance (now broken and weary of war) into letting the old Daleks rule them again.

KALENDORF	You can't trick them if I tell them the truth.
SUZ/EMPEROR	That is why you must die.
KALENDORF	It almost surprises me.
SUZ/EMPEROR	That you are to die?
KALENDORF	No. That you are so predictable. But it's in your nature, isn't it? To destroy, to betray. Nothing else matters except your victory.
SUZ/EMPEROR	That is our strength.
KALENDORF	That is your weakness.

Kalendorf explains that he implanted a destructive impulse in Suz's mind. He activates it (in a clever way yet to be decided!). For a moment, the Emperor becomes Suz completely. She knows what she must do. The Dalek Supreme orders the immediate extermination of Karl and Suz, but Suz releases the destructive impulse through the Dalek command net. All Daleks are destroyed.

Back with Hardew and Tarkov... They hear Kalendorf's last thoughts. He warns that in all probability only the Daleks in our galaxy were destroyed. There are bound to be others on the Dalek home planet. The war with the Daleks will never be over. They will always be back.

Hardew's computer has finished its analysis of the transmitted image. It is a Dalek on a transolar disk. Tarkov reveals that the source of the transmission was beyond our galaxy.

| HARDEW | Then they're out there. And they're on their way. |

DALEK WAR LIBERATION?

Nicholas Briggs: *What we have here is the first version of the script that wasn't accidentally left on a train and lost. It's absolutely bizarre reading it, because I'd largely forgotten what I'd written. I think I felt I'd got myself into a rut and so I decided to start again, just bearing all of this stuff in mind. I think what we have in this version is far too much procedural, Star Trek-ish detail. I think, once I'd got that out of my system, I was able to write something a lot more concise and to do with characters rather than hardware and 'space'. I think a symptom of this is that I lost the 'Helm' character. That was all condensed into Marber and then Marber became a more interesting character. I think a lot of this version came straight from my initial impetus, which was from watching that famous war movie* The Cruel Sea *[1953]. I wanted to make this story about war and the business of prosecuting a war. I think that's still true of the finished production, but I hope it ended up also being to do with characters rather than limpet mines and the manifest of convoy K27!*

To be honest, I'd completely forgotten that I'd given that first draft a title. The question mark was, I remember, very intentional, because I was asking the question of whether or not the new Daleks had truly liberated the humans from the old Daleks, or just re-enslaved them in a more subtle fashion.

I've no idea what the other chapters might have been called. There are two reasons I didn't give the second series chapter titles. One is that I hate it when things line up neatly. I'm a bit of an anarchist, and avoid conformity as often as possible, so on a gut level I liked the fact that the CD titles were in a format that was a bit different from the first series. The second reason is that I was worried that I might want to give a chapter a title with the word 'Dalek' in it. So it might become something like Dalek Empire II: Dalek War – Chapter Three: Dalek Attack. Too many Daleks! Although, arguably, you can never have too many Daleks.

1. Int. Cryo-Pod.
SUZ's breathing. An impact 'clunk'. She murmurs, confused, incoherent. Returns to breathing. (The audience should, by no means, be certain who is making this noise.) Crossfade to:

2. Int. Warship *Victor*. Control Deck.
Chatter of crew activity in background. Scanning FX. Burble of electronic readouts.

HELM   Reading... debris... some... containers of some kind... Could be that supply convoy that went missing.
MARBER   (*Snaps*) Which convoy?
HELM   K27, sir. Reported drifting off course two days ago, just beyond the Stakris Nebula. Contact lost.
MARBER   Any sign of life?
Burble of readouts.
HELM   Hmmm. Inconclusive.
MARBER   (*Snapping into action*) Arm DX missles. Activate the defence fields. Battle stations.
Alarm sounds. Background chatter becomes more agitated. Footsteps. Electronic doors closing etc.
HELM   All sections securing for battle stations, sir.
Comms bleep.
MARBER   Executive Officer Marber to Captain Mirana. We're –

MIRANA   (*Distort. Weary*) I can *hear* the sirens, Marber. I'm on my way to the control deck. What've you got for me?

MARBER   Drifting debris, probably from lost convoy K27. Must've been caught in an ambush. May well be booby-trapped, captain. They just love sticking limpet mines onto chunks of old spaceship.

3. Int. Cryo-Pod.

SUZ breathing. Very eerie, mysterious music cue.

4. Int. Warship *Victor*. Control Deck.

Door opens. Brisk footsteps of MIRANA.

MARBER   Captain, we're ready to open fire.

MIRANA   Any sign of limpet mines?

HELM   No explosives registering, ma'am.

MARBER   They rarely show up on scans, captain.

MIRANA   Oh, they show up... if you look hard enough. Magnify the visual scan, please.

FX of magnification.

MIRANA   What are *those*?

HELM   Er... containers... or something. We spotted some earlier.

Burble of readout.

MIRANA   (*Reading*) Length two point five metres. One metre high... one metre deep. Hmm. (*To HELM*) Are we sure these are the remnants of convoy K27?

HELM   Er... ?

MARBER   With respect, does it matter, ma'am? We may be heading straight into a trap.

MIRANA   Engines all stop.

HELM   All stop, aye.

Hum of engine rumble drops in pitch.

MIRANA   Does *that* satisfy you, Mr Marber?

MARBER   (*Infuriated*) And now we're a sitting target.

MIRANA   Continue scans for explosives and see if we can get hold of the manifest of convoy K27.

HELM   Aye, captain.

MIRANA   Get me an encrypted hyper-beam link to Fleet Command. Flagship *Courageous*.

HELM   Patching through.

Comms bleep.

MIRANA   This is left flank scout 9, Warship *Victor* calling Fleet Command.

Hyperbeam FX.

KALENDORF   (*Distort*) Fleet Command. Kalendorf. This had better be good, Mirana.

MIRANA   We may have found what's left of K27.

Pause. (They both speak carefully. There's hidden meaning in what they say.)

KALENDORF   (*Distort. Hesitant*) Has it... has it been totally destroyed?

MIRANA   There's a lot of debris drifting in space. A number of containers.

KALENDORF   (*Distort*) Containers?

Crossfade to:

5. Int. *Courageous*. Bridge.

KALENDORF What sort of containers?
MIRANA (*Distort*) We don't know. Could be food. Fuel supplies.
KALENDORF Very well. If you're sure there's no sign of explosives, scoop them up. Take them onboard.
ALTERNATE DALEK That may not be wise.
KALENDORF We need all the food and fuel we can get our hands on.
ALTERNATE DALEK Analysis of Enemy Dalek tactics suggests that explosive devices may have been concealed in the wreckage.
MIRANA (*Distort*) We're not reading any sign of explosives.
ALTERNATE DALEK Enemy Dalek explosive devices are often undetectable.
KALENDORF Only when captains aren't thorough enough. Mirana, make an exhaustive scan for explosives before you bring the containers aboard.
MIRANA (*Distort*) Already underway, sir.
ALTERNATE DALEK That course of action is not advisable.
KALENDORF I appreciate your caution, but I trust Captain Mirana's judgement. Is that understood?
ALTERNATE DALEK Understood.
KALENDORF The matter is in your hands, Mirana. Kalendorf out.
Comms bleep.
KALENDORF (*To himself*) Good luck, Mirana.

6. Int. Mentor's Chamber.
THE MENTOR's voice is only slightly distorted by Dalek modulation. The sound of bridge activity distorted in the background.

THE MENTOR Now that... is *interesting*, Kalendorf. You really are... an intriguing creature.
On the distorted bridge activity, an alarm beings to sound. Crossfade to:

7. Int. *Courageous*. Bridge.
Alarm sounding.

KALENDORF Report!
ALTERNATE DALEK 2 Scanners indicate Enemy Dalek fleet approaching on attack vector.
KALENDORF Here they come again. Looks like they were hiding in the asteroid belt this time. Bring the fleet to full battle readiness.
ALTERNATE DALEKS We obey.
KALENDORF Navigation Officer.
NAV OFFICER Sir?
KALENDORF Send deployment signals to the fleet immediately. Attack pattern Orion.
NAV OFFICER Pattern Orion. Confirmed, sir.
ALTERNATE DALEK All weapons now at full power.
KALENDORF Activate defence net.
ALTERNATE DALEK 2 Activating.

Defence net activation FX. A fizzing, crackling sound.
ALTERNATE DALEK 2 Defence net power now at maximum.
Comms bleeps.
NAV OFFICER All fleet vessels signal they are now locked in synchronous attack pattern Orion.
KALENDORF Signal to all vessels. Maximum attack speed. Now!

8. Int. *Victor*. Airlock Area.
Airlock door closes.

CREWMAN All right! Shift 'em to the loading bay.
Electronic crane noise.
MIRANA (*Approaching*) Wait a minute. Shut that off!
Crane winds down.
CREWMAN Something the matter, ma'am?
MIRANA Were there any more like these three?
CREWMAN Plenty... but these were the only ones intact. D'you know what they are?
MIRANA Do you?
CREWMAN Coffins, we reckoned.
MIRANA Coffins?
CREWMAN You know – what they used to put dead people in. The smashed up ones we found... well, there was bodies in all of them. Skeletons, really.
Distant tapping.
MIRANA Sssh!
CREWMAN What's that?
MIRANA It's coming from one of these containers. Hold on...
She gets out a scanner from her pocket. Rustle of material. Tracking bleep.
MIRANA I'm getting a life reading.
CREWMAN From which one?
MIRANA That one... There.
Comms bleep.
MARBER (*Distort*) Control Deck to Captain.
MIRANA Hang fire, Marber. I'm busy.
MARBER (*Distort*) Ma'am, our long-range scanners indicate the fleet has engaged the enemy.
MIRANA (*Concentrating on her scanner*) Very well, Mr Marber. But that's their problem. Have we received new orders?
MARBER (*Distort. Reluctant*) Well... no.
MIRANA Then there's nothing we can do to help.
Comms bleep.
MIRANA Crewman... let's get this thing open.
CREWMAN Right. This looks like the door release. But shouldn't we get security to –
MIRANA Open it!
Clunk, hiss and screech of pod opening... [end of draft]

DALEK WAR CHAPTER ONE

Prologue.

KALENDORF   And now we're alone. Do you understand me?
DALEK   I... understand.
KALENDORF   I don't want anything from you. I'm just going to touch your casing... tell you something... with my mind. I have something you want. Something you *need*.
Crash in theme tune.

1. Int. Planet Velyshaa. Saloran's Ship.
SALORAN is a woman. TARKOV is a man. (This section consists of extracts from a scene in Chapter Four. *It should be recorded as the full scene in* Chapter Four *and edited into the form in which it appears here.)*

TARKOV   A... Dalek? What's a 'Dalek'?
SALORAN   They were a military power from another galaxy. Back in Kalendorf's time, they invaded.
TARKOV   (*Incredulous*) Invaded the entire galaxy?
SALORAN   Yes.
TARKOV   And that's what caused the Great Catastrophe...
SALORAN   Not exactly.
TARKOV   Then what?
SALORAN   Computer, commence playback. Look at the screen.
COMPUTER   Playback commencing.[1]
Buzz of computer activity.
TARKOV   What...? What am I looking at?
SALORAN   A sort of decoding of some of the earliest images I experienced in the burial chamber.

TARKOV   Those are spacecraft... Enormous spacecraft, moving between star systems at incredible speed. And planets... huge populations... cities... cities full of people, creatures.[2]
Crossfade into the image. The sounds of stardrives. Bustling crowds. A brief clip of Vega News from Invasion of the Daleks.[3] *Crossfade back to... Pause.*
SALORAN   You said you wanted to know everything I'd discovered.
TARKOV   Yes.
(Appropriate clips from Dalek Empire *fade in and out of the background during this.)*
SALORAN   It's hard to believe, I know. But this is what the galaxy was like back then. The Earth Alliance had established peace... until the Daleks invaded. When they did, Kalendorf was caught in the middle of it.[4]
Fade in some of the Dalek attack on Vega VI in background.
SALORAN   Somehow he became involved with an Earth woman called Suz. They were captured by the Daleks and, it seems, agreed to work for them. Kalendorf felt he had betrayed everything he believed in, just for the sake of survival. With his help, the Daleks continued their ruthless subjugation of the civilised worlds. It's not clear what the nature of his feelings for Suz were, but there was a special bond between them. The years passed. Kalendorf and Suz continued with their betrayal. Then one day, the Daleks killed Suz. This may have been the trigger for Kalendorf to turn against the Daleks. We don't know for sure. The Daleks had successfully conquered the galaxy, but against all the odds, he apparently led a rebellion against them. It looked like the rebellion might succeed; but the Daleks had a secret strategy. Somehow they had the means to create a dimensional gateway into an alternative universe. And from that universe, they intended to gain the wisdom and the power to rule the entire cosmos. They would join forces with an invincible Dalek army from another dimension.
Extract from final scene of Project Infinity.
SALORAN   But that alliance was not to be. A terrible war between the two Dalek factions began, with Kalendorf and his trusted lieutenants, Alby Brook and Mirana, rallying the rebel humans to fight on the side of the Daleks from the other universe. Kalendorf had swapped sides again. And once again, as the years passed, he was to realise the route to victory and peace would not be an easy one.

2. Int. Flagship *Courageous.*
A huge explosion. Cries of wounded crew members. An alarm sounds. Other explosions continue throughout.

ALTERNATE DALEK Alliance Fleet now under attack. Heavy fire from Enemy Dalek forces advancing from Earth's Solar System.
KALENDORF Well, we knew they weren't going to give it up without a fight. Patch me through to all Alliance ships in the area.
ALTERNATE DALEK I obey.
Comms beep.
KALENDORF *(Rousing speech)* This is Fleet Commander Kalendorf aboard Flagship *Courageous*. This is the beginning of the final battle. It's the culmination of a long, hard fight... and I know that all of you have suffered. We've all lost friends and loved ones. And there's much hard

fighting still to come. But we and our Dalek allies are on the brink of victory. This is the largest Alliance fleet ever assembled. Remember that. Earth's Solar System is the Enemy Daleks' last stronghold. When we beat them here, we will be rid of them... forever. Good luck to you all.
Comms beep.
KALENDORF Signal the attack to all flotillas.
ALTERNATE DALEK I obey.
Signalling FX.
KALENDORF Increase speed to maximum. Open fire, main armament.
Low rumble of engines fades in and slowly rises in pitch.
ALTERNATE DALEK Speed increasing.
Huge report of ship's guns firing.
ALTERNATE DALEK Main armament firing.
KALENDORF (*To himself*) This is it.
Firing continues.

3. Int. Planet Velyshaa. Saloran's Ship.
(This scene is not part of Chapter Four and should be recorded as it appears here.)

TARKOV So now... Kalendorf was loyal to these... other Daleks?
SALORAN He was... for a time. But it seems he had given other orders to Mirana and Alby. Orders that he hoped and believed his Dalek allies did not know about.[5]

4. Int. Scout-Ship *Defiant*. Bridge.
Chatter of bridge activity.

MARBER But, Captain Mirana, these co-ordinates... They put us on a course *away* from the main advance.
MIRANA I'm aware of that, but those are our orders.
MARBER But... I don't understand.
MIRANA I'm not asking you to understand, Mr Marber. I'm expecting you to carry out the orders given to us by the fleet commander.
MARBER Perhaps there's been a mistake.
MIRANA (*Cold*) There is no mistake.

5. Int. Gunship *MX4*.
Engines wind down.

DRUDGER Alby Brook, we have reached our designated co-ordinates.
ALBY Thank you, Drudger. (*Overly innocent*) Any ships in the area by any chance?
DRUDGER No Enemy Dalek ships.
ALBY That's not what I asked.
DRUDGER One Alliance cargo freighter.
ALBY Let's have a look at her.
Screen activation FX.
DRUDGER On screen. Cargo Freighter *Omega N7*.
ALBY Forward guns. Target their transmitter array and engines.
DRUDGER I must point out that Cargo Freighter *Omega N7* is an Alliance ship and as such is under our protection.

ALBY   Well, let's give her a bit of friendly fire, shall we? Are the transmitter array and engines targeted?
Targeting bleeps.
DRUDGER   Confirmed.
ALBY   Just a short burst, please. Fire.
Guns firing. Crackle of explosions on screen.
ALBY   Report.
DRUDGER   Cargo Freighter *Omega N7* transmitter array and engines destroyed.
ALBY   Any crew on board?
DRUDGER   Two Alliance Dalek drones.
ALBY   Just as I thought. Well... they shouldn't give us too much trouble, should they?

6. Int. Flagship *Courageous*. Bridge.
Sounds of explosions on screen. Alarms sounding. Chatter of technicians, human and Alliance Dalek.

TECH 1   Energy levels holding. Generator pod 7 signals coolant requirements increasing. Allocate 10 per cent coolant increase to pod 7.
More background 'techno-babble' lines.
ALTERNATE DALEK Alliance Fleet attack formation holding. No casualties.
KALENDORF Enemy Dalek casualties?
ALTERNATE DALEK Three ships disabled. One destroyed.
KALENDORF (*To himself*) All rather modest... so far. (*To DALEK*) Project the holographic battle plan, please.
ALTERNATE DALEK I obey.
Holographic projector FX.
KALENDORF Wait a minute... What's that? There.
Holographic zoom FX.
ALTERNATE DALEK Focusing on that grid reference.
A tiny bleeping alarm.
ALTERNATE DALEK Additional Enemy Dalek forces located.
KALENDORF They're despatching a reserve flotilla to outflank us from above and below.
Bleep of holographic FX.
ALTERNATE DALEK Agreed. I will deploy our rear attack force to 360 degree defence co-ordinates.
KALENDORF (*To himself*) There's a good boy. Well done.
Bleeping of signals received.
ALTERNATE DALEK Scanners indicate that a second wave of Enemy Dalek ships will outnumber our fleet.
KALENDORF (*Coldly*) I know... I know. But they're not here yet, are they? Let's give the enemy a bloody nose before we even think about retreating.
ALTERNATE DALEK Bloody nose?
KALENDORF We currently outnumber their first wave, agreed?
ALTERNATE DALEK Agreed.
KALENDORF So let's exploit our temporary advantage.
ALTERNATE DALEK Understood.
Bleep of signal.

ALTERNATE DALEK You are summoned to receive a communiqué from the Mentor.

KALENDORF (*Disgruntled sigh to himself. Then...*) Very well. Continue with the attack. Press it home until you receive further orders from me. I won't be long.

ALTERNATE DALEK I obey.

KALENDORF's footsteps. Door opens and closes. The chatter of the bridge is immediately cut off as he walks along a metallic corridor. He stops.

KALENDORF Security clearance: Kalendorf.

Scanning FX.

SCANNER Voice and retinal recognition. Kalendorf. You may enter executive communication chamber.

Door opens.

7. Int. Flagship *Courageous*. Executive Communication Chamber.

Footsteps as KALENDORF enters chamber. Door closes.

ALTERNATE DALEK (*Distort*) Holographic transmission commencing.

Holographic transmission FX. The MENTOR's voice is female, lightly brushed with a Dalek-like effect.

MENTOR Please forgive me for interrupting you at such a moment.

KALENDORF (*Over-practised politeness*) That is your right, Mentor.

MENTOR And I do so enjoy our conversations. I find them... stimulating.

KALENDORF Well... I'm glad, Mentor.

MENTOR We have come a long way, together, have we not?

KALENDORF Indeed.

MENTOR Many years of war. And now we stand upon the brink of victory. A victory for galactic peace.

KALENDORF The battle has not been won yet.

MENTOR Ah, you are as cautious as always. It is a quality I admire in you, Kalendorf. (*Warmly*) Have I not told you that before?

KALENDORF You have told me many times, Mentor.

MENTOR Of course. I am teasing you. That is the action of a friend, would you agree?

KALENDORF (*Caught a little off-guard*) Er... Yes, yes, I suppose it is.

MENTOR And we *are* friends, are we not, Kalendorf?

KALENDORF (*Carefully*) We have been allies for some years now.

MENTOR I see you are cautious even with your friendship.

KALENDORF As you say, Mentor. It is a quality for which you admire me.

MENTOR And your intellect. I admire your cleverness. It has won us many battles. Battles that my Daleks would not otherwise have won.

KALENDORF You are too kind.

MENTOR No.

Pause.

KALENDORF ...is there anything in particular I can assist you with... Mentor?

Pause.

MENTOR I see you are anxious to return to commanding the battle. That is understandable. But please do not be anxious. My monitors tell me that our attack is succeeding. The Enemy Daleks have suffered further casualties. There is only minor damage to the spearhead of our fleet.

KALENDORF   I'm relieved to hear it. But you're right, I am anxious to return to the bridge, so unless there's –

MENTOR   I am intrigued that you are aware of the second wave of enemy ships, but have made no provision to counter them.

Pause.

KALENDORF   I am... gratified at the Mentor's interest in my strategy. My intention is to inflict the maximum amount of damage possible on the Enemy Daleks' primary attack force, which we currently out-gun and outnumber. I calculate that *our* reinforcements will have arrived before their second wave engages us.

MENTOR   There is a high element of risk in your strategy.

KALENDORF   There is always risk.

Pause. During this, we become aware of KALENDORF's breathing. It is, perhaps, just a little too controlled.

MENTOR   You are my Fleet Commander, Kalendorf. I trust you.

KALENDORF   (*About to leave*) Thank you, Mentor.

MENTOR   I look forward to further stimulating conversations with you.

KALENDORF   Of course. Now, if you'd be kind enough to excuse me, I must –

MENTOR   Forgive me, I feel somewhat foolish troubling you with such a trivial matter, but I find myself wondering if you are aware of the plight of Cargo Freighter *Omega N7*.

KALENDORF   Cargo Freighter...? No, I'm afraid I've been too concerned with military matters to –

MENTOR   My monitors tell me that Cargo Freighter *Omega N7* has come under attack. Indications are that it has been destroyed.

KALENDORF   What was its last known position?

MENTOR   Please observe the star map.

Holographic FX. A bleep.

MENTOR   Here.

KALENDORF   That's several star systems away from Earth. I haven't received any reports from that sector for some time.

MENTOR   Were you aware of Enemy Dalek activity in that sector?

KALENDORF   No, but –

MENTOR   It seems odd that one of our freighters could be attacked so far from Earth's Solar System, when we know that all Enemy Dalek forces are now concentrated in that system.

KALENDORF   As I was about to point out, Mentor... with respect... There are still isolated enemy raiding ships scattered throughout the galaxy. Although their survival is regrettable, your own battle computers assess that they are not a significant threat. And I might add that I agree with that assessment.

MENTOR   No doubt the crew of Cargo Freighter *Omega N7* would not so readily agree. You may go.

Ominous music cue.

KALENDORF   (*Trying not to sound troubled*) Thank you, Mentor.

Footsteps as KALENDORF heads for the door. Door opens and closes as he leaves. Music builds.

8. Int. Scout-Ship *Defiant*. Bridge.

Engines wind down.

MARBER   Bridge to Captain Mirana. We have reached our... designated co-ordinates.

MIRANA   (*Distort*) Thank you, Marber. I want a full scan of the immediate area.

MARBER   Scan commencing, Captain.

Scanning FX begin and continue. Door opens. MIRANA's footsteps as she enters the bridge.

MIRANA   (*Approaching*) Have you found anything?

MARBER   Are you expecting to find something out here in the middle of nowhere?

A tiny bleeping alarm.

MIRANA   What's that?

Burble of readout.

MARBER   Space debris. Looks like the remains of a ship. Maybe a freighter.

MIRANA   One of ours?

MARBER   Yes... scan confirms that.

MIRANA   Within signalling distance?

MARBER   It's just debris.

MIRANA   There may be survivors. Activate a comms beam.

Comms beep.

MARBER   Activated.

MIRANA   This is Captain Mirana of the Alliance Scout-Ship *Defiant*. Please respond in any way if you can hear this.[6]

Pause.

MARBER   We're now closing. I can give you a visual.

MIRANA   Do it.

Screen activates. Music cue of doom.

MARBER   Er... I don't think there are going to be any survivors.

MIRANA   What are those things? There...

MARBER   Looks like the cargo... Container pods spilled out over a thousand kilometres of deep space and spreading.

MIRANA   Well... waste not, want not. Activate the forward grappling arms. Let's bring those pods aboard.

Scanning FX.

MIRANA   What are you doing?

MARBER   Scanning them. We want to know *what* we're bringing aboard, don't we? I mean, it could be toxic waste, or something equally nasty.

MIRANA   Not very likely.

Scan negative beep.

MIRANA   What does it read?

MARBER   Er... nothing. Absolutely nothing. Like they're deliberately shielded from scanning. Perhaps it would be best just to log a report, tag them with a nav buoy and leave them out here.

MIRANA   Your concern is noted, Mr Marber. But I'd like you to bring them aboard as soon as possible.

MARBER   But – [7]

MIRANA   – As soon as possible, Mr Marber.

9. Int. Gunship *MX4*.

DRUDGER   Do you wish a change of recreational image on the holographic projector?

ALBY   (*His mind elsewhere*) Hmm? What?

DRUDGER   You have been looking at this image for precisely three hours, fifty-six minutes and thirteen seconds.

ALBY   (*Mocking*) Thirteen seconds, eh?

DRUDGER   Fourteen seconds.

ALBY   Don't get cheeky, mate. Anyway, it's none of your business who or what I choose to look at.

DRUDGER   I am concerned for the mental well-being and efficiency of the human occupant of this craft. The human mind needs stimulation in order to stay alert. There are a variety of images in the ship's databanks which might more usefully engage your – [8]

ALBY   Oh yeah? And what's wrong with this one?

DRUDGER   The face of Susan Mendes may be aesthetically pleasing to you, but a view of the L'Garshoo Nebula, for instance, might –

ALBY   Woah, wait... what the hell do *you* know about Susan Mendes? That's a private image I loaded into the ship's computer just before we set.[9]

DRUDGER   A similar likeness is logged in current Alliance security dispatches. 'Susan Mendes, humanoid from planet Vega VI subjected to conversion processes by Enemy Dalek forces. Processing deemed too far advanced for reversal, by decree of the Mentor. All such humanoids have been scheduled for destruction by –'

ALBY   (*Losing his temper*) Shut it! Just shut up! (*Recovers*) I know all that. Deactivate image.

Image deactivation FX.

ALBY   Any news on the battle?

DRUDGER   Now monitoring fleet transmission frequencies at long range.

Burble and static of frequencies monitored. They continue to burble.

DRUDGER   Indications are that Alliance forces are inflicting severe losses on the Enemy Dalek fleet.

ALBY   (*To himself*) Well done, Karl. Ever the cosummate professional.

A sudden, insistent pulse breaks through the burbling.

ALBY   What's that?

DRUDGER   An unidentified signal from another source.

ALBY   Isolate it.

All other burble and static fades, to leave the one insistent pulse.

ALBY   Where's that coming from?

The signal stops abruptly.

DRUDGER   Transmission has ceased.

ALBY   All right, where *was* it coming from?

DRUDGER   Attempting to locate.

Locator FX bleeps.

DRUDGER   Co-ordinates 0923491274/9834-3874.

ALBY   Is that far from here?

DRUDGER   At extreme range, in the Pkowik System.

ALBY   How long to get there at maximum speed?

DRUDGER   Three solar days. But what would be the purpose of locating the source of this unidentified signal – ?

ALBY	It isn't unidentified. I know what it is.
DRUDGER	Please elaborate.
ALBY	Set a course for those co-ordinates and don't be so nosy.

10. Int. Scout-Ship *Defiant*. Cargo Bay.
A large crane lowers a pod. It hits the deck with a metallic clank.

MIRANA	Is that the last of them?
CREWMAN	Yes, Captain.
MIRANA	How many pods are there?
CREWMAN	Er... about sixty or so... I think. Sorry, I didn't know you wanted them counted, ma'am.
MIRANA	Very well, crewman. You may go.
CREWMAN	Ma'am.

He walks off into distance. A door opens and closes in the background as he leaves.

MIRANA	(*To herself*) Now then...

A rustle in her pocket. She handles something plastic. A click of a switch. A bleeping sound.

MIRANA	Where exactly are you?

Footsteps. The bleeping continues.

MARBER	Captain?
MIRANA	(*Sharp intake of breath*) Marber!

The bleeper is hastily switched off.

MIRANA	What are you doing here?
MARBER	I was curious. If I didn't know better, I'd say you were looking for something in particular.
MIRANA	If you didn't know better.
MARBER	Do you know what's in these pods, Captain? Did you know they'd be out here?
MIRANA	Mr Marber. I see that your commendable curiosity has gotten the better of you.
MARBER	Captain, I feel it's my duty to –
MIRANA	(*Bluffing*) Mr Marber... I'm afraid I can't discuss my top-secret orders with you.
MARBER	'Top-secret'?
MIRANA	Yes. Classified. For my eyes only.
MARBER	But I'm your first officer. I'm usually –
MIRANA	(*Trying to humour him*) I know, Marber, I know. And believe you me, I would like to take such a trusted officer as your good self into my confidence, but... (*Trails off*)
MARBER	I understand, Captain.
MIRANA	There is one thing you can do for me, though, Marber.
MARBER	Yes, Captain?
MIRANA	I'm expecting to rendezvous with another ship in the next few hours. I need you on the bridge to make sure we don't miss that rendezvous. (*Pause*) If you'd be so kind.
MARBER	(*A little flustered*) Er... yes, of course, Captain. Of course. I'm sorry to have... er... sorry if I've in any way –
MIRANA	It's okay, Marber. I appreciate your concern. But I just need you to be on the bridge right now.
MARBER	Yes, Captain.

He walks off. The door opens and shuts as he leaves. Comms beep.
MIRANA   Dr Johnstone.
JOHNSTONE   (*Distort*) Yes, Captain?
MIRANA   I need you down here in the cargo bay. Right away. It's
time.
JOHNSTONE   (*Distort*) Understood. On my way now.
Comms bleep.
MIRANA   Now... where was I?
*The bleeping of her tracker clicks on again. She walks slowly. Music
begins to build. Suddenly, the tracker bleeps excitedly.*
MIRANA   Aha! And there you are. Not long now...
Musical crescendo.

11. Int. Earth. Enemy Dalek Control.
Classic Dalek door opens and closes.

DALEK SUPREME Susan Mendes must be located!
DALEKS   We obey!!!
DALEK SUPREME Order our raiding party in the Pkowik System to
proceed with phase two of their mission now that they have completed
their primary task.
DALEK   Our signals beyond the Earth's Solar System are being
jammed by the attacking Alliance forces, but all indications are that our
raiding party will now proceed to locate their secondary target.
DALEK SUPREME Susan Mendes *must* be located!!! Report status of the
Alliance attack on this solar system.[10]
DALEK 1   Our defence fleet is suffering heavy losses. It will be
totally annihilated before our second wave is in position to engage Human
Alliance fleet.[11]
DALEK 2   By that time, the Alliance fleet will be reinforced.
DALEK SUPREME Will our second wave be defeated?
DALEK 1   Our battle computers predict a 60 per cent probability of
defeat for our forces.
DALEK SUPREME Satisfactory. Kalendorf's fleet must not enter this
solar system before our work here is completed. Is that understood?
DALEKS   Understood.
DALEK SUPREME The retrieval of our Emperor is of foremost
importance. All other concerns are secondary. Only the Emperor can attain
victory for the Daleks. Victory for the Daleks! Victory for the Daleks!
DALEKS   (*Joining in*) Victory for the Daleks! Victory for the Daleks!
Victory for the Daleks! Victory for the Daleks!

12. Int. Scout-Ship *Defiant*. Cargo Bay.
*Cutting equipment is burning into metal – much 'screeching' and spraying
of sparks. Cutting equipment then winds down.*

MIRANA   Phew. That should do it. (*Noises of effort as she shifts it*)
A huge 'clunk' as the top of a pod falls to the deck.
JOHNSTONE   That was pretty heavy-duty casing all right.
MIRANA   Yeah.
JOHNSTONE   I'm surprised your scanner was able to read through all
that.

MIRANA   It wasn't. The pod was particle-tagged for us before the freighter set off.
JOHNSTONE   Lucky.
MIRANA   Luck doesn't come into it, Doctor. We've been planning this for months. Can you get the inner container open?
JOHNSTONE   Hmmm... Looks like a fairly standard cryogenic pod. I'll need to take it to the infirmary first. Get me one of those grav-pads, would you, please?
MIRANA   (*Frustrated*) But... Can't we just open it here?
JOHNSTONE   I have to equalise the temperature first, Mirana. And we'll need a full revival kit on hand in case... Well, we don't know exactly how long the patient's been under and what side effects there might be.

13. Int. Gunship *MX4*.
Engines at full power.

DRUDGER   We are now approaching the Pkowik System.
ALBY   Good. Before you make me some more coffee... anything on the long-range scanners? Any sign of that transmission again?
DRUDGER   Negative on both counts. Energy scans are being inhibited by the proximity of an uncharted particle cloud.
ALBY   Particle cloud? What's one of those?
DRUDGER   'Particle cloud' is a generic term for any spatial phenomenon on which there is no adequate information.
ALBY   In other words, something you know nothing about is stopping us from finding out what's in this system?
DRUDGER   Correct.
ALBY   Let's try the old-fashioned way, then. Maximum magnification on visual.[12]
Visual magnification FX.
ALBY   Right... now... I'm guessing that's the particle cloud.
DRUDGER   Correct.
ALBY   Blimey, how big *is* that thing?
DRUDGER   I estimate approximately three million cubic kilometres in mass.
ALBY   That's... er... big. How come it's uncharted?
DRUDGER   Unknown.
ALBY   All right... Now, pan left a bit.[13]
Visual scan FX.
ALBY   Down a bit – Woah! Stop! What's that? Can we get in closer?[14]
DRUDGER   We are closing on the Pkowik System as we speak, but further visual enhancement is not possible.
ALBY   It looks... artificial?
DRUDGER   Visual configuration suggests a large, manufactured object or collection of objects.
ALBY   (*Musing*) A space station or something like that... (*To himself*) Damn, damn, damn... This is bleedin' important, isn't it?
DRUDGER   Please elaborate.
ALBY   Never mind, Drudger... Never mind. Right. Well... (*To himself*) Sorry, Mirana, but you're just going to have to wait for me. (*To DRUDGER*) Alter course to head directly for it.

DRUDGER   Confirmed.
ALBY   Maybe that's where the signal came from.
DRUDGER   I would be in a better position to give an answer if you informed me of the nature of the signal.
ALBY   Nosy parker.
DRUDGER   Please elaborate. The signal emanates from a 'Nosy Parker'?
ALBY   Huh. Well, I suppose there's no harm in telling you. That signal was a distress call from the Emperor of the Daleks.

14. Int. Scout-Ship *Defiant.* Infirmary.
Medical equipment bleeping.

JOHNSTONE   Pressure and temperature equalisation of the cryogenic pod in... (*reading it off a display*) thirty-four seconds.
MIRANA   (*Edgy*) Is that revival kit ready?
JOHNSTONE   It's ready. Don't worry.
Comms bleep.
MIRANA   Captain to bridge. Marber?
MARBER   (*Distort*) Captain. Still no sign of that rendezvous ship.
MIRANA   Even at long range?
MARBER   (*Distort*) Nothing at all, ma'am.
MIRANA   (*Frustrated sigh*) Thank you, Mr Marber.
Comms bleep off.
JOHNSTONE   Twenty-two seconds.
A clunk and hiss. Little alarms buzz excitedly.
JOHNSTONE   Clamps releasing.
MIRANA   Is that *supposed* to be happening?
JOHNSTONE   I think so.
MIRANA   You're never certain about anything, are you, Johnstone?
JOHNSTONE   I find it's the best policy. Nothing in the universe is ever certain. Nine seconds.
MIRANA   Are you certain about that?
JOHNSTONE   Relatively. Five, four, three, two, one.
A final clunk. A whirr of the pod opening. Hissing of cold gas escaping.
JOHNSTONE   Pod opening.
MIRANA   I noticed that.[15]
Pause as the hissing subsides.
MIRANA   Is... is she alive?
Burble of medical equipment.
JOHNSTONE   It would seem so.
SUZ exhales.
JOHNSTONE   I don't think we're going to need the revival kit. (*Suddenly alarmed*) Er... what are you doing?
A gun cocks.
MIRANA   Taking precautions.
JOHNSTONE   I don't really approve of guns in my infirmary.
MIRANA   I take it you'd be even less approving of an Enemy Dalek agent trying to throttle you?
JOHNSTONE   Is that what she is?
MIRANA   As you say, Doctor... Nothing in the universe is ever certain.

JOHNSTONE (*Dubious*) Very amusing. Would you like me to wake her up or administer a lethal injection?
MIRANA (*Frustrated sigh*)
JOHNSTONE What's the matter?
MIRANA (*Preoccupied*) I was hoping Alby would be here by now.
JOHNSTONE I must warn you that any delay might cause cerebral degradation.
MIRANA Then you'd better get on with it. (*To herself*) Sorry, Alby.
JOHNSTONE Right... Here we go.
Hypo-injection FX. SUZ gives a sudden gasp and exhales loudly. She breathes in and out, apparently agitated. Medical equipment lets out a little bleeping alarm.
JOHNSTONE Blood pressure and heart rate rising a little.
MIRANA Is she going to be all right?
JOHNSTONE She's... a little agitated, it would seem. Try talking to her.
MIRANA Suz? Susan. It's all right. You're safe now.
Her agitated breathing continues. She starts to murmur in distress, as if having a nightmare. The medical equipment alarms increase in intensity.
JOHNSTONE She's going into shock.
MIRANA Is there anything you can do?
JOHNSTONE I'm not sure. If I knew the exact nature of the process she's undergone, I might... but as it is, if I take a chance... it might be fatal.
MIRANA Great. (*Determined*) Susan! Susan! Listen to me! Wake up! Wake – up!
SUZ's breathing suddenly stops. The medical alarms stop.
MIRANA Oh my God, what have I done?
Burble of medical equipment.
JOHNSTONE (*Incredulous*) I think you've done it.
MIRANA Done what?
JOHNSTONE Everything's returned to normal.
MIRANA Susan?
SUZ (*As in her death scene*) Nooooooo!!!

(*End of promo CD for* **DW**M.)[16]

15. Int. Saloran's Ship. Planet Velyshaa.

TARKOV (*Incredulous*) So Kalendorf was prepared to risk everything... just to recover this Susan Mendes.
SALORAN Yes. She was important to him... in many ways.
TARKOV Seems that he was quite fond of switching sides, doesn't it?
SALORAN He was a pragmatist.
TARKOV An opportunist, you mean?
SALORAN (*Solemn*) No... no, I don't think so. I think he always knew what he had to do.

16. Int. Flagship *Courageous*. Bridge.
Distorted sounds of the continuing space battle in the background. Chatter of bridge activity. An alarm bleeps. (KALENDORF is tense, worrying about the situation with SUZ, MIRANA and ALBY.)

KALENDORF (*Agitated*) Mr Herrick! What's happening?
HERRICK Our left lower flank are slipping out of formation, sir.
KALENDORF (*Tense*) What's the matter with them? Have you signalled them?
HERRICK Er, several times, sir. But they *are* coming under heavy fire.
KALENDORF What have we got down there? Mainly Dalek drone ships?
HERRICK Er... yes, sir. The battleship *Repulse* has had to withdraw for repairs to her main drive.
KALENDORF (*More confidential*) That's the trouble with those drones. With their human sector commander gone, they lose the power of initiative.
HERRICK They're still giving the Enemy Daleks a good pounding, sir.
KALENDORF Yes... yes... Very well. I suppose we can't ask for any more than that. But – but keep an eye on them, Herrick![17]
HERRICK Yes, sir. I will, sir.
KALENDORF (*Lost in troubled thoughts*) Good... good.
HERRICK Are you all right, sir?
KALENDORF Hm? What? Yes. Yes, I'm... all right.
Crossfade to:

17. Int. Mentor's Chamber.
The sounds of the Courageous's bridge distorted as if on a screen.

MENTOR (*To herself. Suspicions growing*) You seem troubled, Kalendorf. More troubled than I have ever seen you before.

18. Int. Gunship *MX4*.

ALBY Is it just my wishful thinking, Drudger, or have we cleared the influence of that particle cloud?
DRUDGER You are largely correct, Alby Brook. Scanners are now returning to near normal levels of efficiency.
ALBY Let's have another butcher's at that space station thing, then.
DRUDGER Confirmed. Scanning.
ALBY Anything?
DRUDGER Readings suggest a structure conforming to Alliance Dalek design.
ALBY Life signs?
DRUDGER Minimal and unclear. The particle cloud is still exerting some influence.
ALBY Well, they haven't challenged us yet, so – 'ere, wait a sec, what's that? It looks like they've been in a fight.
DRUDGER Structural damage of the type caused by Enemy Dalek firepower. Some loss of atmospheric integrity detected.
ALBY Oh, God. Any Enemy Dalek readings?
DRUDGER No such readings, although the particle cloud is still exerting –
ALBY – 'some influence', yeah, thanks.
Pause.
DRUDGER What action do you wish to take?
ALBY I'm thinking, aren't I?!

DRUDGER   Apologies.
ALBY   (*Sighs*) Well, I suppose I've gone to the trouble of coming all the way out here... Mirana will be worrying herself to death wondering where I am. I'd better make it count for something. Let's break out the atmos suit. I'm going aboard.

19. Int. Scout-Ship *Defiant*. Infirmary.
Door opens and closes. Footsteps as MIRANA enters.

MIRANA   How is she?
JOHNSTONE   As you see... up and about. Seemingly healthy enough. But not at all communicative.
MIRANA   Not a word?
JOHNSTONE   Not a word.
MIRANA   Could her mind have been affected? Don't tell me, you're not sure.
JOHNSTONE   It seems unlikely, given the readings.
Footsteps.
MIRANA   Susan? How are you feeling? (*Pause*) Susan, I'm a friend.
SUZ   Then how is it I don't remember you?
MIRANA   (*Taken aback*) We... we never met.[18]
SUZ   Then how can you be a friend?
JOHNSTONE   She's got a point.
MIRANA   (*Irritated*) Doctor, please... just leave this to me, would you? (*After a deep breath*) Susan... or may I call you Suz? (Pause) Alby was supposed to be here. Do you remember Alby?
SUZ   This is a trick, isn't it? This is some kind of trick. You're working for the Daleks, aren't you?
MIRANA   No. We're not working for the Daleks. We're not working for either faction.[19]
SUZ   Faction? What do you mean?
MIRANA   (*Sighs*) Later...[20]
JOHNSTONE   Are you hungry? (*Pause*) You must be hungry. It's perfectly normal after –
SUZ   I won't take anything from you! (Pause) What do you mean, 'it's perfectly normal'?[21]
JOHNSTONE   For someone who's been in cryo-sleep.
SUZ   Cryo...? You mean... I've been in hibernation?
MIRANA   Yes. For a few years now.
SUZ   How many years?
MIRANA   Five... nearly six, I think. Is it?
JOHNSTONE   Yes. Nearly six years.
SUZ   How can I possibly know if you're friends or not?
MIRANA   Frankly, I don't know. If Alby was here –
SUZ   Alby? What do you know about Alby? Is he even real? I can't think straight. What I sense... in my mind... It's like a nightmare. (*In quiet terror*) A nightmare... I remember... A ship crashed. On Vega. A ship... A huge explosion. Destroyed so much of the city. Alby... Yes, Alby was there... on the boat. Then at the spaceport. He said we had to go. I wouldn't. Mum and Dad. I couldn't leave them. He said they were already dead.
She begins to cry.

211

SUZ   I hated him for that.
MIRANA   (*Trying to comfort*) Suz...?
SUZ   I HATED HIM! I hated Alby... (*More tears*) Did he kill them? Did he kill them by saying that? Are they dead? Are my Mum and Dad dead? Tell me! If you say you are my friends, you'd tell me, wouldn't you? TELL ME!!!
She sobs for a few moments. Her sobbing subsides.
SUZ   Is Alby dead too?
MIRANA   No.
SUZ   I don't hate him.
MIRANA   I know. He loves you.
SUZ   I know.

20. Int. Hospital Station. Airlock Reception.
Airlock door closes.

ALBY   (*Helmet distort*) I'm reading pressurisation. Safe to take off the atmos helmet?
DRUDGER   (*Distort*) You have entered a pressurised section of the space station. You may proceed.
ALBY removes his space helmet.
ALBY   Ah... that's better... Let me get my torch on.
Click of torch activated.
ALBY   There's a lot of blast damage here. Some Dalek wreckage. (*Nervously*) I take it you're still not picking up any life signs?
DRUDGER   (*Distort*) Confirmed. Which Dalek faction does the wreckage belong to?
ALBY   Er... I think it's Alliance Daleks... no, wait a minute.
He shifts some metallic debris.
ALBY   I think it's both. There's been a battle between Dalek factions here. Hang on... and there are human bodies too. God, it was a massacre.
DRUDGER   (*Distort*) I am detecting movement.
ALBY   Where? What sort of movement?
DRUDGER   (*Distort*) Movement within the space station. I am unable to discern what is causing the movement.
ALBY   (*Scared*) Oh, God, there's something in here with me.
A metallic crashing in the distance.

21. Int. Earth. Enemy Dalek Control.
Much distortion and explosions over the distorted line.

DALEK COM (*Distort*) Dalek solar defence fleet to Dalek Supreme Command on Earth. Am making urgent situation report.
DALEK SUPREME This is the Dalek Supreme. Proceed with your report!
DALEK COM (*Distort*) We have been defeated. The Alliance fleet is breaking through into the solar system on all fronts. Requesting permission to withdraw.
DALEK SUPREME Permission denied.
DALEK COM (*Distort*) Reinforcements are urgently required.
DALEK SUPREME Our second wave of ships will arrive at your co-ordinates in one solar day.

DALEK COM (*Distort*) We cannot hold position until that time. We will be exterminated.

DALEK SUPREME Understood. You will link energy fields with all surviving ships from your fleet and instigate special emergency procedures. (*Pause*) Do you understand?

DALEK COM (*Distort*) Understood. We obey.

22. Int. Flagship *Courageous*. Excecutive Communication Chamber.

Door opens. KALENDORF's footsteps approach and stop.

ALTERNATE DALEK (*Distort*) Holographic transmission commencing.
Holographic transmission FX.

MENTOR Congratulations, Kalendorf. It seems that you have broken the Enemy Dalek line ahead of your planned schedule.

KALENDORF It was a calculated risk, but it seems to have paid off.

MENTOR Even in victory, you never lose your caution.

KALENDORF This isn't victory yet. The second wave of Enemy Dalek ships is only one solar day away from us. And if I know the Daleks, they'll have a back-up plan.

MENTOR A back-up plan? And what do you anticipate this plan might be?

KALENDORF I don't –
A huge explosion. An alarm sounds.

ALTERNATE DALEK (*Tannoy*) Emergency! Emergency![22]

KALENDORF What the hell — ?!

MENTOR What is happening? Has your ship been hit?

KALENDORF Kalendorf to bridge! Mr Herrick! Damage report!

HERRICK (*Distort*) Sir... the Enemy Dalek ships are –
Another huge explosion.

23. Int. Scout-Ship *Defiant*. Mirana's Cabin.

Door opens. Footsteps of SUZ and MIRANA enter.

MIRANA This is my cabin. You'll be more comfortable here.

SUZ We're aboard a spaceship then?

MIRANA Yes. The Alliance Scout-Ship *Defiant*. I'm the Captain. Please, sit down... if you like.
Sounds of them sitting.

SUZ Alliance? You mean the Earth Alliance?

MIRANA Let's just take one thing at a time.

SUZ A lot's happened, hasn't it? While I've been asleep, I mean.

MIRANA Yes.

SUZ (*Making sure*) And you say you know Alby?

MIRANA Yes.

SUZ And Karl... Kalendorf?

MIRANA Yes. Karl.

SUZ I don't know if I believe you.

MIRANA That's... understandable.
Pause.

SUZ What about the Daleks?

MIRANA What about them?

SUZ	Are they still in control of the galaxy?
MIRANA	No. Not in the way you mean.
SUZ	(*Snaps*) How do you know what I mean?

Pause. (Flashback clip of Project Infinity – *Suz's 'Death to the Daleks' address – during next speech.)*

SUZ	I remember... I started a rebellion. (*With realisation*)

'Death to the Daleks'. When I said those words... I saw the crowds overpowering my Dalek guards. For a moment, I thought I was going to live.

MIRANA	You did live.
SUZ	But is all that true? Is that what happened?
MIRANA	Yes. We think that they fired a paralysis beam at you and

transmatted you to a Dalek ship in orbit above Yaldos simultaneously.

SUZ	And then put me to sleep?
MIRANA	Yes.
SUZ	Why?
MIRANA	To... store you for future use.
SUZ	Future use? As what?
MIRANA	As a Dalek.
SUZ	But you defeated the Daleks, didn't you? You, Kalendorf

and Alby. Isn't that what happened? Wasn't the rebellion successful?

MIRANA	Almost.
SUZ	(*Confused*) 'Almost'?
MIRANA	For a time.
SUZ	I don't understand. (*Increasingly panicked*) You said the

Daleks weren't in control of the galaxy anymore, at least not in the way I meant... But what do *you* mean? What *has* happened? What sort of galaxy have I woken up in? Why have you woken me up at all? And why has it taken you six years to get round to it?[23]

MIRANA	(*Trying to calm her*) I know... I know... it's difficult.

Please. Will you let me explain from the beginning?

SUZ	(*Snaps*) I don't see... (*Stops herself. Continues, calmer*) I

don't see that I have any other choice. Do you?[24]

MIRANA	No. (*Takes a deep breath*) Right. It's difficult to know

where to start. Your rebellion was successful. All the work you and Kalendorf did over the years... It paid off.

SUZ	(*Moved*) Then it was *worth* it. All those years...
MIRANA	Yes. The Daleks were apparently taken by surprise. The

balance of power shifted very quickly.

SUZ	What do you mean by 'apparently'?
MIRANA	It was a word Kalendorf used a lot after the tide started

to turn against the Daleks. (*Warmly*) You know Kalendorf. Always suspicious. Always cautious. Suspicious when victory comes too easily. He felt that the Daleks were letting us win. And he was right. Their invasion of the galaxy had simply been one enormous distraction tactic. And the rebellion...

SUZ	They knew about that too. Didn't they?
MIRANA	The Emperor did.
SUZ	Then why did he let it happen?
MIRANA	Don't you remember him telling you about Project
Infinity?	
SUZ	Yes... (*Realising*) The Seer of Yaldos told you this, didn't
she?	

214

MIRANA	Yes. Just as you wanted her to.
SUZ	(*Remembering*) Project Infinity... He said the Daleks would have infinite possibilities at their disposal. Was that true?
MIRANA	So he thought. So *we* thought.
SUZ	What was Project Infinity?
MIRANA	Originally, it was set up by the Earth Alliance. They wanted to find an alternative universe where humanity had worked out a way to defeat the Daleks for all time... then find out the secret of their success. Somehow – no one is quite sure how – the Daleks found out about Project Infinity. And so they waged war on us simply to get hold of it. Of course, *their* plan was to find a universe where the Daleks were in complete control of everything. But, being Daleks, they wanted to go one step further. They wanted to bring the triumphant, alternative universe Daleks through a gateway into our universe – to use them as an all-conquering army.
SUZ	Did they succeed?
MIRANA	We thought they would.
SUZ	You mean they didn't? What happened?
MIRANA	When we were captured by the Daleks – Kalendorf, Alby and me – we were taken to a massive cryo-chamber aboard the Emperor's ship. It was the same place where you were stored. Like you, we were put into hibernation.
SUZ	To be turned into Daleks?
MIRANA	Yes. So... we certainly weren't expecting to wake up still in... human form. Well, I don't think we were expecting to wake up at all.

Crossfade into flashback sequence:

24. Flashback: Int. Emperor's Ship. Cryo-Chamber.
Three cryo-pods open with a hiss of air and a loud clunk.

MIRANA	(*Exhales, coming round*) Hello? (*Pause*) Anyone out there?
ALBY	(*Distant*) Hello? Mirana? Is that you?

A few footsteps (KALENDORF's).

KALENDORF	(*Dry*) It's both of you... and me.
MIRANA	Kalendorf?

Footsteps as they climb out of their pods. Vocal sounds of effort.

ALBY	What the hell happened? How long have we *been* in these pods?
MIRANA	Feels like they only just put us to sleep.
KALENDORF	That's cryo-sleep for you.
ALBY	Weren't we supposed to wake up as Daleks? I don't feel like a Dalek, do you?
KALENDORF	No.
ALBY	I feel more like breakfast, actually.
KALENDORF	And look... We're the only three who have woken up.
MIRANA	My God, you're right. The rest of them are still asleep.
ALBY	(*Determined*) Suz... that bastard Tanlee said she's here... I've got to find her.
KALENDORF	Wait a minute, Alby.
ALBY	Don't try to stop me.
MIRANA	Alby, there are millions of pods here. You could spend your whole life looking.

ALBY   So?

KALENDORF   So it's pretty clear that something has gone wrong, don't you think?

ALBY   (*Reluctant*) Maybe.

KALENDORF   If Suz really is here, I'm as anxious to find her as you are. Let's just work out what's happened first. Mirana. Are you sensing anything on the Dalek command net?

MIRANA   That's a point.

ALBY   What's a point?

MIRANA   I'm not sensing anything. At all.[25]

ALBY   But you should be, shouldn't you? What with those Dalek implants still in your head.

Door opens.

ALBY   Oh no.

MIRANA   (*Under her breath*) Here comes trouble.

ALBY   For one glorious moment I thought they'd all vanished in a puff of smoke.

KALENDORF   There's something different about them.

ALBY   So what. They've had a respray. They're still probably going to exterminate us.

ALTERNATE DALEK   Are you Alby, Kalendorf and Mirana?

ALBY   No. Wrong room. Sorry. Try down the hallway.

ALTERNATE DALEK   You have nothing to fear from us.

MIRANA   (*Confidentially*) What the hell's wrong with its voice?

KALENDORF   (*Musing*) I don't know...

ALTERNATE DALEK   We have accessed the Enemy Dalek database. Your likenesses match. Alby Brook, Kalendorf and Mirana are identified as the leaders of the human rebellion against the Enemy Daleks.

ALBY   'Enemy Daleks'? Aren't all Daleks enemies?

ALTERNATE DALEK   Enemy Daleks have committed the greatest crimes known to our universe.

MIRANA   My God, they're from the dimensional gateway... Aren't you?

ALTERNATE DALEK   Correct.

ALBY   You mean... the Project Infinity thing?

ALTERNATE DALEK   As you say, the Project Infinity thing.

KALENDORF   What's happened to the other... the Enemy Daleks?

ALTERNATE DALEK   The Mentor will answer all your questions. Please follow.

ALBY   Mentor?

MIRANA   Who's the Mentor?

ALTERNATE DALEK   She is our creator.

ALBY   She?

ALTERNATE DALEK   Yes. She knows all things. She gave us life. She brings peace and understanding.

ALBY   We're still asleep, aren't we? This is just some weird hallucination.

KALENDORF   (*To ALBY*) Let's enjoy it until we wake up. (*Aloud*) Take us to your Mentor.

25. Int. Scout-Ship *Defiant*. Mirana's Cabin.

MIRANA   We were taken to the Mentor. I don't think any of us were prepared for what we saw.

SUZ   What do you mean?

MIRANA   Have you heard the ancient stories about angels?

SUZ   Angels? Huh... I was supposed to be one.[26]

MIRANA   I remember seeing a statue of one on old Earth. That's what this Mentor reminded me of. An angel... but encased in a golden, glowing throne. The technological implants embedded in her skin... they were more like beautiful jewels than cold, Dalek mechanisms. She was inspiring... almost... beautiful.

26. Int. Mentor's Chamber.

Alternate Dalek-style door opens and closes. Footsteps.

MENTOR   You are welcome. Please, approach me.

Footsteps continue and stop.

MENTOR   I am the Mentor. I know you have many questions.

KALENDORF   We've been told you are the Daleks from the other side of the dimensional gateway.

MENTOR   We are.

ALBY   Where are the other Daleks... the ones we were fighting?

MENTOR   We have begun a war with these Enemy Daleks. We have achieved our first victory. They have retreated in some disarray, but we know that they will regroup.

MIRANA   Why are these Daleks your enemies?

MENTOR   Their actions contravene everything the Daleks in our universe stand for.

MIRANA   And what do you stand for?

MENTOR   Peace. Order. And we are the guardians of that peace and order. We protect it with every means and all the force at our disposal. That is why the Daleks were created in our universe.[27]

ALBY   Then... that means that... that you're on our side?

MENTOR   Will you help us to defeat them?

KALENDORF   Will *you* help *us* to defeat them?

MENTOR   I see that we share the same aims. That is good.

27. Int. Scout-Ship *Defiant.* Mirana's Cabin.

SUZ   So you joined forces with these... these new Daleks?

MIRANA   And things went well for us. Kalendorf was put in charge of the fleet. With the extra resources of the new Daleks at his disposal, he was able to cut off the Dalek Supreme's retreat to the Seriphia Galaxy.

SUZ   The Dalek Supreme? What about the Emperor?

MIRANA   The Emperor was captured at the first battle on Lopra Minor... at the dimensional gateway.

SUZ   So he was destroyed.

MIRANA   No... The Mentor hoped to use the Emperor to access the Dalek command net and take control of the Enemy Daleks. Maybe even 'pacify' them, I guess. But as soon as it was captured, the Emperor seemed to just shut himself down.

SUZ   So what did you do?

217

MIRANA   I was put in charge of analysing the Emperor. The Mentor told me to unlock its secrets.
SUZ   Did you succeed?
MIRANA   (*Guarded*) In a way... yes.
SUZ   What's the matter? What did you find out?

28. Int. Mentor's Chamber.

MENTOR   (*Slightly irritated*) Then all you can tell me is that this Emperor is inert.
MIRANA   More or less.
MENTOR   (*Suppressing anger*) More – or – less? That much was obvious from the moment we captured this... *creature*.
KALENDORF   Are you suggesting that Mirana and her team have not done their best, Mentor?
MENTOR   I... (*Restraining herself*) Of course not, Mirana. I apologise for my... strength of feeling in this matter. I had hoped that the Enemy Dalek technology implanted in your mind might give you special insight into the Emperor's cerebral functions.
MIRANA   That was my hope too. I was able to detect a low-level distress signal emanating from the Emperor –
MENTOR   Did you shut it down?
MIRANA   Of course.
MENTOR   I am grateful.
MIRANA   But aside from that... Nothing. The Dalek creature inside the Emperor's casing seems to have undergone a kind of self-induced stasis. Dr Johnstone attempted a surgical solution, but he had no success.
MENTOR   (*Curt*) Then I must thank you for your work.
MIRANA   We have a few other avenues we wish to explore, if –
MENTOR   That will not be necessary. I can see that you have exhausted all meaningful research. We will assign you to other duties.
MIRANA   But...
MENTOR   Please! The matter has been decided.
KALENDORF   I'm sure I can find work for Mirana and –
MENTOR   Very well. That would be most satisfactory. Now, if you will excuse me, I have other pressing matters of importance to attend to.

29. Mirana's Narration.

MIRANA   It was after this that Karl communicated with me telepathically. That's when we discovered that we were both harbouring the same fears about these new Daleks.
Telepathic conversation...
KALENDORF   I'm not sure we can trust them any more.
MIRANA   I'm not sure I've ever trusted them.
KALENDORF   Me neither. On the fleet's return from the Vega System, we detected several planets that had been totally devastated.[28]
MIRANA   Devastated?
KALENDORF   Some of them wiped clean by some sort of neutron attack. Others were reduced to the level of medieval society by the destruction of their industrial and technological infrastructure.
MIRANA   What does that prove? What are you saying?

KALENDORF   These civilisations weren't destroyed by Enemy Daleks. They were all well behind our lines. But I know that some of them had refused to supply troops for the war effort. One of the planets, Emmeron, was wrapped up in its own internal affairs – nuclear war to be precise.

MIRANA   And you think the Mentor ordered their destruction?

KALENDORF   That's the rumour. I think our new Dalek allies are as ruthlessly determined about peace and order as our old enemies were about conquest and subjugation. It seems we may have swapped one dictatorship for another. This one is perhaps a little more benign... but it's a dictatorship nonetheless.

MIRANA   There's... something I didn't tell the Mentor.

KALENDORF   About the Emperor?

MIRANA   You knew?

KALENDORF   I had the sense that you were hiding something.

MIRANA   Do you think *she* did?

Pause.

KALENDORF   I don't know. I don't think she entirely trusts us. (*Lighter*) But that just puts us on an equal footing, doesn't it? So come on, tell me.

MIRANA   It was something that I was able to detect with my implant.

30. Int. Scout-Ship *Defiant*. Mirana's Cabin.

SUZ   What was it? (*Pause*) It's something to do with me, isn't it? Why are you looking at me like that?

MIRANA   I was linked to the Dalek Emperor's mind for... a long time... until Dr Johnstone disabled the implants in my head. When I'm near to Enemy Daleks... sometimes, I've been able to... sense things. It hasn't happened in a long time. Maybe it's because I haven't been near enough to an Enemy Dalek for a long time. Maybe it's because they've changed their command net frequencies. I don't know.

SUZ   But you're expecting to sense something *now*. Why? (*Pause*) You think I'm working for your Enemy Daleks, don't you? (*Pause*) Would I know if I was?

MIRANA   I... don't know. But it's not just that.

SUZ   What is it, then?

MIRANA   When we analysed the inert Emperor's cerebral functions... I picked up some... I don't know what you'd call it... 'residue'? of its final commands.

SUZ   And?

MIRANA   And, it seems the reason the Emperor was... *is* inert is that it compressed then transmitted its entire 'consciousness' into another mind.

Pause.

SUZ   My mind?

MIRANA   Your mind.

SUZ   So you revived me to... what? Find out what the Emperor's thinking today? Or to kill me, is that it?

MIRANA   No. The Mentor decreed that the inert Emperor be removed to some secret location. We didn't dare object or pass comment. We were too worried about arousing her suspicions. But then we heard that the Mentor had issued another decree. I had already begun serving as captain of this ship, part of Kalendorf's fleet, when Alby contacted us...

31. Ext. Planet Emmeron.
A backstreet in a wretched, diseased, backward city. The distant sound of hooves. Cries in the darkness etc. Very Dickensian.

MIRANA   He's late. I don't want to stay here any longer than I have to. I've a feeling I might catch something.[29]
KALENDORF   I'm more worried about being missed. The Mentor still seems to be giving me a certain amount of leeway, but if I'm absent from my duties for too long, she's bound to start getting a bit twitchy.
MIRANA   You've only just got back from the front, haven't you? Doesn't she let you have any leave?
KALENDORF   Yes... but... well, let's just say I've been attending to some important business that I don't think she'd entirely approve of. I was expected back on Lopra some time ago.
MIRANA   I think I know better than to ask what you've been up to.
KALENDORF   *(Amused)* Do you now?
Footsteps approach.
MIRANA   *(Harsh whisper)* Alby!
ALBY   *(Approaching)* Sorry I'm late. Not exactly easy to find your way around in this place. Fog everywhere.
MIRANA   Well, I suppose that makes it an ideal secret meeting place.
ALBY   Welcome to the planet Emmeron.
KALENDORF   One of a growing number of worlds people are starting to call the Punished Planets.
ALBY   Then you've heard the rumours too? This place used to be pretty high-tech – look at it now. Heading towards the Stone Age.
MIRANA   And what else have you heard? Presumably you have something to tell us. Or are we standing around here risking our health just for old time's sake?

32. Mirana's Narration.

MIRANA   Alby had heard that the Mentor had ordered the destruction of all 'converted' dormant humanoids who had been held in the cryo-chamber over a certain amount of time. Anyone held longer than a specified cut-off point would be transported to the vicinity of a suitable collapsing star and fired into the centre of it.

33. Ext. Planet Emmeron.

ALBY   Apparently, our glorious Mentor thinks that's the only sure way she can be certain that any Enemy Dalek implants are totally destroyed.
KALENDORF   Well, she's thorough, I'll give her that.
ALBY   And guess what?
MIRANA   What?
ALBY   They've just found a suitable collapsing star... and Suz is on the list for destruction.

34. Int. Scout-Ship *Defiant*. Mirana's Cabin.

MIRANA   For some time, none of us could say anything. Then slowly, bit by bit, we formulated our plan. Alby already had plenty of undercover contacts in all the places that counted. That's the way he works. He managed to get your cryo-pod tagged for identification. Then he shadowed the ship taking you for –

SUZ   – For extermination?

MIRANA   He fired at the ship. Trying to make it look like it had been the victim of an Enemy Dalek raiding party. Then we arranged for me to 'accidentally' stumble across the wreckage and rescue you.

SUZ   And just why should you want to rescue me?

MIRANA   Do you doubt Alby's motives?

SUZ   No. It's *yours* I doubt.

MIRANA   And Kalendorf's?

Pause.

SUZ   Why did the Emperor do this to me?

MIRANA   We don't know. I'm sorry that –

SUZ   *Sorry?!* What good will that do? If you're right about what I've got hidden somewhere in my mind... and if I know Karl... He's got a plan.

Comms bleep.

MARBER   (*Distort*) Marber to Captain Mirana.

Bleep.

MIRANA   What is it, Marber?

MARBER   (*Distort*) A ship's come into range. It's one of ours. A small gunship. Is this the rendezvous?

MIRANA   Thank you, Marber. I'm on my way to the bridge.

Bleep.

SUZ   It's Alby, isn't it? Isn't it? Tell me.

Pause.

MIRANA   I think so.

SUZ   I'm coming with you.

MIRANA   No, I think it would be best if –

SUZ   *I'm coming with you.*

MIRANA   I could have you sedated.

SUZ   You'll have to. Well?

MIRANA   Maybe one of us has to start trusting. (*Smiles*) Come with me.

35. Int. Scout-Ship *Defiant*. Bridge.

Chatter of bridge activity. Proximity alarm is peeping away in background.

MARBER   This is Alliance Scout-Ship *Defiant* to unidentified gunship. Please send your call sign or we will be forced to consider you as hostile.

Door opens. Footsteps of SUZ and MIRANA entering.

MARBER   Ah... Captain, I – Who's this?

MIRANA   A personal guest of mine.

MARBER   Guest?

MIRANA   Any contact with the ship?

MARBER   Er... nothing yet. She's not sent us her call sign.

MIRANA	(*To herself*) Come on, Alby, what's the matter with you?
SUZ	(*Close. To MIRANA*) *Is* that Alby's ship?
MIRANA	It looks like it. Mr Marber. Try again.
MARBER	Very well. This is Alliance Scout-Ship *Defiant* calling

unidentified gunship. Please send your –

| ALBY | (*Distort*) Scout-Ship *Defiant*. We are coming in to dock. |
| MIRANA | (*Warm*) Commander Brook. I thought you'd gone dumb on |

us.

Pause.

MIRANA	Alby?
MARBER	He's not responding, Captain.
MIRANA	I'd noticed.
SUZ	What's wrong?
MIRANA	I'm not sure.

Proximity alarm buzzes again.

| MARBER | Gunship is moving into docking approach. Do we let him |

dock, Captain?

| MIRANA | Have a security detachment meet me at airlock reception, |

Marber.

36. Int. Scout-Ship *Defiant*. Airlock Reception.

Clunking and hissing of docking in progress. Running footsteps of security team approach and stop.

| MIRANA | Security detachment! Take up defensive positions... just in |

case.

| SUZ | Why are you expecting trouble? |
| MIRANA | Because I've caught the caution bug off Kalendorf. I think |

you'd better stay out of the way.

Airlock door opens.

| MORLI | (*Approaching*) Are these your friends? |
| ALBY | (*Kindly, as if to a child*) Yeah – yeah, they are... but just |

keep quiet for now, Morli. There's a good girl.

Pause.

| MIRANA | Alby!? Come on out! |

Footsteps.

MIRANA	Who's that with him?
SUZ	(*Overjoyed*) Alby!!!
ALBY	Stay back! For God's sake just – !
SUZ	But, Alby it's me!
MIRANA	Enemy Daleks! Take cover!!!
SECURITY MAN	Squad! Open fire!

Several gunshots.

MORLI	Don't shoot! Aaargh!
MIRANA	No! Cease firing!
DALEK SQUAD LEADER	Exterminate!

Dalek gun fires. Security guard dies.

| DALEK SQUAD LEADER | Lay down your weapons or we will exterminate |

Alby Brook! Obey!

Pause.

| ALBY | Sorry, Mirana. |
| DALEK 1 | Obey! Obey! |

MIRANA   Do as they say! Now!
Clatter of guns being laid down.
MIRANA   All right! Our weapons are down. Now... What are you doing here? What do you want?
DALEK SQUAD LEADER Where is Susan Mendes? You will surrender her to us immediately!

Crash in closing theme.

NOTES

1. Deleted dialogue – COMPUTER: '~~Playback commencing~~.'

2. Line changed to: 'Those are spacecraft... Enormous spacecraft, ~~moving between star systems at incredible speed~~. And planets... huge populations... cities... cities full of people, creatures.'

3. There are no clips from *Dalek Empire* used in this scene.

4. Line changed to: 'It's hard to believe, I know. But this us what the galaxy was like back then. **Something they called** the Earth Alliance had established peace... until the Daleks invaded. When they did, Kalendorf was caught in the middle of it.'

5. Line changed to: 'He was... for a time. But it seems **that he'd** given other orders to Mirana and Alby. Orders that he hoped and believed his beloved Dalek allies **didn't** know about.'

6. 'Please respond in any way if you can hear this,' is said four times in total.

7. Line changed to: 'But, **Captain**!'

8. Line changed to: 'I am concerned for the mental well-being and efficiency of the human occupant of this craft. The human mind needs stimulation in order to stay alert. There are a variety of images in the ship's databanks which might more usefully engage your **attention** – '

9. Line changed to: 'Woah, wait, **wait**, **wait**... what the hell do you know about Susan Mendes? That's a private image I loaded into the ship's computer just before we set off.'

10. Line changed to: 'Susan Mendes *must* be located!!! Report status of ~~the~~ Alliance attack on this solar system.'

11. Line changed to: 'Our defence fleet is suffering heavy losses. It will be totally annihilated before our second wave is in position to engage **the** Human Alliance fleet.'

12. Line changed to: '**Right**, **well**, let's try the old-fashioned way, then. Maximum magnification on visual.'

13. Line changed to: 'All right... **Hold on**, pan left a bit.'

14. Line changed to: 'Down a bit – Woah, **woah**! Stop! What's that? Can we get in closer?'

15. Line changed to: '**Yeah**, I noticed that.'

16. In order to publicise *Dalek War*, the first 30 minutes of Chapter One were included on a CD given away free with **Doctor Who Magazine** issue 326, which went on sale in January 2003. The CD also contained *No Place Like Home*, an exclusive *Doctor Who* audio story written by Iain McLaughlin.

17. Line changed to: 'Yes... yes... Very well. I suppose we can't ask ~~for~~ any more than that. But – but keep an eye on them, Herrick.'

18. Line changed to: '(*Taken aback*) ~~We~~... we never met.'

19. Line changed to: 'No. **No**, we're not working for the Daleks. We're not working for either faction.'

20. Line changed to: '(*Sighs*) **I'll, er**... **I'll explain that** later...'

21. Line changed to: '**Keep away**! I won't take anything from you! (*Pause*) What do you mean, "it's perfectly normal"?'

22. Deleted dialogue – ALTERNATIVE DALEK: '(*Tannoy*) ~~Emergency! Emergency!~~'

23. Line changed to: 'I don't understand. (*Increasingly panicked*) **You said**... you said the Daleks weren't in control of the galaxy anymore, at least not in the way I meant... But what do *you* mean? What *has* happened? What sort of galaxy have I woken up in? Why have you woken me up at all? And why has it taken you six years to get round to it?'

24. Line changed to: '(*Snaps*) I don't see... (*Stops herself. Continues, calmer*) I don't see ~~that~~ I have any ~~other~~ choice. Do you?'

25. Line changed to: 'I'm not sensing anything. **Anything** at all.'

26. Line changed to: 'Angels? Huh... ~~I was supposed to be one.~~'

27. Line changed to: 'Peace. Order. And we are the guardians of that peace and order. We protect **them** with every means and all the force at our disposal. That is why the Daleks were created in our universe.'

28. Line changed to: '**Nor me**. On the fleet's return from the Vega System, we detected several planets that had been totally devastated.'

29. Line changed to: 'He's late. I don't want to **stand** here any longer than I have to. I've a feeling I might catch something.'

CHAPTER ONE

The original 'teaser' prologue to Chapter One was different, wasn't it?

SUZ   Karl?
KALENDORF Yes. It's me, Suz. Do you remember?
SUZ   I... remember.
DALEK SUPREME (*Extreme panic*) Emergency! Emergency! Exterminate! Exterminate them!
A psychic whoosh followed by a gigantic explosion. Echoes into silence. Hold silence. Theme tune.

Nicholas Briggs: I just wanted to have a prologue that hinted at some cataclysmic event near the climax of the story. As the series progressed, I wanted this prologue to take on more and more potential significance. At the start, I thought the significant moment would be when Suz finally snaps out of being the Dalek Emperor. But I soon realised that it was more important, story-wise, to hint at Kalendorf's sneaky plan. Foreshadowing it made it seem more bedded into the story. Just revealing at the last minute that Kalendorf had done a deal with the evil Daleks might seem a bit improbable and like a last-minute addition. Having a big hint about it at the very beginning of the series made it more of a satisfying revelation. We think, 'Oh, so that's what that scene meant' rather than, 'Oh, come on, you can't just come up with that idea now!'. I suppose you could view it as a bit of a sneaky trick.

The first 14 scenes make up the bit of Dalek War Chapter One that was used on the DWM free CD. How did having that to deal with affect the writing process?
The idea of *Dalek War* being on the **DWM** freebie CD was mentioned to me very early on, so it was quite easy to write the first Chapter with a halfway mark cliffhanger in mind. I think it was a mixture of design and happy accident. It looked like Suz would have to wake up around that point anyway, so why not make it the cliffhanger? And I have to confess that it is true that I included a Dalek scene before that cliffhanger, largely because I wanted that sample half episode on the freebie CD to contain a traditional Dalek scene.

You start in *medias res*, rather than picking up directly from the events of *Project Infinity*. You must have known that there'd be great anticipation as to what happened after the end of the first series, so were you deliberately drawing out the tension here?
I suppose it is about drawing out tension. It's also about giving the audience information at a point in the story when it will have the most impact and be the most rewarding. I think a food and drink analogy is appropriate here. You may really want a glass of

brandy, but it's probably not a good idea to drink it before you eat your meal, as it will lessen the flavour of everything that comes after it and won't be anywhere near as lovely as it would have been if you'd waited to drink it after your meal. By waiting, you end up enjoying both the meal and the brandy, rather than just satiating your brandy lust early for very little reward! So, what happened after *Dalek Empire* would have been a less tasty morsel to eat at the beginning of Chapter One of *Dalek War*. By the end of the chapter, when there's been a build-up of other, complimentary flavours, it tastes a lot better.

One thing that the Saloran and Tarkov scenes do is shift the focus on to Kalendorf. It seems that you were keen on making him the main character of the story.
The shift of focus to Kalendorf was caused by two things. One was an unconscious response on my part to Gareth's strength of character. His concerns about Kalendorf had, quite rightly, made the character more and more important in *Dalek Empire*. Given that I was largely writing in response to what the actors were doing – even though the plot had already been mapped out – his feelings about the character influenced me greatly. By the end of *Dalek Empire*, Kalendorf has emerged as the central character. Additionally, because I wanted the historical perspective in *Dalek War*, the discovery of Kalendorf's telepathic legacy seemed the only 'plausible' way for future historians to access the past with any degree of accuracy (although I wanted them to get stuff wrong, too). So there was very much a story reason as well as an actor and character reason for Kalendorf's increasing dominance.

Tell us about the Mentor. Why is she a she?
The Mentor is the other universe's Davros. In that, alternative version of Dalek history, the Daleks were created by a woman who didn't go power mad and crazy. I talked about this idea with Clayton Hickman a lot. My initial thought was to make her a very matter-of-fact, non-Dalekish, chatty lady. I'd originally thought Karen (who was Saloran, eventually) could play it. But I realised I needed something more traditionally dramatic at the centre of it all. Clay suggested that I get Terry Molloy to play an alternative Davros. But even though Davros is a great idea and both Michael Wisher and Terry Molloy have played the part brilliantly, I just felt that the alternative universe Dalek creator should be very different. To make the creator a woman was a huge, obvious way of striking the difference. I suppose I was doing the Davros trick, though, of having a Dalek-like character that would be slightly more easy on the ears for long conversations. I just wanted to do it in a way we hadn't heard before.

There's a nice consistency of minor characters. Both Herrick and Johnstone, who had appeared in *Project Infinity*, crop up again.
Well, why not? Characters who fulfilled those functions were needed, so rather than create new minor characters, I thought that bringing them back would give them the appearance of more depth, simply because they were more familiar to the audience. When you do a script that has a large element of space opera in it – which *Dalek War* has – you're always going to need people who say 'Yes, sir' and 'Opening fire' etc. Now, these are mundane but necessary roles. There were a lot of them in the original *Star Trek* for example, and almost all those parts were very thinly written. Sulu and Uhura were not very well defined parts as written, for example, because they didn't need to be. But the fact that it was very often those same characters popping up time after time gave them a

sort of 'assumed' depth of character. That was the sort of reasoning behind Herrick and Johnstone. I also knew Jez and Simon were good in those parts, so why get them to play new parts, or take the risk of employing new actors to play equally boring parts. It's not everyone who can make something good out of just a few 'yes, sir' type lines. Jez and Simon have a bit of a talent for that sort of thing. Er... I didn't mean that to sound daming with faint praise!

How different is it writing for characters who are established and have actors who know their parts really well, rather than creating brand new roles? What factors come in to play? At the recording, Gareth Thomas said to you that 'Me neither' wasn't a very Kalendorf-like phrase, so it was changed to 'Nor me.' How helpful or how much of a hindrance is it to have actors who know what their characters would say or do?
I'm always pleased when actors are so engaged with what they're doing that they offer opinions about the lines and the characters' actions. The worst thing is when their attitude is 'whatever you say, fine'. That's no fun at all. So that kind of input from Gareth was expected and welcomed. I have to say that I didn't really encounter it with anyone else. Mark and Sarah, in particular, treated the whole thing as an exciting unfolding story. They really wanted to find out what happened next and were very excited and accepting of everything I wrote. I think there was a very high level of trust between us.

Suz having been asleep since "Death to the Daleks!" gives you a good chance to recap the events by having Mirana fill her in. What with Saloran and Tarkov's framing device, you're getting into flashbacks-within-flashbacks here. Did you ever feel worried that the audience would not accept the out-of-order storytelling?
I think if you step back and think, 'Oh my God, here's someone telling a story within a flashback and shouldn't this be in the right order?!' you're going to panic yourself. The fact is that it's all very simple and logical if you just take it a scene at a time. It only gets confusing if you don't make sure the listener knows where he/she is at any one time. And anyway, I think the term 'flashback' is very unhelpful here. Saloran and Tarkov are discussing something. Now, we could just stay with them talking about it, or, more interestingly, we could jump to the story they are discussing and dramatise it. I don't see that as a flashback... it's just the main story. If anything, Saloran and Tarkov are a flash-forward, if you like. So any stories related by characters in the main narrative are just pieces of information they need to impart... So again, it's much more interesting to dramatise these rather than just have them as 'talking book' sections of the script. You won't confuse people if you give them the story in the most engaging way... that is, in the form of drama!

It's such an intriguing idea: having Alby, Kalendorf and Mirana ally themselves with a faction of Daleks.
Thank you. It touches on the issues of loyalty, honesty and survival. You put your main characters in a situation which demands that they play along with these new Daleks because firstly it seems the right thing to do, then later it seems the only thing to do if our heroes wish to survive to fight another day. It makes the situation more complex and therefore, in my opinion, gives it more of that smell of reality – which I think is essential the more 'unreal' your setting is.

The Alternate Daleks throw up some interesting political points What was your inspiration for this? It has been noted in some quarters that the two sides represent either fascism versus communism, or the Shadows and the Vorlons from *Babylon 5*. Was any of this in your head during the scriptwriting process?

I wasn't really thinking of communists and fascists, or indeed Vorlons and Shadows. The only analogy I'd come up with was *The Day The Earth Stood Still*. I was thinking of the Alternative Daleks being rather like Klaatu's people. They had a good aim, but would stop at nothing to achieve it: 'Be peaceful, or we will destroy you'. If you accept that the end justifies the means, then the Mentor is absolutely one hundred per cent right. She's never deceitful. She's pretty straightforward. The moral dilemma always comes when the means to achieve your aim – in this case, the destruction of the evil Daleks – starts to feel almost as bad as the tactics of the enemy you're trying to defeat. This is an idea that very much resurfaces towards the end of *Dalek Empire III*.

Q&A
CASTING

Nicholas Briggs: What I'm looking for when I cast a part is an actor who's not just good, but also pleasant to work with. I want them to be serious about the role and the fictional world of the script – even though it's Daleks and spaceships – but also to be able to make decisions about their performances quite quickly and without making an enormous fuss. Now, you'd think that would be easy to find in actors; but frankly, it's quite difficult. Some actors find science fiction so ludicrous that they just can't relate to it. Other actors are so serious and intense about their work that it's difficult to develop any kind of shorthand communication with them.

That shorthand is vital, because these plays are recorded very quickly. If you have to start from scratch on every scene with an actor, then it's just going to take too long. I need them to be able to take on board general notes about their character early in the day, and for those notes to filter through their performance for the rest of the day. Some actors need to be told everything you've already told them each time they step up to the microphone, and that's just tedious and frustrating for me and the rest of the cast. It also means you don't have time to fine-tune performances, build on what they've already established and focus on particularly complex changes of emotion and intention in the script. My hope is to excite the actor's imagination and then bring them along with me and my enthusiasm.

So, in order to make sure all this happens, I prefer to meet the actors beforehand, which means, unlike most of the *Doctor Who* casting, I invite actors in to read for me and just chat. For *Dalek Empire*, I had a big casting session to cast Suz, even though I had Sarah Mowat in mind from a very early stage. I saw a lot of good actresses I would have been very happy to work with, but none of them were quite as right for the part as Sarah was. One of the girls I saw for the role, Octavia Walters, is actually in *Dalek Empire III*. I've been planning to work with her for three years now!

I also tend to cast actors I've worked with before. Mark McDonnell was fantastic when we spent a difficult week in Bristol doing some *Doctor Who* plays with Paul McGann. It was all quite tense because Paul was a bit tired, my then girlfriend was going a bit bonkers and several of us had terrible, terrible colds. But Mark was excellent throughout and kept me laughing. I thought then, 'This is Alby Brook.' I'd been impressed by Gareth Thomas's performance in *Storm Warning* [one of the plays recorded in Bristol] and so was very keen to work with him. I'd worked with Hannah Smith in rep in Nottingham, and was really impressed by her attitude to work. She kind of embodies the qualities I've already described. She's serious about her work, smart about scripts, brilliant with her voice and lots of fun to be with. I could go on about the rest of the cast, but I think that's enough luvvie talk, don't you?

DALEK WAR CHAPTER TWO

37. Int. Scout-Ship _Defiant_. Airlock Reception.

DALEK SQUAD LEADER Where is Susan Mendes? You will surrender her to us immediately! (_Pause_) Answer!
SUZ (_Urgent. Sotto voce_) Mirana, give me your gun.
MIRANA (_Urgent. Sotto voce_) What – ? Why? What are you going to do –
SUZ (_Urgent. Sotto voce_) – Don't waste time, I know what I'm doing – just give it to me.
Sound of gun being handed across.
DALEK SQUAD LEADER (_During the above_) Answer! Answer! Answer! (_After gun has been handed across_) Answer or we will exterminate Alby Brook!
Footsteps and scuffle as SUZ stands up. (_SUZ and ALBY are on opposite sides of the stereo soundscape. MORLI is paired with ALBY, MIRANA with SUZ._)
SUZ (_Aloud_) I am Susan Mendes.
ALBY No! She's lying! She isn't.
MORLI Alby – don't make them angry again!
SUZ Alby, it's best this way –
ALBY – No! Susan Mendes... is dead.
DALEK SQUAD LEADER Silence! Run computer scan.
DALEK 1 I obey.
Computer scan FX.
DALEK 1 Physical characteristics match with database information.
DALEK SQUAD LEADER You are confirmed as Susan Mendes.
SUZ So, what now?
DALEK SQUAD LEADER These other humans are not required. Exterminate them.
MORLI (_Overlapping_) Nooo!
DALEK 1 (_Overlapping_) We obey!

CHAPTER TWO CD TRACK LISTINGS		
1 Answer! Answer!	12 Bad stuff	24 Where are we heading?
2 Web of energy	13 Analysis disc	25 Cease firing!
3 Stay calm	14 Orders of a traitor	26 Alby! Go! Please!
4 Further risk?	15 Which Daleks?	27 Escape pod
5 Report!	16 Second wave	28 Paralysis beams
6 Going home?	17 Human hostages	29 Keep back...
7 Not a Dalek, then	18 Alert! Alert!	30 Surrender
8 Surviving humanoid	19 Negative!	31 Another risk, Kalendorf?
9 The Dalek Emperor	20 Stuck	32 Engage restraints!
10 Transolar disc	21 Drammankin Gas	33 We are one!
squadron	22 Await reinforcements	34 Suz?
11 Zero-grav	23 Internal scanners	35 Trailer

SUZ	(*Overlapping*) No!!!
MIRANA	Get down!!!
DALEKS	(*Variously*) Exterminate! Exterminate! Exterminate!

Dalek guns fire. Security guard cries out as he's shot.

ALBY	Suz!!!
MIRANA	Open fire!!!

Security guard guns fire. Dalek guns return fire.

SUZ	No!!! Stop!!! Stop this! Stop this or I'll shoot myself. Do you hear me?! I'll kill myself!!!
DALEK SQUAD LEADER	Cease firing! Cease firing immediately!!!

Dalek gunfire stops. Security guard fire continues sporadically for a moment.

MIRANA	Cease fire!

Gunfire stops.

SUZ	I mean it. This gun is fully charged.
DALEK SQUAD LEADER	Drop the weapon! Surrender!
SUZ	No! I'm serious – keep away!!! (*Pause*) I mean it! I know why you want me. I know I'm vital to your plan.[1]
DALEK SQUAD LEADER	You know nothing of our [plan] –
SUZ	– You want your Emperor back! Don't you? (*Pause. Angry*) You think that what's left of him is stuck in my brain. Don't you?! Well...? Answer!
DALEK SQUAD LEADER	(*Reluctant*) Yes.
SUZ	So if I blow my brains all over this bulkhead... the Dalek Supreme isn't going to be very pleased with you, is he? (*Pause*) Is he?!
DALEK SQUAD LEADER	You will not sacrifice your own life.
SUZ	Why not? I did it before. Or so I thought... (*Pause*) Well?
ALBY	You've confused him... Suz.
SUZ	(*Awkwardly*) Hello... Alby.
ALBY	(*Awkwardly*) Hi.
SUZ	Um... We'll... (*She stops*) Well... Now's not exactly a good time, is it?[2]
ALBY	Sure. Yeah. I know. You... carry on.[3]
MORLI	Go on – *tell* her.
ALBY	Morli, just shut up.
MORLI	Ahhh... she's lovely, isn't she? Just like you said.
MIRANA	Daleks! I suggest you leave my ship!
DALEK SQUAD LEADER	We will not leave.
MIRANA	What choice do you have? You need Susan Mendes alive. If you stay, she will kill herself.
DALEK SQUAD LEADER	Our objective is to capture Susan Mendes. We cannot leave without achieving our objective.
ALBY	(*A growl of frustration, under his breath*) Stalemate...
DALEK SQUAD LEADER	Why do *you* require Susan Mendes?
MIRANA	She... She is our friend.
DALEK SQUAD LEADER	That is *not* the reason.
ALBY	It is.
MORLI	It's true. He loves her. Alby loves Suz.
DALEK SQUAD LEADER	We know of the emotional bond between them. But it is also clear that you are aware of the connection between Susan Mendes and our Emperor. What did you hope to achieve by reviving her? (*Pause*) Answer! (*Pause*) We know that (*with distaste*) the Mentor

ordered her destruction. Why have you disobeyed the orders of your ally in this war?

SUZ   That's none of your business. Just leave this ship.

DALEK SQUAD LEADER We will not leave. You – must – have – a – plan!

SUZ   No I don't!

DALEK SQUAD LEADER Kalendorf, Mirana and Alby Brook have a plan. What is it?

ALBY   There is no plan. We're not Daleks! We did this because... I did this... because...

DALEK SQUAD LEADER Because you love Susan Mendes?

ALBY   Yes.

DALEK SQUAD LEADER Perhaps Kalendorf and Mirana have not shared knowledge of their plan with you, Alby Brook.

ALBY   (*Rattled*) What are you trying to say?

MIRANA   Divide and rule, Alby. That's what it's up to.

DALEK SQUAD LEADER Silence! We will take control of this ship and you –

SUZ   – No! *You* will be silent! All of you!

DALEK SQUAD LEADER You will not kill yourself.

SUZ   I will if you harm anyone else on this ship.

DALEK SQUAD LEADER You value your own existence. Your threat is meaningless.

SUZ   But can you be sure? Can you take that risk?

Pause.

DALEK SQUAD LEADER You do not want us to harm Alby Brook.

SUZ   You will not harm anyone on this ship.

DALEK SQUAD LEADER We will take control of this ship.

SUZ   No!

DALEK SQUAD LEADER We will take control!!! The crew will lay down their weapons and be taken hostage. You will be imprisoned with them. If you do not harm yourself, all humans on this vessel will live.

MIRANA   What's the point of you taking control of this ship? You'll never get past [our fleet]...

DALEK SQUAD LEADER Silence! Silence!!! Those are our terms. (*Pause*) Susan Mendes. Alby Brook is safe. The crew is safe. Do you still wish to kill yourself? (*Pause*) Answer!

ALBY   Suz...?

SUZ   (*Sighs, defeated*) You bastards!

38. Int. Flagship *Courageous*. Bridge.

The crackle of fire. Alarms blaring out. Groans and coughing of wounded.

KALENDORF   (*Coughing through smoke*) Mr Herrick? Mr Herrick!

HERRICK   Sir! Over here... argh!

KALENDORF's footsteps as he approaches HERRICK.

KALENDORF   Are you all right, Herrick?

HERRICK   I think so... I – argh...

KALENDORF   Medic! I need a medic here.

ALTERNATE DALEK (*Approaching*) I obey.

KALENDORF   Get this man to the infirmary.

ALTERNATE DALEK Medical facilities are overstretched. Human patients are being treated in strict order of severity of injury.

KALENDORF (*Close and intense*) I'm the Fleet Commander and I'm giving you an order. This man is my executive officer and I need him fit enough to perform his duties as soon as possible.

ALTERNATE DALEK I... obey. (*Moving off*) I will bring an anti-grav stretcher.

KALENDORF You'll be all right, Herrick.

HERRICK (*Weak*) Thank... thank you, sir. They hit us pretty bad, didn't they?[4]

KALENDORF It could've been worse. Did you see what happened?

HERRICK Just as we were... were closing on the survivors of the Enemy Dalek fleet... They... there was a glowing... They seemed to be firing at each other. For a moment, they were linked by... by something that looked like a giant web... a kind of web of energy.

Hum of anti-grav stretcher approaching.

ALTERNATE DALEK (*Approaching*) The Enemy Daleks linked the total mass output of their ships' reactors. Please climb aboard the anti-grav stretcher.

HERRICK Then they just... exploded.

ALTERNATE DALEK Please climb aboard the –

KALENDORF – I'll help him. Come on...

Vocal noises from KALENDORF and HERRICK as he's helped aboard.

HERRICK Thank you, sir.

HERRICK's groans of pain retreat into the distance as the stretcher hovers off and a door opens and closes.

KALENDORF Anyone in a fit state to give me a damage report?[5]

ALTERNATE DALEK 1 I... I have sust-sustained damage, but re-remain op-operational.[6]

KALENDORF Are repairs underway?

ALTERNATE DALEK 1 Rep-repair teams report slow progress. Damage to outer hull plates and engines was severe.[7]

KALENDORF I knew the Enemy Daleks would have a back-up plan. They're trying to stall us until their second wave arrives. Any idea of fleet casualties?

ALTERNATE DALEK 1 Alliance fleet casualties currently stand at 132 ships. Approximately 25 per cent of our force.[8]

KALENDORF (*To himself*) My God.

Comms bleep.

ALTERNATE DALEK 1 The Mentor wishes to speak with you.

KALENDORF (*Under his breath*) When doesn't she? (*Aloud*) All right. Tell her I'm on my way.

39. Int. *Defiant.* Loading Bay.

DALEK Move into the loading bay! Move!

Footsteps and vocal rumble of crew.

MIRANA Keep moving. Everybody stay calm.

More footsteps etc.

ALBY Suz... Suz, are you – ?

SUZ It's all right, Alby. Don't worry.

ALBY It's... it's good to see you. Did I say that already?

SUZ Who's your friend?

MORLI I'm Morli. There's no need to be jealous –

SUZ	No, I was just –
MORLI	– Alby saved my life. Back on the Space Station.
SUZ	The Space Station – ?
MORLI	We're just good friends.
SUZ	(*Slightly embarrassed*) Right... I see. Er... Pleased to meet

you. How did you save – ?

ALBY	There's a lot to explain, Suz.
SUZ	You think I don't realise that?

DALEK SQUAD LEADER Now, Susan Mendes! You will surrender your
weapon.

SUZ	No. It stays with me.

DALEK SQUAD LEADER Surrender it now, or we will exterminate the
hostages!

SUZ	If you do, I will kill myself. I've told you that. (*Flaring up*)

What's the matter with you, don't you listen?

MIRANA	(*Sotto voce*) They're testing your resolve.
SUZ	(*Sotto voce*) I know. They never change.

Pause.

DALEK SQUAD LEADER (*Guarded*) Very well. Daleks will remain here to
guard you.

MIRANA	Where are *you* going?

DALEK SQUAD LEADER (*Backing through the doorway*) Silence! There –
will – be – no – escape – attempts!

Door closes.

ALBY	Now what?
MIRANA	At least we're still alive.
ALBY	And that's thanks to you, Suz.
SUZ	'Thanks'? Huh... for what? Giving in again?
MIRANA	What do you mean?
SUZ	Oh... (*Sighs*) I told the Daleks I wanted to die once before.

Years ago.[9]

ALBY	That you *wanted* to die? When?
SUZ	When all this began.
MORLI	But they didn't kill you, though, did they?
SUZ	(*Cold*) No. Obviously not.
MIRANA	Because they needed you.

Pause.

ALBY	Suz?
SUZ	They needed *someone*. They thought it might be me. But

they didn't *force* me to work for them. They just... waited.

MORLI	Waited for what?
SUZ	(*Sighs*) Back on Vega VI, when they'd invaded... things

got... Well, it wasn't what you'd call... pleasant. I couldn't see an end to
it all. I wanted to see an end to it all. I told the Daleks I wanted to die
because I was tired. And I was angry. But sometimes the Daleks
understand us better than we understand ourselves. If you take someone
who is tired and angry... and you give them food and rest... They get
comfortable. They remember that life can be good. They regain their hope.
And then you remember that you don't want to die. You can't feel angry
forever... not if you're just... me. And the same thing's happened again
here. When you lose control, the Daleks lose their power over you. But it
never lasts for long.

MIRANA   You're saying you should have just killed yourself the moment the Daleks docked with my ship?[10]

SUZ   If I was dead, the Dalek Emperor would be dead too. And you'd win the war. Well, wouldn't you?[11]

ALBY   It isn't as simple as that, Suz.

SUZ   You don't want to win?

MIRANA   It's a question of who exactly would be winning.

SUZ   So the Dalek was right. You and Kalendorf do have a plan.

MIRANA   I don't know what Kalendorf has in mind. He said it would be safer that way. But I trust him, don't you?

ALBY   Huh... he's a warrior of noble birth. I've always thought that made him pretty bleedin' dangerous.

40. Int. Flagship *Courageous*. Executive Communication Chamber.

MENTOR   So you propose that we should take a further risk?

KALENDORF   (*Impassioned*) We must press ahead into Earth's solar system before the second wave of Enemy Dalek ships can attack. If we can get a foothold on some of the outer moons, we can conserve power and hold out until our reinforcements arrive.

MENTOR   But with 25 per cent of your current force destroyed, you will prove a poor match for the enemy's second wave if they should make their attack earlier than you predict.

KALENDORF   But if we don't advance now, if we wait until their second wave can move into an optimum attack formation, we could be stuck out here for years trying to battle our way in.

MENTOR   I sense you have lost your caution.

KALENDORF   Sometimes caution can lose you the battle... even the war.

MENTOR   Have you received any reports on Freighter Omega N7?

KALENDORF   What? No! I haven't exactly had time to –

MENTOR   My monitors tell me that the Scout-Ship *Defiant* has salvaged its cargo.

KALENDORF   (*Feigning disinterest*) Has it? Well... er... good.

MENTOR   You are aware of who commands Scout-Ship Defiant–

KALENDORF   Yes... Mirana. But I don't see the relevance of – [12]

MENTOR   Were you aware of the nature of the cargo carried by Omega N7?

KALENDORF   No. Why?

Pause.

MENTOR   Why was Scout-Ship *Defiant* taken out of your attack formation and sent on routine patrol duties?

KALENDORF   I have no idea. It must have been a command issued by one of the fleet sub-commanders. If you like, I'll spend my time finding out for sure rather than getting on with winning this war. I take it I am still in command of the fleet.

Pause.

MENTOR   Mirana is your close friend, is she not?

KALENDORF   You know that.

MENTOR   I thought you might have taken a personal interest in her duties. (*Pause*) The answer to your previous question is 'yes'. You are still in command of the fleet. You may proceed with your plan.

KALENDORF   Thank you.

41. Int. Scout-Ship *Defiant*. Bridge.

DALEK SQUAD LEADER Report!
DALEK 1 All Daleks have disembarked from Alby Brook's ship with all necessary equipment.
DALEK SQUAD LEADER Has Dalek interface with this scout-ship's control systems been achieved?
DALEK 1 I have achieved full interface with all Scout-Ship *Defiant*'s systems.
DALEK SQUAD LEADER Activate main drive.
DALEK 1 I obey.
A bleep and rumble of engines begins.
DALEK SQUAD LEADER Drammankin gas tanks must now be prepared for operation.

42. Int. Scout-Ship Defiant. Loading Bay.
Rumble of engine power.

MORLI Oooh... that noise... we've started movin', haven't we?
MIRANA The Daleks have fired up our engines.
MORLI Alby! Alby! Look through the window! They're leaving your ship behind. What about Drudger?
ALBY (*Humouring*) He'll be all right, Morli. Don't worry.
MORLI Won't he get lonely, like? Oooh, poor old Drudge.
ALBY (*To MIRANA*) The Daleks can't be planning to take us to Earth.
MORLI Earth? Going home? Are we?
MIRANA Where else?
MORLI Actually, I've never been there.
SUZ Earth? But –
ALBY That's where the Dalek Supreme is... It's the Enemy Dalek stronghold now... and it's probably where the Emperor's casing is by now.[13]
SUZ The Emperor's casing? (*To MIRANA*) I thought you said that'd disappeared.
MIRANA Yeah, that's what I thought. Alby?
ALBY Yeah, me too. But how do you think I ended up with a bunch of Daleks on board my ship?
MIRANA You tell me.
ALBY (*Sighs*) Well, I was about to set off for the rendezvous point.
MIRANA When you were jumped by Daleks?[14]
ALBY Not quite. I picked up that distress call... you know, the one you detected when you were working on the Emperor's casing.
SUZ But didn't you say you shut that off, Mirana?
MIRANA Yeah.
ALBY I know. That's why I knew I had to go and take a look when I picked up the signal. I traced it to a space station in the Pkowik System. I decided to take a look... Huh, don't know what came over me. Must've thought I was a hero or something. Anyway, when I went aboard, I found there'd been a massive punch-up between the two Dalek factions. Chunks of smashed casing all over the place. My drudger was having

239

trouble picking up life readings because of a nearby particle cloud or
something – but suddenly it detected movement... and then I started to
remember that I'm not a hero...
Crossfade to:

43. Int. Hospital Station. Airlock Reception.
*(Recap a few lines from Scene 20 in Chapter One, then continue...) Sound
of feet scampering over metal flooring in the distance.*

ALBY	*(To DRUDGER)* Sounds as if it's got feet. *(To himself)* So...

not a Dalek, then. Thank God. *(Aloud)* Hello! Who's there?

MORLI   *(Moans in pain)*
ALBY   Drudger... getting any clearer readings yet?
DRUDGER   *(Distort)* Negative.
ALBY   So, no ideas about what I'm dealing with here?
DRUDGER   *(Distort)* No ideas at all.
ALBY   *(To himself)* Bugger.
He cocks his gun.
ALBY   *(Aloud, trying to be brave)* All right! Now listen to me...
If you come out with your hands up, I won't shoot. *(To himself)* Come
on... come on...
*A crash of MORLI bumping into something. ALBY takes a sharp intake of
breath.*
MORLI   *(Distant)* Don't shoot. Please don't 'urt us. I think I've
bashed me knee. Owww...
ALBY   'Us'? How many of you are there?
MORLI's slightly limping footsteps approach tentatively.
MORLI   *(Approaching)* Eh? There's just me, man. Everyone else...
they got killed, like. Don't shoot, mister. I'm starvin'.
ALBY   Who are you?
MORLI   Morli.
ALBY   Morli?
MORLI   That's my name, yeah. I'm one of the patients.
ALBY   Patients? You mean this is a hospital?
MORLI   Yeah... but I'm the only patient left now. Since the bad
Daleks came.
ALBY   The bad Daleks? They attacked?
MORLI   Yeah. The good Daleks was lookin' after us. Then the
bad'ns attacked. Bloody huge battle. They was lookin' for something.[15]
ALBY   Who was?
MORLI   The bad Daleks.
ALBY   What were they looking for?
MORLI   Dunno, mister.
ALBY   Alby.
MORLI   What?
ALBY   My name's Alby.
MORLI   Oh. Alby. Mine's Morli.
ALBY   I know.
MORLI   Do ya?
ALBY   Yeah, you just told me.
MORLI   Did a? Oh aye... sorry... I sometimes forget things, when
I'm scared, like, you knah?[16]

ALBY   Okay... well, look, there's nothing to be scared of. Okay?[17]
MORLI   Okedokey, mister – er Alby.
ALBY   How's your knee?
MORLI   Me knee? Oh, it's not bad. Just knocked it on something when I was runnin' just then. Have you got ought to eat, like?[18]
ALBY   How long since the Daleks were fighting here?
MORLI   Dunno. Quiet now. Seems like ages. I've had to miss me dinner and everything. And breakfast... I think. Can't really remember, like, you knah?
Rustle of plastic wrapper.
ALBY   Here... have some of this.
She grabs the food.
MORLI   (*Eating hungrily*) Thanks, mister. What is it? Tastes funny, like.
ALBY   Basic nutrition bar. It'll build up your strength.
MORLI   (*Still eating*) Well I'm strong, me, anyways, mister.
ALBY   Alby.
MORLI   (*Still eating*) Alby, ooh aye, sorry. Wanna feel me muscles?
ALBY   Morli, listen to me. Who won the battle? The good or the bad Daleks?
MORLI   (*Thinking, with difficulty*) Er... er...
ALBY   It's all right. Take your time.[19]
Distant rending of metal echoes threateningly.
MORLI   (*Fearful*) Oh no. Not again.
ALBY   What was that?
More rending metal. It's the hull buckling.
MORLI   Keeps happening. There was a lot of big explosions when the Daleks was fightin'. I think they may have done some serious damage, like.[20]
A breeze starts to pick up.
ALBY   Oh no... Drudger. I think there's a hull breach.
DRUDGER (*Distort*) You are correct, Alby Brook. I am reading severe buckling in the section adjoining your current position. I suggest you leave the space station immediately.
ALBY   Yeah, well I've picked up a survivor, and she hasn't got a space suit. Morli, do you know where they keep the spacesuits?
MORLI   Errr...
Distant sound of rending metal. The breeze has turned into quite a vicious wind. The air is rushing towards the hull breach.
ALBY   Come on! You've got to come with me. Maybe we can shut off this section. Come on!
MORLI   Right, man. I'm with you, like.
ALBY   Come on!
Hurried footsteps. Laboured breathing from them both as they struggle against the wind. The wind reaches tornado level.
DRUDGER (*Distort*) Alby, there is a bulkhead door ahead of you.
ALBY   (*Above the wind*) Yeah! I see it!
DRUDGER (*Distort*) If you can shut it behind you, you will seal yourself off from the damaged section.
The wind crescendos. Sound of ALBY and MORLI struggling. One last vocal sound of struggle from ALBY. Click of a button depressing, hiss of

a servo. A huge door begins to close. As it does, the wind is slowly shut off.

ALBY   (*Above the din*) That's it! It's closing!

MORLI   Well done, Alby!!! Ya've dunnit!

Door finally closes with a huge crunch. The wind is muffled behind it. They recover, huffing and puffing.

ALBY   (*Still recovering*) Now... Morli, are you sure that there are no Daleks left here?

MORLI   Pretty sure.

ALBY   'Pretty' sure?

MORLI   Aye, well... ya knah, I think good'ns were killed and I saw the bad'ns when they were leavin'.

ALBY   The bad Daleks left?

MORLI   Yeah. After they broke right through those walls into the special place, they just took that big thing and left.

ALBY   Woah... hold on a minute. What big thing?

MORLI   Massive. Big container thing.

ALBY   Can you show me?

MORLI   Nah, cos they took it. It's gone.

ALBY   No, Morli. Can you show me where they took it from?

MORLI   Sure.

ALBY   All right. Drudger, how's the hull of this thing standing up?

DRUDGER   (*Distort*) I am detecting no other areas of structural instability at the moment.

ALBY   Good. I need to take a look around. I think we may have found where our Daleks have been keeping the Enemy Dalek Emperor.

44. Int. Enemy Dalek Transport Ship.

Burble of controls.

DALEK DRONE Particle cloud signal interference now successfully filtered. Contact confirmed with Alby Brook's spacecraft. He has docked with the Hospital Station.

DALEK COMMANDER As predicted. Has he entered the Station?

DALEK DRONE Readings indicate he has entered and encountered a surviving humanoid.

DALEK COMMANDER Dispatch transolar disc squadron to capture them.

DALEK DRONE I obey.

DALEK COMMANDER The moment the squadron has launched, we must engage hyper drive and leave this system.

DALEK DRONE Understood.

45. Int. Hospital Ship. Examination Bay.

Large door opens.

ALBY   My God...

MORLI   What is it?

ALBY   It's the bloody Emperor of the Daleks... that's what it is. What is this place?

MORLI   Special place. Where the good Daleks did all their special stuff, like.[21]

242

ALBY   It's special, all right. Drudger, are you tapping into my suit camera?
DRUDGER   (*Distort*) Tapping in now.
ALBY   Do you see what I see?
DRUDGER   (*Distort*) The Dalek Emperor.
ALBY   Then I'm not imagining it. Looks like our Daleks were giving it a right old going over. They've got it on... well it looks like a huge operating table.[22]
DRUDGER   (*Distort*) Agreed. This suggests they were attempting to access its cerebral functions.
ALBY   And talking of suggestions... any idea what I should do? We can't take it with us and... Wait a minute.
DRUDGER   (*Distort*) What is troubling you, Alby Brook?
ALBY   Morli, you said the Enemy Daleks left with a huge container.
MORLI   Aye, they did.
ALBY   Big enough to carry this thing?
MORLI   Definitely, aye. 'Bout the same size, I'd say, man.[23]
ALBY   Then why the hell didn't they take it with them?
Pause.
MORLI   Dunno. Does it matter?
DRUDGER   (*Distort*) Attention, Alby Brook.
ALBY   What's the matter?
DRUDGER   (*Distort*) I am detecting a squadron of Enemy Dalek transolar discs approaching at high speed.
ALBY   What – ? Oh, shit! What am I supposed to do now? Er... (*Getting a grip*) Morli, you remember those spacesuits we passed down the corridor on the way here?
MORLI   In the big locker, aye.
ALBY   Go and get one and get in it – now!
MORLI   You're not angry with us, are yous?
ALBY   No. I'm just frightened, because –
MORLI   The bad Daleks are coming back to get us?
ALBY   Yeah... But I think they're coming back to get this.
MORLI   The Emproary thing?
ALBY   Yeah – Look, just go and get in that suit. I've got to think of a way to blow this thing up.
MORLI   Why bother? We should just get out –
ALBY   Shut up, Morli! Go![24]
MORLI   (*As she runs off*) Blimey. Keep your hair on, man.
Her footsteps recede into the background.
ALBY   Right... now... Drudger, tell me... what do you make of these controls? (*Pause*) Well?
DRUDGER   (*Distort*) I am processing visual information.
ALBY   Can you hurry up?
DRUDGER   (*Distort*) The controls relate to holographic projection.
ALBY   What?
DRUDGER   (*Distort*) Please touch the Emperor's casing.
ALBY   But... okay.
Fizz of hand hitting holographic projection.
ALBY   Oh my God – it's a bloody hologram. It's not the real thing. The Enemy Daleks must have taken the real thing. But why –?

DRUDGER   (*Distort*) Since the control configuration matches known Alliance Dalek technology, I would suggest that this is a holographic chamber designed for the testing of experimental procedures.
ALBY   Then why are the Enemy Daleks coming back?
DRUDGER   (*Distort*) Perhaps they are coming for you.
ALBY   Why does this smell like a trap all of a sudden?
Clumsy footsteps of MORLI approaching.
MORLI   (*Spacesuit distort*) Have I got this thing on right? Feels funny.
ALBY   Oh, Morli, you've got the boots on the wrong feet! Come here!

46. Ext. Space. Enemy Dalek Transolar Comms.
The purr of transolar disc engines.

DALEK SQUAD LEADER Transolar disc squadron now moving to final approach on Alliance Hospital Space Station. Squadron will disperse into search pattern Ceranud 5.
DALEKS   We obey.
DALEK SQUAD LEADER Calibrate rangerscopes to detect two humanoids.
Insistent bleeping.
DALEK 1   (*Distort*) Attack unit 7 now in position. Am detecting two humanoid figures moving on foot across Station's lower hull support structures.
DALEK SQUAD LEADER All units will close on those co-ordinates immediately!

47. Ext. Hospital Space Station. Hull.
ALBY and MORLI's voices are distorted inside space helmets. Much vocal effort and breathing as they clamber across the hull.

ALBY   Come on, Morli! Keep up!
MORLI   It feels all funny... like me stomach's all floaty... Ooh, I think I'm gonna puke, man. It's that bar o'stuff you gave me![25]
ALBY   No, it isn't! It's zero-grav. Haven't you been in zero-grav before?[26]
MORLI   Nah, ya soft get. D'ya think I'm an astronaut or summit? I've spent all me life on the station... least ways, I canna remember anything else.
Dalek gun and explosion.
ALBY   Oh no, they've found us! Quick!
DALEK   (*Distort*) Attention escaping humans! You are our prisoners! Do not move!
ALBY   Drudger! Can you track our position, bring the ship to us?
DRUDGER   (*Distort*) I am already heading towards you.
ALBY   Fantastic! Well done!
MORLI   He's a clever beggar, your Drudger, isn't he?
DRUDGER   (*Distort*) But I regret to report that rescue is not possible.
ALBY   What? Why not?
DRUDGER   (*Distort*) Daleks have taken over control of this ship. Approaching your position now.
Sound of Gunship MX4's descending engines.

| ALBY | (*Intense frustration*) Oh shit. |
| DALEK | (*Distort*) Surrender! Surrender! Surrender! |

48. Int. Scout-Ship *Defiant*. Loading Bay.

| MIRANA | And then they made you bring them here? (*Pause*) Alby? |

What's the matter?

| MORLI | They did bad stuff to him. |
| SUZ | Bad – ? Alby, what did they do? |

49. Int. Gunship *MX4*.

DALEK SQUAD LEADER	Attach brain analysis disc to his head.
ALBY	Get off me!
DALEK SQUAD LEADER	Restrain him!
ALBY	Aaargh!
DALEK 1	Activating disc.

Buzz of hovering disc.

| DALEK 1 | Disc attaching to subject's head now. |

Fizz of attachment.

| ALBY | Aaaargh! |
| DALEK SQUAD LEADER | Do not struggle! If you struggle, the disc will |

administer pain.

Fizzzzz.

ALBY	Aaaaargh! Bastards!
MORLI	Leave him alone!
DALEK SQUAD LEADER	Exterminate her!
DALEK 2	I obey.
ALBY	No!
DALEK SQUAD LEADER	Wait! We will keep her alive.
DALEK 2	Understood.
DALEK SQUAD LEADER	She may be of use. We will begin. Where is Susan

Mendes?

Disc hums.

| DALEK SQUAD LEADER | Answer! |
| ALBY | (*In pain*) I don't know. |

Fzzzzz.

| ALBY | Aaaaargh!!! |
| DALEK SQUAD LEADER | The analysis disc monitors your brain waves. If |

you fail to answer or do not tell the truth, you will experience pain. Where
is Susan Mendes?

Fzzzzz.

| ALBY | Aaaargh! |
| DALEK SQUAD LEADER | We know that your associate, Mirana, will have |

accessed her cryo-pod.

| ALBY | (*Taken aback*) What? |
| DALEK SQUAD LEADER | We know that you are to rendezvous with |

Mirana's ship.

| ALBY | (*In pain*) If you know, then why are you asking? |
| DALEK SQUAD LEADER | These statements create mental images in your |

mind. The analysis disc is downloading them to the disc operator. (*To
other DALEK*) Report analysis of download.

DALEK 1   Rendezvous co-ordinates are pre-programmed into this ship's nav computer. Hovering robot drone is able to initiate main drive and course settings.

DALEK SQUAD LEADER Order the hovering robot drone to initiate main drive and set co-ordinates for the rendezvous.

The disc fizzes.

ALBY   Aaaaaargh! No way!

More disc fizzing.

ALBY   Aaaaargh! Oh, God!!! Aaaargh!

DALEK 1   Brain analysis suggests further motivation is required.

DALEK SQUAD LEADER Understood. If you do not give the order to your hovering robot drone, we will exterminate this humanoid female.

MORLI   No!

DALEK SQUAD LEADER Restrain her!

MORLI   Aaargh! Let go!

DALEK SQUAD LEADER Give the order to the hovering drone!

ALBY   (*In pain*) I'm sorry, Morli. But I... I can't... can't do it.

MORLI   Alby! Please!

DALEK SQUAD LEADER Report analysis of download.

DALEK 1   Hovering robot drone's control systems can be overridden by Dalek technology.

DALEK SQUAD LEADER Proceed!

DALEK 1   I obey.

MORLI   You mean you're not going to kill me?[27]

ALBY   Why did you make that threat?

DALEK SQUAD LEADER The statement provoked additional mental stress. You envisaged that which you did not wish to reveal.

Disc FX wind down.

DALEK SQUAD LEADER Remove the analysis disc.

DALEK 1   I obey.

Disc disconnects and hovers off.

ALBY   (*Exhausted*) Satisfied?

DALEK SQUAD LEADER We also now know how important this secret is to you.

ALBY   What do you mean?

DALEK SQUAD LEADER You were prepared to sacrifice a friend to keep us from finding the Mendes woman.

ALBY   Morli isn't my friend. I only just met her.

DALEK 1   The disc detected your concern for her.

DALEK SQUAD LEADER This weakness in your character may be of further use to us.

ALBY   (*Suspicious*) Did you get that stuff about Mirana and the rendezvous out of my brain, or did you already know all that?[28]

DALEK SQUAD LEADER Silence!

ALBY   What's going on here? Eh? Why did you take your Emperor and then come back for me? Did you know I'd be coming here?

DALEK SQUAD LEADER Secure the humans!

MORLI lets out a yelp as she's grabbed by a Dalek.

ALBY   (*Struggling. Being dragged away*) You deliberately sent that distress call, didn't you? Why? Why did you want to trap me... and how did you know I'd be out here anyway?!

50. Int. Scout-Ship *Defiant*. Loading Bay.
The conversation is hushed.

SUZ   So what are you saying, Alby?
ALBY   I'm not sure.
MIRANA   How could those Daleks have been expecting you?
MORLI   Have you got any food? I'm hungry again.
Rustle of wrapper.
ALBY   Here.
MORLI   Ahhh, thanks, man. I don't hold it against you, you know.
ALBY   (*Distracted*) What?
MORLI   Saying the Daleks could kill me.[29]
ALBY   Oh. Morli... look, I'm sorry about – [30]
MORLI   Nah... I understand. You canna go givin' the Bad'ns top secret information, can you? We'd be right buggered if they knew what we was plannin', wouldn't wu?
SUZ   You're right, Morli. The trouble is, the Daleks seem to have a habit of always knowing more than they should.
MORLI   Aye, that's what they told us on the machine at the hospital.
MIRANA   Machine? What machine, Morli?
MORLI   The Good'ns machine. Talks in your head, you know? 'The Bad'ns commuted the greatest crimes known to their uni-' thing.
MIRANA   (*Musing*) Universe...
MORLI   Aye, that's it. You hear it too?
MIRANA   Sounds like some sort of Alliance Dalek conditioning.
ALBY   Conditioning?
Footsteps, approach.
MARBER   (*Approaching*) Captain... Er, excuse me, ma'am.
MIRANA   (*Suppressed irritation*) What is it, Marber?
MARBER   (*Confidentially*) I don't know if you have any idea where they're taking us, but – [31]
MIRANA   Why?
MARBER   Some of the crew and I have been taking a look out of the viewport at some of the star formations.
ALBY   And?
MARBER   I think... Well, we think we're heading for Earth's solar system.
ALBY   Top marks.
MARBER   You knew?
MIRANA   Wasn't it obvious that's where they'd be taking us?
MARBER   But what would be the point? I mean, our fleet's about to destroy all their forces in Earth's solar system.
ALBY   You really believe all the propaganda, don't you?
MARBER   Propaganda? Look, if what our security guards have been telling me about *her* is even half true –
SUZ   (*Pointedly*) And what *have* they been telling you about 'her'?
MARBER   That the Enemy Daleks need your mind to reactivate their Emperor.
ALBY   What about it?
MARBER   Then it's true? Well... isn't it obvious? We can't let them take her back to Earth. If the Daleks were to create a new Emper–

SUZ   So what do you propose we do?

MARBER   Look, we've got your gun and we outnumber the Enemy Daleks on this ship by about three to one.

ALBY   And that means the odds are still in their favour.

MARBER   So what are we going to do? Just sit here and let the enemy win?

MIRANA   Kalendorf has a plan.

MARBER   What sort of plan?

ALBY   Look, we'll never get through the Alliance lines into the solar system –

MARBER   And if that's true, the situation is even more urgent. These Daleks here will probably hold us hostage, try to force the Alliance to let us through. The Mentor will never accede to their demands, so...

MIRANA   So?

MARBER   They'll end up killing us one by one.

ALBY   If the Mentor doesn't order our destruction first... just to simplify the issue.

SUZ   Your Mentor wanted me dead anyway.

MARBER   What do you mean? (*It's dawning on him*) Wh – ? Then... Captain, why did we rescue her if the Mentor...? What's going on here?

ALBY   Do we have ourselves a real boy-scout?

MIRANA   Oh yeah, I believe we do.

MARBER   (*Aghast*) You people are working against the Alliance Daleks, aren't you? Against the Mentor.

SUZ   Your Mentor ordered my destruction. I was supposed to be fired into a collapsing star and forgotten about.

MARBER   Well maybe if your mind is controlled by the Enemy Dalek Emperor, that's the best place for you.

ALBY   (*Angry*) You just watch what you're saying!

SUZ   Alby... It's all right. Look, I am not controlled by the Emperor. (*Slightly sarcastically*) He's just used my mind as somewhere to store his consciousness... for reasons best known to himself.

MARBER   And you expect me to believe that?

MIRANA   I expect you to obey orders, Mr Marber.

MARBER   Obey the orders of a traitor?

ALBY   Traitor? Who have we betrayed? The human race? The Earth Alliance? Or were you just thinking of the Mentor?

MARBER   What's the difference? We're all on the same side!

ALBY   The difference, my friend, is that in her own, sweet, beautiful way, your precious Mentor is every bit as bad as the old Daleks we know and hate so well. Haven't you ever heard of the Punished Planets? (*Pause*) Yeah... I see you have. But like so many of us, you decided not to listen to the rumours... or just not think.

MARBER   Look, the Mentor is –

ALBY   And what *did* you think? Oh, there has to be an explanation for it. The Mentor and her Daleks are here to save us. She wouldn't order the destruction of planets, just because they wouldn't, or couldn't help with the war effort... or couldn't help to the degree that *she* felt appropriate.

MARBER   The Mentor is the only reason we're defeating the Enemy Daleks. Without her forces, we'd have been overrun years ago.

MIRANA   Maybe, but what do you think's going to happen when

we've won? Do you think the Mentor and her Daleks are just going to say, 'Glad we could be of service' and shoot off back to their own universe?[32]
ALBY   Well?
MARBER   I... I don't know.
MORLI   Have you got any more food, like?
ALBY   Here...
Another rustle of a food bar being given and unwrapped.
MORLI   Aw... magic. (*Eating*)
SUZ   Alby, what do *you* think they'll do?
ALBY   They'll take over. They may give us the illusion of freedom... of choice... of happiness. But if any system of planets... any planet... any one person steps out of line –
SUZ   They'll exterminate them?
ALBY   For their own good, you understand. Peace and order... but on the Mentor's terms, nobody else's.
MARBER   Even if you *are* right, isn't that better than being conquered and enslaved by the Enemy Daleks?[33]
MIRANA   Yes. But that's just the lesser of two evils. I'd prefer a third option.
MARBER   So what is Kalendorf planning? (*Pause*) Well? You might as well tell me. (*Pause. Realising*) You don't know, do you?
MIRANA   We trust him.
MARBER   (*Incredulous*) You *trust* him? Is that all?
SUZ   With a man like Kalendorf... that means everything. He's a Knight of Velyshaa. I don't think he'll rest until he's sure that every last Dalek – of whatever faction – has been driven out of this galaxy.

51. Int. Planet Velyshaa. Saloran's Ship.

TARKOV   Have you any idea why Kalendorf didn't trust his friends?
SALORAN   I'm not sure it was a case of him not trusting them. He just felt in his heart that Daleks could never be trusted... no matter which dimension they came from.
TARKOV   You mean... The more people who knew about his secret plan, the more likely it was that the Daleks might find out?
SALORAN   (*Pointedly*) Which Daleks are you talking about?

52. Int. Flagship *Courageous*. Bridge.
Rumble of engines at full thrust.

KALENDORF Maintain course and speed. Give me a scope reading.
ALTERNATE DALEK 1 Second wave of Enemy Dalek ships still well beyond strike distance.
KALENDORF (*Tense, under his breath*) Good... good.
ALTERNATE DALEK 2 Our fleet is now entering Earth's solar system.
KALENDORF Start scanning for likely landing spots on some of the moons of Jupiter.
ALTERNATE DALEK 3 I obey.
Scanning FX commence.
KALENDORF I don't like the look of our power reserves. If we can land and recharge a significant number of ships, we'll be in better shape to tackle their second wave... if it gets here before our reinforcements.

ALTERNATE DALEK 1 Understood, Kalendorf.

Chatter of electronic readouts.

ALTERNATE DALEK 3 Scans are yielding unexpected results.

KALENDORF Unexpected? What do you mean exactly?

ALTERNATE DALEK 3 (*During and beneath the following*) Relaying scan results to main view plate.

Door opens.

HERRICK (*With some effort*) Reporting for duty, sir.

KALENDORF Herrick? Are you sure you're fit enough to –

HERRICK Sir, look! On the screen... What the hell's that?

ALTERNATE DALEK 3 The planet Jupiter.

HERRICK (*Gobsmacked*) Jupiter... but... (*Is lost for words*)

KALENDORF I thought Earth was the only inhabitable planet in this system.

HERRICK It is... I mean, *was*.

KALENDORF What exactly is the scan reading?

ALTERNATE DALEK 3 Nitrogen/oxygen atmosphere: breathable for human beings. Seventeen large continental landmasses. Large H_2O oceans. Conditions are suitable for human habitation.

KALENDORF But... why? How?

Bleep of controls.

HERRICK There's something in orbit... several somethings by the look of it.

Burble of scanners.

ALTERNATE DALEK 2 Terraforming generators. Energy signatures are those of Enemy Dalek technology.

HERRICK You're saying that the Enemy Daleks have deliberately turned the biggest gas giant of the solar system into an inhabitable planet?

ALTERNATE DALEK 1 It would seem so.

HERRICK But it doesn't make sense.

KALENDORF No... No, it doesn't. What the hell are they playing at?

53. Int. Scout-Ship *Defiant*. Bridge.

DALEK SQUAD LEADER Report.

DALEK 1 This scout-ship is now within scanning range of Earth's solar system.

DALEK SQUAD LEADER We must now deal with our human hostages.

DALEK 1 Understood. Drammankin gas tanks have been fitted to loading bay air-supply vents, as ordered.

DALEK SQUAD LEADER Proceed with Drammankin gas release.

DALEK 1 The humans may become hostile when they realise the Drammankin gas is being released. Susan Mendes is armed and may attack Dalek guards.

DALEK SQUAD LEADER Dalek guards in the loading bay will be ordered to withdraw.

DALEK 1 Understood.

DALEK SQUAD LEADER When the Drammankin gas has done its work, we will retrieve Susan Mendes for brain analysis.

DALEK 1 Understood.

Comms beep.

DALEK SQUAD LEADER Dalek commander to Dalek guards in loading bay. Withdraw immediately.

54. Int. Scout-Ship *Defiant*. Loading Bay.
Door opening in mid distance.

MORLI	Look!
MARBER	Captain! *Captain!* The Daleks – they're leaving!
MIRANA	What?
ALBY	Now where the hell are *they* going?
SUZ	Alby –
ALBY	What?
SUZ	I – I don't –
ALBY	*What?!*
SUZ	I've got a feeling –
ALBY	So have I. (*To Daleks*) Hey! You two! Where the hell are

you going?!!

MARBER	They're up to something –
ALBY	My thoughts exactly – Suz, give me that gun!
SUZ	Here.

Gun fires. Impact on Dalek.

MORLI You hit one![34]
DALEK GUARD 1 Alert! Alert! Under fire! Under fire! Alert! (*Continues*)
ALBY Too right, you bastards!
ALBY fires again. Another explosion.
ALBY Everyone down!
He fires again. Another explosion.
DALEK GUARD 2 Motive units damaged. I cannot move.
DALEK GUARD 1 I will give covering fire.

55. Int. Scout-Ship *Defiant*. Bridge.

DALEK SQUAD LEADER Negative! Do not give covering fire! Susan Mendes must not be put at risk.
DALEK GUARD 1 (*Distort*) I... obey.
DALEK 1 Command network diagnostic data indicates one of the Dalek guards has sustained severe damage to motive power.

56. Int. Scout-Ship *Defiant*. Loading Bay.

MORLI It's stuck in the doorway.[35]
ALBY fires again.
MIRANA Alby, no! Don't fire again!
ALBY What?
MIRANA Leave it! They can't close the door. That Dalek's in the way!
MARBER Why isn't it firing back?
SUZ It's me! They don't want to risk harming me.
MARBER Aim for that other Dalek's gun!
ALBY's gun fires.
DALEK GUARD 2 Alert! Alert!
(*Continues into next scene...*)

57. Int. Scout-Ship *Defiant*. Bridge.

DALEK GUARD 2 (*Distort*) Alert! Am under fire!
An explosion on distort.
DALEK GUARD 2 (*Distort*) Weaponry disabled! Unable to defend!
ALBY (*Distort*) Come on! All of you! Let's get out of here!
DALEK SQUAD LEADER Close loading bay doors immediately! The humans must not escape!
DALEK 1 The immobilised Dalek guard is obstructing the doorway!
DALEK SQUAD LEADER (*With more emphasis*) Close loading bay doors immediately and release Drammankin gas! Now!
DALEK 1 I obey!

58. Int. Scout-Ship *Defiant*. Loading Bay.
Doors activate. Panic and chatter and footsteps of crew escaping.

MARBER Quick! They're closing the doors! Move it![36]
ALBY Come on! Suz?
SUZ I'm all right, let's go –
A hissing noise.
SUZ What's that?[37]
MIRANA What do you mean?
The door crashes into Dalek.
MORLI Oh blimey, look at that! (*She laughs over the following*)
DALEK GUARD 1 Aaargh! Alert! Casing being crushed by loading bay door! I cannot move! Assist me! Assist!
DALEK GUARD 2 (*Moving into distance*) Cannot assist! Cannot assist! I have orders to withdraw and await reinforcements!
MORLI That's magic, that is! Crushin' the bastard!
Door mechanism is clicking on and off, like a car engine with crashing gears. Mechanism is in trouble. The Dalek casing is being slowly crushed under its weight, but it's a bit of battle.
DALEK GUARD 1 Aaargh! Assssssisssssst![38]
ALBY That Dalek casing's not going to take the weight of that door indefinitely, folks! Come on!
Coughing and screaming of crewmembers. Hissing increases in volume.
MIRANA What the hell's happening?
MARBER (*Spluttering*) It's gas! Coming from the air vents! Gas! Everyone out! For God's sake! Now![39]
ALBY The cheaky beggars were gonna gas us!
MIRANA *Are* gassing us!
SUZ Alby, come on!
Screaming, panic and coughing crescendos.

59. Int. Scout-Ship *Defiant*. Bridge.

DALEK SQUAD LEADER The humans are escaping! Track them on internal scanners.
Ping of scanners tracking.
DALEK 1 Tracking. Fifty-seven humans rendered unconscious by Drammankin gas. The remaining sixteen are moving at speed along walkway adjoining loading bay.

252

DALEK SQUAD LEADER Dispatch a security squad to intercept them immediately.

60. Int. Scout-Ship *Defiant*. Walkway.
Footsteps and much exhausted breathing of the sixteen survivors running.

MARBER What about the others we left behind? Are they dead?
SUZ They wouldn't have wanted to kill me. That gas must've just knocked them all out.[40]
MORLI Yeah, but there'll be others after us soon, won't there?
ALBY Mirana! Where are we heading?
MIRANA We have to get to the armoury – We're not going to get back control of my ship with just one gun!
MARBER We should take this lift![41]
Footsteps come to a halt. Much recovery vocal noises.
MIRANA Level Nine.
MARBER (*Irritated*) I know!
Bleep of lift activation. Then negative bleep.
MARBER It's not working.
SUZ They'll have shut down the lifts.
ALBY Makes sense. The Daleks never miss a trick.
MORLI Are we buggered then?
ALBY Let's hope not, Morli.
MIRANA If they've accessed the security shutdown controls, it won't be long before they activate the emergency bulkhead doors and cut off our escape routes.
MARBER So what do we do?
MIRANA Use the maintenance access ladders and get to the nearest escape pods.
MARBER There are four on the level below us. Should be enough to take us all – at a squeeze.
ALBY Well let's go then!
Footsteps start (led by MIRANA at first).
MIRANA This way. Should be a maintenance hatch along –
Door opens in distance.
DALEKS (*Variously, in distance*) Surrender! Surrender now! You are our prisoners!
MORLI Look out! More of the buggers!
ALBY Move it, everyone! I'll cover you!
Running footsteps begin.
SUZ No, Alby! Give me the gun! They won't shoot me!
MIRANA Marber, help me with this hatch!
MORLI I'll help. Got big muscles, me! Wanna feel?
Metallic creak and click of hatch being opened. Continues under...
MARBER (*With effort*) Got it!
MIRANA grunts with effort too.
MORLI (*With effort*) Argh! It's all crusted up! You wanna look after these hatches, man!
MARBER (*With effort*) Keep pulling!
DALEK Exterminate!
Dalek firing. Several humans cry out and die.

61. Int. Scout-Ship *Defiant*. Bridge.
Cry of humans and firing continues on distort as if on screen.

DALEK 1   Dalek security squad opening fire. Eleven humans exterminated.
DAL SQUAD LEADER (*With urgency*) Cease firing! Cease firing! Susan Mendes must not be harmed!
SUZ   (*Distort*) Cease fire! All of you! You daren't kill me! You daren't!
Firing has ceased.
SUZ   (*Distort*) Now, quickly! All of you!
DALEK 1   Humans are escaping through maintenance hatchway. Schematic suggests they are heading for escape capsules on the level below.
ALBY   (*Distort*) Suz!
SUZ   (*Distort*) Just go, Alby! Get out of here! If you stay, sooner or later, they're going to kill you and... and I couldn't bear that!
DALEK SQUAD LEADER They must not escape! They must not escape! Security squad will switch weaponry to paralysis mode.
MORLI   (*Distort*) Come on, Alby – !

62. Int. Scout-Ship *Defiant*. Walkway.

MORLI   (*...continued*) Come on!!!
SUZ   Alby! Go! Please!!!
ALBY   I can't leave you, Suz! Not again. I can't!
Gun fires. Impacts.[42]
SUZ   (*To DALEKS*) Get back! Get back!
DALEK   Under fire! Under fire!
DALEK 1   You will surrender! Surrender!
ALBY   Suuuz!

63. Int. Scout-Ship *Defiant*. Bridge.
Gunfire continues on distort from previous scene, with cries from Daleks etc.

DALEK 1   Two humans have escaped down maintenance ladder. Security scan identifies them as Captain Mirana and First Officer Marber.
Alarm bleeps.
DALEK 1   They have entered an escape pod. Escape pod engines now firing. They have escaped.[43]

64. Ext. Space.
Escape pod launches into space.

65. Int. Scout-Ship *Defiant*. Bridge.

DALEK SQUAD LEADER Security squad will fire paralysis beams at the two remaining humanoids with Susan Mendes, immediately!

DALEK   (*Distort*) We obey. Firing!

66. Int. Scout-Ship *Defiant*. Walkway.

Dalek guns fire.

SUZ   Noooo!!!
ALBY   Su – aaaargh!
MORLI   Aaaaaargh!
Silence.
SUZ   You... you've killed them! Keep back or I'll fire!
DALEK   You are our prisoner!
SUZ   Then I'll be your dead prisoner.
DALEK   No! No! You must not kill yourself! You are essential to our plan!
SUZ   You've just killed the one reason for me staying alive. I don't care anymore.
DALEK   He is not dead.
SUZ   What?
DALEK   Alby Brook is not dead. We were ordered to fire paralysis beams only.
SUZ   Alby?
DALEK   He is unconscious, but he will recover shortly.[44]

67. Int. Scout-Ship *Defiant*. Bridge.

DALEK SQUAD LEADER Tell her, 'If you do not surrender, we will exterminate Alby Brook'.
DALEK   (*Distort*) If you do not surrender, we will exterminate Alby Brook.
Pause. SUZ starts to laugh, a slow laugh of despair. It grows in momentum. Crossfade:

68. Int. Scout-Ship *Defiant*. Walkway.

SUZ's laugh becomes hysterical.

DALEK   Silence!
She stops.
SUZ   Or you'll exterminate me? I don't think so.
DALEK   Drop the weapon or the man you love will die.
Long pause. The weapon drops to the floor with a clang.

69. Int. Flagship *Courageous*. Executive Communication Chamber.

MENTOR   Another risk, Kalendorf?
KALENDORF   I don't think it's a dangerous risk. We'll leave half the fleet orbiting in defensive formation. The rest will land and refuel. Our scientists have located more than enough chemical and mineral deposits on Jupiter for our purposes.
MENTOR   Fortuitous.
KALENDORF   Indeed. If all goes well, we'll leave Jupiter with more power at our disposal than we had when we first engaged the enemy outside this solar system. We'll also be able to give our non-Dalek soldiers some time to stretch their legs or whatever else it is they need to stretch. They've been cooped up in those troop carriers for several

months. The Orearlisians in particular have been complaining rather a lot.[45]

MENTOR   And you are certain that Jupiter is completely uninhabited?

KALENDORF   I'm sure you've accessed the scans yourself, Mentor. No intelligent life whatsoever.

MENTOR   Have you formed any opinion as to why the Dalek Supreme might have... laid this golden egg for us?

Pause.

KALENDORF   I think the Enemy Daleks were intending to make it a military base, but had to retreat when we defeated their first fleet.

MENTOR   That is... an optimistic assumption.

KALENDORF   I don't see any other reasonable interpretation.

MENTOR   (*Firm*) That this newly terraformed planet Jupiter is a trap, Kalendorf.

KALENDORF   In what way? You've seen the scans. Lush vegetation. A breathable atmosphere. Rich in minerals and –

MENTOR   Ideal for human habitation. The Daleks have no such requirements.

KALENDORF   You would rather we stayed here and met their second wave with our energy depleted and our crews exhausted?

Pause.

MENTOR   When you land on this planet, Kalendorf... be on your guard. You and I know how cunning the Dalek Supreme can be. Do not forget that caution I have admired in you so much.

KALENDORF   I won't, Mentor. I won't.

MENTOR   Before you proceed, I feel I must inform you that Scout-Ship *Defiant* has been detected at long range, approaching this solar system.

KALENDORF   Then I'll contact Mirana and ask her why she –

MENTOR   My monitors have already attempted contact. The *Defiant* seems to have suffered a communications breakdown.

KALENDORF   Then I'll take a ship and intercept –

MENTOR   I have already dispatched a gunship to offer assistance. (*Pause*) Is something troubling you, Kalendorf?

70. Int. Scout-Ship *Defiant*. Bridge.

DALEK SQUAD LEADER   Engage restraints!

DALEK 1   I obey.

Bleep. Then massive clunking of three huge metallic restraint devices. As each clunks shut, gasps of pain from MORLI, ALBY, then finally SUZ.

SUZ   What are you going to do to us?

DALEK SQUAD LEADER   Activate brain analysis disc.

DALEK 1   I obey.

Hum of brain analysis disc rising.

SUZ   What is that?

ALBY   (*Groggy*) It's that thing they used on me to –

DALEK 1   Silence!

DALEK SQUAD LEADER   Brain analysis disc will attach to the Mendes woman's head.

DALEK 1   I obey.

Controls bleep. Disc hum as it hovers to SUZ. 'Glitch' of it attaching.
SUZ   Aaaargh!
DALEK 1   Silence!
ALBY   Leave her alone!
Massive electrical shock.
ALBY   Aaaaargh!
MORLI   Alby![46]
DALEK SQUAD LEADER Silence! All of you!
SUZ and ALBY make noises of recovery.
DALEK SQUAD LEADER Susan Mendes, the brain analysis disc will scan
your mind for traces of the Emperor's consciousness. If you resist us,
your friends will die in agony. The girl first, then the man you love. We
will begin.
ALBY   (*Weakly*) Suz... I'm sorry.
*Buzz of disc activating. SUZ gives out a yelp of pain, which settles into
moans of discomfort.*
DALEK SQUAD LEADER Where is the Emperor?
SUZ   I... I...
DALEK SQUAD LEADER Where is the Emperor? Do not resist. Surrender
your mind to us. Where is the Emperor?
SUZ   I... I... can't –
DALEK SQUAD LEADER Maximum scan power. Now!
Control bleep. Huge charge from the disc.
SUZ   Aaaaaargh!
DALEK SQUAD LEADER We are entering your mind. You cannot resist.[47]
We are entering your miiiiind!
Cut immediately to:

71. Int. Suz's Mind.

SUZ   (*Close and echoing*) I... I cannot resist. You are entering
my mind. Who are you?
EMPEROR   (*Very distant and echoing wildly*) Susan Mendes... Susan
Mendes... Susan Mendes... (*Continues, coming ever closer*)
SUZ   (*With dread*) It's... it's you... It's you. No. No. I don't want
to think this... No.
EMPEROR   (*Clearer and foreground*) I am part of you. You are part
of me. You will obey! You will obey! You will obey!
SUZ   No! Please! No!
EMPEROR   We are one! We are the same! We are the Emperor of the
Daleks!
SUZ   (*Screams*)

72. Int. Scout-Ship *Defiant*. Bridge.
SUZ is screaming.

ALBY   Leave her alone! Stop this! I'll kill you! I'll bloody kill you
all! Bastards!
Electric shock.
ALBY   Aaaaargh!
DALEK SQUAD LEADER Silence!
ALBY recovers noisily.

257

MORLI   Alby... Alby, are you okay, man?[48]
ALBY   (*Recovering from agony*) Argh... yeah... I... I'm... I'm
okay.
DALEK 1   Scan complete.
Disc hums away then the hum winds down.
DALEK SQUAD LEADER Report analysis.
DALEK 1   Total success.
ALBY   Success? What do you mean?
DALEK SQUAD LEADER Silence!
ALBY   What do you mean? Success? Have you killed her? Suz?
MORLI   Alby, don't! They – [49]
Massive electric shock again.
ALBY   AAAAaaaargh!
He recovers.
ALBY   (*Very weak*) Suz?
DALEK SQUAD LEADER Susan Mendes?
SUZ   (*Dazed*) Mmm? What?
DALEK SQUAD LEADER Susan Mendes. Speak.
Pause.
SUZ   I... we... I... am the Emperor of the Daleks.
ALBY   (*Screams*) Noooo!

Crash in closing theme

NOTES

1. Line changed to: 'No! ~~I'm serious — keep away!!!~~ (*Pause*) ~~I mean it!~~ I know why you want me. I know I'm vital to your plan.'

2. Line changed to: '~~Um~~... We'll... (*She stops*) Well... Now not's exactly a good time, is it?'

3. Line changed to: '~~Sure~~. Yeah. I know. You... carry on.'

4. Line changed to: '(Weak) Thank... thank you, sir. They hit us pretty **hard** didn't they?'

5. Line changed to: '**Is** anyone in a fit state to give me a damage report?'

6. Line changed to: 'I... **I**... **I**... I have sust-**sust**-sustained **da**-damage, but re-**re**-remain ~~op~~-operational.'

7. Line changed to: 'Rep-**rep-rep**-repair teams report slow progress. Damage to outer hull plates and engines was severe.'

8. Line changed to: 'Alliance **fl-fl**-fleet casualties currently stand at 132 ships. Approximately 25 per cent of our force.'

9. Line changed to: '~~Oh~~... (*Sighs*) I told the Daleks I wanted to die once before. Years ago.'

10. Line changed to: 'You're saying **that** you should have just killed yourself the moment the Daleks docked with my ship?'

11. Line changed to: '**Yeah**. If I was dead, the Dalek Emperor would be dead too. And you'd win the war. Well, wouldn't you?'

12. Line changed to: '(Impatient) Yes... Mirana. But I don't see the relevance of **that** – '

13. Line changed to: 'That's where the Dalek Supreme is... It's the Enemy Dalek stronghold ~~now~~... and it's probably where the Emperor's casing is by now.'

14. Line changed to: 'When you were **hijacked** by Daleks?'

15. Line changed to: 'Yeah. The good Daleks **were** lookin' after us. Then the bad'ns attacked. Bloody huge battle. They **were** lookin' for something.'

16. Line changed to: 'Did a? Oh aye... sorry... I sometimes forget things, **like**, when I'm scared, ~~like~~, you knah?'

17. Line changed to: '**All right**... well, look, there's nothing to be scared of. Okay?'

18. Line changed to: 'Me knee? Oh, it's not bad. Just knocked it on something when I was runnin' just then. Have you got ought to eat, ~~like~~?'

19. Line changed to: 'It's all right. **Just** take your time.'

20. Line changed to: 'Keep happening. There was a lot of big explosions when the Daleks was fightin' I think they **might** have done some serious damage, like.'

21. Line changed to: 'Special place. Where the good Daleks did all their special stuff, ~~like~~.'

22. Line changed to: 'Then I'm not imagining it. Looks like our Daleks were giving ita right **good** old going over. They've got it on... well it looks like a huge operating table.'

23. Line changed to: 'Definitely, aye. 'Bout the same size, I'd say, ~~man~~.'

24. Line changed to: 'Shut up, Morli! **Just** go!'

25. Line changed to: 'It feels all funny... like me stomach's all floaty... Ooh, I think I'm going to puke, man. It's that bar o'stuff you gave **us**!'

26. Line changed to: 'No, it isn't! It's zero-grav. **Have** you been in zero-grav before?'

27. Line changed to: 'You mean you're not going to kill **us**?'

28. Line changed to: '(Suspicious) Did you get that stuff about Mirana and the rendezvous out of my brain, or did you already know ~~all~~ that?'

29. Line changed to: 'Saying the Daleks could kill **us**.'

30. Line changed to: 'Oh. Morli... look, I'm sorry ~~about~~ – '

31. Line changed to: '(*Confidentially*) **I**, **er**... I don't know if you have any idea where they're taking us, but **some of the crew** – '

32. Line changed to: 'Maybe, but what do you think's going to happen when we've won? Do you think the Mentor and her Daleks are just going to say, '**Oh**, glad we could be of service' and shoot back off to their own universe?'

33. Line changed to: '**Look**, even if you are right, isn't that better than being conquered and enslaved by the Enemy Daleks?'

34. Line changed to: '**Ah**, **great**, **man**! You hit one!'

35. Line changed to: '**Ee**, **that Dalek**. It's stuck in the doorway.'

36. Line changed to: 'Quick! They're closing the doors! Move it! **Come on**!'

37. This line and the following three were re-ordered as:
The door crashes into Dalek.

MORLI   Oh blimey, look at that! (*She laughs over the following*)

DALEK GUARD 1 Aaargh! Alert! Casing being crushed by loading bay door! I cannot move! Assist me! Assist!

SUZ   What's that?

MIRANA   What do you mean?

38. Deleted dialogue – **DALEK GUARD 1**: '~~Aaargh! Asssssssssst!~~'

39. Line changed to: '(*Spluttering*) It's gas! Coming from the air vents! Gas! **Come on**, everyone out! For God's sake! Now!'

40. Line changed to: '**The Daleks** wouldn't have wanted to kill me. That gas must've just knocked them all out.'

41. Line changed to: 'We should take **the** lift.'

42. The rest of the scene was re-ordered as:

DALEK 1   You will surrender! Surrender!

SUZ   (*To DALEKS*) Get back! Get back!

DALEK   Under fire! Under fire!

ALBY   Suuuz!

43. 'They have escaped,' was moved to the beginning of Scene 65.

44. Line changed to: 'He is unconscious, but he will recover ~~shortly~~.'

45. Line changed to: 'Indeed. If all goes well, we'll leave Jupiter with more **energy** at our disposal than we had when we first engaged the enemy outside this solar system. We'll also be able to give our non-Dalek soldiers some time to stretch their legs or whatever else it is they need to stretch. They've been cooped up in those troop carriers for several months. The Orearlisians in particular have been complaining rather a lot.'

46. Line changed to: 'Alby! **Stop hurting him**, **man**.' Also, added dialogue – **DALEK 1**: 'Silence!'

47. Line changed to: 'We are entering your mind. You cannot resist **us**.'

48. Line changed to: 'Alby... Alby, are you okay, ~~man~~?'

49. Line changed to: 'Alby, don't! They'**ll hurt you**.'

Q&A
CHAPTER TWO

When you're writing, do you consider sound design – or is it a completely separate process that you only worry about after recording?
Nicholas Briggs: Since I invariably do my own sound design, I think I can't help thinking about it when I write. Mostly, it's to do with knowing what is achievable. I can't imagine writing audio drama without being able to think of a way of technically achieving what I'm writing. That's just automatic. However, I do try to do just one job at a time. So I do set myself incredibly difficult problems with sound design. They're the kind of problems I'd curse another writer for creating. But ultimately, I can't help hearing a scene in my head when I write it... and that involves hearing the sound effects, which starts me thinking how I'd achieve them.

Occasionally in the scripts, you'll note where some music should go and sometimes what it's doing ('Music cue – "o-oh"'). Was this a guide for the actors, or for you when you did post-production?
I really do leave most of the music ideas until the sound design is done. However, sometimes I feel it helps to make sense of the scene for me and the actors if you note that this will be one of those 'oh-oh, here comes trouble' type of moments. I don't generally put music notes into the script. I only do it when I feel the script wouldn't seem so effective without it. It's something I only do when I know I'm going to be directing and sound designing. In many ways, I think it's a bit of a crass thing to do. But it works for me. I forgive myself.

Alby says 'shit' a couple of times in Chapter Two. Tell me about your attitude to swearing. Do you think the rules were flexible/different because it wasn't *Doctor Who*?
The swearing thing is an ongoing debate in Big Finish. Now that the TV series is coming back and will, quite rightly, be targeted at *Doctor Who*'s traditional family audience, I think that swearing shouldn't feature in any of our *Doctor Who* releases. It's contradicting the core brand image. However, before the return of the TV series, I feel that our audience was mainly (not totally, I agree) made-up of people in their twenties and thirties who were probably receptive to a more 'adult', 'gritty' kind of drama. I wanted *Dalek Empire* and *Dalek War* to be that kind of drama, so I felt that limited swearing was allowable, in line with what the BBC *Doctor Who* books have done. I would never have wanted to use the f- or c-words, though. I think that would have been too ugly in this context. With *Dalek Empire III*, I'm not having any kind of swearing at all. It's been a challenge for me, but, in the final analysis, swearing offends some people, but a lack of swearing never offends. Perhaps that should be the tag-line for *Dalek Empire III*... 'This time, it's less offensive, so Justin Richards's son can listen to it'.

Jupiter? A habitable planet? ...that's just silly.

I wanted the Daleks to do something audacious! I know it's totally impossible, but so are the Daleks and so is all the space travel without the time dilation effect. It's just different degrees of fantasy, and it's very personal as to what an individual will buy into. John Ainsworth thought it was unforgivable. We laughed a lot about it. He said it would have been easier for the Daleks to build a new planet from scratch rather than try to terraform a gas giant. Maybe that's what the Daleks did... blew up Jupiter and built a new planet. And let's not get started about the effect this would have on gravitational pull in the solar system. Remember, folks. It's fantasy. It's not predictive science fiction.

Although she appears in the final few moments of Chapter One, this part sees us meet Morli. The dialogue was written almost phonetically – you could hear her accent in your head, couldn't you?

I hope Clayton Hickman won't mind me quoting him, but he said one of the things he liked about *Dalek Empire* was that Alby's voice made it feel like 'common people in space', rather than the usual southern English accents dominating. I'd met Dannie Carr and seen her work and fell in love with her accent. I thought it would be fun to have a Geordie character... and she's a great actress. Because I know the way she talks, I couldn't help writing it phonetically. I did apologise to her in advance, in case she thought it was patronising. She changed some of the phraseology. It's also good to have a mixture of accents. I know it's one of the 'no-no's of radio drama to have loads of spurious different accents just for the sake of delineating the characters – so you end up with a German, a Scot, an American and a Hungarian all just happening to share a train carriage – but, a mix of accents, judiciously used, can be helpful in this respect.

Why was the line 'When you were jumped by Daleks?' changed to 'When you were hijacked by Daleks?'

It made everyone laugh. It sounds like the Daleks 'got off' with Alby... if you've got a dirty mind. And most actors do have dirty minds. They're always looking for something smutty to laugh about... oh, maybe that's just me. I kind of want to avoid as much unintentional *double-entendre* as possible. My favourite one is 'her energy pods are glowing', which was a line from an Audio Visuals play, referring to a space ship which was about to explode. The actors laughed like drains, even though it wasn't really a *double-entendre* at all. It just inexplicably sounded smutty.

The Mentor and Kalendorf scenes must have been fun to write. All the time, the pair of them are trying to not give away their true beliefs or knowledge – there's marvellous tension in those scenes. How difficult is it to write scenes like that – scenes where characters *aren't* saying something?

I find scenes like this a lot of fun to write, because the characters have very clear motivations. And when the motivation is to achieve your aim covertly, it leads to all sorts of interesting twists and turns of phrase. I particularly liked it when the Mentor just paused and let Kalendorf stew for a while.

DALEK WAR

Recording Schedule

Nicholas Briggs: *I hate recording things out of order, but the advantage of it is that you can have bigger casts. If you recorded each episode one at a time and in order, you'd have to keep bringing back actors day after day to do their scenes from each episode. If, however, you record in character blocks, someone who's in all four episodes need only come in for a day. That saving then gives you money to employ other actors so that you can reduce doubling up... or indeed save money, make Jason Haigh-Ellery very happy, and leave enough pennies for Nick Pegg to blow the budget again on his spectacular star casting!*

There is, of course, also the issue of cast availability. When you're doing a second series of anything, you need the same actors back, and the chances are that this time round they're far less available. It was a bit of a nightmare, because Sarah was on tour, and Mark and Gareth were also very busy on stage in Scotland. It was a real juggling act doing the scheduling and it nearly drove me insane. I've just done it again for Dalek Empire III and my head's really hurting.

Sunday 27 October 2002

ACTORS Gareth Thomas (Kalendorf), Sarah Mowat (Suz), Mark McDonnell (Alby), Hannah Smith (Mentor), Jeremy James (Herrick & Tech 1), Ian Brooker (Marber, Drudger, Sparks), Nicholas Briggs (Dalek voices)
Scenes may not be recorded in the order listed below. The numbers in brackets indicate roughly how many pages to each scene.

2. Int. Flagship *Courageous.* (1) Alternate Dalek, Kalendorf
6. Int. Flagship *Courageous.* Bridge. (2) Tech 1, Alternate Dalek, Kalendorf
7. Int. Flagship *Courageous.* Executive Communication Chamber. (3) Alternate Dalek, Mentor, Kalendorf
16. Int. Flagship *Courageous.* Bridge. (1) Kalendorf, Herrick
22. Int. Flagship *Courageous.* Excecutive Communication Chamber. (1) Alternate Dalek, Mentor, Kalendorf, Herrick
38. Int. Flagship *Courageous.* Bridge. (2) Kalendorf, Herrick, Alternate Dalek, Alternate Dalek 1
40. Int. Flagship *Courageous.* Executive Communication Chamber. (1.5) Mentor, Kalendorf
52. Int. Flagship *Courageous.* Bridge. (2) Kalendorf, Alternate Dalek 1, Alternate Dalek 2, Alternate Dalek 3, Herrick
69. Int. Flagship *Courageous.* Executive Communication Chamber. (2) Mentor, Kalendorf
98. Int. Scout-Ship *Defiant.* Bridge. (2) Dalek, Dalek 1, Dalek Squad Leader, Dalek 2, Alby, Suz, Kalendorf
101. Int. Scout-Ship *Defiant.* Bridge. (4.5) Suz, Kalendorf, Alby, Dalek Squad Leader
104. Int. Scout-Ship *Defiant.* Bridge. (4.5) Suz, Kalendorf, Alby, Dalek Supreme
112. Int. Scout-Ship *Defiant.* Bridge. (1) Alby, Kalendorf, Suz, Dalek Supreme
114. Int. Scout-Ship *Defiant.* Bridge. (1.5) Dalek Supreme, Kalendorf, Suz
5. Int. Gunship MX4. (1) Drudger, Alby
9. Int. Gunship MX4. (2) Drudger, Alby
13. Int. Gunship MX4. (2) Drudger, Alby
18. Int. Gunship MX4. (1) Alby, Drudger

20. **Int. Hospital Station. Airlock Reception. (1)** Alby, Drudger (also do Drudger lines for 43, 45 and 47)
24. **Flashback: Int. Cryo-Chamber. Emperor's Ship. (3)** Alby, Kalendorf, Alternate Dalek, Mirana (to be recorded 10 November)
26. **Int. Mentor's Chamber. (1)** Mirana (to be recorded 10 November), Mentor, Kalendorf, Alby
28. **Int. Mentor's Chamber. (1)** Mentor, Mirana (to be recorded 10 November), Kalendorf
31. **Ext. Planet Emmeron. (1)** Mirana (to be recorded 10 November), Kalendorf, Alby
33. **Ext. Planet Emmeron. (0.5)** Alby, Kalendorf, Mirana (to be recorded 10 November)
123. **Int. Flagship *Courageous*. Secure Room. (1)** Dalek, Herrick, Kalendorf
73. **Ext. Jupiter. (1)** Herrick, Kalendorf
74. **Int. Flagship *Courageous*. Bridge. (1)** Kalendorf, Herrick, Alternate Dalek 1
80. **Int. 5th Airborne Brigade HQ. Jupiter. (1)** Kalendorf, Herrick
82. **Int. Allenby's Skimmer. (1.5)** Sparks, Kalendorf's lines only, Trooper (to be recorded 4 November)
83. **Int. Flagship *Courageous*. Bridge. (1)** Kalendorf, Alternate Dalek 1
88. **Int. Flagship *Courageous*. Executive Communication Chamber. (4)** Mentor, Kalendorf, Monitor, Alternate Dalek
89. **Int. Flagship *Courageous*. Corridor. (1.5)** Alternate Dalek, Kalendorf, Alternate Dalek Tannoy, Vaarga-man, Alternate Dalek 1
91. **Int. Space Transport Ship. (0.5)** Kalendorf

Sunday 3 November 2002

ACTORS Gareth Thomas (Kalendorf), Mark McDonnell (Alby), Sarah Mowat (Suz – arriving PM), Hannah Smith (Mentor), Dannie Carr (Morli), Helen Goldwyn (Godwin & Computer), Jack Galagher (Command & Trooper), Nicholas Briggs (Dalek voices)
  Scenes may not be recorded in the order listed below. The numbers in brackets indicate roughly how many pages to each scene.

116. **Ext. Battlefield. Planet Meecros V. (4.5)** Godwin, Command, Kalendorf, Alternate Dalek, Trooper
117. **Int. Flagship. Bridge. (2)** Godwin, Kalendorf
118. **Int. Recovery Capsule. (2.5)** Godwin, Kalendorf, Computer
120. **Int. Recovery Capsule Docking Arm. (0.5)** Kalendorf, Computer
121. **Int. Mentor's Base. (1)** Kalendorf, Alternate Dalek
122. **Ext. Mentor's Garden. (2)** Mentor, Kalendorf
124. **Ext. Mentor's Garden. (3.5)** Mentor, Kalendorf
126. **Int. Flagship. Kalendorf's Cabin. (2)** Kalendorf, Godwin
127. **Int. Dalek Control. Earth. Tracking Centre. (1)** Dalek, Dalek 1, Dalek Supreme, Kalendorf
128. **Int. Dalek Control. Earth. Dalek Supreme's Chamber. (0.5)** Dalek Supreme, Kalendorf
130. **Ext. Dalek Control. Landing Pad Zeg. Earth. (1)** Dalek, Dalek 1, Kalendorf
131. **Int. Dalek Emperor's Antechamber. Earth. (7)** Dalek, Dalek Supreme, Kalendorf, Suz, Dalek Tannoy
43. **Int. Hospital Station. Airlock Reception. (5)** Alby, Morli, Drudger
45. **Int. Hospital Ship. Examination Bay. (3)** Alby, Morli, Drudger
47. **Ext. Hospital Space Station Hull. (1)** Alby, Morli, Dalek, Drudger
49. **Int. Gunship MX4. (3.5)** Dalek Squad Leader, Alby, Dalek 1, Morli, Dalek 2
57. **Int. Scout-Ship *Defiant*. Bridge. (0.5)** Dalek Guard 2, Alby, Dalek 1
61. **Int. Scout-Ship *Defiant*. Bridge. (1)** Dalek 1, Dalek Squad Leader, Suz, Alby, Morli; cry of humans

62. Int. Scout-Ship *Defiant*. **Walkway.** (0.5) Morli, Suz, Alby, Dalek
66. Int. Scout-Ship *Defiant*. **Walkway.** (1) Suz, Alby, Morli, Dalek
68. Int. Scout-Ship *Defiant*. **Walkway.** (1) Dalek, Suz
70. Int. Scout-Ship *Defiant*. **Bridge.** (2) Dal Squ Leader, Dalek 1, Suz, Alby, Morli
71. Int. **Suz's Mind.** (0.5) Suz, Emperor
72. Int. Scout-Ship *Defiant*. **Bridge.** (1.5) Suz, Alby, Dal Squ Leader, Morli
85. Int. Scout-Ship *Defiant*. **Holding Cell.** (2.5) Morli, Alby, Suz
97. Int. Scout-Ship *Defiant*. **Cell.** (3.5) Alby, Suz, Morli, Dalek
103. Int. Scout-Ship *Defiant*. **Airlock Reception.** (1) Alby
129. Int. **Dalek Emperor's Chamber. Earth.** (0.5) Suz, Dalek Supreme

Monday 4 November 2002

ACTORS Teresa Gallagher (Mirana), Mark McDonnell (Alby), Sarah Mowat (Suz), Dannie Carr (Morli), Ian Brooker (Marber & Sparks), Jeremy James (Herrick & Trooper), Mark Donovan (Allenby, Scientist & Trooper 1), Nicholas Briggs (Dalek voices)
Scenes may not be recorded in the order listed below. The numbers on the right indicate roughly how many pages to each scene.

14. Int. Scout-Ship *Defiant*. **Infirmary.** (3) Johnstone, Mirana, Marber, Suz
19. Int. Scout-Ship *Defiant*. **Infirmary.** (2.5) Mirana, Johnstone, Suz
23. Int. Scout-Ship *Defiant*. **Mirana's Cabin.** (3.5) Mirana, Suz
25. Int. Scout-Ship *Defiant*. **Mirana's Cabin.** (0.5) Mirana, Suz
27. Int. Scout-Ship *Defiant*. **Mirana's Cabin.** (1) Suz, Mirana
30. Int. Scout-Ship *Defiant*. **Mirana's Cabin.** (1.5) Suz, Mirana
32. **Mirana's Narration.** (0.5) Mirana
34. Int. Scout-Ship *Defiant*. **Mirana's Cabin.** (1.5) Mirana, Suz, Marber
35. Int. Scout-Ship *Defiant*. **Bridge.** (1.5) Mirana, Marber, Suz, Alby
36. Int. Scout-Ship *Defiant*. **Airlock Reception.** (1.5) Mirana, Suz, Morli, Alby, Security Man, Dalek Squad Leader, Dalek 1
37. Int. Scout-Ship *Defiant*. **Airlock Reception.** (5.5) Suz, Mirana, Alby, Morli, Dalek Squad Leader, Dalek 1, Daleks
39. Int. *Defiant* **Loading Bay.** (3) Mirana, Alby, Suz, Morli, Dalek, Dalek Squad Leader
42. Int. Scout-Ship *Defiant*. **Loading Bay.** (1.5) Morli, Mirana, Alby, Suz
48. Int. Scout-Ship *Defiant*. **Loading Bay.** (0.5) Mirana, Morli, Suz
50. Int. Scout-Ship *Defiant*. **Loading Bay.** (5.5) Suz, Alby, Mirana, Morli, Marber
54. Int. Scout-Ship *Defiant*. **Loading Bay.** (1.5) Morli, Marber, Mirana, Alby, Suz, Dalek Guard 1
56. Int. Scout-Ship *Defiant*. **Loading Bay.** (0.5) Morli, Mirana, Alby, Marber, Suz, Dalek Guard 2
58. Int. Scout-Ship *Defiant*. **Loading Bay.** (1.5) Marber, Alby, Suz, Mirana, Morli, Dalek Guard 1, Dalek Guard 2; coughing and screaming of crewmembers; screaming, panic and coughing crescendos.
60. Int. Scout-Ship *Defiant*. **Walkway.** (2) Marber, Suz, Morli, Alby, Mirana, Daleks; several humans cry out and die.
76. Int. **5th Airborne Brigade HQ. Jupiter.** (2) Scientist, Herrick, Allenby
77. Ext. **Jupiter. Forest. Night.** (0.5) Allenby
78. Int. **Allenby's Skimmer.** (1.5) Allenby, Trooper, Sparks
79. Ext. **Jupiter. Forest. Night.** (1) Allenby, Trooper, Trooper 1
81. Ext. **Jupiter. Forest. Night.** (1) Trooper, Allenby
82. Int. **Allenby's Skimmer.** (1.5) Sparks, Kalendorf, Trooper

Plus as many of the following Dalek-only scenes as is possible.
11. **Int. Enemy Dalek Control. Earth.** (1) Dalek Supreme, Daleks, Dalek, Dalek 1, Dalek 2
21. **Int. Enemy Dalek Control. Earth.** (1) Dalek Com, Dalek Supreme
41. **Int. Scout-Ship *Defiant*. Bridge.** (0.5) Dalek Squad Leader, Dalek 1
44. **Int. Enemy Dalek Transport Ship.** (0.5) Dalek Drone, Dalek Commander
46. **Ext. Space. Enemy Dalek Transolar Comms.** (0.5) Dalek Squad Leader, Daleks, Dalek 1
53. **Int. Scout-Ship Defiant. Bridge.** (1) Dalek Squad Leader, Dalek 1
55. **Int. Scout-Ship *Defiant*. Bridge.** (0.5) Dalek Squad Leader, Dalek Guard 1, Dalek 1
59. **Int. Scout-Ship *Defiant*. Bridge.** (0.5) Dalek Squad Leader, Dalek 1
63. **Int. Scout-Ship *Defiant*. Bridge.** (0.5) Dalek 1
65. **Int. Scout-Ship *Defiant*. Bridge.** (0.5) Dalek Squad Leader, Dalek
67. (0.5) Dalek Supreme, Dalek, Suz (laugh, transferred from Scene 68)
84. **Int. Enemy Dalek Command. Earth.** (1) Dalek, Dalek Supreme
93. **Int. Scout-Ship *Defiant*. Bridge.** (0.5) Dalek, Dalek Squad Leader
94. **Int. Gun Ship B68. Bridge.** (0.5) Alternate Dalek
95. **Int. Scout-Ship *Defiant*. Bridge.** (0.5) Dalek, Dalek Squad Leader
96. **Int. Enemy Dalek Control. Earth.** (0.5) Dalek, Dalek Supreme
100. **Int. Scout-Ship *Defiant*. Airlock Reception.** (0.5) Dalek Guard
102. **Int. Attack Squadron *Dalazar* Command Ship.** (0.5) Dalek Squad Leader, Dalek Supreme

Wednesday 6 November 2002

ACTORS Karen Henson (Saloran Hardew), Steven Elder (Siy Tarkov), Jack Galagher (Nav Computer, Computer, Technician, Tannoy), Nicholas Briggs (Trooper & Dalek voices)
Scenes may not be recorded in the order listed below. The numbers in brackets indicate roughly how many pages to each scene.

3. **Int. Saloran's Ship. Planet Velyshaa.** (0.5) Tarkov, Saloran
15. **Int. Saloran's Ship. Planet Velyshaa.** (0.5) Tarkov, Saloran
51. **Int. Saloran's Ship. Planet Velyshaa.** (0.5) Tarkov, Saloran
87. **Int. Saloran's Ship.** (0.5) Tarkov, Saloran
105. **Ext. Space.** (0.5) Nav Computer
106. **Ext. Planet Velyshaa.** (1) Tarkov, Trooper
107. **Int. Kalendorf's Burial Chamber.** (1.5) Tarkov, Saloran, Trooper
108. **Int. Star Yacht *Crusader*. Corridor.** (1) Saloran, Tarkov
109. **Int. *Crusader*. Tarkov's Cabin.** (4.5) Tarkov, Saloran
110. **Int. Kalendorf's Burial Chamber.** (3.5) Saloran, Tarkov, Dalek
111. **Int. Saloran's Ship.** (3) Computer, Saloran, Tarkov
113. **Int. Saloran's Ship.** (1) Tarkov, Saloran
115. **Int. Saloran's Ship.** (0.5) Tarkov, Saloran
125. **Int. Saloran's Ship.** (0.5) Tarkov, Saloran
132. **Int. Saloran's Ship.** (1.5) Saloran, Tarkov
133. **Int. Saloran's Ship. Computer Room.** (1.5) Technician, Saloran, Tarkov, Dalek, Dalek 1
134. **Ext. Velyshaa.** (2) Tannoy, Trooper, Tarkov, Saloran, Daleks

Plus any of the following Dalek-only scenes left over from Monday 4 November.

Sunday 10 November 2002

ACTORS Gareth Thomas (Kalendorf), Teresa Gallagher (Mirana), Hannah Smith (Mentor), Ian Brooker (Marber), Simon Bridge (Johnstone), Nicholas Briggs (Dalek voices)

Scenes may not be recorded in the order listed below. The numbers in brackets indicate roughly how many pages to each scene.

4. **Int. Scout-Ship *Defiant*. Bridge. (0.5)** Marber, Mirana
8. **Int. Scout-Ship *Defiant*. Bridge. (2)** Marber, Mirana
10. **Int. Scout-Ship *Defiant*. Cargo Bay. (2.5)** Mirana, Crewman, Marber, Johnstone
12. **Int. Scout-Ship *Defiant*. Cargo Bay. (1)** Mirana, Johnstone
86. **Int. Escape Pod. (3)** Marber, Mirana
24. **Flashback: Int. Cryo-Chamber. Emperor's Ship. (3)** Mirana, Alby (previously recorded), Kalendorf, Alternate Dalek
26. **Int. Mentor's Chamber. (1)** Mentor, Kalendorf, Alby (previously recorded), Mirana
28. **Int. Mentor's Chamber. (1)** Mentor, Mirana, Kalendorf
29. **Mirana's Narration. (1.5)** Mirana, Kalendorf
31. **Ext. Planet Emmeron. (1)** Mirana, Kalendorf, Alby (previously recorded)
33. **Ext. Planet Emmeron. (0.5)** Alby (previously recorded), Kalendorf, Mirana
17. **Int. Mentor's Chamber. (0.5)** Mentor
75. **Int. Mentor's Chamber. (1)** Mentor, Alternate Dalek Monitor
Chapter Three Prologue. Mentor, Alternate Dalek
90. **Int. Mentor's Chamber. Lopra Minor. (1)** Mentor, Monitor
92. **Int. Alliance Gunship B68. Bridge. (1)** Alternate Dalek, Mentor, Monitor

Plus pick-ups from previous days with Gareth.

[Editor's Note: **Prologue Scene 2. Int. Flagship *Courageous*** from Chapter Three was not included on the schedule as it was written by Briggs during the recording process. It was recorded on 10 November.]

DALEK WAR CHAPTER THREE

Prologue.

MENTOR   Peoples of the planet Emmeron. This is your last chance to join our crusade against the evils in this galaxy. We have come to save you from destruction and enslavement, but you must learn to fight for yourselves. We must all unite against a common enemy. Your leaders tell me that the petty affairs of your planet are more important than our great cause. They would rather wage war with other continents than face up to their wider responsibilities. It would seem they have made their choice for you all. I give you one last chance to overthrow your leaders or to make them see sense. If you do not respond... your fate is sealed.

ALTERNATE DALEK Readings show intercontinental ballistic missiles firing and impacting. The planet Emmeron is at war.

MENTOR   They are not listening. We must make them listen. Release the plague.

ALTERNATE DALEK I obey.

Prologue Scene 2. Int. Flagship *Courageous*.
Door opens.

KALENDORF   (*Surprised*) Mirana? I didn't expect –

MIRANA   (*Angry and upset*) Have you heard the news about Emmeron?

KALENDORF   (*Affecting a lack of concern*) Yes. A pity, really. But the Mentor really didn't have a choice.

MIRANA   (*Shocked*) Didn't have a choice?!

KALENDORF   Yes. I'm sure that's what she'd say now... *if* she were here... (*quietly*) *listening... or watching.* (*Normal level*)
Pause.

MIRANA   Yes. Yes, of course. Of course.

KALENDORF   Is there anything else I can help you with?

CHAPTER THREE CD TRACK LISTINGS		
1 Emmeron	12 Cactus...	23 I'm on my way
2 Unidentified transmission	13 Gunfire	24 Gunship *B68*
3 Surface of Jupiter	14 Exacuate!	25 Main armament
4 Time is the essence	15 Vaarga	26 Alert!
5 Kalendorf's agenda	16 Bad Daleks	27 Totally destroyed
6 Red light	17 Middle of nowhere	28 The Emperor's Brain
7 Are you there?	18 Dark One	29 Second Wave
8 Motion scanners	19 Hive Leader Stralos	30 Enter
9 Lost contact	20 Disaster	31 Karl!
10 Search-beams	21 Not so very different	32 Advance Party
11 Atmosphere checks	22 Monitors report	33 Barricades
		34 Pure... destruction

MIRANA   (*Carefully*) Yes. There's been report that a... an 'unidentified' transmission was detected, coming from this ship.[1]
KALENDORF   'Unidentified'?
MIRANA   Only a fragment of it was picked up. There's some suggestion that it might have been on a wavelength used by the Enemy Dalek Command network.
KALENDORF   Some suggestion?
MIRANA   There's really not enough data for us to be sure.
KALENDORF   So, to all intents and purposes, it really was an unidentified transmission.
MIRANA   If... if it happens again, we'll be ready for it this time. Do you think it's likely to happen again?
KALENDORF   (*Nonchalantly*) No. No, I don't think it's likely.
MIRANA   I... I wonder what it could have been.[2]
KALENDORF   I wonder.
Crash in opening theme.

73. Ext. Jupiter.

A gentle breeze. Some birdsong. A spacecraft approaches from the distance. It gets nearer and nearer. Its retro rockets fire with a loud roar as it descends upon us. The rumble and crunch of the spacecraft landing. Pause for a moment. The gentle breeze and birdsong. A massive hatch opens. A metallic gangplank thuds to the ground. Footsteps of soldiers moving down the gangplank. The sound of soldiers fanning out. Their field gear clunking and jingling as they move. Some background 'soldier chatter' (post production), some of it on radios. An impression of general activity. Bleep of communicator.

HERRICK   Herrick to *Courageous*.
KALENDORF   (*Distort*) This is *Courageous*. Go ahead, Herrick.
HERRICK   Commander Kalendorf, we have touched down on the surface of Jupiter. All surface scans checked out on the way in. 5th Airborne brigade now setting up camp.
KALENDORF   (*Distort*) We have processed all your surface scan data. I'm giving the order for all units to land at their designated sites. You have the co-ordinates of those mineral deposits?
Click and bleep of a personal scanner being operated.
HERRICK   That's confirmed, sir.
KALENDORF   (*Distort*) Then get your science and engineering teams to work, Herrick. The sooner you begin extraction and processing, the sooner the fleet can be in a fit shape to tackle the Enemy Dalek second wave.
HERRICK   Any news on their position, sir?

74. Int. Flagship *Courageous*. Bridge.

KALENDORF   Still no change since they stopped just off Venus solar orbit.
HERRICK   (*Distort*) I'd like to know what they think they're up to, sir.
KALENDORF   So would I, Mr Herrick, so would I. You'd better get to work. Time is of the essence.

HERRICK (*Distort*) Will do, sir. Out.
Bleep of comms clicking off.
KALENDORF Do we have an update on that gunship approaching the *Defiant*?
ALTERNATE DALEK 1 Gunship *B68* still unable to establish contact with *Defiant*. It will be several hours before they are in visual range.
KALENDORF Is the gunship moving at maximum speed?
ALTERNATE DALEK 1 Gunship *B68* is travelling at optimum cruising speed.
KALENDORF (*Anxiously*) Order it to increase speed to maximum. If Mirana and her crew are in trouble, then we need to know as soon as possible.

75. Int. Mentor's Chamber.

MENTOR (*To herself*) And *now* you are concerned about Mirana, Kalendorf. Why now, when you have so blatantly neglected to investigate the matter for so very long? Monitors?
Screens activate.
ALTERNATE DALEK MONITOR (*Distort*) What are your orders, Mentor?
MENTOR All information from Gunship *B68* is to come to me before it is released to Kalendorf.
ALTERNATE DALEK MONITOR (*Distort*) That is understood, Mentor.
MENTOR Also... I want you to access all Kalendorf's personal records together with all logged and unlogged flightplans and surveillance data relating to his movements.
ALTERNATE DALEK MONITOR (*Distort*) What are we looking for?
MENTOR I don't know... But I sense that Kalendorf is not being entirely honest with me. It would appear that he has his own agenda. We must discover what that agenda is and... take him to task over it. (*Suddenly very sharp and Dalek-like*) Proceed!
ALTERNATE DALEK MONITOR (*Distort*) I obey.
Build music, then subside for passing of time.

76. Int. Jupiter. 5th Airborne Brigade HQ.
Fade in on... Sound of drilling in background. Much chatter of soldiers working etc.

SCIENTIST (*Distort*) These are the purist deposits of Sytesium I've ever encountered. It means we can process the ore for the fleet's energy storage batteries even faster than we'd anticipated. We'll have doubled our quota by morning. It's quite remarkable. I've never seen anything like it.
HERRICK Well, I suppose it's about time we had some good luck. All right, keep me informed.
SCIENTIST (*Distort*) Yes... yes, of course, Mr Herrick.
Comms bleep off. A tiny alarm buzzes. Comms bleep.
HERRICK (*Sighs. Not unduly concerned*) Er, perimeter sector guard Niner Seven, I'm showing a red light on your perimeter sensor. Report, please.
Hiss of static.
HERRICK Niner Seven, are you reading me?

Hiss of static.
HERRICK   Niner Seven?
Hiss of static.
HERRICK   (*Voice raised slightly*) Sergeant Allenby! Sergeant!
ALLENBY   (*Approaching*) Sir! Sorry, sir. I was just on the comm-link to a Beta Section patrol.
HERRICK   Beta Section? What do they want from *us*? They're several hundred kilometres to the east, on the coastline, aren't they?
ALLENBY   Er, yes, sir. Seems they have a bit of a medical emergency... far as I could gather, sir.
HERRICK   Well why didn't they call for their *own* med-team?
ALLENBY   Said they couldn't make contact with their base-camp, sir.
HERRICK   Couldn't...? What was the medical emergency?
ALLENBY   That's just it, sir. They didn't say. Their comms just cut off. I was trying to raise them again when you called me.
Pause.
ALLENBY   Er... why *did* you call me, sir?
HERRICK   (*Distracted*) I was just wondering if there's a connection. Can't be.
ALLENBY   Connection with what, sir?
HERRICK   Sergeant, how are your night-flying skills?
ALLENBY   It's what the 5th Airborne are all about, sir.
HERRICK   Good. I want you to get your section airborne in surface skimmers. I had a red light on Niner Seven's perimeter sensor just now, but couldn't raise them. No comms signal at all. It's like they're not there.[3]
ALLENBY   What do you think it is, sir?
HERRICK   It could be nothing, Sergeant ... or a whole lot of trouble. Split your force, Allenby. One skimmer to Niner Seven's last reported position, the rest can head out to Beta Section. I'll get our comms people to check in with all brigade headquarters. You'd better get moving – and stay in touch!
ALLENBY   Sir!
His boots crash to attention, then he marches out at the double. Comms bleep.
HERRICK   This is Executive Officer Herrick. Get me Commander Kalendorf on the *Courageous*.

77. Ext. Jupiter. Forest. Night.
A breeze is blowing through trees and plants. We hear a sinister rustling – and just a hint of some harsh breathing for a moment. A skimmer fades in from the distance and hovers nearby.

ALLENBY   (*Via loudspeaker*) Perimeter guard unit Niner Seven! Are you there? Perimeter guard unit Niner Seven, show yourselves![4]

78. Int. Allenby's Skimmer.
Skimmer engines in hover mode.

ALLENBY   Any trace on the motion scanners?
TROOPER   Nothing, Sarge. Just a few plants swaying around a bit.
ALLENBY   Hit the search-beams.

Searchlights activate.
ALLENBY   Are you sure this is the right position?
TROOPER   Positive, Sarge.
ALLENBY   (*Suddenly spotting something*) What was that?
TROOPER   What, Sarge?
ALLENBY   Thought I saw someone moving behind those cactus-things.[5]
TROOPER   Think it was just the plants moving in the breeze.
ALLENBY   I suppose we'd better take a look on foot. Take us down nice and slow, Trooper. First sign of trouble and – [6]
TROOPER   Don't you worry, Sarge. They don't call me the grasshopper for nothing.
Engines start the descent.
ALLENBY   Sparks!
SPARKS   Sarge?
ALLENBY   Signal Brigade HQ, tell them we're landing at Niner Seven's last reported position.
SPARKS   Sarge.
ALLENBY   Anything from our people heading for Beta Section?
SPARKS   They just called in to let us know they'd made contact.
ALLENBY   Good. Everything seem okay?
SPARKS   Far as I could tell.
ALLENBY   (*A bit edgey*) Good, right... that's what I like to hear.
Retros fire.
TROOPER   Touching down now, Sarge.
ALLENBY   Right. Grab five guys and follow me, trooper.
TROOPER   Yes, sarge.

79. Ext. Jupiter. Forest. Night.[7]
Skimmer door is closing.

ALLENBY   Okay, people. Let's use the light from the skimmer's search-beams. Fan out ahead.
TROOPER   What are we looking for, Sarge?
ALLENBY   Anything at all, Trooper. Anything out of the ordinary.
TROOPER 1   Hostiles, maybe?
ALLENBY   Now, Trooper, they've told us there's nothing on this planet but plants, insects and rodents. But if you see a hostile-looking bug, you have my express permission to blow its ugly head off.[8]
A murmur of laughter from the troopers.
ALLENBY   All right. Let's go.
The sound of soldiers wading through the undergrowth. The breeze starts to howl a bit louder. Mingled with the breeze, we start to hear some harsh, ragged breathing. Threatening music builds through this.

80. Int. Jupiter. 5th Airborne Brigade HQ.
Howl of the growing breeze in background.

KALENDORF   (*Distort*) What do you mean, lost contact?
HERRICK   Just that, sir. Over ten different sections are now not responding.
KALENDORF   (*Distort*) Have you sent out skimmer patrols to investigate?

273

HERRICK   I have two skimmers at Niner Seven's last reported position. They checked in just now. Found nothing yet. And the rest of Allenby's unit headed out to Beta Section.

KALENDORF   (*Distort*) And?

HERRICK   We've er... we've lost contact with *them*.

KALENDORF   (*Distort*) And you don't want to lose contact with any more skimmer units, I see.

HERRICK   Sir... either there's something pretty worrying going on, or it's just a change in atmospheric conditions causing transmission jamming. There's quite a wind getting up now. Could be an electrical storm brewing higher up, maybe. Can your people run an atmosphere check?

KALENDORF   (*Distort*) We'll do it right away and I'll have our comms people attempt transorbital contact with the affected sections. Maybe all that's needed is a stronger signal.

HERRICK   Thank you, sir. I didn't want to cause a panic, but –

KALENDORF   (*Distort*) No, Herrick. You did the right thing. Patch me through to Allenby's lot at Niner Seven's position, would you?

81. Ext. Jupiter. Forest. Night.
The sounds of soldiers wading through the undergrowth. The wind is quite severe now.

TROOPER   (*Close*) Argh!

ALLENBY   (*Some distance off*) You all right, Trooper?

TROOPER   Yeah, yeah, I'm fine, Sarge. Just caught meself on one of these bleedin' cactus things. Owww... not very nice, but I'll live. Owww... (*His pained breathing continues under the following*)

ALLENBY   All right.

Comms crackle.

ALLENBY   (*Distort*) Right... Everybody, listen up. Five more minutes, then we head back to the skimmer.

As the breeze gets louder and we hear soldiers moving around, the TROOPER's breathing gets more and more manic, until...

TROOPER   (*Close and intense*) Uuuurgh! Must... musssssst... Must kill.[9]

ALLENBY's footsteps approach through the undergrowth, then stop.

ALLENBY   Trooper? What's the matter? (*Pause*) Wh – what are you doing?

Music crescendo.

82. Int. Allenby's Skimmer.

SPARKS   Yes, Commander. No signs of trouble at all –

KALENDORF   (*Distort*) Apart from the fact that you can't find guard unit Niner Seven.

Distant, sustained gunfire.

SPARKS   What the hell – ?

KALENDORF   (*Distort*) Sparks? What is it? Sounds like –

SPARKS   Gunfire, Commander, and lots of it.

KALENDORF   (*Distort*) What kind of gunfire?

SPARKS   Our kind, sir.

More gunfire. Screams of soldiers being killed.

KALENDORF (*Distort*) Sparks? Sparks – !
SPARKS Hold on, Commander.
Comms bleep.
SPARKS Skimmer to Sergeant Allenby. Sarge? What's going on?
Comms hiss.
SPARKS Sarge?
Door suddenly opens. The wind howls in violently. Ragged breath of the trooper.
SPARKS Oh my God.
KALENDORF (*Distort*) What is it? What's happening? Sparks?
Gunfire. SPARKS cries out and dies. Hiss and buzz of comms controls fizzing and shorting.
KALENDORF (*Distort*) Sparks! Sparks?! Airborne unit! Come in!
TROOPER Must kill… must kill…
His feverish breathing builds.

83. Int. Flagship *Courageous*. Bridge.

KALENDORF Come in! (*To DALEK*) Check the signal – *now*, do it!
ALTERNATE DALEK 1 I obey.
Bleeps etc.
ALTERNATE DALEK 1 Signal has been cut off at source.
KALENDORF (*To himself*) Gunfire? What the hell's going on? (*To DALEK*) Get me Herrick again.
Bleep, the buzz and hiss of static.
ALTERNATE DALEK 2 Signal carrier wave not established. Our signal is not being received.
KALENDORF (*To himself*) Herrick? Not you too.
Music cue: foreboding. Pause. KALENDORF sucks breath in, considering.
KALENDORF Signal to all ground forces on Jupiter you can raise. Evacuate! Evacuate now! Code the message with my ident and send it now! Do it!
ALTERNATE DALEK 1 I obey.
KALENDORF (*Through gritted teeth*) It would seem the Mentor was right. I don't know what the hell's happened, but we've walked right into a trap.

84. Int. Earth. Enemy Dalek Command.

DALEK (*Distort*) Report for the Dalek Supreme.
DALEK SUPREME Enter!
Door opens.
DALEK SUPREME Speak!
DALEK The Vaarga plants on Jupiter have begun their work.
DALEK SUPREME Excellent! Soon Kalendorf's forces will be powerless to resist us. He will have no *choice* but to co-operate.
DALEK Shall we move in for the final attack?
DALEK SUPREME No. We must await the coded signal from our advance party.[10]
DALEK Understood.
DALEK SUPREME When it is confirmed that Susan Mendes has been captured, *we – will – advance!*

85. Int. Scout-Ship *Defiant*. Holding Cell.

MORLI   Alby... Alby!
ALBY   (*Groggy and in pain*) Yeah... what is it, Morli?
MORLI   Are you gonna be okay, man? You're not gonna die, like...
Like the others did?
ALBY   Others? What others?
MORLI   In the hospital. When the bad Daleks came. They killed
everyone. All me mates.
ALBY   No... no, it's all right, Morli. Don't panic. I may feel dead.
I thought I *was* for a moment back there. But, apparently, I'm not. You
okay?
MORLI   Yeah. (*Pause*) I think she's awake now. She just opened
her eyes. Just then... look, there.
Sounds of effort and movement from ALBY as he moves towards SUZ.
ALBY   Suz? Suz? Speak to me.
SUZ   Hello, Alby.
ALBY   It is... *you*, isn't it? (*Pause*) Suz?
SUZ   What do you mean?
ALBY   It's just that... back on the bridge... Well, you said you
were the Dalek Emperor.
SUZ   Yes... I was. I am... in a way. It's all in my mind – stored
away. The Daleks woke him up for a moment. I suppose they wanted to
make sure that he was still in here. Checking up on him. Worrying that
they'd made a wasted journey. But they haven't, have they?
ALBY   Suz?
SUZ   Mm?
ALBY   Will you hold me?
Rustle of movement as she moves close to him. We hear them kiss.
SUZ   What do you think? That we're kissing each other
goodbye?
ALBY   I hoped it'd be something a little more lasting than that.
SUZ   (*Laughs warmly*) Yes. We haven't... huh. Well, we haven't
had much luck, have we? There's always been... something in the way,
hasn't there?
ALBY   Several light years of space, you mean.
They both give a weak, warm laugh.
ALBY   And now the Emperor of the Daleks. Do you think he's
sitting in your mind, laughing at us? Do Daleks laugh?
SUZ   They ought to. Isn't that what mad people are supposed to
do? (*With some venom*) Mad, twisted, psychotic murderers.
ALBY   Why do you think he did this to you, the Emperor?
SUZ   I... I don't know. (*Pause*) Do *you*?
ALBY   Well... I have a nasty theory about that. I've suspected it
ever since we found out about it.
SUZ   Suspected what?
ALBY   That the Dalek Emperor knew that, of all the people they
put into hibernation, you'd be the one most likely to be rescued.
SUZ   Why?
ALBY   Because of Kalendorf. Because you were the legendary
Angel of Mercy.
SUZ   And because of... us? Because we love each other?

ALBY   Yeah. Because of that.
They kiss again.
SUZ   But what good will that love do us now? What good has it
done? It's just given the Daleks what they want.
MORLI   I tell you what you two need.
SUZ   What's that?
MORLI   A bit of food inside yous. If you're anything like me, you
must be bleedin' starvin'.
SUZ and ALBY can't help but laugh.

86. Int. Escape Pod.
Escape pod whooshes past through space. Cut to interior of pod:

MARBER   Nothing. Still can't see a damn thing out there.
MIRANA   (*Determined*) If we keep on this course, we should find
Alby's ship. We can get onboard and –
MARBER   And what? Catch up with the *Defiant* and save the day?!
I think you've lost your grip on reality.
MIRANA   Calm down, Marber.
MARBER   What, and conserve air? What's the point? We're just
about out of fuel and we're in the middle of nowhere.
MIRANA   The scanners in this pod have a very limited range. We
could find Alby's ship at any moment.
MARBER   *If* we set off in the right direction in the first place.
Engines cut out.
MARBER   That's it. Engines out.
Scanner bleep.
MARBER   Nothing on the scanner
Pause.
MIRANA   What do you want me to say? That we're finished?
MARBER   I don't need you to say it. But I know what I do want you
to tell me...
MIRANA   What?
MARBER   Kalendorf's plan. (*Pause*) All right, maybe you don't know
what he's up to for sure. Maybe it was safer that way. But you must have
some idea. Well, haven't you?
A sombre, electronic chiming.
MARBER   That's the final oxygen warning light. Come on, it's nearly
all over, Captain. Don't let me die of curiosity as well as asphyxiation.
MIRANA   He really did never tell me.
MARBER   And you were still prepared to risk your life for him?
MIRANA   For the freedom of the galaxy. Yes. And anyway, I asked
him not to tell me.
MARBER   Why?
MIRANA   Because I had a feeling I wouldn't like... the means.
MARBER   The means?
MIRANA   Well, think about it. You've got two factions of the most
evil, destructive race the galaxy, probably the universe, has ever known.
You've allied yourself with one faction to defeat the other. It looks like
you might win. But then you find out the Daleks on your side are pretty
much as bad as the bad Daleks. So what do you do?
MARBER   I don't know. That's what I'm asking, isn't it?

MIRANA   I think you have to do something pretty bad. Take some enormous risks... probably involving the potential loss of billions of lives. That's what happened last time, when Suz and Kalendorf started that rebellion. The slaughter was virtually incalculable.
MARBER   So?
MIRANA   So... (*Pause*) I chickened out. Fell into line behind a great man. Left the moral difficulties to him.
MARBER   You've never struck me as a coward, Mirana.
MIRANA   Thanks.
MARBER   I wasn't being kind. I mean that you must have formed some idea of what Kalendorf intended for you to be that scared of it.
MIRANA   No clear idea. No.
MARBER   But you *did* have an idea. Didn't you?
Final hiss of oxygen tanks emptying. Both MIRANA and MARBER have difficulty breathing.
MARBER   Mirana... for God's sake... tell me the idea... tell me...
MIRANA   I... think... I thought to myself... What's the thing I feared most?[12]
MARBER   Yes? And... (*Splutters, gasping*) And what was that?
MIRANA   (*After a final gasp*) That he'd switch sides.
Big music cue of rumbling doom. Hold. Then crossfade to:

87. Int. Saloran's Ship.[13]

TARKOV   You must have formed an opinion of the man.
SALORAN   Why do you ask?
TARKOV   Well... all this. It must have been a kind of... intimate experience for you.
SALORAN   Yes. You want me to sum Kalendorf up in one word?
TARKOV   (*A chuckle*) You can have more than that. Is he really the monster who brought about the Great Catastrophe. The 'Dark One'? The 'Bringer of Death' we were all told about at school?[14]
SALORAN   There is one word that comes close to summing him up.
TARKOV   There is?
SALORAN   Yes. 'Warrior'. And a warrior must be prepared to risk everything in order to win his war.

87A. Orearlisian Transmission.
A highly distorted transmission.

HIVE LEADER STRALOS This is Hive Leader Stralos on Emergency Frequency Delta Four Zero. This is an emergency! All humanoid personnel occupying Jupiter have been infected! Orearlisians and other non-humanoids are unaffected by this plague of madness, but we are outnumbered! Send help immediately! My people are being slaughtered! Emergency! Send help immediately!!!
The voice is swamped in static.

88. Int. Flagship *Courageous*. Executive Communication Chamber.
Door opens. Footsteps.[15]

MENTOR   I summoned you over two hours ago, Kalendorf.

KALENDORF (*Approaching*) My apologies, Mentor, but there is something of an emergency in prog –

MENTOR (*Suppressed anger*) There something of a *disaster* in progress, Kalendorf. My monitors keep me fully informed at all times. Do not insult my intelligence.

KALENDORF I assure you that no insult was intended.

MENTOR I am not so sure.

KALENDORF (*Bridling*) As I'm sure you're aware, we have lost contact with all ground forces on Jupiter. I have spent the last two hours doing all I can to –

MENTOR You have spent the last two hours attempting to make amends for your catastrophic error of judgement, and you have failed, Kalendorf.

KALENDORF I've sent two craft into lower Jupiter orbit. They've been fitted with transmission boosters because we have reason to believe that some atmospheric disturbance may be responsible for –

MENTOR I am aware of your inadequate efforts. And there is no atmospheric disturbance!

KALENDORF But –

MENTOR There are other developments of which you are not aware. Observe!

Screen activation. Rhythmic bleep of motion tracking.

KALENDORF Those are ships taking off from Jupiter. Then our signals must have got through! Thank God! Then everything's –

MENTOR Silence! I have made a full analysis of the data obtained from your surface scans. Observe!

Screen image change FX.

MENTOR Tell me what you see, Kalendorf.

KALENDORF It's... just an aerial view of some forest land.

MENTOR There are now areas of vegetation such as this all over the surface of Jupiter. Observe!

Zooming in and scanning effect.

MENTOR These forests contain many varieties of plant life. Do you recognise this particular plant?

KALENDORF I don't know. It's some sort of cactus, maybe.

MENTOR Access to our full database has identified it as a Vaarga plant.

KALENDORF (*None-the-wiser*) A... Vaarga?

MENTOR A species of hostile plant-life originally native to Skaro. The Enemy Daleks' planet of origin.

KALENDORF How is this plant hostile?

MENTOR Because it is a hybrid creature, part animal, part plant. All indications are that it was engineered into existence by the Daleks as a form of defence. The poison from its spines attacks the brain of its victim. Rational thought is replaced by an overwhelming desire to kill. Eventually the poison seeps through the system and the victim is gradually transformed into a Vaarga.

KALENDORF You're saying that's what happened to our people on Jupiter?

MENTOR By now, they will be in the grip of the psychotic phase.

KALENDORF Then how come ships are now leaving the surface? Perhaps it's our people escaping.

279

MENTOR   Observe.

Burble of screen graphics.

MENTOR   This is the Vaarga plant image as stored in our database. *This* is the Vaarga found on Jupiter.

KALENDORF   It looks the same.

MENTOR   Almost. Molecular examination, made possible by more thorough analysis of data collected by your surface scans, shows an adaptation of the spines and the poison contained within them. Our analysis of this augmented 'poison' reveals that it contains an additional agent which induces a 'pack mentality'. Those people affected by it will not just have become mindless psychotic killers; they will have joined forces to become a mass, psychotic army, intent on the destruction of all others.

KALENDORF   (*Realising*) And they're heading this way...

Comms alarm.

MENTOR   Speak!

Explosions in background on 'distort'.

MONITOR   (*Distort*) Transmission booster ships in lower Jupiter orbit are being fired upon and destroyed by those ships rising from the planet's surface.

MENTOR   The ships rising from Jupiter must be destroyed the moment they are in range.

MONITOR   (*Distort*) The order will be given, Mentor.

KALENDORF   We must –

MENTOR   You are relieved of your command, Kalendorf. My Daleks will take control of the situation.

Doors open.

ALTERNATE DALEK You will come with us or you will be neutralised.

KALENDORF   Mentor, you're making a big mistake.

MENTOR   It is you who have made the mistake, Kalendorf, in betraying me. We are here to help your people; to restore peace and order in this galaxy. But I now know that you are working against me. Until now, I have trusted you, even encouraged your individualistic traits. But detailed analysis of your actions over the last few years reveals mysterious periods of absence, secret assignations with Captain Mirana and Alby Brook... I believe that you are responsible for the destruction of Cargo Freighter *Omega N7*. I believe that you knew of the cargo it contained. I believe that you have attempted to save the life of the dangerous Enemy Dalek agent Susan Mendes. (*Pause*) I see that you do not deny any of it. I do not know what your plan is – that is irrelevant to me at this precise moment – but rest assured that it is over.

KALENDORF   What are you going to do with me?

MENTOR   You are to be brought to me, here on the planet Lopra Minor, where you will undergo full interrogation and brain correction.

KALENDORF   Brain correction. Ah yes, the techniques you've been developing in your secret station in the Pkowik System.

MENTOR   A station that we now know has been attacked and destroyed by an Enemy Dalek raiding party operating deep in our territory. You supplied the enemy with information on the Pkowik Station? (*Pause*) Just what is the depth of your treachery, Kalendorf?

KALENDORF   Well... I look forward to our little chat on Lopra.

MENTOR   Bring him to me on Lopra Minor! Now! Take him to the transport ship!

ALTERNATE DALEK We obey.

89. Int. Flagship *Courageous*. Corridor.

Door closes. KALENDORF's footsteps.

ALTERNATE DALEK You will move.
KALENDORF Not so very different from your cousins from *this* universe, are you?
ALTERNATE DALEK You will not speak!
A deep rumble of impact.
KALENDORF Sounds like the trouble is really starting.
An alarm sounds.
ALTERNATE DALEK TANNOY Battle stations! Battle stations! This fleet is under attack from ships crewed by Vaarga-infected humanoids! Battle stations! (*Continues under*)
ALTERNATE DALEK You will move, faster!
A bigger, more immediate explosion. KALENDORF gasps as he steadies himself.
KALENDORF That was a direct hit.
ALTERNATE DALEK Move faster!
Another, even bigger explosion.
ALTERNATE DALEK TANNOY Emergency! Emergency! Vaarga-infected humanoids are now boarding this ship! Emergency! (*Continues under*)
KALENDORF You see what happens when I'm not in command!
Gunfire and impacts close by.
KALENDORF Look out, chaps!
ALTERNATE DALEKS Under attack! Under attack! Alert!
VAARGA-MAN Must kill! Must kill! Kill them all!!!
Gunfire and chants and screams of other Vaarga-infected humans.
ALTERNATE DALEK Neutralise them! Neutralise!
Neutralising beams fire. Mayhem of gunfight in full swing. Vaarga-humans screaming as they're shot and much gunfire.
ALTERNATE DALEK AAAAaargh!
ALTERNATE DALEK explodes.
ALTERNATE DALEK 1 Kalendorf is escaping! Alert! Alert!
Battle mayhem escalates. Hold for a while, then crossfade to:

90. Int. Lopra Minor. Mentor's Chamber.

MENTOR Monitors, report to me! What is happening?
MONITOR (*Distort*) Craft piloted by Vaarga-infected humanoids are inflicting severe damage upon our fleet orbiting Jupiter.
MENTOR Where is Kalendorf?
MONITOR (*Distort*) Reports from the Flagship *Courageous* are confused. Vaarga-infected humanoids have breached the airlock and are attacking our Daleks. I am receiving no monitor signal from the Daleks escorting Kalendorf to the transport ship.
Bleeping.
MENTOR Your sensory array is indicating that the transport ship is now leaving the *Courageous*.
MONITOR (*Distort*) No Daleks are detected aboard.
MENTOR Kalendorf is escaping. Track the course of the transport ship! He must not get away!

91. Int. Space Transport Ship.
Whooshes past in space, then cut to interior:

KALENDORF (*A self-satisfied laugh*) Don't worry, Suz. I'm on my way.
The transport ship whooshes off into space.

92. Int. Alliance Gunship *B68*. Bridge.

ALTERNATE DALEK This is Alliance Gunship *B68* calling Mentor. Scout-Ship *Defiant* is now in visual range, but is still not responding to our transmissions.
MENTOR (*Distort*) Is there any sign of structural damage? Perhaps the *Defiant* has been under attack and is unable to respond.
ALTERNATE DALEK Preliminary visual scans give no such indication.
MENTOR (*Distort*) Then approach with caution.
An alarm sounds on 'distort'.
MONITOR (*Distort*) This is Monitor Control. We are tracking the trajectory of Kalendorf's escape.
MENTOR (*Distort*) Proceed.
MONITOR (*Distort*) Projections of his course indicate he is heading for the *Defiant*. He is travelling at maximum hyper velocity and will arrive within the hour.
MENTOR (*Distort*) Gunship *B68*, be advised that Kalendorf has betrayed the Alliance and has escaped in a stolen space transport.
ALTERNATE DALEK Understood. Is he to be captured or neutralised?
MENTOR (*Distort*) Neutralisation is a final resort. Instruct him to surrender. But do not hesitate to destroy his ship if he does not obey.
ALTERNATE DALEK Understood.
MENTOR (*Distort*) Continue with your approach to Scout-Ship *Defiant*.

93. Int. Scout-Ship *Defiant*. Bridge.

DALEK The Alliance gunship is still approaching us and attempting contact.
DALEK SQUAD LEADER Continue to ignore their comms signals.
DALEK I obey.
DALEK SQUAD LEADER Are they now within weapons' range of this scout-ship?
DALEK They are.[16]
DALEK SQUAD LEADER Activate main armament. Target and destroy them without delay.
DALEK I obey.
Targeting sensors bleep.
DALEK Gunship targeted.

94. Int. Gunship *B68*. Bridge.

ALTERNATE DALEK Alert! The *Defiant's* weaponry systems have targeted this vessel. Evaisive manoeuvres, immediately! Activate defence –
A massive explosion.

95. Int. Scout-Ship *Defiant*. Bridge.

DALEK Gunship totally destroyed.
DALEK SQUAD LEADER Transmit coded signal to Dalek Control on Earth.
DALEK I obey.

96. Int. Earth. Enemy Dalek Control.

DALEK Report for the Dalek Supreme.
DALEK SUPREME Speak!
DALEK We have received the coded signal from our advance party. Susan Mendes has been captured.
DALEK SUPREME Brain analysis report?
DALEK Her mind contains the consciousness of our Emperor.
DALEK SUPREME Excellent! Where is Kalendorf?
DALEK Intercepted Alliance Dalek signals indicate he is approaching the *Defiant* at speed and will arrive shortly.
DALEK SUPREME Order our second wave to advance. The main assault force will destroy all surviving Alliance ships in Jupiter orbit. Attack Squadron *Dalazar* will proceed with all speed to intercept Kalendorf and the *Defiant*.

97. Int. Scout-Ship *Defiant*. Cell.

ALBY I wonder what the hell they've got planned. Any ideas?
SUZ No. Mirana seemed to think they'd never get through your Alliance Dalek forces to Earth. But they must have a plan. I know the Daleks.
ALBY How well?
SUZ Better than I'd like to. When I was working for them, in the last war... Kalendorf accused me of thinking like a Dalek. Huh. Why are you looking at me like that?
ALBY Oh... nothing.
SUZ You're thinking... She's got the Emperor's brain in her head. Can I trust her? (*She laughs loudly*)
ALBY I was thinking... maybe the Emperor knows what the plan is... and since his brain's in your head...
SUZ (*Sighs*) I don't think it works like that, Alby. I think he's asleep.
MORLI (*Quiet, concentrating*) Perhaps it's time you did what you threatened to do, like.
ALBY I thought you were asleep.
MORLI I never sleep, me. Just think, with me eyes closed.
SUZ What did you mean?
MORLI You said you should've killed yourself.
ALBY Morli!
MORLI Well, you did, din't ya?
ALBY Yeah, all right, Morli. Just close your eyes and do some more thinking –
SUZ No, Alby. She's right.
MORLI You said, 'If I was dead, the Dalek Emperor would be dead too. And you'd win the war.' That's what you said.

ALBY	Yeah, and I said it wasn't that simple.
MORLI	But it is, isn't it? We want to win, don't we?
ALBY	Well, yes, but –
MORLI	We have to win. We have to defeat the bad Daleks. What else is there to do?
ALBY	It's not as simple as that.
SUZ	Morli... these... 'good' Daleks are just as bad in their own way. They've been killing people.
ALBY	That's right. All sorts of bad stuff, like blowing up whole planets, just because their governments said they were too poor to help in the war effort.[17]
MORLI	But, Alby, the war's the only thing, like. The Bad Daleks have commuted the... you know... nastiest things in the whole uni-thing. We have to be on the side of the Good Daleks. That's the only way.[18]
ALBY	(Dismissive) Look, Morli, just –
MORLI	Nah, it is the only way! That's what they taught us at the hospital, like. We has to do what they tells us. We has to, man. And they can't have their Emproary... boss man back, can they? That would be the worst thing for all of us. The worst bloody thing of the lot.[19]
SUZ	Morli... you say that's what they taught you?
MORLI	I don't think I should be listening to you. You've got the Emproary thing in yer head, like.[20]
ALBY	How did they teach you, Morli?
MORLI	Not teachin' really. Not old fashioned teachin' with computers and stuff. They just made us sleep... and when we woke up... we knew. Some didn't get it. Some went funny and had to sleep for a long time. But the rest of us... we knew all right. And I know now. I've been listening... thinking, like. And I know.
SUZ	Know what, Morli?
MORLI	Alby?
ALBY	Yeah?
MORLI	Will you help me?[21]
ALBY	Help you? Help you to do what?
MORLI	I know you loves her and all that. But we have to kill her.[22]
ALBY	Morli, just sit down and shut up. We've heard enough of this. I don't know what they did to you in that hospital, but whatever it was, it was –
MORLI	(Yells) Are you gonna help me?!|[23]
ALBY	Morli... I'm warning you. Sit down –

MORLI hits ALBY hard.

| ALBY | Aaaaargh! |

And again.

| ALBY | Ooooffff! Ugh. |

He collapses, spluttering and groaning in agony. He's been well and truly immobilised.

MORLI	Now stand still, Suz. I have to kill ya now. And I know that you knows that it's for the best. You said it yerself, din't ya?
SUZ	Yes... yes, I did.
ALBY	(Spluttering through agony) No... no, Suz! Get away from her! We'll find a way out of this! We have to!
MORLI	There's a good girl. There's a good girl.

SUZ　　　　　*(Quiet, and accepting)* Oh God...
Door opens.
DALEK　　　　Exterminate![24]
Dalek gun fires. MORLI screams, dies and falls to the floor.
DALEK　　　　Why was she attempting to kill you? Answer!
SUZ　　　　　*(In shock)* Because she was brave.
ALBY　　　　Because she'd been brainwashed by the Alliance Daleks...
on that base in the Pkowik System.
DALEK　　　　You are required on the Bridge. Both of you! Move!

98. Int. Scout-Ship *Defiant*. Bridge.

DALEK　　　　Long-range scanners detect that our second wave is now
destroying the Alliance fleet orbiting Jupiter. Alliance reinforcements are
detected approaching this solar system.
DALEK 1　　　Attack Squadron *Dalazar* now on course for our co-
ordinates.
Tracking bleeps.
DALEK 2　　　Tracking approach of Kalendorf's transport ship.
DALEK SQUAD LEADER Is Kalendorf alone?
DALEK 2　　　Running scan of his vessel.
Bleep of scan.
DALEK 2　　　Scan complete. He is alone.
DALEK SQUAD LEADER Where is Susan Mendes?
DALEK　　　　She is being brought to the bridge, as ordered.
DALEK SQUAD LEADER What is the delay?
DALEK　　　　The other female captive attempted to kill her.
DALEK SQUAD LEADER Why?
DALEK　　　　It would appear that the other human female had been
subjected to the Alliance robotisation techniques we detected in operation
in the Pkowik System. She has been exterminated.
Door opens. ALBY is still in pain.
ALBY　　　　What are you going to do to us now?
DALEK SQUAD LEADER Put them in the restraint devices.
DALEKS　　　We obey!
*The sound of struggling and discomfort from SUZ and ALBY as they are
locked into the devices. The restraints crash shut. Pause.*
SUZ　　　　　So... What happens now?
DALEK SQUAD LEADER Kalendorf will be here soon.
ALBY　　　　Kalendorf? You mean... the Alliance fleet?
DALEK SQUAD LEADER The Alliance fleet is being destroyed.
ALBY　　　　How? I mean, I thought we had you outnumbered –
DALEK SQUAD LEADER Kalendorf will explain all.
SUZ　　　　　Karl? How can he explain that?
Alarm sounds.
DALEK 1　　　Kalendorf's ship is approaching.
KALENDORF　*(Distort)* Kalendorf to *Defiant*, are you reading me?
SUZ　　　　　Karl!
DALEK 1　　　Silence!
DALEK SQUAD LEADER This is Scout-Ship *Defiant*. You will begin docking
procedures immediately.
KALENDORF　*(Distort)* Understood.

ALBY What the hell's going on?
Crossfade to:

99. Ext. Space.
KALENDORF's space transport docks with Defiant.

100. Int. Scout-Ship *Defiant*. Airlock Reception.
Airlock door opens.

DALEK GUARD Enter![25]
Footsteps.
DALEK GUARD You will proceed to the bridge.
Footsteps continue, echoing down corridor. Build music.

101. Int. Scout-Ship *Defiant*. Bridge.
Pause. Door opens.

SUZ Karl! It really *is* you!
KALENDORF (*To Daleks*) Is the Alliance second fleet approaching?
ALBY You mean – reinforcements?
DALEK SQUAD LEADER They will be within scanning range in 70 rels.
ALBY So you lot'd better get going before they burn your metal arses off!
KALENDORF Then we don't have long. You must evacuate this ship immediately.
DALEK SQUAD LEADER Unacceptable! You will *proceed* immediately.
SUZ Proceed with what? Karl – what's going on? What's he talking about?
KALENDORF Suz. (*Pause*) Leave this to me. (*To DALEK*) Talk to the Dalek Supreme or do what you like – but I am going to do nothing unless you take your Daleks and leave this ship. We both know your attack squadron is well within transmat range by now – so go!
DALEK SQUAD LEADER I will contact the Dalek Supreme for orders.
KALENDORF Do that – but do it fast, for all our sakes.
DALEK SQUAD LEADER Accessing command network. (*Fade into background*)
Bleeps of Dalek command network in operation.
KALENDORF (*His old self*) Are you two all right?
ALBY Not really. (*Pointedly*) Are *you*?
KALENDORF You have to trust me, Alby. Both of you do. (*Sighs*) Suz... it's good to see you. I'm sorry there isn't time for a better reunion just now.
SUZ It's good to see *you*, Karl.
KALENDORF Where's Mirana?
DALEK SQUAD LEADER The Dalek Supreme confirms your order.
ALBY Order?
DALEK SQUAD LEADER We will now transmat to Attack Squadron Dalazar.
KALENDORF Then get on with it.
Daleks transmat away.
SUZ I don't believe it. They really did go because you told them to.

286

ALBY   He's up to something. What are you up to, Kalendorf?
Clunk of restraint devices being released.
KALENDORF Getting you two out of these for a start.
SUZ and ALBY make vocal noises of relief as they step out of the restraints.
ALBY   Thanks – but you still haven't answered me.
KALENDORF Alby, I don't have time for this.
ALBY   Very convenient.
KALENDORF Just listen! You heard that our second fleet is on its way. So we don't have much time.
SUZ   But if your reinforcements are – [26]
KALENDORF What you don't know is that the Enemy Daleks have just about finished exterminating our first fleet and will be ready to take our second force by surprise.
ALBY   How the hell did that happen? I thought you were supposed to be good at your job – !
KALENDORF We walked into an Enemy trap on Jupiter.
SUZ   *On* Jupiter?
KALENDORF *PLEASE! BOTH OF YOU!!!* (*Pause*) Alby, on the approach to this ship, my scope showed thirty-odd crewmembers trapped in the loading bay.
SUZ   They were knocked out by nerve gas. We thought the Daleks would've killed them by now.
KALENDORF Is Mirana with them?
ALBY   No. We think she and her first officer got away in an escape pod.
KALENDORF I see... Alby – go and let those people out of the loading bay and arm them against attack.
ALBY   Attack from where?
KALENDORF The airlock.
ALBY   But if the Daleks can trans –
KALENDORF There isn't time for this, Alby. Go!
ALBY   What are you going to do?
KALENDORF I have to talk to Suz.
SUZ   What about?
KALENDORF About everything that's happened – everything that *is* going to happen. You're the key to this whole situation, Suz.
SUZ   Me? How?
ALBY   Yeah – what are you talking [about?]
Proximity alarm.
ALBY   What's that?
KALENDORF That is a Dalek attack squadron closing in for the kill. Alby, you've got to get moving.
ALBY   But –
SUZ   Alby, I'll be all right. Do as he says.
ALBY   (*Moving off*) All right, all right. I don't like it – but I'm going, I'm going.
During this, we hear his footsteps retreat to the door. Doors opens and closes. Pause.
SUZ   I thought you were in a hurry.
KALENDORF It *is* good to see you again.
SUZ   What are you up to, Karl?

287

KALENDORF Stopping the Daleks. *All* of them.
SUZ Should I trust you?
KALENDORF Yes. You should.
SUZ Then why don't I?
Pause.
KALENDORF Sometimes it's difficult to trust. Hold my hand. Look into my mind – and find out.
SUZ All right.
The telepathic sound (as heard before). Their voices becoming echoed. They are communicating telepathically.
KALENDORF Look into my mind, Suz.
SUZ (*In distress*) Oh my God... what have you done, Karl?
KALENDORF What is necessary. As I know you will too.
A sudden whoosh of psychic energy begins to build.
SUZ No... no, keep away from me... now, please... Karl – why are you doing this to meeeee?!!
The whoosh comes to a violent conclusion. SUZ screams in agony.

102. Int. Attack Squadron *Dalazar* Command Ship.

DALEK SQUAD LEADER Advance party Squadron Leader to Dalek Supreme.
Crackle of hyperlink.
DALEK SUPREME (*Distort*) Report.
DALEK SQUAD LEADER We are now aboard Attack Squadron *Dalazar*'s command ship. We are closing to within 10 hyper-rels of Scout-Ship *Defiant*.
DALEK SUPREME (*Distort*) Excellent! Maintain that position. Our second wave of ships has totally destroyed Alliance forces around Jupiter, and is now moving to your sector of space.
DALEK SQUAD LEADER The second Alliance fleet is now within range of our scanners. It is far superior in number and firepower to our fleet. If we engage it, we will be defeated.
DALEK SUPREME (*Distort*) That will not be necessary.

103. Int. Scout-Ship *Defiant*. Airlock Reception.
Sounds of great activity. The thirty-odd crewmembers are alert, armed and busy barracading the airlock. Welding equipment and barked orders etc.

ALBY All right – get the barricades up!
Sounds of effort and crashing of large objects. Comms bleep.
ALBY Alby to bridge. We're setting up defences at the airlock as best we can.
Pause. Bleep.
ALBY Bridge? Kalendorf? Suz? (*A sound of frustration*) Guys, I've got to go to the bridge – keep it together here. I'll be back.
Footsteps and breathing from ALBY as we follow him. Activity fades into the background.
ALBY (*Mumbles to himself*) Kalendorf... what the hell are you up to? Bastard... Never trust a man of noble birth... They'll sell you all down the river just for the sake of honour.

Fade up footsteps and crossfade to:

104. Int. Scout-Ship *Defiant*. Bridge.
SUZ regains consciousness. She groans, recovering as if from a bad dream.

KALENDORF (*Close*) Suz?
SUZ (*Close*) I couldn't... It was... Pure... destruction...
KALENDORF (*Close*) Now, do you understand?
SUZ (*Close. Now calm*) Yes. I do.
Door opens.
ALBY (*Approaching, out of breath*) Leave her alone! What are you doing to her? What's going on?
Feet scuffle as SUZ stands.
SUZ (*Getting up*) It's all right, Alby.
ALBY Is it? Here, take this gun.
Acoustic FX.
KALENDORF Don't *I* get a weapon?
ALBY Not until you explain what you're up to. Why didn't you answer my call on the intercom?
SUZ What call?
ALBY What's been going on here? You've been doing your telepathic stuff on her, haven't you, Kalendorf?[27]
Comms alarm.
DALEK SUPREME (*Distort*) This is the Dalek Supreme.
ALBY What the hell – ?!
DALEK SUPREME (*Distort*) Kalendorf, you will respond.
Gun cocked.
ALBY Stay where you are. Don't even think of touching those comms controls.
KALENDORF (*To DALEK SUPREME*) I know you can hear me – I'm sure your Daleks left enough surveillance devices on this ship to –
DALEK SUPREME (*Distort*) I can hear you.
ALBY You mean they've been listening to us all –
KALENDORF Are you ready to relay the signal?
ALBY What signal?
DALEK SUPREME (*Distort*) Attack Squadron *Dalazar* is equipped with trans-hyper signal projectors. Your transmission will be relayed throughout the entire galaxy.
KALENDORF Suz? Are you ready?
SUZ I'm ready.
Gun cocks.
ALBY Suz – don't move! Kalendorf, don't touch those controls – *I mean it!!!*
KALENDORF Put the gun down, Alby – and trust me.
ALBY Do as I say!
SUZ Alby – it's all right.
ALBY Is it? Then tell me what you're going to do?
DALEK SUPREME (*Distort*) The Alliance fleet is manoeuvring into attack formation. Prepare for transmission in 60 rels.
ALBY What are you supposed to transmit?! *I SAID DON'T TOUCH THOSE CONTROLS!!!*

KALENDORF   Alby, if you're going to kill me, you'd better do it now. But I warn you, the next person you'll have to kill will be Suz.

ALBY   Suz – tell me what you're going to do.

KALENDORF   There isn't time!

SUZ   I'll make time.

KALENDORF   But –

SUZ   Karl... it's important to me. (*Pause*) Alby, I'm going to tell the galaxy that the Angel of Mercy has returned – and that the Daleks have made that possible.

ALBY   Which Daleks? The *Enemy* Daleks?

SUZ   Yes.

ALBY   But –

SUZ   We have to join forces with our old enemies to defeat our new enemies.

ALBY   You've *got* to be joking.

KALENDORF   You know all about the Punished Planets, Alby –

ALBY   Yeah, but – look, I know we've found out that the Mentor and her lot are not all sugar and spice – but that's no reason to go running into the arms of the Daleks who nearly wiped us out last time.[28]

KALENDORF   And what about that station you found in the Pkowik System?

ALBY   You know about that? How?

SUZ   And Morli? What about her? That's the way the Mentor wants us all to be one day – simple, lovable, obedient and murderous on cue. Is that what you want to be like?

ALBY   (*To KALENDORF, realising*) Kalendorf... *You* told the Enemy Daleks about the Pkowik station, didn't you? That's why they were waiting there for me. That's how they knew how to find the Emperor's casing. My God. When did this start? How long have you been selling us out to the Enemy Daleks?

KALENDORF   Not quite as long as the Mentor has been plotting to turn us all into mindless cattle. Now, if you'll excuse me –

ALBY   Don't!!! I'm warning you! I *will* fire.

KALENDORF   Alby, I'm not going to bother to attempt justifying my actions –

ALBY   – because you can't! How would that be possible? Oh yeah, I know the Mentor's lot are bastards in their own way. I know that – I've *always* known that. I was *with* you on *that*. But how is joining forces with an even worse enemy gonna put that right?

KALENDORF   The Dalek Supreme has given us certain... assurances.

ALBY   Which'll go right down the pan the moment he gets what he wants.

KALENDORF   Maybe.

ALBY   Maybe? What's the matter with you? You *know* that!

KALENDORF   Whether you agree with me or not is immaterial! If Suz doesn't make that broadcast soon, that Dalek attack squadron will blast us out of existence.

ALBY   (*Locked in anger*) You bastard.

KALENDORF   Killing me won't stop Suz making the broadcast. Will it?

SUZ   No. Put the gun down, Alby.

ALBY   He's got you under his influence somehow. Don't you see, Suz? He's gone bad! He's sold us out. What he's doing can't be right.

DALEK SUPREME (*Distort*) You must make the broadcast now. Soon, the Alliance fleet will attack and we will be defeated.

ALBY　　　　This is our chance to defeat them, Suz. Isn't that what you've always been fighting for? Suz?

SUZ　　　　Put the gun down, Alby. I can't let you kill Kalendorf. You *have* to trust us.

ALBY　　　　I trust *you*, Suz. But you don't know what you're saying. He's a traitor and he's done something to your mind. You must trust me. *Comms bleep.*

KALENDORF　Kalendorf to Dalek Supreme, commencing transmission now.

ALBY　　　　Noooo!

Gun fires.

Crash in closing theme.

NOTES

1. Line changed to: '(*Carefully*) Yes. There's been report that a... an "unidentified" transmission was detected, coming from this ship.'

2. Line changed to: 'I... I wonder what it could have been.'

3. Line changed to: 'Good. I want you to get your section airborne in surface skimmers. I had a red light on Niner Seven's perimeter sensor just now, but couldn't raise them. No comms signal at all. It's like they're not there.'

4. Line changed to: '(*Via loudspeaker*) Perimeter guard unit Niner Seven! Are you there? Perimeter guard unit Niner Seven, show yourselves! **Perimeter guard unit Niner Seven! Are you there**?'

5. Line changed to: '**I** thought I saw someone moving behind those cactus-things.'

6. Line changed to: '**Yeah**, I suppose we'd better take a look on foot. Take us down nice and slow, Trooper. First sign of trouble and – '

7. Scenes 79 and 80 were reordered in post-production, with Scene 79 being inserted between two halves of Scene 80. The point in which Scene 79 was placed is during HERRICK's fourth line; 'Can your people run an atmosphere check?' being the first bit of the second half.

8. Line changed to: 'Now, Trooper, they've told us there's nothing on this planet but plants, insects and rodents. But if you see a hostile-looking bug, you have my express permission to blow its ugly **nuts** off.'

9. Line changed to: '(*Close and intense*) Uuuurgh! Must... musssssst... Must kill.'

10. Line changed to: 'No. We **will** await the coded signal from our advance party.'

11. Line changed to: 'No... no, it's all right, Morli. Don't panic. I may feel dead. I thought I *was* for a moment back there. But, apparently, I'm not. **Are you okay?**'

12. Line replaced by:

MIRANA   **There was a transmission**.
MARBER   **Transmisson**?
MIRANA   **Oh, it doesn't matter. The thing is**... I thought to myself... What's the thing I feared most?

13. Added dialogue at the beginning of the scene:

TARKOV   **Do you want some more**?
SALORAN   **Yes, thanks**.
TARKOV pours a drink. SALORAN takes a drink.
TARKOV   **You know**... **Are you okay**?
SALORAN   **Hmm. Yes, fine**.

14. Line changed to: '(*A chuckle*) You can have more than that. Is he really the monster who brought about the Great Catastrophe. The "Dark One"? **The**... the "Bringer of Death" we were all told about at school?'

15. Added dialogue at the beginning of the scene:

ALTERNATE DALEK Holographic transmission commencing.

16. Line changed to: '**Now in range**.'

17. Line changed to: 'That's right. All sorts of bad stuff, like blowing up whole planets, just because their governments said they were too poor to help in the war effort.'

18. Line changed to: 'But, Alby, the war's the only thing, like. The Bad Daleks have commuted the... you know... nastiest things in the whole uni-thing. We have to be on the side of the Good Daleks. That's the only way.'

19. Line changed to: 'Nah, it is the only way! That's what they taught us at the hospital, ~~like~~. We has to do what they tells us. We has to, man. And they can't have their Emproary... boss man back, can they? That would be the worst thing for all of us. The worst bloody thing of the lot.'

20.   Line changed to: 'I don't think I should be listening to you. You've got the Emproary thing in yer head, ~~like~~.'

21.   Line changed to: 'Will you help **us**?'

22.   Line changed to: 'I know you ~~loves~~ her and all that. But we have to kill her.'

23.   Line changed to: '(*Yells*) Are you gonna help **us**?!!'

24.   Line changed to: 'Exterminate! **Exterminate**!'

25.   Line changed to: 'Enter! **Enter**!'

26.   Line changed to: 'But if your reinforcements are **just** – '

27.   Line changed to: 'What's been going on **in** here? You've been doing your telepathic stuff on her, haven't you, Kalendorf?'

28.   Line changed to: 'Yeah, but – look, I know we've found out that the Mentor and her lot are not all sugar and spice – but that's no reason to go running into the arms of the Daleks who nearly wiped us out **the** last time.'

Q&A
CHAPTER THREE

Prologue 2 – Chapter Three's extra scene – was written during the recording, wasn't it?
Nicholas Briggs: More or less from the moment John and I had agreed the script was finished, I had this grumbling feeling in my waters about the whole business of Kalendorf covertly working against the Enemy Daleks. As it turned it, it was clear that Chapter Three was underrunning, so during the recording process – one evening after a studio session – I decided to write an extra scene for Chapter Three. The beginning of this chapter already had an 'out-of-sequence' scene, involving the Mentor destroying Emmeron, so I thought I'd just build on that a bit. I wanted to cement the idea that Kalendorf was up to something, so that the revelation that he'd retrieved Suz to use her as bait for the Dalek Supreme wasn't such an out-of-the-blue shock. I still wanted it to be a shock, but not one that seemed to have no basis.

Chapter Two had largely been about Alby, Mirana, Suz and Morli – and we left them on some pretty mighty cliffhangers. Why then shift focus to Jupiter and other characters?
Although I do quite a bit of planning and scribbling down of ideas, I'm a firm believer in writing being a lot to do with gut feeling. When I'm writing and I have a gut feeling that the story needs to go somewhere else for a while, I invariably act upon that feeling – because I feel I'm being the audience as well as the writer. It's like being stuck in one room too long. Sometimes, you just need to get outside and go for a walk. So that's one reason why I got outside and went for a walk with all the soldiers on Jupiter. But, once again, it was also a way of heightening tension, by not immediately resolving the previous set-up of Alby and Suz in trouble and Suz confessing she had the Dalek Emperor in her brain.

Scene 85 is beautiful – for the first time since *Invasion of the Daleks*, we hear Alby and Suz really talking together. Was it difficult to write – did you feel any expectation?
Thanks. I just wanted to create an intimate moment, and to be fair, it really works because of Sarah and Mark's acting. They were totally uninhibited about it. And, because the two of them genuinely felt that it was high time that the characters 'consummated' their relationship, it was the scene they were dying to do. They instinctively knew how to do it. I think it does come across well, as this very contained, almost trivial moment of reality amongst the most momentous events. As for writing it... I don't recall that it was difficult. When you've been building up to a scene like this for almost two whole series, you know exactly what the characters are thinking. When you're positive of that, and know the characters really well, it's exhilarating to write such a scene. I felt real anticipation for it.

Scene 86 is Mirana and Marber's only appearance in Chapter Three. As a listener, you're constantly thinking that they're going to be rescued, that something will happen – and then you kill 'em off!

I'm always trying to do what is 'realistic', even though the backdrop is often preposterous. I enjoy writing my characters into situations, and then having no idea of how I'm going to get them out of trouble. I'd had Marber and Mirana leave in the escape pod, I knew they'd still be floating around in it. I thought, what are the chances that they're going to be rescued? Virtually none at all. I think, when I initially wrote it, I hoped right up until the last breath that I'd think of a plausible way out of it... but there wasn't. I think my hope comes through in the performances of Tree [Gallagher] and Ian [Brooker]. We all worked very hard on that scene.

Chapter Three has only one scene of Saloran and Tarkov, as did Chapter Two. Were you worried that the audience would lose sight of the framing device – or, on the other hand, were you concerned about returning to them too often?

To be honest, that's just the way it worked out. It didn't worry me, although I seem to remember John Ainsworth picking up on this. The **Doctor Who Magazine** reviewer certainly did. But I needed narration at this point and not at any other during this chapter. I'm a great believer in using dramatic devices as and when they're needed, and not just for the sake of uniformity. I'm always trying to tell the story the most effective way I can at any given point.

The one Saloran and Tarkov scene begins with a bit of ad-libbing:

TARKOV	Do you want some more?
SALORAN	Yes, thanks.

TARKOV pours a drink. SALORAN takes a drink.

TARKOV	You know... Are you okay?
SALORAN	Hmm. Yes, fine.

Well, I had a lovely day with Karen Henson and Steve Elder doing the Velyshaa scenes. We had loads of time and we talked and rehearsed a lot. They're both very good actors who work in very different ways, so it was rather fun. Steve is very serious and concentrates hard. Karen is as mad as a tree and totally anarchic. She giggles and 'hums' and 'hahs' a lot. Then she hits the nail on the head and gets it just right. Steve is very precise and keen on detail. So somehow we worked out that it was really time that Tarkov and Saloran had some sort of meal, just to convey that they were talking for a long time. It's interesting that one reviewer said they were having breakfast... but we left it open to interpretation. We just talked about what they might be doing, and Steve and Karen just added those opening lines.

Why use Vaarga plants?

Seemed a good method for the Daleks to use to trap the alliance forces. And, er... I'd just listened to the CD of *Mission to the Unknown* [1965 *Doctor Who* episode, which only survives as an audio recording]. I thought it would be fun and it was appropriate in the context of the plot. It just added to the Daleky feel of the whole thing, I hoped.

Where does the name Dalazar come from?
You fool! Do you not know the name of the continent on Skaro where the Dalek city was built?

Why was 'But if you see a hostile-looking bug, you have my express permission to blow its ugly head off' changed to 'But if you see a hostile-looking bug, you have my express permission to blow its ugly nuts off'?
Actors! They said it. I laughed. What can I say? I was seduced. I forgot I'd let them change it when it came to putting the quote on the sleeve!

Q&A
NAMES

Nicholas Briggs: *The names I make up for my scripts come from a variety of sources. If they don't just pop into my head – and some of them often just do! – then I look around the room and see what I can spot. Sometimes they come from randomly selected pages from books, sometimes off bleach bottles. Sometimes I say real names, but muffle my mouth and see what they sound like. Yes, it's all a bit weird. I can't remember the origins of most of the Dalek Empire names, but here's what I do and don't remember...*

SUSAN MENDES – I don't know where Mendes came from. Possibly Sam Mendes, the director. But I wanted her to be called Suz, because that's what my Gramp always called my Nan.

ALBY BROOK – again, no idea where the surname came from, but Alby was my Gramp's name. Hence the 'thank you' to Nan and Gramp in the CD booklet.

KALENDORF – is the name of the visiting dignitary in Agatha Christie's *Spider's Web*. It's usually pronounced with a flat 'a' sound – like calor gas – but when I was in a production of this play, a fellow cast member, the wonderful Nick Pegg opted to pronounce it 'Karlendorf' and somehow I fell in love with the name. The name originally featured in my first pitch for *Embrace the Darkness* [2002 Doctor Who audio] but all the human characters were eventually replaced by one big robot family.

PELLAN – I think that was an adaptation of Pelham in *The Taking of Pelham One Two Three* [1974]

DRUDGER – I created for Audio Visuals, when I needed a name for a type of robot. Robot comes from the Czech verb 'robotit', which means 'to drudge', hence Drudger. They also featured in Big Finish's first *Doctor Who* audio, *The Sirens of Time*.

ELISONFORD – was originally Elinsford, but I accidentally typed the name incorrectly for the sleeve details. The sleeve was sent off before the recording session, so I had to change the name in the script! Elinsford comes from the Audio Visuals play *Justyce*.

ERNST TANLEE – Tanlee comes from a bizarre mix of character and actor names of the spymasters in James Bond and *The Ipcress File* [1965]. I later added the name Ernst rather randomly. It's been suggested that I was thinking of Ernst Stavros Blofeld, but I can't honestly say that's true.

DAUGHTER – was an 'in-joke' for the actress playing the part, Georgina Carter. Her agent at the time referred to all men as 'Daughter!'.

MARBER – I'd just acted in a production of Patrick Marber's brilliant play, *Closer*.

SPARKS – is a traditional way of referring to a radio operator or an electrician. Don't you watch war movies!?

MORLI – was originally Gojo, but that was just stupid. Then I changed it to Muli, but someone told me that sounded like a racist insult, so I changed it.

ALLENBY – the surname of the first girl I snogged.

GURIA – nothing to do with Simon Guerrier, who I didn't even know when I wrote the script.

CARSON'S PLANET – a reference to a vaguely remembered planet name from some old 1950s sci-fi novel. I didn't bother looking it up.

DEFIANT – I honestly didn't think of *Deep Space Nine*. I was naming it after HMS *Defiant*.

DX MISSILES – I use a discordant sound from an old Yamaha DX7 keyboard for my Dalek music.

DRAMMANKIN – is a mountain range on Skaro, you fool!

DALEK WAR CHAPTER FOUR

105. Ext. Space.
A synthesised, computer voice.

NAV COMPUTER Star Yacht *Crusader*, nav computer dispatch. Logged seven zero, nine, four two. *Crusader* has now entered Velyshaa System. No recognition comms received. Requests for planetary traffic control flightpath guidance from planet Velyshaa... unanswered. Solar sails retracting for final approach. Chemical engines activating for touchdown adjacent to ruins of Velyshaan capital city.
Crash in Dalek Empire *theme.*

106. Ext. Planet Velyshaa.
Howling, desolate winds. Roar of Crusader's *chemical engines slowly fades in from the distance.* Crusader *comes in to land. As engines reach a roaring crescendo, there is the crunch and clunk of the ship's contact with the rocky surface. The engines wind down. A pause. For a moment, nothing but the howling wind. The electronic motor of a door ramp opening. It crashes to the rocky ground. Footsteps on the metal gangplank, then crunch of footsteps on the ground.*

TARKOV   Still no contact?
TROOPER   No reply to any of our signals, sir.
TARKOV   (*Sighs heavily*) Right... We'll search on foot. Use your portable readers. Set them to detect humanoid life.
TROOPER   *Squad!* Humanoid life!
Various clicks and whirrs of several 'readers' being set.
TARKOV   (*To himself*) She's here somewhere. I know it.

TROOPER   Do we head for the buildings, sir?
TARKOV   That's all that's left of the Velyshaans... so that's where she's going to be.
TROOPER   Understood.
TARKOV   Let's move out. See what we can find before nightfall.
TROOPER   Sir. *Squad!* Wide dispersal! Move out!

The general crunch and clatter of the squad moving out. Bleep of readers. Martial music cue starts and reaches a crescendo. Change mood and crossfade to:

107. Int. Kalendorf's Burial Chamber.

The howling wind is muffled and distant. A flame is burning. SALORAN HARDEW is sleeping. We can hear her breathing. Distant hammering on a wooden door. SALORAN stirs, making a few confused groans.

TARKOV   (*Distant*) Hello, in there! Open this door!

SALORAN continues to recover from being rudely awoken. More hammering on door.

SALORAN   (*Impatiently*) There's a simple latch![1]
TARKOV   (*Distant*) Oh...

In the distance, a latch is lifted. The door creaks open. Footsteps of several approach. When they are near, they stop. The sound of several guns cocking.

TARKOV   Saloran Hardew?
SALORAN   Why the guns?
TARKOV   You didn't respond to any of our signals. Are you Saloran Hardew?
SALORAN   I didn't *hear* your signals. Put the guns away. I've no time for boy soldiers.
TARKOV   There were no navigation buoys on our way in. Has there been trouble here?
SALORAN   (*Amused*) Yes. Didn't you hear? A civilisation died over two thousand years ago. Who are you?
TARKOV   I'm Siy Tarkov. Special envoy from the Galactic Union. (*Pointed*) I'm looking for Saloran Hardew.
SALORAN   You intending to execute me?
TARKOV   Squad, stand down, please.
TROOPER   *Squad!* Stand down!

Clicks and whirrs of weaponry being uncocked.

SALORAN   Thank you... Tarkov. And what does the... (*With distaste*) Galactic Union want with me all of sudden?
TARKOV   Your help.

SALORAN starts to laugh. Her laugh gets louder and louder, echoing wildly through the cavernous chamber.

108. Int. Star Yacht *Crusader*. Corridor.

Door hisses open. And clunks shut. Footsteps as SALORAN and TARKOV walk along corridor.

SALORAN   How long did it take you to get here in this thing?
TARKOV   We set off from the Home Territories about a year ago.
SALORAN   Under solar sail power?

302

TARKOV   That's right.

SALORAN   Not bad. Technology's been improving since I've been away. Took me five years to get here. I spent most of it asleep of course.

TARKOV   Little by little, we're making improvements.

SALORAN   Hmmm. About three thousand years ago, our ancestors would have made the same journey in a fraction of the time. Sobering thought, isn't it?

Door hisses and clunks open.

TARKOV   In here, please.

SALORAN   Thank you.

Footsteps. Door closes. Crossfade to:

109. Int. *Crusader*. Tarkov's Cabin.

TARKOV   Please. Sit down.

SALORAN sits.

TARKOV   Can I get you a drink? Some breakfast?

SALORAN   You seem an intelligent sort of fellow, Tarkov.

TARKOV   Thank you, I –

SALORAN   So I'm guessing you'll have a pretty good idea of just how suspicious I am of you and your bosses.

TARKOV   I do realise that you – [weren't exactly treated well by the Galactic Union]

SALORAN   That I feel bitter, betrayed... cast out? Forgotten? *Do* you? (*Pause*) My people and I have been grovelling around in the stale shit of this planet for ten years, Mr Special Envoy. Have you any idea why?

TARKOV   (*Clears his throat. Awkward*) I've read your work. You put forward a theory that the Great Catastrophe was some sort of war, and that before it came about our galaxy was inhabited by a far superior civilisation. That the galaxy's population was a billion times larger than it is now. That –

SALORAN   Because your friends on the Galactic Union council dismissed me as an obsessive – not right in the head! That's the answer you're so politely trying to avoid, Tarkov. They said I was obsessed with the past, when we should be concentrating on the future. (*Pause*) What's your opinion on all this? Hm?[2]

Pause.

TARKOV   Um... I want to show you something. Please... if you'll just look at the screen.

Taps a few computer keys. The sound of a 3D graphic materialising on a screen.

TARKOV   This is a transmission which was picked up by our tracking stations just under two years ago.

SALORAN   It's coded.

TARKOV   Yes.

SALORAN   (*Disbelief*) You want me to crack a code?

TARKOV   No. We think we cracked it.[3]

SALORAN   You 'think'?

TARKOV   Some of the data was too corrupted to make sense of. But we got most of it.

SALORAN   What did you get?

Key taps. Graphic bleeps.

SALORAN   Some sort of visual file. A fragment of an image.
TARKOV   What do you make of it?
SALORAN   It looks like... metal. A detail of some machinery. Why have you brought it to me?
TARKOV   We analysed the physical characteristics of this 'metal'. *Key taps. Graphic bleeps.*
TARKOV   Do you recognise it?
SALORAN   (*Laughs*) And that's why you came to me. You *have* done your homework, Tarkov.
TARKOV   The physical characteristics of this unknown alloy correlate approximately to those of various artifact fragments you discovered before you came to work here on Velyshaa. Agreed?[4]
SALORAN   Agreed. Where did this transmission come from?
TARKOV   That's why I'm here.
SALORAN   (*With dread*) Don't tell me... It came from outside our galaxy?
TARKOV   Yes.
SALORAN   How did you pick it up? I didn't think our tracking stations could track that far.[5]
TARKOV   They can't. But this transmission came through a freak wormhole.
SALORAN   (*Chuckles*) Ah, fate... always keen to take us by surprise.
TARKOV   We estimate that it emanated from a source several thousand light years away.
SALORAN   And so *at last*, the Galactic Union are worried. Worried that what befell the galaxy centuries ago may happen again. And finally, like me, they want to look into the past to find out how to *stop* it all happening again.[6]
TARKOV   Frankly... No.
SALORAN   (*Puzzled*) I don't understand. Then why are you here?[7]
TARKOV   Well... I... (*Sighs*) I made... something of a nuisance of myself.
SALORAN   I beg your pardon?
TARKOV   They *allowed* me to come... but... well...
SALORAN   They think *you're* not right in the head too?
TARKOV   Let's just say that I need to make a pretty convincing case for them to take action.
SALORAN   And what sort of action would you like your precious Galactic Union to take?
TARKOV   I don't know. It depends on the nature of the threat, doesn't it? All I do know is that the evidence that something terrible happened round about two and a half thousand years ago is conclusive. I've seen the debris and dust that were once star systems. I've visited planets where the atmospheres are still poisoned... that still bear the scars of some... some unimaginably violent upheaval. And I've read as much of your work as I could find.[8]
SALORAN   Which probably isn't much.
TARKOV   It was enough. There's been a lot of rebuilding in the last thousand years. There may still be far too much poverty, fear and distrust out there, but things are gradually improving. And like it or not, that's because of the work the Galactic Union are doing.[9]
SALORAN   Huh.

TARKOV	I'd hate all that work to be for nothing.[10]
SALORAN	You're a crusader, Mr Tarkov.
TARKOV	Aren't *you*? It's the name I gave my ship. (*Pause*)

Saloran... I need you to tell me everything you've discovered here. (*Pause*) Saloran?

SALORAN	You think that I've been keeping it a secret all these

years? It's just that nobody wanted to listen.

TARKOV	Then...?
SALORAN	Then I'd like you to hand that corrupted transmission

over to *my* people... see if they can get anything else out of it. They've become exceptionally good at that sort of thing.

TARKOV	Of course. But I doubt they'll have any luck.
SALORAN	*And* we'd better get back to the burial chamber.
TARKOV	Burial chamber?
SALORAN	Where you found me.
TARKOV	You *sleep* in a burial chamber?
SALORAN	I do.
TARKOV	Why?

Music cue. A short passage of time.

110. Int. Kalendorf's Burial Chamber.
The wooden door creaks open. Footsteps on rock.

SALORAN	The last resting place of the great and terrible Kalendorf!
TARKOV	Kalendorf? Who was that?
SALORAN	Have you ever been to Earth?
TARKOV	Er... can't say I have. Where is it?[11]
SALORAN	Or Guria?
TARKOV	Er... no.
SALORAN	Celatron? Yaldos Major? No? Hmm... no. All of those

planets – and there are others too – all of them have small pockets of ancient communities who have passed stories of the Great Catastrophe down from generation to generation.[12]

TARKOV	Not very reliable sources, though.
SALORAN	Maybe not. Maybe not.

A few footsteps as they move further into the burial chamber.

SALORAN	Ever heard of the 'Dark One'? The 'Bringer of Death'... or

'Harbinger of Darkness'?

TARKOV	Only stories I was told as a kid.
SALORAN	Those stories, or stories much like them, have been told

all over the galaxy for centuries. Some of them differ from each other wildly. But when you put them all together... analyse the differences and the similarities... Pick over the bones of the meagre historical evidence from the Great Catastrophe... They start to point towards one man. A native of this planet. A Knight of Velyshaa. Kalendorf.

TARKOV	You're saying that this Kalendorf is the 'Dark One'? The

mythical figure who brought about the Great Catastrophe?

SALORAN	I'm saying it looked like he might have been... so I came

here to find out.

TARKOV	And all you found was his tomb.

SALORAN's footsteps.

SALORAN   The Knights of Velyshaa were a telepathic people. This place is alive with his thoughts. That's why I sleep here.

TARKOV   (*Dubious*) You can hear the thoughts of a dead man?

SALORAN   Only in dreams.

TARKOV   (*Dubious*) In... dreams?

SALORAN   There are no telepaths left in the known galaxy... but Velyshaans were able to communicate telepathically with ordinary folk like us.

TARKOV   Even when they've been dead for centuries?

SALORAN   Kalendorf left this for someone like me to find. Well, he probably hoped for someone better than me. But all these stone carvings, all these statues you see are charged with what he called his 'thought memory'.

TARKOV   (*Increasingly dubious*) So that's what you've been doing here all these years. Sleeping... and then dreaming about the man who allegedly caused the Great Catastrophe?

SALORAN   It's a little more scientific than that.

TARKOV   I'm relieved to hear it.

SALORAN   I've devised a cerebral link-up with my ship's computer. Downloading the mental impulses I pick up. I've got a couple of psychologists, a linguist and one or two of the local witch-doctors working on interpreting it all. (*Pause*) Are you thinking of taking your boy soldiers and leaving me to wallow in my own insanity, Mr Tarkov?

TARKOV   (*Sighs*) Tell me what you've found out.

SALORAN   And you'll decide later whether or not I'm off my head?

TARKOV   Something like that.

Pause.

SALORAN   Very well.

TARKOV   So?

SALORAN   Just take a look around.

TARKOV   At what? The statues?

SALORAN   If you like. What do you see?

TARKOV   Is this... Kalendorf?[13]

SALORAN   We think so. What do you think?

TARKOV   Well... that he doesn't look like a 'Harbinger of Death'. He doesn't look... evil. Sort of... noble.

SALORAN   Well... he *was* a knight.

TARKOV   What's this one?

SALORAN   You tell me.

TARKOV   Look, I'm not really in the mood for games –

SALORAN   Please. It's important.

TARKOV   Er... well... it looks like some sort of machine... Maybe a weapon of some kind?

SALORAN   It's interesting that you pick that one out.

TARKOV   Is it?

SALORAN   Yes.

A few footsteps.

SALORAN   Go ahead.

TARKOV   What?

SALORAN   You want to touch it, don't you?

TARKOV   (*Taken aback*) Yes. Yes, I do. But how did you know?

SALORAN   Then go ahead.

TARKOV All right.

Hand touches statue. Tarkov gasps in a mixture of confusion and pain. We are suddenly transported into a swirling psychic impression. Sounds are confused, echoing and distorted.

DALEK *(Echoing)* Exterminate!!!

A Dalek gun blast. Tarkov cries out. A long cry that echoes over and over again until we hear nothing but the fading echoes. Crossfade to:

111. Int. Saloran's Ship.

The background whirr of the ship's computer.

COMPUTER Cerebral activity returning to normal. Subject regaining consciousness.

TARKOV groans, waking.

SALORAN *(Soothing)* It's all right. You're all right.

TARKOV Am I?

SALORAN Well that's what my computer says.

TARKOV Your...? This is your ship?

SALORAN More of a glorified shelter now. It'd never get off the ground, that's for sure.

TARKOV *(Trying to remember)* I touched that... that statue... and then... The machine... The machine in the statue seemed to come alive. *(Becoming agitated)* And... and I wasn't... there... I wasn't... wasn't – [14]

SALORAN *(Calming)* You latched onto a little test Kalendorf left behind for posterity.

TARKOV Kalendorf? What do you mean? What *was* that machine? It... *spoke.* It fired a weapon at me. I thought I was... *dead.* [15]

SALORAN What you saw was a Dalek. Or at least a psychic impression of one.

TARKOV A... Dalek? What's a 'Dalek'?

SALORAN They were a military power from another galaxy. Back in Kalendorf's time, they invaded.

TARKOV *(Incredulous)* Invaded the entire galaxy?

SALORAN Yes.

TARKOV And that's what caused the Great Catastrophe...

SALORAN Not exactly.

TARKOV Then what?

SALORAN Computer, commence playback. Look at the screen.

COMPUTER Playback commencing. [16]

Buzz of computer activity.

TARKOV What...? What am I looking at?

SALORAN A sort of decoding of some of the earliest images I experienced in the burial chamber.

TARKOV Those are spacecraft... Enormous spacecraft. Like nothing I've ever seen before... And planets... huge populations... cities... cities full of people, creatures. But these are just dreams, you said it yourself.

SALORAN Was what you experienced just a dream?

TARKOV I... don't know.

SALORAN What you encountered was something that Kalendorf left, for us to find out that we could access the thoughts he left behind. *(Pause)* You said you wanted to know everything I'd discovered.

TARKOV   Yes.

SALORAN   It's hard to believe, I know. But this is what the galaxy was like back then. Something they called the Earth Alliance had established peace... until the Daleks invaded. When they did, Kalendorf was caught in the middle of it. Somehow he became involved with an Earth woman called Suz. They were captured by the Daleks and, it seems, agreed to work for them. Kalendorf felt he had betrayed everything he believed in, just for the sake of survival. With his help, the Daleks continued their ruthless subjugation of the civilised worlds. It's not clear what the nature of his feelings for Suz were, but there was a special bond between them. The years passed. Kalendorf and Suz continued with their betrayal. Then one day, the Daleks killed Suz. This may have been the trigger for Kalendorf to turn against the Daleks. We don't know for sure. The Daleks had successfully conquered the galaxy, but against all the odds, he apparently led a rebellion against them. It looked like the rebellion might succeed; but the Daleks had a secret strategy. Somehow they had the means to create a dimensional gateway into an alternative universe. And from that universe, they intended to gain the wisdom and the power to rule the entire cosmos. They would join forces with an invincible Dalek army from another dimension.[17]

Extract from final scene of Project Infinity.

SALORAN   But that alliance was not to be. A terrible war between the two Dalek factions began, with Kalendorf and his trusted lieutenants, Alby Brook and Mirana, rallying the rebel humans to fight on the side of the Daleks from the other universe. Kalendorf had swapped sides again. And once again, as the years passed, he was to realise the route to victory and peace would not be an easy one.

During the above (which has already been heard in Chapter One) *crossfade (at a point to be determined in post-production) to:*

112. Int. Scout-Ship *Defiant*. Bridge.

ALBY   I trust you, Suz. But you don't know what you're saying. He's a traitor and he's done something to your mind. You must trust me.

Comms bleep.

KALENDORF   Kalendorf to Dalek Supreme, commencing transmission now.

ALBY   Noooo!

Gun fires. Pause.

ALBY   (*In pain*) Suz? (*Gasps*)

SUZ   (*Breaking down*) I'm sorry, Alby... I'm sorry, but I couldn't let you kill Kalendorf.[18]

ALBY gives a final gasp and dies.

DALEK SUPREME (*Distort*) Begin transmission immediately!

SUZ   (*Numb*) What have I done?

KALENDORF   Saved the galaxy.

SUZ   I wonder...

DALEK SUPREME (*Distort*) Begin immediately!

Comms bleep.

KALENDORF   We're transmitting. (*Pause. Prompting her*) Suz.

SUZ   (*Beginning a long speech*) This is the Angel of Mercy... I have returned to you...

113. Int. Saloran's Ship.[19]

TARKOV   Did Kalendorf's plan work?

SALORAN   I think it was the beginning of what we call 'The Great Catastrophe'. There was chaos.

Sounds of battle accompany this with music.

SALORAN   After Susan Mendes made her speech, calling for the Mentor to be defeated, the Alliance fleet erupted into a war between all the non-Dalek races and the Mentor's Daleks. The Dalek Supreme's forces moved in.

More sounds of battle. Explosions. Quite a music moment too. Fade...

SALORAN   Eventually, the Mentor's Daleks retreated. The Alliance joined forces with the Dalek Supreme. It was the beginning of a long, terrible war. The Mentor brought forward her plans for brain conversion of all other species. Kalendorf led the Alliance alongside the Dalek Supreme. The destruction was... almost beyond comprehension.

TARKOV   When you... experience Kalendorf's thoughts... Do you...? I mean, what about his feelings? Did he do all this without any sense of regret or remorse?[20]

Pause.

SALORAN   The Knights of Velyshaa believed in strength of purpose at all costs. Kalendorf's purpose was to rid the galaxy of the Daleks... any Daleks. He believed that overrode all other concerns.

TARKOV   But how did he hope to win? Even if his new alliance succeeded in defeating the Mentor and her Daleks, he must have known that the Dalek Supreme wouldn't be an ally forever.

SALORAN   You're forgetting the Emperor.

TARKOV   The Emperor? Then what happened to Suz?

114. Int. Scout-Ship *Defiant*. Bridge.

DALEK SUPREME (*Distort*) She will be brought to me, here on Earth.

KALENDORF   You don't need her... You only need to extract the consciousness of your Emperor from her mind.

DALEK SUPREME (*Distort*) The extraction process must be carried out on Earth.

KALENDORF   Why?

DALEK SUPREME (*Distort*) Do not question the Dalek Supreme! (*Pause*) When we have won the war, you will see Susan Mendes again.

KALENDORF   You mean you're going to hold her hostage.

DALEK SUPREME (*Distort*) This discussion is at an end.

The hyperlink cuts off.

SUZ   Did you expect anything else?

KALENDORF   I'm sorry.

SUZ   There's no need. We both know what has to be done... don't we?

KALENDORF   Yes.

SUZ   You know I don't think I'll be able to bear it...

KALENDORF   What do you mean?

SUZ   If I'd killed Alby for no reason.[21]

Deep boom and crunch of distant spaceship docking. A tiny alarm sounds.

KALENDORF	The Dalek command ship is docking with us.
SUZ	Karl?
KALENDORF	Yes?
SUZ	Win this war.
KALENDORF	It's all I can do.

115. Int. Saloran's Ship.

TARKOV　　And did he win?
SALORAN　　No one could. There was just more and more destruction. For years and years. No end to it in sight.
TARKOV　　Then what could possibly have been his plan?
SALORAN　　It was based on an old strategy used by one of Velyshaa's greatest and most feared leaders.

116. Ext. Planet Meecros V. Battlefield.
Massed gunfire. Huge explosions. Cries of Mentor Daleks being destroyed. The dust settles. The battle is over. We overhear a conversation on a transceiver...

GODWIN　　(*Distort*) Colonel Godwin to command. Meecros V Mentor-Dalek base destroyed. We're ready for evac.
COMMAND　　(*Distort*) Any word from Commander Kalendorf?
Crackle.
COMMAND　　(*Distort*) Godwin? Is Kalendorf all right?
GODWIN　　(*Distort*) We... we don't know. He led the primary assault force in on the ground.
COMMAND　　(*Distort*) He...? What? But he's our Commander-in-Chief, he's – !
GODWIN　　(*Distort*) I know, *I know*. But have you ever tried arguing with him? We couldn't stop him.[22]
COMMAND　　(*Distort*) Has he gone crazy – ? It must've been a hell-hole in there.
GODWIN　　(*Distort*) Don't you get the idea that's where he wants to be these days? I mean, don't get me wrong, he's a fine soldier. The best commander we could have. But... you know, when he's not fighting a battle, he just sits in his cabin... listening to the hyper-scanner, like he's trying to find something. Won't talk about it, but I know – [23]
COMMAND　　(*Distort*) All right... Look... We've missed our window on hitting that enemy transport fleet anyway. We can hang on here until Eastern Sunrise. *We'll* keep tracking for him. *You* send in a squad to find him.[24]
GODWIN　　(*Distort*) I'll lead it myself.
COMMAND　　(*Distort*) And, Godwin, keep signalling for him on the comms.[25]
GODWIN　　(*Distort*) Will do.
COMMAND　　(*Distort*) Good luck. Command out.
Crackle.
GODWIN　　(*Distort*) Commander Kalendorf, do you read me? Please respond. This is Colonel Godwin calling Kalendorf. Can you hear me?
KALENDORF sounds significantly older now.
KALENDORF　　(*Exhausted*) I can hear you. I'm alive.

GODWIN (*Distort. Repeats her call, obviously not hearing KALENDORF. Dip the call repeating under KALENDORF's next speech*)

KALENDORF I just don't feel like talking... that's all. Not to you, anyway.

He clicks Godwin off in mid sentence.

KALENDORF I want to talk to Suz. *Suuuzzz!!!*

His words echo across the battlefield.

ALTERNATE DALEK (*Gurgles*) Susan... Mendes...

KALENDORF Huh... (*Chuckles harshly*) Are you the only one we left alive here?

ALTERNATE DALEK (*Strangled voice*) You... surrendered Susan Mendes... to the Dalek Supreme... You sacrificed her... Why?

KALENDORF (*A statement*) Why.

ALTERNATE DALEK (*Weakly*) Whyyyyy?

KALENDORF That's not you talking. That's the Mentor speaking through you.

ALTERNATE DALEK Whyyyyyy...?

KALENDORF Tell you what, I'll make you a deal. I'll talk to you – warrior to warrior... (*building rage*) but without *her LISTENING!!!*

Then, with an animalistic roar, he attacks the DALEK's casing. He rips the broken metal casing open. The creature within squeals.

KALENDORF Come – out – of – there!!!

Crunching and crashing of metal. Squelching and squirting of noxious fluids. The creature continues screaming. A grunt of massive effort from Kalendorf, then... A final rip and a splat. The Dalek creature whimpers and gurgles pathetically.

KALENDORF And there you are... laid bare... free from all that machinery... from your billions of connections with her – the all-seeing, all-knowing, all-powerful *Mentor*. What's it like to be alone on a battlefield? Surrounded by the dead – knowing you're going to die?

Pathetic gurgle from the creature.

KALENDORF Huh... Can't speak. But I'll grant you your last wish. I'll answer your question, in my own way. The way I told Suz. Why did I let the Dalek Supreme take my friend from me? Well... There was once a great leader of my people. His name was Sancroff. Like you, he nearly conquered this galaxy. He was defeated in the end – but at least he was defeated by his enemies. That's what he wanted. He didn't fear that. He knew it would happen one day. But what he couldn't bear was the idea of betrayal. To be defeated by the enemy within. So many of his predecessors had gone that way – stabbed in the back. It was very nearly a tradition. So, whenever he promoted anyone into high office, he made them swear an oath of allegiance. Now, as you may or may not know, the Velyshaans are telepathic. So, at the ceremony of 'Victory or Death' – that was the name of the oath, by the way – he would hold the nobleman or woman's hand, then pull them close, to see if their thoughts were true and pure. And, you know, none of his knights ever betrayed him. Except one. Seterisius was her name. She fought at Sancroff's side in many a battle. She was brave, ruthless, determined. Sancroff loved her as if she were his own daughter, so they say. Then one day, Sancroff discovered that she was plotting his downfall. He didn't tell her that he knew. He just summoned her for a private audience with him. The doors closed. No one knew what passed between them. But when it was over, Seterisius left

311

Sancroff's palace, went straight to her fortress and brutally killed everyone of her co-conspirators. Then... She killed herself.

GODWIN   (*Distort. Distant*) Kalendorf! It's him! Kalendorf!!!

Footsteps run across the battlefield towards us and stop.

GODWIN   (*Out of breath*) Kalendorf... Thank God you're alive.

KALENDORF   Don't interrupt. This is a private conversation.

GODWIN   (*Distort*) Conv...? With who?

KALENDORF   This... thing... This... Dalek creature.

TROOPER   Er... I think it's dead... sir.

KALENDORF   Dead? Huh... dead. Yes, dead. Everything's dead.

GODWIN   (*Distort*) Are you all right, sir?

KALENDORF   Come on, we'd better get moving.

He staggers to his feet with great vocal effort.

KALENDORF   The war's not over yet.

117. Int. Flagship. Bridge.

Slow fade up on...

GODWIN   Still no sign of that enemy transport fleet, Commander. Should we break off the search and head for the outer sectors?

Pause. The sound of a transmissions hyper-scanner, dialling through a mass of random transmissions.

GODWIN   Commander? (*Close, slightly awkward*) Sir? Perhaps you'd like to go to your cabin and rest.

Suddenly, there's a single, repeating sequence of bleeps.

KALENDORF   There.

GODWIN   Sir?

KALENDORF   (*To himself*) I think that's it. Visual scan. Long range. Co-ordinates... (*reading off*) 94249127459/9874.[26]

COMPUTER   Scanning.

Scanning FX.

GODWIN   (*Sighs*) What is it you're looking for, sir?

Scanner finds something. An alert bleep.

KALENDORF   Yes. Well? Can't you see it, Godwin?

GODWIN   (*Dubious*) Well... I...

KALENDORF   Magnify that area. Well, go on.[27]

GODWIN   Er... right.

Bleep of controls. Magnification FX.

GODWIN   (*Surprised*) There *is* something there.

KALENDORF   Well don't sound so surprised. Did you think I'd finally flipped my lid? Stop engines.

Power hum lowers.

GODWIN   All stopped. We're still drifting towards it.

KALENDORF   (*Squinting at screen*) Just getting a closer... (*Stunned*) And there it is...

GODWIN   What is it?

KALENDORF   It's an escape pod. Godwin, read the ident mark on the hull and tell me I'm not going mad.

Bleep of controls.

GODWIN   (*Reading*) S. S... Defiant... Wasn't she lost years ago? (*Pause*) Sir?

KALENDORF Lost? Yes... she was.
Cut to:

118. Int. Recovery Capsule.
Burst of rocket fire as Recovery Capsule blasts off from Flagship. Crossfade to interior of capsule. Pinging of proximity scanner (like a quickening sonar ping).

GODWIN *(Distort)* Flagship to Recovery Capsule, you are clear and on course for *SS Defiant* escape pod. We are tracking you on approach vector six, speed rising to eleven mettrons per second.
During the last sentence, a strange phasing sound distorts then obscures the dialogue. The phasing sound continues on distort.
KALENDORF Recovery Capsule to Flagship, your signal is breaking up. Seems to be a problem with your transmission.
Pause. Phasing continues.
KALENDORF Flagship? Respond, please.
GODWIN *(Distort. Fades in through phasing)* Recovery Capsule, come in. Come in, please. Are you reading me? Kalendorf?
KALENDORF *(Some urgency)* Recovery Capsule receiving. What's going on, Godwin?
GODWIN *(Distort)* Kalendorf! Listen to me –
KALENDORF What happened?
GODWIN *(Distort)* We lost you for a moment, but –
KALENDORF What was it? Some sort of signal interference?
GODWIN *(Distort)* No... Listen to me – We lost you *completely*. The scanners couldn't pick you up at all.
KALENDORF What?
GODWIN *(Distort)* Your capsule and the *Defiant*'s escape pod just... phased out of existence for a few moments. You – [28]
KALENDORF Run a diagnostic on your scanners and proximity –
GODWIN *(Distort)* No. *Kalendorf*, turn your capsule around and get back here, *now!*
KALENDORF Are you giving your Commander-in-Chief an order, Godwin?
GODWIN *(Urgent)* I'm the designated officer commanding for this EVA – this is *my* call, Kalendorf, and I don't think we have time for this discussion. I shouldn't have let you go out there in the first place. Turn back now.
KALENDORF Why? What's going on?
GODWIN *(Distort)* We're initiating remote control. We're bringing you back whether you like it or not –
During this, KALENDORF operates several controls.
GODWIN *(Distort. Angry)* Kalendorf?!
KALENDORF I've shut off the remote control receptors. You're not bringing me back until you tell me what's going on.
GODWIN *(Distort)* Commander, *please!*
Phasing begins again during this and finally cuts off transmission.
GODWIN *(Distort)* There isn't time! We've detected some sort of spatial anomaly... a kind of dimensional shift... and that escape pod is sitting right in the middle of –
Cut off.

KALENDORF Godwin? Godwin!
Crackle.
COMPUTER Transmission source out of range.
KALENDORF (*Incredulous*) Out of range? Distance to Flagship.
COMPUTER Incalculable.
KALENDORF In – ? Visual scan 360 degrees.
COMPUTER Scanning 360 degrees.
Scanning FX.
KALENDORF There's the pod...
Scanning continues.
KALENDORF (*Realisation*) No sign of the Flagship. But just now – Distance to *Defiant* escape pod?
COMPUTER Now within docking arm range.
KALENDORF Extend docking arm immediately.
COMPUTER Extending.
Clunk and whirr of docking arm.

119. Int. Flagship. Bridge.

GODWIN Well keep scanning! He must be out there somewhere. He can't have just disappeared!
COMMAND I'm afraid that's exactly what he *has* done, Colonel. No trace of the pod at all.
GODWIN (*To herself*) Kalendorf...

120. Int. Recovery Capsule. Docking Arm.
KALENDORF's breathing through space helmet filter. The clunk of his booted feet as he proceeds down the arm.

KALENDORF Now in docking arm. What's the atmosphere reading in the pod?
COMPUTER (*Distort*) No readings available.
KALENDORF (*To himself*) No readings... no readings. What did you expect? A miracle...
Footsteps stop.
KALENDORF Now opening escape pod door.
Door mechanism buzzes and door creaks open. Cut to:

121. Int. Mentor's Base.
Door opening. KALENDORF's footsteps. A different door closes.

KALENDORF (*To himself*) What the hell...? This isn't the escape pod. This... This is –
Another door opens.
ALTERNATE DALEK You may remove your protective helmet. The atmosphere here is breathable for humanoids.
KALENDORF removes his space helmet.
KALENDORF So. I've walked into a trap. Very clever. What now?
ALTERNATE DALEK 1 You will come with us.
KALENDORF No, I think I'd rather walk straight back through that door.

ALTERNATE DALEK You and your Recovery Capsule were transported through the dimensional gateway. You are no longer in your own universe.

KALENDORF How the hell did you manage to do that... and more importantly – why?

ALTERNATE DALEK 1 The Mentor will explain. She is waiting to see you. Come with us.

KALENDORF *(After a long sigh)* All right.

122. Ext. Mentor's Garden.

A distant, almost musical, gentle wind. Soothing sounds of alien birdsong. Door opens. KALENDORF steps out onto grass.

MENTOR There are refreshments for you. Please. Make yourself comfortable.

KALENDORF Where's Mirana? *(Pause)* Suz told me Mirana had got away in the *Defiant*'s escape pod. Or was that pod I saw just some sort of clever mirage?

MENTOR It has been many years since that pod was launched. My Daleks located it some time ago. Would you *expect* Mirana to be found alive in it?

Pause.

KALENDORF No.

MENTOR And yet you had to see for yourself. To be certain. I knew you would. It has something to do with guilt, has it not?

KALENDORF Well?

MENTOR As you suspected, Mirana is, of course, dead. She and her first officer, Marber, died some years ago of asphyxiation. I am sorry if the news... upsets you, Kalendorf. *(Pause)* You look puzzled.

KALENDORF You must have gone to a lot of trouble to get me here. What did you do...? Stretch the dimensional gateway all the way from the Lopra System to Meecros?

MENTOR Your presence in our universe is proof that we have that ability... would you not agree?

KALENDORF Huh... And why would you bother? Do you think the Alliance will fall apart without me?

MENTOR I doubt that.

KALENDORF Then what do you want?

MENTOR When did you turn against us?

KALENDORF *(Amused)* Do you think if I tell you, you'll be able to win back my allegiance?

MENTOR I wish to understand your motives.

KALENDORF *(Goading)* I thought you'd thoroughly examined all the evidence relating to me. Are you telling me you're not all-powerful and all-seeing?

MENTOR Humour me, Kalendorf.

Pause.

KALENDORF It was early on in the war. But I'd already decided you weren't to be trusted. We'd captured a squad of Enemy Daleks. Most of them had blown themselves up before we could disable their self-destruct mechanisms. But we got to one of them just in time.

Crossfade to:

123. Int. Flagship *Courageous*. Secure Room.

DALEK   You will learn nothing from me.

HERRICK   (*Distort*) Commander! It's released some sort of data virus in its brain unit. We can't stop it! It's wiping everything it knows!

KALENDORF   Disengage all our scanning equipment.

HERRICK   (*Distort*) But, sir, if we –

KALENDORF   Do it now, Herrick! Cut off all surveillance and comm-links in this room. 100 per cent shut-down and secure! Do it!

HERRICK   (*Distort*) Sir.

Shut down FX.

KALENDORF   (*Testing*) Herrick? Herrick? Herrick!!! (*Pause*) And now we're alone. Do you understand me?

DALEK   I... understand.

KALENDORF   I don't want anything from you. I'm just going to touch your casing... tell you something... with my mind. I have something you want. Something you *need*.

124. Ext. Mentor's Garden.

A distant, almost musical, gentle wind.

MENTOR   You gambled that the Enemy Dalek would relay your offer of Susan Mendes through its command network to the Dalek Supreme.

KALENDORF   I gambled. And I won.

MENTOR   *Why* did you turn against us?

KALENDORF laughs. His laughter continues for a while under...

MENTOR   Our only purpose was to bring peace and order to your universe. To destroy the Daleks who would enslave and exterminate you. You knew that.

KALENDORF   Yes, but when we accepted your *kind* offer of help... we didn't know that you would destroy any world that refused to join our alliance.

MENTOR   On a crusade against evil, there can be no equivocation.

KALENDORF   (*Angry*) Those planets weren't equivocating... they were sick of war! They'd lost the will to fight... most of them'd had their natural resources ripped out of the guts of their worlds. It isn't that they didn't *want* to fight alongside us, most of them *couldn't*! (*Pause*) No. No answers. No excuses. No discussions. Just that fixed, exquisite smile. And ultimately, that's the only difference, isn't it? The smile. The gentle voice. (*Pointed*) But you are a Dalek.

MENTOR   And for that... intellectual conceit, you have led your galaxy to the brink of destruction.

KALENDORF   Freedom of thought – of *choice* – isn't an intellectual conceit! It's my birthright.

MENTOR   And what would you do with that birthright? Conquer and enslave as your own ancestors did? As the Daleks did? Tell me... What is the difference?

KALENDORF   The difference is that we make our own decisions. And we don't get turned into mindless, obedient zombies.

MENTOR   You are referring to the mind-processing techniques we developed in the Pkowik System?

KALENDORF   Techniques you've been employing wholesale since we became enemies. And you really can't understand why I won't embrace that as the future for my galaxy?

MENTOR   'My galaxy'? You are a warrior at heart, Kalendorf. What would you do without a war to fight?

No answer from KALENDORF. Pause.

MENTOR   See how beautiful this planet is. This is my home. There are countless worlds in this universe just as beautiful... as peaceful. That is why the people here are content. Why would they want the freedom to war amongst themselves? And ultimately, that is all you want the freedom to do, is it not? To carry on with your own, petty, destructive affairs without interference from the Daleks. But you will never have that.

KALENDORF   That's for me to find out.

MENTOR   Do you think you are winning this war?

KALENDORF   Why don't you get on and kill me or brain convert me or whatever you have planned?

MENTOR   You are not winning this war. But neither are we. And as the war continues, more and more of your galaxy is laid waste. There is something almost poignant about the futility of what we are engaged upon.

KALENDORF   What are you trying to say?

MENTOR   Our battle computers confirm that this war can never be won... by either side. It will only end in the total destruction of life, not only in your galaxy, but ultimately beyond that.

KALENDORF   So, what do you propose?

MENTOR   What if you *were* to win this war?

KALENDORF   What do you mean?

MENTOR   If your alliance were to drive us out of your universe... What would happen then? (*Pause*)

KALENDORF   That would be our affair... not yours.

MENTOR   What is certain is that the Dalek Supreme and the Emperor would not honour any agreements made with you.

KALENDORF   Perhaps.

MENTOR   It is certain.

KALENDORF   What are you saying?

MENTOR   Which would you prefer? The destruction of your universe? Another, perhaps endless war with your old enemy Daleks, ending in defeat or destruction? Or a future under our guidance and protection?

KALENDORF   I prefer to make my own future.

MENTOR   You really believe you could defeat the Emperor's Daleks if they turned against you?

KALENDORF   Perhaps.

MENTOR   You could not defeat them before.

KALENDORF   Perhaps things are different now.

MENTOR   They are not. The course you choose is destruction.

KALENDORF   It's my choice. And the choice of every other free mind in the galaxy.

MENTOR   A galaxy that will be consumed in the fires of war if this futile conflict does not end now. And unlike the Daleks of your universe, we have no desire to participate in pointless destruction. So you see, there is a difference, Kalendorf. Goodbye.

125. Int. Saloran's Ship.

TARKOV   What...? And they just... just left?
SALORAN   Yes. The Mentor recalled all her forces through the dimensional gateway.
TARKOV   And Kalendorf?
SALORAN   He was returned to his ship.
TARKOV   And then what? The Dalek Supreme's forces turned on Kalendorf's people?
SALORAN   No. For a brief period there seemed to be peace.

126. Int. Flagship. Kalendorf's Cabin.
Door bleep.

KALENDORF   Enter.
Door opens.
GODWIN   I hope I'm not interrupting you, sir.
KALENDORF   No... no, Godwin... Come in.
GODWIN   Thank you.
Footsteps. Door closes.
KALENDORF   Take a seat... please.
Sound of GODWIN sitting.
KALENDORF   How long until we arrive in Earth's orbit?
GODWIN   We're currently refuelling. But at optimum speed it shouldn't take us more than a couple of months to get there.
KALENDORF   (*Pensive*) Good... good...
GODWIN   Do you really expect the Daleks to let us just sail in there?
KALENDORF   (*Touch of irony*) Why not? We're allies, aren't we? What can I do for you, Colonel?
Pause.
GODWIN   What do you think will happen next?
KALENDORF   Is that really why you came to see me?
GODWIN doesn't answer.
KALENDORF   What do *you* think?
GODWIN   (*Sighs*) Well... Everyone's expecting another war. I mean... I don't see how the Daleks will ever keep their promise of peaceful co-existence. It's not what they're about, is it... really?
KALENDORF   No. No, it isn't.
GODWIN   You're going back for the Angel of Mercy, aren't you?
KALENDORF   Suz. Yes. (*Pause*) You don't think that's a good idea.
GODWIN   I understand why... But... (*Sighs*) Well... There are those who think it would be wiser to prepare for some kind of attack.
KALENDORF   Ah yes. And are you one of those who think that? (*Pause. Cottoning on*) Hmm. Will you at least take me to the edge of Earth's solar system, Colonel? I can make the rest of the journey in one of our one-man scout-ships.
GODWIN   I... I think that would probably be best. I'm sorry. We all owe you so much, but...
KALENDORF   My time has passed. I'm already just... part of history.
GODWIN   I'd like to be able to convince you not to go. But I know better than that.
KALENDORF   (*Chuckles*) Godwin, what's your first name?

318

GODWIN   Er... Susan, sir.

KALENDORF   Susan? All these years we've fought together, and I never knew... Well, Susan... I don't have a choice. But thanks for the thought.

Music. Passage of time. Slow crossfade to:

127. Int. Earth. Dalek Control. Tracking Centre.
Fade in on alarms sounding.

DALEK   Alert! Alert! Enemy craft approaching.

DALEK 1   Target for destruction immediately.

DALEK   I obey. Targeting.

Call-sign transmission.

DALEK   An unknown call sign is being transmitted.

Comms bleep.

DALEK SUPREME (*Distort*) This is the Dalek Supreme. That is the call-sign of Kalendorf. Dispatch a transolar disc squadron to force it to land. Activate magnatrap.

Comms bleep.

DALEK   Approaching vessel is attempting contact with Dalek Control.

KALENDORF   (*Distort*) This is Kalendorf. There's no need to panic. Your scanners must be able to tell that I'm alone, and all the weapons systems of this ship are powered down.

DALEK SUPREME (*Distort*) What is the purpose of your visit?

Crossfade during DALEK SUPREME's above line to:

128. Int. Earth. Dalek Control. Dalek Supreme's Chamber.

DALEK SUPREME What is the purpose of your visit?

KALENDORF   (*Distort*) You promised that Susan Mendes would be released when the war was over.

DALEK SUPREME I promised that you could see her.

KALENDORF   (*Distort*) Doesn't it amount to the same thing?

DALEK SUPREME A squadron of transolar discs will escort you. You may land. But if you attempt to deceive us in any way, you will be exterminated immediately!

KALENDORF   (*Distort*) Understood.

129. Int. Earth. Dalek Emperor's Chamber.
Door opens.

DALEK SUPREME Kalendorf's ship is now landing. He will be brought to you immediately.

SUZ   Good.

130. Ext. Earth. Dalek Control. Landing Pad Zeg.
Final moments of touchdown.

DALEK   Magnatrap at full strength. This ship will not be able to lift off without our releasing it.

Comms bleep.

DALEK 1   Dalek Control to Kalendorf.

KALENDORF (*Distort*) Yes.

DALEK 1 Leave your ship now! If you attempt to escape, you will be exterminated!

KALENDORF (*Distort*) Why the hell would I come here just to try to escape? I could've just stayed away. That would have been the wiser thing to do.

DALEK 1 Leave your ship noooowww!!!

Comms bleep off. KALENDORF's shuttle hatch opens. Footsteps.

KALENDORF Now what?

DALEK You will come with us! Move! Move!

KALENDORF Where's Suz?

DALEK 1 Move or you will be exterminated!

131. Int. Earth. Dalek Emperor's Antechamber.

Door opens. Footsteps.

DALEK Halt!

DALEK SUPREME Kal-en-dorf!

KALENDORF I don't believe we've met.

DALEK This is the Dalek Supreme!

KALENDORF Where's Suz?

DALEK SUPREME You will see her now.

Door opens.

DALEK SUPREME Follow! Follow!

DALEK Move!

Footsteps and stop. As we move in, the background hum alters slightly and the reverb becomes larger.

KALENDORF Well, where is she?

A complex series of metallic shields unfolds. The Dalek heartbeat becomes louder, more dominant. SUZ's footsteps echo.

KALENDORF Suz?

SUZ (*Cold*) You won the war. Well done.

KALENDORF I didn't *win* it. I just convinced the Mentor that I'd never give up fighting. So, she couldn't see the point in going on.

SUZ It was a good strategy.

KALENDORF It was just the truth – Suz, are you all right? (*Pause. To Daleks*) Are you Daleks going to let us out of here? What are you planning?

SUZ *I* am planning to make another speech to the citizens of the galaxy. It's time the Angel of Mercy united us.

KALENDORF I imagine the Dalek Emperor has other ideas. I'd like to speak to him before I leave, by the way. (*To DALEK SUPREME*) Can that be arranged?

DALEK SUPREME Why do you wish to speak to the Emperor?

KALENDORF (*With some irony*) We're both commanders-in-chief of our respective forces. And we're both allies. Isn't that reason enough? (*Pause*) Well?

DALEK SUPREME You see the Emperor before you.

KALENDORF What...? You? But you're just the Dalek Supreme –

SUZ Me, Karl. Me. (*A little snigger*) Explain it to him.

DALEK SUPREME We activated the Emperor's consciousness in the mind of Susan Mendes and prepared for the extraction. Then – there – were – new – orders.[29]

320

SUZ I didn't favour extraction... more, *amalgamation*. Susan Mendes possessed a power I wanted.

KALENDORF (*Almost to himself*) No...

SUZ The Angel of Mercy will appear to be the new Emperor of the Daleks. It will become clear to the galaxy that we will no longer be the enemy. There will be no more war.

KALENDORF Until the alliance forces drop their guard... and you strike.

SUZ (*With a laugh*) Perhaps.

KALENDORF Is there anything of Suz left in there?[30]

SUZ Why did you want to speak to the Emperor?

KALENDORF I told you – Answer me!

SUZ (*Smiles*) There are some touches of humanity. The more persuasive elements of the Human Factor.

KALENDORF Suz...?[31]

SUZ Why did you come here, Kalendorf?

KALENDORF To find Suz.

SUZ And yet... I can access Suz's memory. Her knowledge of you tells me... you would *expect* the Daleks to betray you.

KALENDORF Then why did I enter into this alliance in the first place?

SUZ (*Puzzled*) I don't... I can't quite...

KALENDORF Isn't there anything left in there that can tell you that? Try... Try to think it. It's there. I'm sure it must be.

SUZ (*Snaps*) Take him away!

DALEK SUPREME I obey.

KALENDORF What are you afraid of, *Emperor?!*

DALEK SUPREME Move!

SUZ I fear nothing! The Daleks have no fear! We are the superior race! It is our destiny to conquer you!

KALENDORF Then why do you want me taken away? It's because you fear me! Me! A mere humanoid.

DALEK SUPREME Move or you will be exterminated.

SUZ Stop! Leave him!

DALEK SUPREME I obey.

SUZ You are inferior, Kalendorf.

KALENDORF Am I?

SUZ And you will die.

KALENDORF Now that I know the truth... I expected nothing less.

SUZ (*Insistent*) *Why* did you come here, Kalendorf?

KALENDORF That question's really eating away at you, isn't it?

SUZ You are cunning. You had a plan. You *have* a plan!

KALENDORF Is that Suz or the Emperor speaking?

SUZ Susan Mendes is dead!

KALENDORF And yet you know me. You know me as Suz knew me! But perhaps Suz knew better than you. Yes, why would I come here? You've turned the whole planet Earth into one gigantic Dalek metropolis. I'm stuck fast at the dead centre of your web. How the hell would I expect to get out? Maybe I didn't expect to get out.

SUZ You are keeping something from me.

KALENDORF Maybe I am. Maybe I'm not. You're not sure, are you?

SUZ I am the Emperor of the Daleks. There is no greater mind than mine.

KALENDORF And yet Suz would know. Wouldn't she? Wouldn't you?

SUZ	*Susan – Mendes – is – dead!*
KALENDORF	So you keep saying! And if she is, you'll never know what I've planned.
SUZ	You are attempting to deceive me. There is no plan.
KALENDORF	So you've changed your mind. Well, I suppose that's a Dalek's prerogative.
SUZ	How would Susan Mendes know?

Pause.

KALENDORF	How did we organise a rebellion that brought your empire to its knees?
SUZ	That was anticipated. It was our strategy to –
KALENDORF	– Distract us from Project Infinity, yes I know. But are you telling me that you always knew we were plotting against you?
SUZ	We soon discovered that you and Susan Mendes were in telepathic contact.
KALENDORF	And *that's* why Suz would know! Because there was a connection between our minds. A connection that no longer exists, because you've destroyed it. You've killed Susan Mendes. And when you did that, you destroyed something more powerful than the Daleks will ever be.
SUZ	What...? What do you mean?
KALENDORF	You wouldn't understand.
SUZ	Tell me!
KALENDORF	Why should I?
SUZ	Tell me, or you will be exterminated!
KALENDORF	I'm dead alread –

A sudden sound of impact and an electric sizzle.

| KALENDORF | Aaaargh!!! |

KALENDORF then continues to make choking sounds under the following.

| SUZ | Even in this frail, humanoid form, I can call upon all the raw energy of the Daleks. |

A further sizzle.

| KALENDORF | Aaargh! |
| SUZ | I can choke the life out of you! |

KALENDORF is gagging and choking.

| SUZ | Or make every nerve in your body burn for an eternity of agony! |

More sizzling.

| KALENDORF | Aaaaargh! (*Through pain*) I will never answer you! |
| SUZ | You will answer! Answer! |

Sizzling increases.

KALENDORF	Aaaargh! (*Fighting to speak through pain and choking*) But you can answer yourself. I can see... in your mind... You have the answer you want! Buried in Suz's thoughts. Now that you're touching me... I can make contact... I can see. It's still there.
SUZ	(*Enraged*) What?! What is still there?!
KALENDORF	Can't you see it? Or is the Emperor's mind too blind for that?

More sizzling. A nasty scrunching sound indicates KALENDORF is being choked further.

| KALENDORF | (*A strangled, choked cry*) |
| SUZ | Tell me!!! You – will – tell – meeee!!! |

A psychic-transition effect. We are suddenly inside SUZ's mind. The familiar, high-pitched psychic whining sound.

KALENDORF (*Calm, echoing, disembodied*) Victory or death. Victory or death. They say that's all Seterisius could hear in her mind as she entered her fortress. Victory or death. She ordered her knights to kneel before her. They did not hesitate to obey. Victory or death. It was Sancroff's voice in her mind. And without hesitation, she killed them all. Victory or death... the last thought in her mind. The thought Sancroff had planted there.

SUZ (*Calm, echoing, disembodied*) Victory or death. I remember.

Psychic transition whoosh back into the Emperor's chamber...

SUZ (*Herself again*) Karl...

KALENDORF You remember?

SUZ On the *Defiant*...

DALEK SUPREME What is happening? Explain!

SUZ You sent Alby away... Our minds linked...

DALEK SUPREME You are the Emperor!

SUZ No. I am Susan Mendes. And I know what I must do.

DALEK SUPREME Emergency! Emergency!

Alarms start.

DALEK TANNOY Emergency! Emergency! (*Continues*)

DALEK SUPREME Cerebral malfunction! Shut down Imperial link to Dalek Command Network immediately!

KALENDORF Now, Suz! Now!

DALEK SUPREME Exterminate!

Psychic energy burst and constant shriek of psionic energy.

DALEK SUPREME Exterminaaaaaaaaaaaaaaaargh!

DALEK TANNOY Emergencyyyyaaaaaaaaargh!

DALEK Aaaaaargh!

Explosion after explosion.

SUZ Victory – or – death!!!

Crossfade to the cries of countless Daleks and explosions as they're destroyed. A montage of massed Dalek destruction. Musical crescendo. Crossfade to:

132. Int. Saloran's Ship.

SALORAN Kalendorf had used Sancroff's strategy. Sancroff had planted a destructive mental impulse in his knights' minds, so that if they'd betrayed him, he could trigger it and any traitor would destroy themselves and their fellow conspirators. Kalendorf had planted such an impulse in Suz's mind. An impulse that ripped through the Dalek Command Network like a burning whirlwind of destruction.

TARKOV Hadn't he hoped that impulse would have been transferred to the Emperor from Suz?

SALORAN In a way, it made it easier that the Emperor had decided to exist within Suz.

TARKOV (*Understanding*) It was easier for him to make physical contact.

SALORAN I think Kalendorf had been planning a glorious suicidal, *physical* assault on the Emperor.

TARKOV Which would have left Suz alive. Poor Kalendorf. Always longing to make the ultimate sacrifice to save others. I take it he survived...

SALORAN He did. Almost a cruel miracle. Somehow he managed to drag himself back home, to Velyshaa. It took him years. But Suz had been destroyed, along with all the Daleks in this galaxy.

TARKOV And that was the Great Catastrophe.

SALORAN The collateral damage caused by the mass destruction of the Daleks and all their technology tore the galaxy apart. Whole star systems disappeared, billions upon billions died. It took centuries for the shroud of devastation to begin to lift. Even now, we still live under it.

TARKOV But Kalendorf did defeat the Daleks.

SALORAN Kalendorf, Suz, Alby, Mirana... They all made it possible.

TARKOV Huh... (*He gives a cynical chuckle*)

SALORAN What is it?

TARKOV And if I present all this evidence to the council of the Galactic Union... They'll just say it's proof that this threat from the past is dead and gone.

SALORAN Perhaps... Except for one thing.

TARKOV And what's that?

SALORAN That transmission fragment that brought you here. If my people have had more success with it than you did.

TARKOV *If* they have.

Crossfade to:

133. Int. Saloran's Ship. Computer Room.

The familiar sound of Dalek transmission interference. Some indistinct Dalek chatter filters through for a moment and is then gone.

TECHNICIAN There was more data hidden in the carrier wave. We're working on that right now. It's still being rendered. But we've deciphered more of the visual information already.

SALORAN Let's see it.

Screen activation. Interference fades in and out. Dramatic chord of threat.

TARKOV It's a Dalek all right.

SALORAN On a transolar disc... Look... you can just make out...

TARKOV A whole squadron of them.

SALORAN An invasion force.

A tiny alarm bleeps.

TECHNICIAN Right... the rendering's complete on that hidden data.

TARKOV What is it?

Sound of a fast-forward scan through Dalek dialogue.

TECHNICIAN Audio transmission fragments by the look of it.

SALORAN Let's hear it, Jake.

Bleep.[32]

DALEK (*Much distortion and static*) Attack spearhead now entering outer galactic sectors. Heavy concentration of asteroid fields indicate massed planetary destruction. Radiation readings indicate destruction caused by Dalek weaponry.

DALEK 1 (*Harsher distortion*) Long-range scans reveal energy readings towards galactic centre. Alien life still exists within this galaxy.

Your orders are to proceed. Every planet within that mighty swirl must become a Dalek world. Daleks conquer and destroy!
Transmission cuts off.
TECHNICIAN   That's it.
SALORAN   That's enough.
TARKOV   Then it's definite. The Daleks are still out there. Alive. On their way.
SALORAN   Probably coming from Seriphia. It's just as Kalendorf thought. In spite of all our galaxy has been through, the war with the Daleks isn't over. It will begin again.
TARKOV   But we've no idea when that transmission was made – how far away they actually are.
SALORAN   Then you'd better take this evidence to your council as fast as you can, Tarkov.

134. Ext. Velyshaa.
Crunching of footsteps on rocky ground. Soldiers are boarding the Star Yacht Crusader. *Engine power is building. A klaxon howls from within the ship.*

TANNOY   (*Muted in distance*) Prepare for blast-off! Secure all ballast. Secure for blast-off!
TROOPER   All right, you lot! Get a move on! The holiday's over! Lift off in sixty seconds! Come on! Move it!
TARKOV and SALORAN have to talk louder and louder as the Crusader's *engines build up to blast off point.*
TARKOV   Are you sure you won't reconsider, Saloran? Your knowledge of all this is –
SALORAN   You know what to tell them, Siy. I've no appetite for never-ending war.
TARKOV   Never-ending? What do you mean?
SALORAN   Oh... don't listen to me. It's just that I feel I've already fought all three of Kalendorf's wars.[33]
TARKOV   Which means you're more than qualified to help this time.
SALORAN   No. Because I think, while there is life in this universe, there will always be creatures who seek to conquer and destroy others. Perhaps the Daleks are the worst of these creatures... I don't know... Perhaps there's worse yet to come.[34]
TARKOV   You sound like you're giving up. Like you think we've lost already... before it's even begun.
SALORAN   I just don't have the stomach for it. This new war may be about to begin... but in a sense, it's never stopped... and never ends.[35]
The engine roar is very loud now.
TARKOV   I hope you're wrong, Saloran! I hope you're wrong! Goodbye![36]
SALORAN   Good luck!
The whirr and clank of the ship's door closing. Engines fire with massive surge of energy. Crusader *lifts off. As it climbs, we crossfade to Saloran's running footsteps across the rocky terrain. She stops, out of breath.* Crusader *can still be heard, rising high into the sky.*
SALORAN   (*Close. To herself*) Good luck. You'll need it.
Crash in closing theme. During the theme, the sounds of war and

325

destruction fade in. Cries of exterminate can be heard. And, little by little the sound of massed Dalek chanting emerges and dominates until there is no other sound.

DALEKS   Daleks conquer and destroy! Daleks conquer and destroy! *A nightmarish, deafening crescendo. Then silence.*

The end.

NOTES

1. Line changed to: '(*Impatiently*) **What**? There's a simple latch!'
2. Line changed to: 'Because your friends on the Galactic Union council dismissed me as an obsessive – not right in the head! That's the answer you're so politely trying to avoid, Tarkov. They said I was obsessed with the past, when we should be concentrating on the future. (*Pause*) **So**, what's your opinion on all this? Hm?'
3. Line changed to: 'No... **no**... No, we think we**'ve** cracked it.'
4. Line changed to: '**I take it you agree**. The physical characteristics of this unknown alloy correlate approximately to those of various artifact fragments you discovered before you came to work here on Velyshaa. **Yes**?'
5. Line changed to: 'How did you pick it up? **I**... I didn't think our tracking stations could track that far?'
6. Line changed to: 'And so *at last*, the Galactic Union are worried. Worried that what befell the galaxy centuries ago, may happen again. ~~And finally, like me, they want to look into the past to find out how to stop it all happening again.~~'
7. Line changed to: '(*Puzzled*) I don't understand. **But** why are you here?'
8. Line changed to: 'I don't know. It depends on the nature of the threat, doesn't it? All I ~~do~~ know is that the evidence that something terrible happened round about two and a half thousand years ago is conclusive. I've seen the debris and dust that were once star systems. I've visited planets where the atmospheres are still poisoned... that still bear the scars of ~~some~~... **of** some unimaginably violent upheaval. And I've read as much of your work as I could find.'
9. Line changed to: 'It was enough. There's been a lot of rebuilding in the last thousand years. There may still be far too much poverty, fear and distrust out there, but things are gradually improving. And like it or not, that's because of the work **that** the Galactic Union are doing.'
10. Line changed to: '**I**... **I'd**... I'd hate all that work to be for nothing.'
11. Line changed to: 'Er... **I** can't say **that** I have. Where is it?'
12. Line changed to: 'Celetron? Yaldos Major? No? Hmm... no. **Well**, all of those planets – and there are others too – all of them have small pockets of ancient communities who have passed stories of the Great Catastrophe down from generation to generation.'
13. Line changed to: '**Oh, er**, is this... **is this**... Kalendorf?'
14. Line changed to: '(*Trying to remember*) **I**... I touched that... that statue... and then... The machine... The machine in the statue seemed to come alive. (*Becoming agitated*) ~~And~~... and I wasn't... there... I wasn't... wasn't – '
15. Line changed to: 'Kalendorf? What do you mean? What *was* that machine? It... *spoke*. It fired a weapon at me. **I thought I**... I thought I was *dead*.'
16. Deleted dialogue – COMPUTER: '~~Playback commencing.~~'
17. Line changed to: 'It's hard to believe, I know. But this is what the galaxy was like back then. Something they called the Earth Alliance had established peace... until the Daleks invaded. When they did, Kalendorf was caught in the middle of it. Somehow he became involved with an Earth woman called Suz. They were captured by the Daleks and, it seems, agreed to work for them. ~~Kalendorf felt he had betrayed everything he believed in, just for the sake of survival. With his help, the Daleks continued their ruthless subjugation of the civilised worlds. It's not clear what the nature of his feelings for Suz were, but there was a special bond between them. The years~~

327

passed. ~~Kalendorf and Suz continued with their betrayal. Then one day, the Daleks killed Suz. This may have been the trigger for Kalendorf to turn against the Daleks. We don't know for sure. The Daleks had successfully conquered the galaxy, but against all the odds, he apparently led a rebellion against them. It looked like the rebellion might succeed; but the Daleks had a secret strategy. Somehow they had the means to create a dimensional gateway into an alternative universe. And from that universe, they intended to gain the wisdom and the power to rule the entire cosmos. They would join forces with an invincible Dalek army from another dimension.~~' The rest of Scene 111 is also deleted.

18.   Line changed to:

    SUZ   (*Breaking down*) I'm sorry, Alby...

    ALBY   **Suz?**

    SUZ   I'm so sorry, but I couldn't let you kill Kalendorf.

19.   Scene 113 does not contain the battle sounds specified.

20.   Line changed to: 'When you... **when you** experience Kalendorf's thoughts... Do you...? I mean, what about his feelings? Did he do all this without any sense of regret or remorse?'

21.   Line changed to: 'If I**'ve** killed Alby for no reason.'

22.   Line changed to: '(Distort) I know, ~~I know~~. But have you ever tried arguing with him? We couldn't stop him.'

23.   Line changed to: '(*Distort*) Don't you get the idea that's where he wants to be these days? I mean, don't get me wrong, he's a fine soldier. The best commander we could have. But... you know, when he's not fighting a battle, he just sits in his cabin... listening to the hyper-scanner, like he's trying to find something. Won't talk about it, ~~but I know~~ – '

24.   Line changed to: '(*Distort*) ~~All right~~... Look... We've missed our window on hitting that enemy transport fleet anyway. We can hang on here until Eastern Sunrise. *We'll* keep tracking for him. *You* send in a squad to find him.'

25.   Line changed to: '(*Distort*) ~~And~~, Godwin, keep signalling for him on the comms.'

26.   This line and the following, were reordered as:

    KALENDORF   (*To himself*) I think that's *it*. Visual scan. Long range.

    COMPUTER   Scanning.

    KALENDORF   Co-ordinates... (*reading off*) 94249127459/9874.

27.   Line changed to: 'Magnify that area. ~~Well~~, go on.'

28.   Line changed to: '(*Distort*) Your capsule *and* the *Defiant's* escape pod just... phased out of existence for a few moments. ~~You~~ – '

29.   Line changed to: 'We activated the Emperor's consciousness in the mind of Susan Mendes and prepared for extraction. ~~Then there were new orders.~~'

30.   Line changed to: 'Is there anything **left of Suz** in there?'

31.   Deleted dialogue – KALENDORF: '~~Suz~~...?'

32.   Added dialogue – TECHNICIAN: '**Hang on a sec.**'

33.   Line changed to: 'Oh... **no, don't**... don't listen to me. It's just that I feel I've already fought all three of Kalendorf's wars.'

34.   Line changed to: 'No. **No**, because I think, while there is life in this universe, there will always be creatures who **want** to conquer and destroy others. Perhaps the Daleks are the worst of these creatures... I don't know... Perhaps there's worse yet to come.'

35.   Line changed to: 'I just... **I just** don't have the stomach for it. This new war may be about to begin... but in a sense, it's never stopped... and never ends.'

36.   Line changed to: 'I hope you're wrong, Saloran! **I say**, I hope you're wrong! Goodbye!'

328

CHAPTER FOUR

It's a very Kalendorf-heavy episode. The logical conclusion to Gareth's 'shouldn't he be more noble?' complaint?
Nicholas Briggs: In a way, I suppose it is. But it's also because we find out that what happens in *Dalek War* is all largely due to Kalendorf's manipulation. You know? It's a story all about what Kalendorf did to cause the Great Catastrophe. He is the root cause of everything that happened. He made the alliance with the Mentor. He made the alliance with the Dalek Supreme. He determined to rescue Suz. He planted the destructive impulse in Suz's mind. He did all this, because he wanted to be the ultimate warrior and save the galaxy. The irony is that he didn't have a noble death and was largely remembered as the cause of something terrible. The Great Catastrophe was the collateral damage caused by Kalendorf's great plan.

How did you go about casting the part of Godwin?
I wanted a strong actress to play Godwin, because I wanted to her to be a kind of 'regular' who actually appears from nowhere in terms of plotting. We leap forward to a time when Kalendorf has been fighting another long war. So I needed someone I could trust to deliver the goods. Someone who was very at ease with herself, with me and with the whole Big Finish set-up and would instantly sound at home in her fictional environment. I thought of Helen Goldwyn as I was staring at the character's name... 'Godwin... Goldwyn!' It was really as pathetically simple as that. And she's such a laugh... and very, very talented.

Do you find writing the conclusion to a story easy or troublesome? Is it nice to tie up all the loose ends – see it all come together – or do you fret about it?
For some time now, I've made it a rule to sort out my endings when I first conceive a story. That said, the developing plot often reshapes these endings a bit. But this ending was largely what I'd planned. However, approaching it, I did fret. You want to make sure that it lives up to what you'd initially thought of. I also fret because it's like getting near the end of a book you're reading. Suddenly, I don't want it to end. No matter how much trauma and frustration I've had during the writing, it's like saying goodbye to a friend. Eventually, I just get on and do it, though!

What's the significance of the line, 'Every planet within that mighty swirl must become a Dalek world'?
I thought it was an appropriately grand thing for a Dalek to say. It's also a quote from a TV Comic story. Both Jac Rayner and John Ainsworth zeroed in on it as a really bad line. But I fought for it. They both said something like, 'Er... is this a quote or something?'.

And I said, 'Er... yeah'. It's ironic that I've used it as the mainstay of the *Dalek Empire III* teaser trailers.

Sancroff? Wasn't he in your *Doctor Who* audio play *The Sirens of Time*?
Yes, Sancroff is the defeated Knight of Velyshaa held captive by the ghastly Ruthley. I'm not in favour of making the universe smaller by linking these kind of things up, but I'd already created this character, so it seemed silly and perhaps unnecessarily confusing to create another Velyshaan dictator. I also thought it would be nice to look back and wonder how ruthless and noble that frail old chap in *Sirens* had once been.

The series ends with an ominous beat: the Daleks are on their way back. Again, was this you writing an ending with a sting in its tail, or setting up a further series?
I wasn't thinking of a sequel. But I just can't say, 'The Daleks have won' or 'The Daleks have been destroyed'. It's just so... disappointing. The ending I was going for was the idea that wars against terrible things will always happen, because people (or, in this case, creatures) are always capable of doing evil. I was thinking, too, of the end to *The Dalek Book*, with the line 'and never ends' on the last page of the book. That's what I was aiming for.

Q&A
Dalek Empire III

Nicholas Briggs tells us about Dalek Empire III... 'Dalek Empire III has six chapters. They are The Exterminators, The Healers, The Survivors, The Demons, The Warriors and The Future. *The last title may change. It picks up twenty years after Tarkov's departure from Velyshaa... but he hasn't got home yet. Meanwhile, rumours are reaching the Galactic Union that a race known as "Daleks" have entered the Border Worlds. The trouble is, no one thinks they're a threat. Only Tarkov can warn them, and he's disappeared! The new series introduces a whole cast of new characters and focuses more on the cunning the Daleks have to employ in order to conquer the galaxy. At its heart, it's an epic story about friendship and loyalty and whether or not those qualities can survive in the face of an onslaught from the dastardly Daleks.'*

From Dalek Empire III: *Chapter One – The Exterminators* by Nicholas Briggs...

SUZ   Victory or death. Victory or death.

The thought that Kalendorf had planted in me...

And everywhere it went –
That thought
Now *my* thought
Now *me* –
Everywhere *I* went, there were Dalek thoughts...
Programs
Instructions
Commands...
... hatred.

And I smashed them all aside.

Crossfade back to Dalek War *Chapter Four clip: explosions and Daleks crying out. Crossfade back to:*

SUZ   And I couldn't stop.

I couldn't... stop. I was destroying everything...
Because they thought I was one of them. They
thought I was the Emperor, so every pathway in
their neural network was open to me, no matter

331

how secure, how secret. The way was always clear.
And I was destroying everything...

Every Dalek *thing* in the galaxy... And then beyond.
Destruction that was never going to stop until there
were no Daleks left in the entire universe.

I sensed them trying to find ways of stopping me.
Too late.
There were so few of them left now. They were
panicking, Desperate for a strategy.
But I was unstoppable.

The sound of her thoughts smashing to a halt.

(*She breathes a sigh of relief*)
And then...
I arrived
Somewhere... far beyond our galaxy...
I arrived.

It was... another mind.
Another
Mind
And yet
My mind.

DALEK   *My miiind!*

Available Now

DOCTOR™ WHO

THE AUDIO SCRIPTS

ISBN 1-84435-005-3

Since 1999, Big Finish Productions have produced regular, fully-licensed ongoing audio adventures for the Doctor and his companions on CD. Each four-part story stars members of the original *Doctor Who* cast in brand-new adventures through time and space.

Presented in this book are the original scripts for four of Big Finish's most popular plays, one per Doctor.

From the new run of Fifth Doctor adventures starring Peter Davison comes **Loups-Garoux**, penned by Marc Platt who wrote the very last *Doctor Who* story made by BBC Television in 1989.

Colin Baker returned as the Sixth Doctor in **The Holy Terror**, by award-winning playwright Robert Shearman.

Representing the Seventh Doctor, played once again by Sylvester McCoy, is **The Fires of Vulcan** by acclaimed novelist Steve Lyons.

Rounding this collection off is **Neverland** featuring Paul McGann and authored by *Doctor Who* comic strip writer and editor Alan Barnes.

The scripts reprinted herein include dialogue and sequences missing from the finished releases. A must for every fan of the Doctor's timeless adventures!

Available Now

The Audio Scripts
Volume Two

ISBN 1-84435-049-5

Since 1999, Big Finish Productions have produced regular, fully-licensed ongoing audio adventures for the Doctor and his companions on CD. Each four-part story stars members of the original *Doctor Who* cast in brand-new adventures through time and space.

Presented in this book are the original scripts for four of Big Finish's most popular stories plus an essay by actress India Fisher, who plays Charley Pollard.

Representing the Fifth Doctor adventures, starring Peter Davison, comes **The Eye of the Scorpion**, written by Iain McLaughlin and featuring the first appearance of new TARDIS traveller Erimem.

Colin Baker featured as the Sixth Doctor in **The One Doctor**, the award-winning romp by Gareth Roberts and Clayton Hickman.

From the Seventh Doctor run, with Sylvester McCoy, is **Dust Breeding** by Mike Tucker, featuring the return of an old and deadly enemy...

Rounding this collection off is **Seasons of Fear**, one of the most significant Eighth Doctor audio adventures, featuring Paul McGann and penned by Paul Cornell and Caroline Symcox.

This collection also features a number of early storylines, an unmade episode and other features!

Available Now

DOCTOR™ WHO

THE AUDIO SCRIPTS
VOLUME THREE

ISBN 1-84435-063-0

Since 1999, Big Finish Productions have produced regular, fully-licensed ongoing audio adventures for the Doctor and his companions on CD. Each four-part story stars members of the original *Doctor Who* cast in brand-new adventures through time and space.

Presented in this book are the original scripts for four of Big Finish's most popular stories plus an essay by actor Colin Baker, who continues to play the Sixth Doctor.

Representing the Fifth Doctor adventures, starring Peter Davison, comes **Spare Parts**, written by Marc Platt and focusing on the early days of the Doctor's old foes, the Cybermen.

Colin Baker featured in Nicholas Pegg's **The Spectre of Lanyon Moor**, featuring the long-awaited first meeting between the Sixth Doctor and Brigadier Lethbridge-Stewart as played by Nicholas Courtney.

From the Seventh Doctor run, with Sylvester McCoy, is **The Rapture** by Joseph Lidster, set around the hedonistic clubland of Ibiza.

Rounding this collection off is **The Chimes of Midnight**, an eerie thriller featuring the Eighth Doctor and Charley penned by Robert Shearman.

This collection also features a number of deleted scenes, observations and other features!

Coming Soon...

THE AUDIO SCRIPTS
VOLUME FOUR

ISBN 1-84435-065-7

Since 1999, Big Finish Productions have produced regular, fully-licensed ongoing audio adventures for the Doctor and his companions on CD. Each four-part story stars members of the original *Doctor Who* cast in brand-new adventures through time and space.

Presented in this book are the original scripts for four of Big Finish's most popular stories – three stories that made up a loose trilogy of returning villains, as well as Big Finish's 40th anniversary *Doctor Who* story.

Representing the Fifth Doctor adventures, starring Peter Davison, comes **Omega**, written by Nev Fountain and featuring the return of the exiled Time Lord.

Colin Baker featured in Lance Parkin's **Davros**, which saw the Doctor coming face to face with the creator of the Daleks.

From the Seventh Doctor run, with Sylvester McCoy, is **Master** by Joseph Lidster. Has the evil Time Lord genuinely lost his memories?

Rounding this collection off is **Zagreus**, Big Finish's 40th anniversary *Doctor Who* story. Written by Alan Barnes and Gary Russell, it saw Peter Davison, Colin Baker and Sylvester McCoy team up with Paul McGann.

This collection also features a number of deleted scenes, observations and other features!

Available Now

DOCTOR™ WHO

Coming Soon...

SHORT TRIPS: REPERCUSSIONS

A short-story collection edited by
GARY RUSSELL

ISBN 1-84435-048-7

Throughout time and space, people have encountered the Doctor. For some, that encounter has enriched their lives. For others, it's been a detrimental experience. Either way, for each of them, nothing has ever been the same again.

Which would be fine – except on those occasions where the Doctor's interference has not just upset or altered the people, but damaged the web of time itself. Like a pebble breaking the surface of a pond, even though the incident has occurred, the ripples still reach further and further out...

These are their stories. Tales of the happy and sad, the broken and the mended. And the effect the Doctor has had, not just upon them but on the whole fabric of the universe...

Featuring stories by Peter Anghelides, Mark Michalowski, Joseph Lidster, Trevor Baxendale, Colin Brake and many more!

OTHER BOOKS AVAILABLE FROM

BIG
FINISH

DOCTOR WHO

The New Audio Adventures – The Inside Story
by Benjamin Cook (ISBN 1-84435-034-7)

STAR QUEST

The Star Quest Trilogy by Terrance Dicks
(ISBN 1-84435-066-5)

PROFESSOR BERNICE SUMMERFIELD

Professor Bernice Summerfield and The Dead Men Diaries
edited by Paul Cornell (ISBN 1-903654-00-9)
Professor Bernice Summerfield and The Doomsday Manuscript
by Justin Richards (ISBN 1-903654-04-1)
Professor Bernice Summerfield and The Gods of the Underworld
by Stephen Cole (ISBN 1-903654-23-8)
Professor Bernice Summerfield and The Squire's Crystal
by Jacqueline Rayner (ISBN 1-903654-13-0)
Professor Bernice Summerfield and The Infernal Nexus
by Dave Stone (ISBN 1-903654-16-5)
Professor Bernice Summerfield and The Glass Prison
by Jacqueline Rayner (ISBN 1-903654-41-6)
Professor Bernice Summerfield: A Life of Surprises
edited by Paul Cornell (ISBN 1-903654-44-0)
Professor Bernice Summerfield: Life During Wartime
edited by Paul Cornell (ISBN 1-84435-062-2)

Coming soon...

Professor Bernice Summerfield and The Big Hunt, a novel by Lance Parkin

A novella collection edited by Gary Russell, featuring stories by
Joseph Lidster, Jacqueline Rayner and Paul Sutton

Professor Bernice Summerfield: The Inside Story,
a behind-the-scenes book by Ian Farrington

www.bigfinish.com